Praise for The Gardella Vampire Chronicles

Rises the Night

"A Buffy-esque vampire hunter living in an Austen-style Regency world. . . . A tense plot line and refreshingly diverse supporting characters complete the package, giving series fans plenty to sink their teeth into—and plenty more to look forward to." —*Publishers Weekly*

"Excuse me for one moment while I give Colleen Gleason a standing ovation. The second book in the Gardella Vampire Chronicles, *Rises the Night*, is a superb sequel in a series that is unique, sexy, and definitely very intense."
—Romance Reader at Heart

The Rest Falls Away

"Sophisticated, sexy, surprising! With its vampire lore and Regency graces, this book grabs you and holds you tight to the very last page!" —J. R. Ward, *New York Times* Bestselling Author of *Lover Unbound*

"So, what would Buffy as a debutante death-dealer, Buffy in a bonnet, have been like? . . . You can see the result in *The Rest Falls Away*, Gleason's publishing debut that turns vampire stories—and romances—on their ear with a decidedly dark, decidedly unsentimental Regency heroine who stakes the undead with the best of them." —*Detroit Free Press*

continued . . .

THE BLEEDING DUSK

DUSK

The Gardella Vampire Chronicles

Colleen Gleason

A SIGNET ECLIPSE BOOK

SIGNET ECLIPSE
Published by New American Library, a division of
Penguin Group (USA) Inc., 375 Hudson Street,
New York, New York 10014, USA
Penguin Group (Canada), 90 Eglinton Avenue East, Suite 700, Toronto,
Ontario M4P 2Y3, Canada (a division of Pearson Penguin Canada Inc.)
Penguin Books Ltd., 80 Strand, London WC2R 0RL, England
Penguin Ireland, 25 St. Stephen's Green, Dublin 2,
Ireland (a division of Penguin Books Ltd.)
Penguin Group (Australia), 250 Camberwell Road, Camberwell, Victoria 3124,
Australia (a division of Pearson Australia Group Pty. Ltd.)
Penguin Books India Pvt. Ltd., 11 Community Centre, Panchsheel Park,
New Delhi - 110 017, India
Penguin Group (NZ), 67 Apollo Drive, Rosedale, North Shore 0632,
New Zealand (a division of Pearson New Zealand Ltd.)
Penguin Books (South Africa) (Pty.) Ltd., 24 Sturdee Avenue,
Rosebank, Johannesburg 2196, South Africa

Penguin Books Ltd., Registered Offices:
80 Strand, London WC2R 0RL, England

First published by Signet Eclipse, an imprint of New American Library,
a division of Penguin Group (USA) Inc.

First Printing, February 2008
10 9 8 7 6 5 4 3 2 1

For Marcy

Thanks for hanging in there with me and making it happen.

Acknowledgments

I realize more and more with each book how much it's not a solitary process. There are many people to thank each time, and my heartfelt gratitude goes out to each of them.

First, always, thanks to Marcy Posner for holding my hand, keeping me from going off the deep end, and for celebrating the good stuff.

And to Claire Zion, whose brilliance makes the Gardellas that much better . . . every time.

Thanks to everyone at NAL who has helped bring Victoria and her story to the market—Sandra Devendorf, Hilary Dowling, Kara Welsh, and the incredible, amazing art department, which just blows my mind with their cover and promotional designs. They just keep getting better and better! Thanks, too, to the sales reps, who have done a fabulous job getting the books out in unexpected places everywhere.

Big thanks to my blogger friends who have helped along the way, especially Carl V. (who is constantly going out of his way to support me), Cheya, Nancytoes, Zeus and Marina,

Bam, Susan Helene, Chris, Mary F., Kailana, the Smart Bitches, Heather Harper, Megan F., and everyone who hangs out at my blog. Also to Jeff for the great pictures!

Thanks to my writer friends, especially Jackie Kessler, Diane Gaston, Janet Mullany, Anne Mallory, and all of the Wet Noodle Posse.

I couldn't do it without Holli and Tammy holding my hand through the whole creative process, and also Jana DeLeon, whose shoulder to cry on and ear to celebrate in has made it all so much easier.

Thanks to Christel for the Italian and French assistance, and to Beth, Debi, Danita, and Jen for all their support. And also to the Brighton Borders, for hosting me and my Mambo addiction nearly every day during deadline time, and to Paperback Outlet, for two of the best signings ever!

And, lastly, to Steve and my three lovelies for understanding the whole concept of the writing process, and letting me do it . . . even when we'd all rather be hanging out together. I love you all, and thank you for your love, enthusiasm, and plot help!

THE BLEEDING
DUSK

Prologue

In Which Max Faces the Vampiress in Her Den

The lair of the Queen of the Vampires was tucked away in the snowy mountain range of Munṭii Făgăraş.

The only reason Maximilian Pesaro had been able to find the hideaway was because of the two bite marks on his neck. Permanent ones left by Lilith herself.

They burned and tingled as he approached the entrance to the interior chamber. The throbbing never fully went away, but there were times when it ebbed enough that he could forget about the fact that he was permanently linked to the vampire queen.

The back of his neck felt as though a brick of ice rested on it; but it was not because of the winter that blustered outside of the stone-cut chambers in the mountain. The howling winds and blinding snow that came much too early and stayed too long in these Romanian mountains had nothing to do with the chill that burned his neck, and everything to do with the fact that there were vampires nearby. As he was a

Venator, it was his way of sensing the presence of the undead.

Coming here was foolish and brazen. Max was never foolish, although he had his brazen moments. But after what he'd been through in the last months, he was willing to accept the consequences of this visit. Even if it resulted in his death, he chanced it—because it could also result in his freedom.

The only reason he'd made it so far into the bowels of Lilith's refuge was the fact that he bore her markings. Her branding of him was an obscene protection from the undead that guarded her compound.

Max passed yet another of Lilith's Guardian vampires, ones that had eyes that burned pale ruby and fangs that released a strong poison at will. She opened the heavy wooden door to Lilith's private chamber and stepped back to allow him in.

"Maximilian." Lilith's voice was a purr, and her red-ringed blue eyes were avid as she cast her gaze over him. "I believe this is the first time you have ever come to me of your own accord. What a pleasure."

Carved in the deepest part of the mountain, Lilith's sanctuary was as far as possible from the sunlight that would peel the skin from her body. Its interior was otherwise like any well-appointed house in the civilized world of London, Rome, or Budapest, with the exception of its lack of windows.

Comfortable furnishings were arranged throughout the large, high-ceilinged room. Tables held lamps and sheafs of parchment; settees were covered with thick pillows and cushions. Thick Persian rugs warmed the cold stone floor. A large tapestry hung on the wall depicted the immortalization of Judas Iscariot, the first true vampire. Another showed him slaying the first vampire hunter, Gardeleus the Venator.

That was the first time a vampire had killed a Venator, and, Max thought grimly, it had not been the last. Fortunately there had been other vampire hunters born from Gardeleus's blood over the ages—arising randomly from far-flung branches of the family tree. And then there had been a very few—like Max himself—who were not of Gardella blood, but had chosen the path of a vampire slayer and had passed the life-or-death test that allowed them to wear the holy empowering amulet of the Venators, the *vis bulla*.

Nor were Venators protected from being turned by a vampire, although the power of the *vis bulla* made it more difficult for the vampire's blood to take hold in the Venator and to make one undead. Max had always felt that Gardeleus's fate of death was preferable to being turned into a vampire.

The chamber was warm, and the lighting burned low. A massive blaze roared in the fireplace, taking up the entirety of one long wall and casting black and red shadows into the room.

Lilith herself was arranged casually on a long chaise, her filmy ice-blue gown draping from her hip to the floor, leaving her white feet and arms bare. Her red hair, so shiny and bright that it appeared to burn, poured over her fair skin in sensual coils that reminded Max of the locks of a copper-haired Medusa. Although she had been on the earth for more than a millennium, Lilith had the beautiful elfin face of a thirty-year-old, and a body that matched. Her pose appeared nonchalant, but a fleeting glance at her dangerous eyes told Max a different story.

He was glad for at least the advantage of surprise.

The doors closed behind him, and he stopped in the center of the room. Wanting to keep what little leverage he had, he waited.

"You're not dead," Lilith said after the silence stretched.

She followed suit and arched her long, lithe body as she drew herself into a seated position. One of control.

"Then you're aware that I've destroyed Akvan's Obelisk. That I've kept my part of our agreement to stop your son, Nedas, from using its power." Lilith had raised Nedas, who was the son of one of her consorts from the tenth century, from an infant, and had turned him to an undead when he was twenty.

She smiled. Her upper fangs glinted. "So that is why you have come."

Now she stood and moved toward him, bringing with her a renewed burning in the bites on his neck and the scent of roses. Max felt her presence as it seeped into him, cloying and close, and noticed the way his breathing became . . . heavier . . . controlled.

Although he kept his eyes averted from hers, he felt the first hint of a muscle tremor deep beneath his skin.

"You agreed to release me from your thrall if I succeeded." He drew in his breath slowly, keeping it steady with effort. "You didn't expect me to."

Lilith tilted her head, turning her face away while keeping her gaze on him in a sly manner. "On the contrary, Maximilian. I was certain that you would succeed. I had no doubts. After all"—she reached for him, brushing her long-nailed finger along one of his cheekbones—"those very characteristics attract me to you. Your strength, your determination, and your integrity."

Max didn't flinch as the nail, death-sharp, cut a thin line into his skin. His heartbeat was still his own, and though his throat was dry, he was still steady. He wanted to step away, but he didn't. He'd faced Lilith before; he'd face her this time.

Now her hand had come to rest on one side of his chest, and they stood face-to-face, the vampire as tall as he, the weight of her hand burning through his shirtwaist. "Along with . . . this . . ." she added, smoothing her palm over his firm pectoral. With her touch came the strength of her thrall, battling to capture his breathing, the race of his heart, the surge in his veins. His desire.

"Will you not keep your word and release me?" Max closed his eyes. He knew it had been foolish to come here, but he'd been willing to try. He had little to lose. He'd even told Victoria he never believed Lilith would release him.

Both of her hands were on him now, flat palmed, sliding up and over his shoulders to cup the bare skin of his neck. Max felt the tiny, warm drip of blood from his cheek where she'd cut him, and the unbearable closeness when she leaned forward and pressed an openmouthed kiss to the edge of his jaw, over the trickle of blood.

The flood of sensation staggered him. Her lips—one cool and firm, the other warm and soft—bussing against his skin set his fingers to trembling against the sides of his trousers. Her teeth were slick and smooth as they slid against his jaw, ending in a tiny nibble. His breath caught, and he drew it in sharply, deeply, and felt the beginnings of response simmering low inside him, behind the weakness in his knees, and his lips parted with a soft puff of air.

When she kissed him he tasted his own blood, and he kissed her back, unwillingly, yet willingly.

Then through the haze of desire that pummeled him, Max remembered who he still was, and managed to slide his hand up between them, brushing against her breasts as they pressed against his shirt. He tore at its ties and at last closed his fingers over the tiny silver cross that hung from his areola.

Strength from the *vis bulla* surged through him, and he drew in his first clear breath since she'd stepped near him. He pulled his face away as she realized what had happened and stepped back. Her fingers tore at his shirt, pulling it open, and with a shriek of surprise, she jerked away.

"So you have come armed." At first she could not look at him, could not look at the large silver cross that hung on a heavy chain around his neck. Hidden beneath his shirt, it was the only weapon he'd been able to bring into her presence aside from the tiny *vis bulla*. It wasn't as effective as an ash stake, but it had produced the effect he'd desired.

"I am not so foolish as to come to you unprepared," Max replied, his voice easier now, although his blood still leaped and his chest was tight. "A stake would have been preferable, but your Guardians would not allow me to pass with one. I tried."

"I would expect nothing less from you, Maximilian." She kept her distance, kept her eyes slightly averted, but was not the crumpled heap of weakness a lesser vampire would have been. The surprise had sent her spinning away, but the mere vision of the cross was not enough to frighten a vampire of her caliber for long. As one's eyes became used to sudden light in darkness, so would she soon be able to look at him again.

But the large cross would keep her from touching him— or touching him much. And the delicate silver *vis bulla*— blessed with holy water and forged of silver from the Holy Land—gave him his Venator speed, strength, and fast-healing capabilities. But neither would damage Lilith in any other way.

Now, as she looked at him again, her eyes narrowed and seemed to focus on his half-bare chest. "That is not your *vis bulla*," she said suddenly, her eyes widening.

Max looked at her.

"You are surprised that I would have noticed. Why should you be, Maximilian? I notice everything about you." The purr was back in her voice again, and despite the hand-size cross hanging there, she stepped toward him. "This one is different. It is smaller."

"But no less powerful." It was true. He'd given his *vis bulla* to Victoria, then walked away from her on the streets of Roma a month ago. And later, when he'd decided to make this mad trip, he'd replaced it with this one, one that did not belong to him.

"No, I would expect not. But still." Her eyes narrowed again, and she tried again to catch his gaze, but he would not play. "Not dead, and wearing someone else's *vis bulla*," Lilith mused. "And demanding that I comply with your wishes. Maximilian, you absolutely fascinate me. Are you quite certain you do not wish to remain here with me? Forever?"

"I have no wish for immortality."

"But you did at one time."

"I did. Long ago." There was no glossing over it. Max had learned to live with his choices.

"Not that long ago. Merely fifteen, perhaps sixteen years ago. And this last year you spent living among the members of the Tutela did not raise that desire in you again?"

The mark of the Tutela had first been burned into the back of his shoulder when he was a young, naive man of sixteen and had foolishly joined them and their cause: to protect and serve the vampires in the hopes of attaining immortality and power. Now the tattoo of the writhing dog— for that was really what the Tutela were: mortals who acted as bitches and whores for the undead—seemed to itch on his skin.

This last year when he'd lived among the Tutela again had been Hell on earth. Max had had to pretend not only to be one of them, desiring power and immortality while bowing and scraping to the vampire Nedas, but he had also carried on the charade of being engaged to Sarafina, the daughter of Conte Regalado, who had been the mortal leader of the Tutela.

He replied to Lilith, "I did what you asked because of your promise to release me if I succeeded with the task you set me to. Now I am here to collect on it."

"And what of the woman you love? You left her?"

Max lifted an eyebrow in question, but did not speak.

"The girl you were to marry? Shall I be jealous of her? Is that why you wish to be released?"

His breathing smoothed. "I would not expect you to be jealous of a mere mortal."

"Her father is a vampire now, and he might well sire her in his footsteps."

"But she will be young and weak."

"True." Lilith looked at him, reached out her hand to touch his arm. "I cannot let you go, Maximilian, my Venator pet."

"You lied, then." He'd known it, known she would not release him. "I did your bidding and you never intended to do as you promised."

"Come, now, Maximilian. You are fully aware that the secrets I gave you, the knowledge you had that enabled you to see to the destruction of Akvan's Obelisk, were just as much to your benefit—and that of your race—as they were to mine. I would not say you have come out of this so very badly."

Black bile burned the back of his throat. Oh, but what he had been forced to do to carry out Lilith's desires and to save Roma—and the world—from the malevolent power of Akvan's Obelisk . . . executing Eustacia, accepting her willing sacrifice by swinging the sword himself in the presence of Nedas. It had been the only way to prove his loyalty to the Tutela, the only way to get close enough to destroy the obelisk.

And Victoria. She'd seen it happen. She'd never forgive him.

Yes, he'd done the right thing, the only thing . . . but it had been repugnant. Heartbreaking.

And that was why he'd removed his *vis bulla*, walked away from Victoria and the rest of the Venators . . . and why he'd been reckless enough to come here.

A hero he'd been, true, but a repulsive one at that.

"Ah, Maximilian." Lilith was speaking again, touching him again. Her fingers wove into the hair that brushed his shoulders, sending little frissons of unease into his scalp. "I do like your hair long like this. It makes you look so much more . . . savage. You would be a magnificent vampire."

He closed his eyes. Waiting. Ignoring the leap in his veins, the obstinate awareness of her pull, the way his fingers trembled. The unbearable smell of roses from the hideous creature in front of him. The way his body responded to hers, and the knowledge that it wasn't only because of the bites.

"I'll never drink your blood."

Lilith sighed against him, her breath not putrid, as one might expect from an undead . . . but tinged with the same floral scent that clung to the rest of her. But then, of course, she hadn't just been feeding. "And that, my pet, is my greatest disappointment of the century. All right, Maximilian. I will allow you to be released from my thrall. Much as it will annoy me to do so."

She released him and he opened his eyes. Wary.

Lilith stepped away, suddenly breezy in her demeanor. "I will release you. There is a salve, a balm you can apply to the bites . . . my bites," she added, her blue-red eyes narrowing. "It will heal them permanently. We will no longer be bound."

"And?"

Her smile came all the way to her eyes, drawing them

tight at the corners and tightening the tops of her cheeks. But it barely touched her lips. "And . . . with the dissolution of my markings on you will also be the destruction of your Venatorial powers. The *vis bulla* will be useless to you. You will no longer sense those of my race."

But he'd chosen to be a Venator; he could choose it again. He'd willingly go through the life-or-death test to regain any powers he lost.

As if reading his mind—perhaps it was as simple as her sensing the change in him—Lilith continued: "But, of course, since you are not of Gardella blood, my bites that you so disdain have tainted you and your blood. As such, you will not be able to pass the test to regain your lost powers. They would be gone from you forever. But never fear—along with the loss of your strength, you will be relieved of any memory of our times together, of your time as a Venator. It will all go away."

"I will recall nothing of the Venators, of the vampires?"

"Nothing. Your ignorance will be your bliss."

He could forget what had happened. Live a normal life.

"You've done your duty, Maximilian. Beyond your duty. You've done everything that's been asked of you, and more. I would miss you, of course. . . ."

Then he understood. "And, of course, I would be ripe for your plucking."

"Oh, no, Maximilian. You would be just like any other mortal man. No longer a challenge. No longer exciting, a mixture of pleasure"—she stroked a hand over his cheek—"and pain"—and slipped her hand down under his shirt to brush against his *vis bulla*. And then she jerked away with the shock, and a breathless laugh. "I would have no further interest in you."

His heart thumped quietly. "Why?"

Lilith placed both hands on his chest. "I would no longer have to contend with my greatest threat: you as a Venator."

He took her wrists—the first time he'd ever touched her of his own volition—and forced them away.

"So what shall it be, Maximilian? A free, ignorant life . . . or the *vis bulla* and me?"

One

In Which Our Heroine Is Rearmed

On the west bank of the Tiber, in Rome's fourteenth *rione*, lay a small quarter known as the Borgo. Beyond its narrow streets, farther to the west, perched the Basilica of Saint Peter, and just to its east was the massive fortress of Castel Sant'Angelo. But within the small crisscross of *borghi,* a peaceful collection of hostels, shops, and churches attracted pilgrims from all over the world. Rosary makers, or *coronari*, had shops intermingled with *osterie*—the small eateries that offered meat and pastries—alongside the homes of artisans who worked at the Vatican.

Down one of the narrow *borghi*, near enough to smell the unpleasant aroma of oiled silk from the umbrella makers, was situated the unassuming church of Santo Quirinus. Made of yellowing plaster with curved terra-cotta tiles for its hipped roof, it was barely large enough to be considered a church rather than a chapel. In the shadow of the brilliant St. Peter's and the low but imposing presence of Santa Maria in Traspontina, Santo Quirinus attracted no more attention than might a Roman cockroach.

But deep beneath this tiny, simple church was a large, circular room. In the center of the secret subterranean chamber rumbled a fountain that spilled into a red-veined marble pool about the size of a bed. The water that tumbled from a slender column of pink marble was pure and clear and shimmered as though mixed with diamonds.

The chamber itself was accessible through a well-hidden spiral staircase. It acted as the hub to other rooms and galleries, reached by hallways that shot off like spokes through arched entryways, each flanked by two columns of black-and-gray-streaked white marble.

Lady Victoria Gardella Grantworth de Lacy, who back in her homeland of England was also the Marchioness of Rockley, stood at the fountain. Two tiny silver crosses dangled from her fingertips. The silk skirt of her long navy-and-black gown brushed up against a table behind her, where a piece of parchment that tended to curl back into itself was kept open by the weight of an inkwell and a small book.

She had not yet fully come to terms with the grief of losing her great-aunt Eustacia so horrifically a month ago, for it had happened only a year after her beloved husband, Phillip, had been turned into a vampire. It seemed sometimes too much for her to bear, to think about losing two people whom she'd loved so briefly, yet so deeply—two people who each understood a single side of her bilateral life.

"Why do you not wear both of them?"

"Wear two *vis bullae*?" Victoria watched as the woman next to her trailed just the tip of her forefinger in the brilliant water. "Is that permissible?"

Wayren, a tall, slender woman with hair the color of wheat, pulled her dripping finger from the water. As she had been every time Victoria had seen her, she was dressed in a long, simple gown gathered loosely at the waist with a woven leather belt. Her sleeves, fitted tightly at the tops of her arms, flared into wide points and hung from her wrists nearly to the floor. She looked like a medieval chatelaine, and even though she was wearing fashions centuries older than the flounce-hemmed, ankle-length gown Victoria wore, she did not look out of place.

"*Permissible* is an odd choice of word for the Gardella to use," Wayren replied with a beatific smile. With her customary ease and grace, she moved the leather-wrapped braid that fell from her temple back over her shoulder, where it merged with the rest of her long hair.

Wayren was not a Venator. She was . . . Victoria wasn't ever exactly certain who or what Wayren was, except that her library of old books and scrolls seemed infinite, and she was the one to whom the Venators always turned when they needed information and advice. "A single *vis bulla* is forged specifically for each Venator as he or she is called. As it is created for each one individually, there are no two alike, and the amulet becomes an intimate part of them. When possible, the *vis* is always buried with the Venator, but of course this didn't happen in the case of your aunt. I've not known a Venator to wear two *vis bullae*, but there has probably not been a time when one has had the opportunity to *have* two of them. It is not as if there are extras lying about. And as you are the new Gardella, there is no one who should say you nay."

"I can scarcely comprehend that less than two years after I had the dreams that led to my calling to be a Venator, I'm now the one to whom everyone will turn. Even those who have been Venators far longer than I." Victoria's aunt had been eighty-one, one of the longest-living vampire hunters ever, when she died. As the only other person bearing the direct bloodline of the Gardella family, Victoria had inherited the title—and responsibility—of *Illa* Gardella: the Gardella.

"You may be younger—in fact, you may be our youngest Venator," Wayren told her with that same smile, "but you are well deserving of your title. What you have accomplished in the last eighteen moons would have been a challenge for even your aunt when she was in her prime fighting years."

Victoria looked away from Wayren's serene gaze, focusing on the spill of glittering holy water next to her. She hadn't accomplished running off Lilith last year in London, or killing Nedas, the vampire queen's son, a month ago, without Max's help.

Wayren was speaking again, perhaps in an effort to draw Victoria from her unpleasant thoughts. "The *vis bullae* are precious amulets. They cannot and should not be destroyed, and they are worth nothing to one who is not a Venator. Did your aunt tell you from whence they come?"

"The crosses are forged from a silver vein under the hill at Golgotha, in the Holy Land," Victoria replied. "And they are held in holy water blessed by the pope"—she gestured at the fountain— "until they are given to the Venator for whom they were intended. But . . . is not each *vis bulla* made for one particular person? Can another Venator wear one not made for herself?"

Wayren was nodding. "Yes, one and only one *vis bulla* is forged for the person for whom it is intended. As you see, the one that belonged to your aunt Eustacia is different from the one that Max gave you. But as you are aware, the power of a *vis bulla* can strengthen any Venator."

Victoria didn't need to look at the small crosses, each of which hung from its own silver hoop, to recall which was which. Aunt Eustacia's had tiny beveled edges, and the ends of each bar of the cross were pointed. Max's was slightly thicker and sturdier, without any ornamentation. Both crosses were no larger than her thumbnail.

Victoria's own *vis bulla* had been torn from where she

wore it pierced through her navel on the same night that Aunt Eustacia had died, during a fierce battle with Lilith's undead son, Nedas. Hers had been slender, with delicate filigree along its edges, so minute she could not comprehend how anyone could have worked silver into such an intricate design.

"Well?" asked Wayren after a moment. "Shall I ask Kritanu to prepare for two of them?"

Victoria nodded slowly, wondering if wearing two amulets would make her feel any different. Would it make her twice as strong? Or would they cancel each other out? She made the decision; if there was a problem she could easily remove one of them. "Yes. I'll wear them both."

During their conversation, the other members of the Consilium had been walking about the chambers, in and out and through, some pausing to dip their fingers in the fountain or to speak to another. They were all men of varying ages and appearance. Victoria was the only female Venator of the hundred in the world, and there were only two dozen Venators in Rome, at the Consilium, at any given time.

"Then I shall inform Kritanu, and we will proceed in a few moments. I know you have missed being on the hunt this last month while your wound healed, and you were closing up your aunt's properties in Venezia and Florence." Wayren gave her another soothing smile, then moved away in such a graceful manner that she appeared to glide.

The reinserting of her *vis bulla* was brief and less painful than Victoria recalled the first piercing being. Perhaps it was because the pain of its being torn away was more prevalent in her memory than the quick, smooth piercing. Kritanu, the elderly man originally from India who had been Aunt Eustacia's companion and Victoria's trainer, was quick and efficient with the long, curved needle. Since Victoria had decided to wear the two amulets, Kritanu inserted them separately, so that they each hung from the top of her navel and brushed against each other as they settled into the small hollow below. The moment the first one slipped into place, Victoria felt a renewal of energy, a familiar surge tingle through her body.

She felt as if she'd become whole again.

And, now that she was wearing something from her aunt, perhaps she would not only have her aunt's strength of spirit with her, but also begin to heal her grief.

"Beheaded dogs and cats?" Victoria said, looking from Ilias, the keeper of the Consilium and one of the eldest Venators, to Michalas, one of the Venators who lived permanently in Rome. It was nearly two months since Victoria had had the two *vis bullae* inserted, and although she'd been out several times after sundown searching for vampires, things had been relatively quiet.

Michalas nodded, his russet curls so tight they moved but a whisper. With his fair skin and very blue eyes, he looked more like a young boy than a feral warrior, despite the fact that he was a decade older than Victoria. "A pile of them— perhaps three dozen. In various stages of decay, so it appears the pile was started some time ago, and has been added to. I saw it two weeks ago, but many of the carcasses had been there much longer. Perhaps two or three months."

"That doesn't sound like vampires," she said, looking at Ilias for confirmation. "They prefer human blood, and certainly would have no reason to cut off the heads of their victims, at any rate."

"Yes, and it's for that reason that I waited until today's gathering to apprise you of it," Michalas said, glancing at Victoria and then back at Ilias. "There's no urgency, nothing to indicate any connection to the undead or any other non-human threat."

The older man nodded his head in agreement. Ilias was well over fifty, perhaps approaching sixty, and had watery yet wise eyes that crinkled at the corners, matching the furrows on his forehead. When he was deep in thought, as now, he pinched the end of his sharp nose with his thumb and forefinger. "*Vero,* not vampires. But something unpleasant, to be sure. It could be as simple as the leftovers from a butcher shop—some of the Oriental pilgrims have unusual eating habits. This was two weeks ago? Has the pile grown?"

Michalas smiled ruefully. "I confess, I didn't deem it important enough to check on it again. With the city preparing for Carnivale, and all of the tourists arriving for the festivities, I've been busy in the more populous areas."

"Where did you find this?"

"In the Esquiline," Michalas said. "I saw no undead in the area, but there were some about. I could sense them."

"The Esquiline. That's near the Villa Palombara," Ilias said, his pale blue eyes suddenly sharp. Sometimes they appeared rheumy, but that affect seemed to disappear when something of interest presented itself.

Victoria looked at both of the men, natives of Rome, and waited for an explanation. Having lived her first twenty years in England, she was at a disadvantage in this city, the home and birthplace of the Venators. Nevertheless, despite the fact that she was a woman, and much younger than either of them, they were respectful and forthcoming with whatever information she needed. She was the Gardella.

"The Villa Palombara has been empty for a hundred and forty years, since its *marchese* disappeared under unusual circumstances. He was an alchemist, and had quite a popular salon with others of his inclination—trying to find the way to transmute any metal to gold, that process which, of course, is believed to be the source of immortality."

Victoria felt that it would be in poor taste to mention that one could easily achieve immortality by having a vampire turn one undead. Of course, there was the disadvantage of being damned for all eternity and being relegated to drinking human blood if one was turned. Instead, she said, "Perhaps we could go tonight and see if anything has changed. As well, I'm not familiar with that part of the city and would like to see it with someone who knows it well."

"That would be a pleasure," Michalas said with a genuine smile. "I would enjoy hunting with you."

They were interrupted from their conversation, which had taken place in one of the alcoves adjoining the fountain chamber, by a handsome man with red-gold hair. His arms were heavily muscled, a feature that Zavier tended to display by wearing unfashionable shirts with the sleeves cut off, much as he might have on the farm his father and brothers worked back in Scotland. It made him look slightly barbaric, and Victoria felt mildly embarrassed at all of his exposed skin.

"Come, ye gabblers—Wayren is gathering us in the Gallery. Victoria, 'tis good to see your bonny face again. Ilias, Michalas, come along with ye."

"Zavier." She turned toward him, smiling. "I knew you wouldn't miss our celebration today! I can only imagine how delighted you'll be to see Aunt Eustacia's new portrait unveiled in the Gallery."

Though his brawny physique bespoke great strength, his blue eyes were kind and his smile warm, particularly when he was in Victoria's presence—a fact that had not been lost on her. He'd left Rome just after Aunt Eustacia died to investigate rumors of vampire activity in Aberdeen. Wayren, with the use of the well-trained pigeons that clustered around Santo Quirinus, had learned that Zavier was on his way back to Rome, but she hadn't been certain he'd be there in time for the portrait unveiling, a bittersweet tradition that honored

each Venator after his or her death. But she should have
known Zavier wouldn't have missed the honor to the oldest
Venator.

Somehow, as he ushered her out of the alcove, he managed to place himself between her and Michalas and Ilias,
drawing her back to walk behind them. "And you ken that I
have been attemptin' to wheedle out of Wayren whether the
painting of Eustacia is one of her in her younger years or as
we ken her."

Victoria slipped her hand into the tiny crook of his arm,
aware of the unusual fact that her fingers were touching a
man's bare skin. He'd been the first of the Venators to be-
friend her when Aunt Eustacia brought her to the Consilium
for the first time. Not that the rest of them had been stand-
offish or looked down on her for being a woman—only Max
had done that, and only until he'd seen her at her most vul-
nerable moment—for they were all well aware of the power
and skill her aunt had wielded, and thus they held no preju-
dice against the female gender.

"She hasn't told me either," she replied, glancing at him.

"Well, soon enough. Tell me, when will ye be having
your *vis bulla* replaced, and be able to go out on the hunt?"

"I have already done so, Zavier. Whilst you were gone
back to Scotland."

"Och! And I meant to be there for it," he said, a gleam of
humor in his cornflower eyes. "I would have offered to hold
your hand."

Victoria couldn't stay the blush—and, truly, it was mortifying for her, a Venator, to blush over something like
this!—and she looked away.

Despite the fact that every Venator wore his *vis bulla*
somewhere on his body, pierced through the skin so that it
became one with the being of the person, Victoria had not
relished the thought of being surrounded by a group of men

whilst her belly was bared and her navel poked. And along with that resolution, she'd also made it a point not to consider where Zavier—or any other Venator—wore his. She felt it was a private thing.

"Well, you were not, and Kritanu and Wayren were the only ones there. Just as I preferred."

Zavier chuckled. "Ye canna blame a man for tryin' his best."

Victoria changed the subject as they wandered past the fountain and through the alcove that led to the Gallery where portraits of all of the Venators through the years were hung. "Did you dispatch the vampires in Aberdeen?"

"Indeed I did. Five of the demmed leeches were living beneath the construction of the new Music Hall, coming out at night to feed on the locals. I never heard of any undead that far north before; I thought Scotland was too cold and rough for them."

Victoria smiled. "I'm certain it was pleasant to have a reason to visit home, after living here for several years. I've been in Italy for only six months, but already I do miss London. Have you had any more thought on the paintings? Perhaps the months away from them have given you a different theory."

"No matter how I look at it, and study the portraits in the Gallery, I can only come to the conclusion that they have all been painted by the same artist."

"Even though some of the paintings of the Venators are centuries old?" Victoria let the humor into her voice. "It must be a family of painters, perhaps a father-to-son-to-grandson sort of talent . . . not so unlike that of the Venators."

"Ye are most likely correct, but I still canna get beyond the fact that they are so similar. And Wayren persists in being mysterious about it all. Ah, well, 'tis nothing more than a legitimate opportunity for me to study our artifacts."

"Which is no hardship for you."

"Indeed not." He looked at her, his eyes suddenly warm enough to cause her face to heat. "Perhaps now that I am back we can hunt together some night. Carnivale begins in three days, and we will all need to be watchful during the festivities."

"So I hear," she replied. "I am looking forward to experiencing the great Roman Carnivale."

"Since I have been here these last five years, I have learned to greatly enjoy it. Most especially the roasted chestnuts and *brunetti*, which they sell on every street corner."

With that, they entered the long, narrow portrait gallery, which was lined on each side with the pictures of every Venator from Gardeleus on. Most of them were men, but there were a few women in the ranks. Zavier, who was particularly interested in the female slayers, had told her that each of the women Venators were direct descendants of Gardeleus—as Victoria herself was, and her aunt before her, and unlike himself and Michalas, who were from other branches of the family. One of her favorite portraits depicted Catherine Gardella, whose laughing green eyes and brilliant red hair gave her a mischievous look that made Victoria wish she'd known her.

Other Venators, like Zavier, were also from the Gardella family tree, but had sprung randomly from far-flung branches that often went for three or more generations without producing a potential Venator.

Ilias gathered their attention with three sharp claps of his large-knuckled hands. "Since I believe that Zavier is about to expire on the spot with curiosity, it is time to unveil and honor our beloved Eustacia Gardella, mistress of the Venators, gracious lady of the Gardellas."

With a quick flick of his wrist, he whipped the lush white covering from the large portrait, revealing a life-size painting.

Victoria felt the sting of tears in her eyes as she looked on the beautiful, wise face of the woman who had mentored her through her first year as a Venator. The artist, who in keeping with his mystery did not sign a name to any of the portraits, had captured the liveliness in her eyes, the gentle crinkles at their corners, and the gleam of her black hair. Aunt Eustacia's white forehead showed nary a wrinkle, despite the fact that the painting depicted her just as she had been before she died—eighty-one years old, and still beautiful and strong.

Zavier bumped a handkerchief in front of Victoria's hands and she took the wadded cotton, dabbing at her eyes—hardly remembering the last time she'd wept. Her hand moved down over the front of the loose tunic and split skirt she'd taken to wearing now that her mother wasn't nearby to insist upon more conventional garb, pressing through the material to the pair of *vis bullae* that hung from her navel. Aunt Eustacia's was on the right, and Victoria closed her fingers around it for a moment . . . and missed her aunt.

Two

Wherein Our Heroine Is Privy to a Repulsive Discovery

"I do believe Zavier is smitten with the new *Illa* Gardella," Michalas said to Victoria. He cast her a sly grin from under his hat brim as they walked quickly along the Via Merulana. "Perhaps I should have invited him to join us."

Victoria was glad it was dark, for she would have been mortified for him to see the warm flush on her cheeks. Although perhaps he would have written off the slight color to the bite in the February air, for the tip of her nose was cold and likely just as red. "Perhaps you should have, although we'd likely be treated to a history lesson if you had."

Michalas chuckled softly, then gestured ahead. Fortunately the air wasn't cold enough to show the puff of air from his laugh. "You're likely quite correct."

Victoria was, of course, well aware of the interest the Scot had shown toward her, but she was a bit mortified that others had noticed as well. But why should it matter? Zavier was kind and gentle, and so very different from the easy propriety of her husband, Phillip . . . and the golden, overbearing charm of Sebastian.

The thought of Sebastian, and how she'd let him seduce her last autumn in the carriage, made Victoria's stomach squiggle, and so she picked up her pace as she walked along with Michalas.

Sebastian was the great-great-great-(she didn't know how many generations)-grandson of the legendary vampire Beauregard. Because Beauregard had been turned undead after he'd had his own son, there had been no vampire blood passed down through the generations. Sebastian was just as mortal as Victoria herself, but despite their intimacies, she didn't and couldn't fully trust him, for he seemed to come and go on a whim—usually when there were vampires or other danger about—and it was obvious his loyalties were divided.

As such, Sebastian had spent the past year, since meeting Victoria, trying to balance his loyalty to his grandfather with his . . . how would he describe his relationship with Victoria? A fascination? Attraction? Game of cat and mouse?

She suppressed a snort that would have sent her mother into spasms, if she'd been there to hear it. But she was safely back in London, undoubtedly being squired about by the smitten Lord Jellington and exchanging gossip with her two cronies, fondly known as Lady Nilly and Duchess Winnie.

But what would *Victoria* call it—her relationship with Sebastian? A tryst gone bad? Or good . . . depending on how one looked at it. An *affaire*?

She'd tried to give as little thought to him as he likely gave to her these days, now that his great-grandfather was stalking the streets of Rome, attacking and feeding where he would and taking great care not to get caught. Regardless of whatever her feelings were toward Sebastian, Victoria had a duty and a responsibility to hunt down Beauregard and slam a stake into his centuries-old chest.

But Sebastian had apparently thought of her at least once since last autumn, for somehow he had obtained her Aunt Eustacia's *vis bulla* after the horrific events of that long, bloody night and sent it to Victoria. How he'd obtained it she couldn't guess, but the fact that he had sent it on to her was a miracle.

And then there was Max, from whom she'd heard nothing since he handed her his own *vis bulla* and walked away. Almost four months ago.

That *vis*, in combination with her aunt's strength amulet, had given Victoria even greater strength and speed than her own single amulet. Instead of canceling each other out or even maintaining her level of expertise, the dual *vis bullae* had made her faster, stronger, and healthier—if the training she'd been doing with Kritanu was any indication.

Michalas stopped, drawing Victoria abruptly from her maze of thoughts. It was a good thing a vampire hadn't leaped out in front of her, as she'd been distracted more than was prudent.

"Eh, now, look here," he said. "This great stone wall encloses the Palombara estate. It reaches all along this block and then around in a sort of elongated pentagonal shape. We're at the very rear, at the farthest point from the villa, which sits near the front, at the fifth corner of the wall. It's just a bit up this street that I came upon the pile of animal carcasses."

The sun had just set, and the graying light in the sky allowed her to see the crumbling rock of the barrier. Along the top of the enclosure—which was half again as tall as she was—high, sharp stones had been set in the mortar so that their edges discouraged anyone from climbing over. But there were cracks, and one large one where an oak branch had grown against the wall and caused it to buckle, then split halfway down so it would be possible to climb through.

Via Merulana was lined by narrow residences that appeared to be more well-kept than the Palombara estate, yet it wasn't a busy thoroughfare. A few carriages drove by, and several pedestrians moved quickly along—heads bent against the chill, or in an effort to remain unseen and unnoticed. It was a bit eerie, made more so by the fact that she and Michalas didn't carry a lantern as if in fear of attracting attention.

"No one has lived here for more than one hundred forty years," Michalas told her, examining the crevice where the tree trunk thrust through. "Apparently the *marchese* had a secret laboratory where he and some of his fellow alchemists conducted their experiments. He claimed he was about to unveil the secret of transmutation after two more nights of work in his workshop, but he disappeared that very night. The laboratory, which presumably contains the results and remnants of his experiments, has remained locked since his disappearance."

Victoria looked thoughtfully at the broken wall. "I don't suppose he was turned into a vampire," she said, a note of humor in her voice.

Before Michalas could reply, they both stilled. "Speaking of the bloody creatures," he murmured, sliding a stake from his belt. Victoria followed suit and they looked at each other, then waited.

She felt the brush of cold air over the back of her neck, raising the prickles of awareness that always accompanied the presence of an undead. "It's back there," she said, gesturing to the wall. "Behind the wall."

Michalas nodded, and they moved toward the crack in the enclosure. "First or last?" he asked.

"First," Victoria said, pleased he hadn't tried to keep her behind. Some of the male Venators, particularly the younger ones who hadn't fought beside Aunt Eustacia, still had to be reminded that she was as capable—more so, in fact, due to her dual *vis* and direct Gardella lineage—as they in defending herself.

Despite that, Michalas had to help her through the crevice when her wide-legged trousers, designed to look like a skirt, got caught on a low branch. He followed behind her.

The sensation at the back of her neck was getting stronger, so she knew they were going in the right direction. The sun's last gasp of light was disappearing rather quickly, and it was too dark on the other side of the wall to see any details of the overgrown terrain. Tall, skeletal trees mingled with thick bushes, and the tangled brown-leaved vines and brush of a long-forgotten garden left little room to pass.

Michalas pointed to the remnant of a pathway marked only by a smattering of stones. It was a pale streak in the dark, and nearly obstructed by tall grass that had fallen over it through the years. They were silent as they moved along the old trail. Victoria found herself peering ahead in the direction she expected the villa to lie, somehow assuming she'd see lights or other illumination, but knowing that there would be none. It was just odd to have a large estate in the middle of a city, empty and unused. This would never occur in London.

The sensation at the back of her neck was growing stronger; Victoria knew they were close when they came upon a lower stone wall that appeared to bisect the estate, separating the back, with its more natural gardens, from the front, where the villa, stable, and more formal gardens would lie.

She sensed three or four of the undead nearby, perhaps just on the other side of the wall. She and Michalas either needed to find a gate or another way over it.

She silently grabbed Michalas's arm to get his attention and showed him four fingers, now barely visible, backlit by an anemic moon. He nodded and pointed to a large gap where the two walls should have connected—a space they could easily walk through.

But as they moved toward it, Victoria heard the sound of rusty metal: a gate, opening and clinking back into place. She and Michalas waited for a moment, then began to creep silently toward the undead.

Eight red eyes glowed in the darkness, and they appeared to be talking excitedly among themselves; probably planning where and when to stalk the victims for their evening feed. She hated to interrupt their dinner plans, but . . . she lunged from the covering of a pine tree, the needles brushing over her cheek, her stake raised.

The element of surprise allowed her to stab one of the undead before the others realized they weren't alone. When her stake plunged through to the creature's heart, he froze, then poofed into the malignant pile of ash and dust that was the final result of a life of damned immortality. Michalas was just as quick with his weapon, and it was really too simple for both of them to dispatch the other three vampires with barely the flicker of an eyelash or a disruption of breath. They were easy targets—taken by surprise as they were, and, from the looks of them, had not been undead for very long.

When she'd stabbed her second and final vampire, Victoria stopped, silent and still for a moment. The back of her neck was no longer cold and prickling, so she slipped her stake back into the deep pocket of her man's coat.

"They came from this way," Michalas said, starting off into the darkness.

Victoria was glad to follow. One could hardly call that brief skirmish a battle—she could have done it in full court dress, without Michalas. Perhaps they would find something more interesting if they continued.

She finally saw the shape of the villa, rising wide and dark in front of them, just past the lower gated wall through which the vampires had come. It was dark as a tomb, large and black and quiet.

"It must be here somewhere," Michalas said from the darkness. She realized he was walking along yet another wall, this one angling off from the shorter one and stretching into the darkness, toward the back corner of the villa.

"What?"

"*La Porta Alchemica*," he said as she joined him. "The Door of Alchemy—the door to Palombara's laboratory. I've not seen it, but I've heard about it."

"It's too dark," Victoria said, peering up at a particularly overbearing pine that obliterated every bit of residual light from the moon. "I don't know how we'll find it."

Michalas *tsk*ed. "If only we had some source of light . . . Why does Miro not invent something practical like that for us? How many times have I wished for something that I could turn on or inflame at a moment's notice. We spend so much time in the dark and cannot see. All the fancy weapons he spends his time on—pah! An ash stake is all I need. Or perhaps a little bit of something that could be set to explode at will." His smile flashed at her.

Privately, Victoria agreed with him that the best weapon was a stake, but since the Venator weapons master was working on a special garment for her, she felt it would be inappropriate to complain.

"Eh, perhaps this is it. Feel here," Michalas said.

She moved next to him and felt around the great stone lintel that framed a massive stone door set into the wall. The moon peeked out from behind the trees and clouds just enough to illuminate the smooth white door and the shadowy carvings on it and its frame.

"It's locked with three keys, and I understand it cannot be

opened without all three of them," Michalas told her. "This must be it. Feel the round disk in the center? And the carvings on it? There are more carvings on the lintel, and legend has it that the symbols and words there are taken directly from an alchemical journal that came into the possession of Palombara before he disappeared."

"Do these symbols contain the secrets to immortality, then?" she asked in a wry voice, feeling the moss and dirt beneath her fingers as she felt the crevices of the carvings.

Michalas was moving around in the dark behind her now, back in the direction from which they'd come. Suddenly she heard the unmistakable sound of him tripping and then the "Oof!" when he fell.

Even Venators, apparently, had moments of gracelessness.

"By the bloody rood," swore Michalas quietly.

"What is it?" she asked, coming toward him where he crouched not far from the gate through which the vampires had passed.

"You . . . perhaps you don't want to see this," he said, straightening and turning as if to block her view. "Eh, it is not a pleasant sight."

Remembering the carnage she'd seen at Bridge and Stokes, a private club in London, Victoria shook her head. "What is it?"

She nearly stumbled over them herself in her effort to show she wasn't hesitant. There were four of them. She could barely make out the details in the low light, but she could see enough.

Still clothed. One in a dress. The other three in breeches and shirts.

Humans.

Headless.

Just like Aunt Eustacia.

The memory shot into her mind. Blood everywhere.

Victoria took a deep breath, closed her eyes. Her heart was slamming hard. Her stomach roiled, but she managed to keep from losing control. She waited a moment, swallowing hard. "What are they doing? Why cut off their heads?"

"They were taking them somewhere, probably out of the estate."

Victoria looked at Michalas. "No coincidence that there's a pile of beheaded animal carcasses nearby. Let's go see if . . . if there are other bodies there. But . . . we can't leave them here."

"No . . . eh . . . shall we bring them somewhere outside these walls so they'll be found? So perhaps they'll be identified? I've not heard any reports in the city about finding headless corpses," Michalas added. "I've a cousin who works with the *polizia*, and he tells me of all the goings-on."

"But why take off their heads? They're vampires," Victoria asked again, if only to keep her mind from thinking about the morbid task at hand. They certainly couldn't leave the bodies; Michalas was right.

In the end they moved the four corpses and left them in a small courtyard several blocks away from the Palombara estate. Michalas would suggest to his cousin that he might wish to investigate that particular *viuzza*, and then the police could at least attempt to find the families of the victims.

By the time they completed the task of moving the bodies, Victoria was filthy and bloody and quite nauseated, but she still wanted to see the pile of animal carcasses, so Michalas took her to where he'd found it, which was only two streets away from the broken wall of the estate.

The pile was still there, in the darkest corner of an overgrown courtyard behind a half-burned-out apartment. She had no idea how Michalas had ever come upon it.

According to him, the pile was larger now. Rotted. The

stench was stomach-turning. And it was composed only, as far as they could tell, of dogs and cats, perhaps a wolf or two.

But it would be too much of a coincidence to believe that the four dead humans were not intended to be added to the pile.

"Now we know there are undead involved," Victoria said as she and Michalas walked away from the dark courtyard, still on the alert for more undead. "But the question becomes: What are they doing with the heads?"

Three

In Which Victoria's Idyll Is Invaded

Victoria and Michalas finished the night by patrolling the rest of the *rione* near Villa Palombara. They staked a measly three more vampires before returning to the Consilium at sunrise to report their findings to Ilias. They found him on his way to speak with Wayren.

After their brief discussion, Ilias suggested that Victoria join him with Wayren in her private library. Michalas appeared relieved to be dismissed, saying with a crooked grin that he was ready to return home to his own bed.

Victoria would have been pleased to do so herself, but of course she did not. She followed Ilias to the library. It smelled of old books—of paper and papyrus, of ink and leather. She had been there only once before—very briefly—so as she came into the dome-shaped room that was accessed by a locked door with hidden bolts, she took the opportunity to reexamine the chamber.

The ceiling of the round room was high above her head, and rows of books sat on shelves that appeared to be carved into the circular walls. On closer look, however, she saw that the shelves were stone ledges, and carved with letters or symbols in a language Victoria didn't recognize. She presumed the symbols were some sort of code by which the books, scrolls, and laced-together parchments were organized.

Victoria stepped onto a thick white rug that covered half of the chamber floor and selected a straight-backed chair for her seat. In the center of the room was a large piece of glass situated like a tabletop. Wayren sat behind the desk, her square spectacles resting neatly on a wooden tray next to a spread-eagled book. Ilias, who'd followed Victoria into the room, closed the door behind him and sank into the final seat.

The room wasn't as large as she would have imagined, knowing how many tomes Wayren had access to. A bevy of candles burned from sconces on the walls and some of the lower shelves, and from stands with multiple tiers and holders placed throughout the room. Despite being a deep flight of stairs underground, the room was lit as if it were noon in July.

Ilias glanced at Wayren. "Where is Ylito? Is he not joining us?"

She bowed her head easily. "He is in the midst of a procedure. I have already spoken with him, and he urges us to continue without him."

"Ylito?" Victoria was surprised at the unfamiliar name. She knew of all of the Venators by name, even if she hadn't met them all, and the Comitators, their martial-arts trainers, but this was one she'd never heard mentioned.

"He is not a Venator, but an herbalist and alchemist who studies the properties of plants and metals and is very talented with his work."

Victoria looked at Wayren. "Do you mean to say he's a wizard?"

The older woman looked pained for a moment, then

smiled slightly. "He prefers to be called a hermetist, a sort of spiritual alchemist, which is a bit more palatable to him than the moniker of wizard or sorcerer." When Victoria continued to look at her with clear question in her eyes, she continued, "As powerful and daunting as our Venators may be, we've found over the years that someone like Ylito often provides skills beyond what a Venator can do: casting protections, creating infusions or distillations, and even drawing forth the energies and inherent powers of gold and silver—all for the purpose of annihilating the malevolence brought on this earth by Lilith and her kind."

"It is not surprising that you haven't met Ylito, or perhaps even heard his name spoken," added Ilias. "He prefers to remain cloistered in his workshop unless needed. Which is why he's chosen not to grace us with his presence at this time." He shifted in his seat and raised a hand to scratch his chin. "So let us get to the matter at hand, Victoria. We have vampires who are cutting the heads off small animals and now, apparently, humans." He looked at Wayren. "That would be behavior more like that of a demon, so I am at a loss as to why the undead would do such a thing, particularly since they abhor demons."

"I shall have to study it," Wayren told them when they described in more detail the headless corpses. "But I would suggest that a visit to the Door of Alchemy—*la Porta Alchemica*—during the daylight would be in order. Perhaps we will find some evidence that you could not see in the dark."

Ilias turned to Victoria. "There are three keys that open the Magic Door, as it is also called. Each one must be inserted in its proper slot and, once inserted, cannot be retrieved until the door is open. Palombara had one of the keys, he secreted a second one somewhere in the villa, and the third one was given to Augmentin Gardella shortly before the *marchese* disappeared."

"A Venator." Victoria's skin began to prickle.

"Indeed. Unfortunately Augmentin wasn't able to save Palombara from whatever befell him before he completed his quest. But he did keep the key. And passed it down through the family. Your aunt Eustacia was the last person to have it."

"It's not here, and we'd best find it before the vampires do," Wayren said, looking at Victoria. "I believe your aunt wore it on her person. Do you recall a silver armband? It was made specifically to hold the key, which is quite small—not much larger than the first knuckle of your finger."

"She wore it high on her arm, and never took it off. That and her *vis bulla*." Victoria chewed on her lip, not liking where her thoughts were leading her. Not at all. Best to change the subject. "What's behind the door that's so important to the vampires? They already have immortality."

"The papers and journals of the alchemist must contain something of value to them. After Palombara disappeared, there was much activity about the door, as the undead—and some of the mortal alchemists—tried to force their way in. But the only way in is with the three keys, and they were in possession of none of them, even, presumably, the one kept by the *Marchese* Palombara." Ilias was rubbing his nose again, pinching it between a thumb and forefinger.

"They gave up after a time, and the Door of Alchemy has remained untouched and unbothered for a hundred and forty years. But now, with this undead activity in the area—as well as the death of your aunt and the possibility that the key might fall into the wrong hands—it's imperative that we keep our attention on the door. In fact, the very great possibility is that somehow the key was removed from her person . . . after the events last autumn, and that it has already been put to use." Wayren's face, unlined and ageless, was a pale moon of seriousness. "The fact that the undead want what's behind the door is more than enough reason for us to be concerned."

"Yet another reason to visit the door, to see if any of the keys have been turned," Ilias said.

"Yes. Ylito will want to accompany you," Wayren said, to Victoria's surprise. "Perhaps you will be able to ascertain what is so important behind that door, or at least whether there is indeed anyone trying to get inside it."

Late that afternoon Oliver, Victoria's driver and the bane of her maid's existence, stopped the little barouche in front of the Gardella villa. As Victoria stepped out, she realized she hadn't been home or slept since leaving yesterday morning for the portrait unveiling at the Consilium. She was bone-tired, yet energized with purpose in a way she hadn't been for months. Her mind was racing down a myriad of avenues, and she felt as though she could barely keep up with it. At the same time she was still dirty and mussed from her evening of moving headless corpses with Michalas.

But she had a task, and felt for the first time since Aunt Eustacia's death that she was back in full form.

Still, she wanted nothing more than to get into the quiet of her room and practice some of the meditation and breathing that Kritanu had taught her. Tomorrow she would meet the mysterious Ylito and they would go to examine *la Porta Alchemica*.

The front door opened just as she reached it, Aunt Eustacia's Italian butler looking slightly more harried than usual.

"*Grazie*, Giorgio," Victoria said, walking in and directly toward the stairs as she pulled off her gloves and began to unhook the fastenings of her spencer. "Please ring for Verbena and ask that she wait upon me in my chamber."

"*Si*, milady," Giorgio said. "But perhaps you might wish to take a moment to visit the parlor?"

"The parlor?" Victoria, her hand on the newel post at the bottom of the steps, halted reluctantly—only a flight of stairs from the haven she sought. She glanced toward the parlor and saw that the door was closed.

But before Giorgio could reply, the door in question opened. "Victoria!" came a familiar shrill greeting. "Victoria, we have arrived!"

Victoria couldn't move. Her fingers froze like a cap over the stairwell post as she looked at her mother, Lady Melisande Gardella Grantworth, rushing toward her from the sitting room, skirts and ruffles and lace bouncing and flouncing in all directions.

"We?" Victoria managed to ask, all thoughts of a quiet rest disintegrating along with the peacefulness of her home. No wonder Giorgio had looked out of sorts.

"Indeed! Lady Nilly and Duchess Winnie and myself, we're all here. Just in time for the week of Carnivale. And for you, you poor dear, of course. Poor darling, to have to handle all of this on your own. I am only sorry I couldn't have arrived sooner." Lady Melly gathered Victoria into her maternal embrace even as her daughter desperately clutched the stairwell post.

And as her mother's two bosom friends spilled into the hall behind her, arms outstretched in greeting, high-pitched voices exclaiming over everything from Victoria's simple hairstyle to her sunken cheeks to the mild Italian weather and how it was so warm for February, so why were her hands so cold and her gown—was that even a gown?—so dirty and mussed? My goodness!—had she been hurt? . . . she could do nothing but let them fuss and hug and pat and croon as they'd done since she was a little girl.

With a weary glance over her shoulder, she told Giorgio, "Please tell Verbena I shall be a while."

A long while.

Two hours later Victoria sank onto the stool in front of her dressing mirror. Two hours.

All that time listening to her mother and the ladies Winnie and Nilly prattle on about the circles under her eyes, the gauntness of her cheeks (although Lady Nilly thought it wasn't so terrible, she of the hollow cheeks herself), and the paleness of her skin. Not to mention the droopiness of her plain hairstyle and unfashionable clothing.

And that wasn't all. There were unveiled hints about her returning to London to find another husband. And how her dear friend Gwendolyn Starcasset was now the toast of the ton, with her new betrothal to an earl with more than fifty thousand a year, and how her brother, George, would be a perfect match for Victoria. (Victoria had had to bite her tongue particularly hard on that topic, for the last time she'd seen George Starcasset he'd been here in Rome with Nedas, as a member of the Tutela, and had been intent on ravishing her.)

There had been Lady Melly's grievances about the erstwhile Lord Jellington, who had, apparently, failed to meet her expectations of what a beau should do and be, and was thus the impetus for her visit to Italy.

Then followed opinions on Italian biscuits (too dry and crusty), Italian streets (crowded and confusing and filled with pilgrims), and the beauty of the little fountain in front of the villa.

She'd had to keep the ugly red calluses on her left hand— her tea-pouring and stake-wielding hand—hidden while playing hostess, for, of course, she wasn't wearing the gloves she would have been wearing had she been home in London. Nor was she garbed in a proper gown, the lapse of which still had her mother in horrified raptures.

The entire event had culminated in one big problem that led somewhere she wasn't sure she wanted to go. She rested her head on the dressing table in her chamber.

"Now, milady, no sense in lettin' em make it any worse'n it already is. Ye have important things to attend to."

Victoria lifted her head to look in the mirror. All she saw at first were two puffs of orange-colored hair on either side of her own dark head, and then her maid, Verbena, looked up from where she'd been unfastening the buttons of Victoria's tunic. Her face bore pity, but also a glow of interest.

"Did ye see that massive crucifix the duchess was wearing? I swear, even m'cousin Barth wouldn't be wearin' one that size, though he's been known to drive vampires around himself. Pardon me for sayin' so, but the duchess's cross looks bigger than the pope's."

As she spoke, Verbena drew the tunic up and over Victoria's head, leaving her droopy-eyed mistress to sit at the table in merely her split-skirt and chemise.

Victoria sighed. "I cannot believe they're here," she said wearily. "Without a word of warning Mother has arrived with them, and now I haven't any idea how I'm going to get out at night without their knowing." Sundown—vampire-hunting time—was in a matter of hours, and Melly expected her to join them for dinner, and likely more conversation. Surely she would also expect Victoria to join them in other activities, both during the day and in the evening.

In fact, the dearth of calling cards on the front table of the villa had sent Lady Melly into yet another soliloquy about how cloistered Victoria had allowed herself to become since Aunt Eustacia died, and how terrible it was that her social life had gone to null. And how glad Melly was to be here to set things right.

But that was the least of Victoria's worries.

Verbena loosened Victoria's hair from its casual mooring at the back of her head. "An' ye'll have to give more attention to your hairdressing and gowns, now that your mama is here. She won't tolerate ye lookin' less than a marchy-ness, now that ye finally got the title." She sounded magnificently pleased with this new development, which was no surprise, as Verbena lived for the opportunity to get creative with Victoria's coiffure and toilette whilst finding ways to incorporate the tools her mistress Venator might need.

Recently Victoria's choice to wear the split skirt and long tunic favored by Kritanu for both training and rest had nearly given Verbena fits. But since Victoria had rarely left the villa except late in the day to go to the Consilium and then to search the streets for vampires, it was her opinion that it mattered not what she wore. Since she knew few people in Rome, there were no social obligations requiring her attendance. And, quite honestly, Victoria preferred it that way.

Her days of balls and soirees and musicales (thank goodness) were over. She was a Venator, and that was her life.

But all that would change now that Lady Melly and her cohorts were here.

"Mother's horror at my choice of attire and coiffure was made abundantly clear, but at least the neglect was attributed to grief due to Aunt Eustacia dying." Victoria looked longingly toward her bed. Perhaps she would have two hours to rest, if she could keep the list of worries at bay. "However, sadly, that topic brought an even larger problem to mind." She looked in the mirror at her maid's crystal blue eyes.

"I've no fear ye can't handle yer mama an' her biddies. I heard her say ye should come back to London and rejoin Society . . . she wants ye to marry again so ye can give her some little bunnies in nappies."

Victoria was shaking her head. "No, no . . . that I can

manage. I think. 'Tis even a bigger problem." She closed her eyes for a moment, then rose to move toward her bed. "The silver armband that my aunt always wore . . . I must find it. As soon as my mother remembers it she'll want it—but the bigger problem now is that the vampires are already looking for it, because it holds a special key."

Their gazes met again in the mirror, Verbena's eyes rounding in her cherub face, and her mouth following suit.

"That, my lady, is a bloody mess of a pro'lem."

"Indeed it is, since my mother believes Aunt Eustacia died in her sleep. Thus, she expects that the bracelet would have been on her arm, readily available for me to retrieve."

"Per'aps yer auntie gave it to Kritanu."

Victoria shook her head. "No, she did not, for he gave me all of her personal effects, and it was not there."

The apple-cheeked maid *tsk*ed, pity curving her lips down at the corners. Then they tilted up. "But, my lady, ye've forgotten someone did see th' body after. He must've, in order to send ye her *vis bulla*. Perhaps—"

"I know," Victoria said again, rising to go to the bed, her head suddenly aching. "That is the biggest part of the problem."

Not only would she have to keep the vampires from finding the keys and opening the Magic Door . . . but now it appeared she would have to find some way to contact Sebastian and ask for his help.

Then he would, as usual, expect her to demonstrate some form of gratitude for said help.

And, truth be told, she could think of worse things to do. Much worse.

Victoria's meeting with Ylito was delayed to just before noon on a rainy morning two days after her mother and friends arrived. Even so, it was pure luck that she'd actually been able to slip out of the villa that day, for Melly had planned to take her to see the Colosseum, but had developed a headache. Victoria had quickly seized upon a similar excuse, retreating to her room and instructing Verbena to allow no one to enter until the next morning.

"This is the first day she's not dragged me about shopping, viewing the sights, parading around the city," Victoria hissed as she slipped back down through the servants' hall to the exit. "Pray God she has the headache all afternoon and misses dinner as well."

"Now, milady, ye shouldn't wish such stuff on yer mama," Verbena cautioned. "She can' help it if she jus' wants t' show ye off and dress ye pretty."

"*Marry* me off is rather more accurate," Victoria mumbled, tamping away the guilty feeling. She paused with her hand on the back door. "And for someone so concerned with propriety, the fact that it's been only three months since Aunt Eustacia died and we're not expected to be in mourning is surprising."

"'T might be so, milady, but close as ye were to her, she was still jus' yer great-aunt. Not so long fer mournin', even back in Lunnon, but ye're in Rome now. An' if Lady Melly was in mournin' she wouldn't be able t' go to Carnivale this week." Verbena looked up at her, and Victoria saw sympathy in her cornflower eyes. "Ye're still so young and pretty, milady. Yer mama jus' wants ye to find happiness. She wants t' erase that sadness in yer eyes."

Happiness. Victoria wasn't sure it was possible.

Perhaps not happiness, then, but contentment. Or at least satisfaction that her place on earth was as more than merely one half of a marriage, a womb to bear an heir, or a showpiece for her mother to flaunt.

Victoria had a more important, more difficult role than most women—or men—could imagine. If she could find the same satisfaction and peace her aunt had as *Illa* Gardella, Victoria could ask for little more.

Because her mother delayed her, Victoria was late meeting Ylito at what was left of the Villa Palombara. Despite the early February chill and dampness, she had Oliver drive a circuitous route in the city in order to make certain no one was following her from Aunt Eustacia's villa. When the barouche stopped in front of the crumbling wall shaded by the old oak that had grown through it, Oliver turned to look at her.

"This the meeting place?" He looked at her questioningly. Not only was his driving gentler than that of Barth back in London, but his care for her safety was as well. Unlike Barth, Oliver wasn't as keen on leaving a woman alone on the streets, particularly in areas that could be considered dangerous.

Of course, unlike Barth, Oliver had never seen Victoria fight vampires.

"Yes, you may let me off here and return to the villa."

She'd never seen a person with such dark skin as Ylito. Even Kritanu, who had the mahogany skin and sleek dark hair of his Indian heritage, had lighter coloring than the hermetist.

"So, you are the new *Illa* Gardella," he said, looking at her soberly. Victoria was surprised at his low, smooth voice; for some reason she'd expected him to sound as exotic as he looked, with his walnut skin and hair that spun out in tight, finger-length coils all over his head. His family was originally from Egypt, Wayren had told her, but Ylito's grandfather had left the land of the pyramids and come to study with the Venators in Rome nearly a century ago.

"And you are the mysterious Ylito," she replied, and felt compelled to make a brief bow to him. "I am delighted to meet you, particularly since I understand you rarely venture out."

He looked as if he was at least two decades, or more, older than her own twenty-one years. He was dressed in boots and breeches and a coat and shirtwaist, as any other man of the times would be, but with his dark skin and regal bearing, he still looked exotic. He gave her a formal bow in return. "Come, let us look at this strange door."

Now, in the daylight, Victoria could really see the deep split in the wall. It was caused by a low branch of the large oak growing through what had likely been a small crack at one time, but as the oak's branch and trunk filled out, it had opened the wall. The shadow of the large tree, along with a mess of leafless vines, had helped to camouflage the opening.

With Ylito's help, Victoria climbed through the crack, turning sideways so she could slip through the wet stone. She couldn't help but think it was best that Zavier wasn't there, for he would never have fit his bulky muscles through the slender opening. As soon as Ylito stepped both feet on the ground, they started off, Victoria leading the way.

The ground was wet and muddy, seeping into Victoria's slippers, and the budding leaves had begun to shoot into green furls that would soon thicken the view even more.

Ylito made a disgusted comment under his breath as he paused to wipe mud from the side of his boot, but then he followed behind Victoria as they traipsed through thigh-high grass toward an awkward-looking gray-brick building. What must have been the main part of the villa loomed high behind it, and was made of the yellowish stone most common in Rome.

As Victoria trudged along, she turned her mind from the chill of her cold, wet gown to something nearly as uncomfortable: how to find Sebastian.

In London she had been able to go to his pub, the Silver Chalice, to contact him, but it had been destroyed. The last time she'd seen him was here in Rome, when, with his usual talent, he'd simply shown up when she didn't necessarily want him to. Short of putting a notice in the newspaper, there was little she could do to find him.

But then a thought struck her. Sebastian had introduced her to two young women, twins named Portiera and Placidia. Perhaps if she called on them she might be able to learn how to find Sebastian in this city.

Not to mention the fact that her mother would love to see her interested in making social calls.

Since Lady Melly had arrived, Victoria had spent the last two nights at home with her aunt and friends, playing whist, catching up on gossip, and generally doing the things she thought she'd left behind when she married and moved from her mother's home. Even as a marchioness she was expected to have social obligations—but at least they would be under her own terms.

"There it is," Victoria said, gesturing to the wall made of slim gray stones stacked atop one another as she and Ylito passed through the same gate that the vampires had used two nights before. Off to the right was the smooth white lintel framing a solid stone door.

"*La Porta Alchemica*," said Ylito, stepping toward it.

Victoria's sodden skirt brushed against him as she too moved toward the door. It was not a particularly large one, now that she saw it in full daylight. Just an average size, low enough that someone as tall as Max might have to duck to cross the threshold.

She watched as Ylito smoothed his dark hand over the white marble as though reading with his fingertips the symbols carved there. Above the door was a large circle carving, within which were two triangles superimposed on each other, one pointing up and the other pointing down, and a cross stamped on top of them.

"Jupiter . . . tin . . . *diameter sphaerae thau . . . circli . . . non orbis prosunt . . .* Venus . . . copper . . ." murmured Ylito, moving his hand down the right side of the doorway.

"What does it say?"

"Alchemical symbols—this is for the planet Jupiter," he said, showing her the top carving that looked like a cross with an arrow pointing to the right, "and represents the metal tin. Below it, the symbol of feminity, or Venus, the circle with the cross below it. There is Mercury and Mars . . . " he added, gesturing to the other side.

"What does it all mean?"

Again Ylito flashed his white teeth. "I do not know, and apparently neither did Palombara. As the story goes, he found the papers of an alchemist who came to Rome searching for a mysterious herb. After the alchemist disappeared, Palombara studied his journals and had some of the content engraved on the door. For example, under the Jupiter symbol it says, 'the sphere's diameter, the circle's tau, and the globe's cross are of no use to the blind.' It simply means one might have the tools, but if one doesn't know how to put them to use, they're worthless."

Victoria, looking at the odd symbols, couldn't agree more.

A large dial was set into the stone of the portal, covering about the center half of the entrance. The round disk, which was flush with its setting, was formed of a different color stone and had the shape of a triangle carved into its face. At each of the three corners was a small rectangular notch, no more than two fingers wide and one thumb-length long. Victoria could see that the dirt and moss had been scraped away from the bottom right-hand notch, as though someone had recently slipped something into the hole.

She pushed her fingers in, examining the stone around the opening of what must be one of the keyholes, though it looked nothing like any keyhole she'd ever seen. Which made her realize that the key was perhaps not a long metal one with notches carved on one side, but something different. More of a small tab that would slide into the small opening. "Ylito, look at this."

He crouched next to her with a faint pop in one of his knees and thrust his fingers sideways into the notch. They disappeared up to his second knuckles, and his dark eyes lit up with interest. "The key. One of the keys has been found." He looked up at her, more animation in his face than she'd seen yet today. Obviously this was a fascination to him. "*Si*, that slot has the key slid in, unable to be retrieved until the door is opened. It has been fitted into place, and there it will stay. Each key fits in its slot and lifts the insides of the lock, and thus allows the disk to turn. That will open the door."

Victoria nodded, her heart filling her chest. Was the missing key the one that had been given to Augmentin Gardella and then passed down to Aunt Eustacia? How could they know? Had the others been found?

Then she noticed that the moss and dirt had been cleaned off just above the notch, and that there was a faint carving on it.

Ylito was already looking at the etched lettering, his quick, dark hands passing over it as if it would help him to read it. "That is the name of the key. '*Deus et homo,*' God and man. And see, there: its symbol—a large circle with rays like the sun, with a smaller circle inside it, resting at the bottom. It will be carved on the key itself, so that the user knows where it fits."

"And the other two?" Victoria crouched so she could look at the bottom left corner of the triangle, using her nails to scrape away the moss, feeling the grit of moist dirt. "They're named as well?"

"They are all noted here, in this symbol above the door," Ylito said, drawing her attention to the large circle above the door. "See, it names the keys—'*tri sunt mirabilia: Deus et homo, mater et virgo, trinus et unus*,' that means 'three are the wonders: God and man, mother and virgin, the one and three.' The wonders are represented by the three keys that will give access to this secret laboratory."

Victoria saw the words carved around the circle, and bent back down to the lower left key slot, scraping the dirt away. She uncovered enough to see that it was the "*mater et virgo*"—mother and virgin—key, and then sat back on her heels, heedless of the wet grass bleeding into her thighs and rump, her heart thumping hard in her chest. "And this?" she asked, relief beginning to creep through her muscles.

"This is the slot for the '*mater et virgo*' key," he said easily, tracing the symbols. "A slender crescent moon to the left, representing the virgin, curving away from and touching the full, ripe circle of the mother." He looked up. "It's two parts of a common ancient symbol of the three goddesses: virgin, mother, crone."

"Aunt Eustacia's armband is marked with that very same symbol of mother and virgin. They haven't found her key yet."

Ylito's face settled into a smooth mask. "But we see here evidence that someone is looking for it now."

Four

In Which Victoria Develops an Acute Dislike of Sugarplums

"So how do you find your first Roman Carnivale?" asked Zavier, looking down at Victoria as he was jolted into her side by an overzealous celebrant.

Since it was at least the dozenth time he'd bumped into her, or she into him, Victoria hardly noticed the shove; she was concentrating on keeping her papier-mâché mask in place. "It is like nothing I've ever experienced," she replied with abject honesty. "The people seem to have gone insane!" While she could fully understand why it was important for the Venators to be out in the streets during the eight nights of Carnivale, she wasn't as convinced of the necessity of wearing a mask.

If the jostled eyeholes weren't obstructing her view, the long beak of her bird-face was bumping into the person in front of her, or being knocked to the side by someone throwing a plaster sugarplum.

Or being hit by one, which had happened more than once, as evidenced by the white marks on her mask and clothing.

Zavier laughed easily, but she noticed his attention didn't falter from the activity going on around them. With all of the revelry and masquerading on the wide street of Corso spilling into the smaller, darker side streets, the night was rife with the possibility of vampire attacks—or worse, kidnappings by members of the Tutela for their vampire masters. And now the new threat of being taken off and beheaded, for some inexplicable reason. So far neither of them had encountered any undead, but it was barely midnight, and dawn was a long way off on this February night.

Although Carnivale had been going on for almost a week, this was the first night Victoria and Zavier had gone out patrolling for undead together. It was also the first time she'd gone hunting since her mother arrived, and since she and Ylito had visited the Magic Door . . . other than the time she'd surreptitiously slipped a stake into the chest of a vampire who'd dared to sneak up on Lady Nilly when they were going home after a late Carnivale party.

To Lady Melly's great joy, Victoria had put her secret plan to find Sebastian into action by looking up the Tarruscelli twins, Portiera and Placidia. Unfortunately an afternoon of tea with them had turned into a series of invitations to Carnivale parties, races, and the sharing of their balcony overlooking the Corso, where all of the festivities took place. Victoria felt odd being thrust back into a world of society and parties after turning her attention—and her life—to her Venator duties. It felt foreign to her in a way it hadn't even after she'd rejoined Society following Phillip's death.

Perhaps she really had left all of that behind.

In return for having to sit and make conversation, while chafing about the other things that needed to be tended to,

Victoria had had no luck in turning the conversation with the twins to Sebastian or learning of his whereabouts.

Perhaps he wasn't even in Rome anymore.

At any rate, tonight Victoria had managed to dislodge her mother's manipulative fingers ("But the *Barone* Zacardi is ever so smitten with you!") and plead exhaustion so that she could stay home. Ilias had explained that tonight was Rose Monday, the second-to-last night of Carnivale, and the fever pitch of excitement—and danger—would continue to grow until it reached its peak tomorrow night.

Lady Melly and the others planned to join the Tarruscellis, along with some other new acquaintances—including the bound-to-be-disappointed *Barone* Zacardi—in their red-draped balcony, so they could watch the street below. Victoria was relieved to be out on the street with her stake—masked or otherwise—and doing her job. Plus, she had another idea about how to contact Sebastian, and she was going to attempt it tonight.

The smell of roasting chestnuts tinged the air, drawing her from her thoughts, and Victoria felt a sudden pang of hunger. The fragrant nuts reminded her of Christmases spent at her family's estate of Prewitt Shore with her mother and her two friends, long before any of their husbands had died. At that house at least one of her meals during the holidays would be made up only of hot nut meats and warm milk.

"Zavier." She turned to look at him, but her mask was knocked askew again. She reached up and pushed the long, narrow bird-beak back into place, and when her eyeholes were realigned, she saw that Zavier was nowhere in sight.

If she were a normal woman, with normal strength and no capability to defend herself, she might be terrified at being separated from her male companion in the middle of the boisterous festival at midnight. But instead Victoria directed herself to the side of the broad, thronged Corso, where a man and his wife were selling hot chestnuts. Her stake was safely in the deep pocket of her loose costume, and Verbena had made certain that Victoria's other pocket included a pistol, along with a few *écus* for such an occasion as this.

She pulled out one of the coins to pay for the chestnuts, and just as she turned back to look toward the wide thoroughfare, Victoria felt another sugarplum slam into the back of her shoulder. This one was harder than any of the others; as if it had been thrown from close proximity.

She whipped around, her hand going automatically to her stake even though the back of her neck wasn't any colder than it had been moments before . . . and even though this was all supposed to be in the name of revelry. This time, miraculously, her mask stayed in place, and she turned to see a slight figure twisting away to slip through the crowd.

She started after the figure, a sense of recognition niggling deep in her mind with an impression of dark eyes behind a peacock mask, and a certain familiarity of movement.

Suddenly something grabbed her arm from behind, and Victoria pivoted back, hand groping for her pistol. "Zavier."

"Where were you going?" he asked. "I lost ye for a moment there."

"I . . . went to get some chestnuts, but I couldn't find you, and then someone threw a sugarplum at me. Again."

He laughed and turned her away. "I see it. Another powdery white spot on your shoulder." He slipped an arm around hers, as naturally as if he'd always done so. "I've seen not one vampire here tonight, nor felt—"

His voice trailed off as the hair lifted at the back of her neck in a definite chill. They looked at each other. "This way," Victoria said, starting off in the direction the figure had gone.

Whether it was a coincidence or not, she didn't know. But

they went off through the crowds, pushing through the revelers, on the trail of the first vampire they'd sensed all night.

Moving through the streets, they soon left the celebration behind them, and Victoria realized they were walking up a small hill. At the top she could see the outline of monuments and gravestones.

A cemetery. Not a bad place to find an undead.

She took off her mask and adjusted the stake she now held as they walked through the open iron gate.

"Do ye hear something?" Zavier asked, stopping next to her.

Up here, in the yard of death away from the insanity of the festival below, the night was quiet but for the occasional shout or shrill laugh far in the distance. Monuments and headstones made tall, stark shadows over the dark grass.

"No," she replied, walking on, mask dangling from her hand. The fresh air felt good on her face, now that it was uncovered, but the back of her neck had warmed slightly, and the fine hairs there had flattened. She'd lost the scent.

"Nae many vampires during Carnivale this year," Zavier said, walking along with her. His shoulder bumped against hers, then drew away as he kept on. "Perhaps they've all cloistered away since the death of Nedas, trying to get organized again."

Victoria had killed Lilith's son, Nedas, at the same time Akvan's Obelisk had been destroyed. Nedas had been a powerful leader among the vampires in Rome who'd been served by the Tutela. With his destruction, the fate of his followers and the Tutela had been thrown into question, along with the issue of who would succeed him.

"I hardly think that Beauregard would lose his opportunity to gain control of the vampire underworld in Rome," Victoria replied, stepping over a low iron fence. Its spike caught at the hem of her trousers—thank heaven her mother hadn't been around to see her wearing them. "He was fairly salivating at the news of Nedas's death, and intended to execute Max that night while the vampires looked on." Her fingers were cold, but the air was only chilly. "We barely made it out alive."

"Was there not another vampire who wished to succeed Nedas?"

"Indeed, the Conte Regalado, who was the leader of the Tutela, wanted it very badly. He is a newly turned vampire, and young in his power, but it seems as if he may have not only the support of the Tutela, but also of some of Nedas's followers. It was partly due to Regalado's interference that Max and I were able to escape from Beauregard." Regalado was also the father of the woman Max had intended to marry, a woman who enjoyed being fed upon by vampires.

Victoria wondered, fleetingly, if Sarafina's father ever fed on her, now that he was a vampire. He was vulgar enough to do so.

And Sarafina was indecent enough to let him.

The truth was, Victoria wouldn't have escaped the battle between the two factions of vampires without the assistance of Sebastian Vioget. But at least now she thought she had a way of finding him.

Lost in her thoughts, Victoria didn't realize Zavier had stopped walking until something snagged her sleeve. Dropping her mask, she whirled around, stake raised, and nearly drove it into his barrel chest.

Instead of being surprised or taken aback by her offensive stance, he looked at her with a glint of humor in his expression. "Ye can put that down for a minute."

"No, I can't," Victoria replied, spying a movement in the shadows behind him. The hair on the back of her neck lifted, and the chill intensified again.

Stake in hand, she started off after the glowing red eyes,

leaping over a gravestone and slipping a little when she landed on the damp grass.

The vampire must have thought he'd come upon two lovers strolling through the graveyard, taking a quiet moment away from Carnivale; for until Victoria landed in front of him, stake at the ready, he'd remained hovering in the bushes. When he saw that she'd fearlessly come after him, he turned and ran.

Elated, Victoria followed. She loved the feeling of letting herself go, of running, leaping over the stones and low fences, dashing around a crumbling mausoleum, and finally throwing herself at the vampire. She crashed into him, barely feeling the impact, and they tumbled to the ground. The loose legs of her costume wrapped around their calves as he rolled on top of her, fangs bared.

His eyes were red, the color of Chianti, glowing as he bent his face down toward her. She could smell blood on his breath, and she dropped her stake, reaching up to grab him by the shoulders and fling him onto his back. He was young and relatively weak, and would be perfect for the message she needed to send.

But suddenly there was a whistle of movement and the vampire jerked, then froze, then burst into a cloud of dust and musty ash. It poofed onto her face and into her hair and lashes, and Victoria looked up to see Zavier standing over her. He was offering a hand to help her up.

"Why did you do that?" She ignored his hand and rolled easily to her feet, barely breathing hard, stake again in hand. For a moment she wanted to plant it in that big barrel chest in front of her. *Damn and blast!* The first vampire she'd seen in a week, and he was gone before she could talk to him. Now she'd have to find another one tonight—although it shouldn't be hard, really, since they were bound to be out on the Corso.

"Why, I was helpin' ye."

"I had things well in hand. I didn't need help. I wanted to talk to him, not kill him." The thrill of the fight had gone out of her and left Victoria with a rumbling annoyance and the feeling of unfinished business. Not to mention covered with vampire dust.

"Ye appeared to be in danger, so I wasna going to stand by and watch him maul you."

Victoria looked at him as she brushed the dank ash from her hair and clothes. They were nearly the same height, although he was much bulkier than she. "I am capable of staking a single vampire," she said slowly and distinctly, her nerves still wanting to jump. "I've done it many times before. In fact," she said, closing her eyes to finger away the dust on her lashes as much as to retain the evenness of her voice, "I have fought five at a time, and won. I purposely didn't kill him because I needed him to take a message for me." A message to Beauregard that she was looking for his grandson.

But, of course, Zavier wouldn't have—couldn't have—known that. He didn't even know anything about the Door of Alchemy.

When she opened her eyes, Zavier was still looking at her. But instead of bafflement or chagrin or even annoyance, his expression was filled with admiration. "Of course," he said. "Fool that I was, I forgot that you of all women dinna need protection."

The smile he gave her there, in the cold cemetery, warmed Victoria from her cheeks down to her toes, and she had to glance away for fear her face would start to glow. Although fighting her way through undead immortals and evil demons was becoming second nature to her, she was less sure of herself when interacting with men.

She'd debuted into London Society just about a year and

a half ago, and had been in mourning for her husband, Phillip, for a twelvemonth of that period, during which, of course, she'd worn black and stayed cloistered in her husband's home—far away from members of the opposite sex. No fetes, no balls, no theater engagements. She'd been lonely and grieving and trying desperately to determine how to fit the two parts of her life together.

She had come to the realization that there was no way to have a real life, with a real relationship with a man. Her life was with the Venators, especially now, as *Illa* Gardella. She would touch Society from time to time, but she would never be immersed in it as she once had been. She'd never marry again, never have a child, much as her mother might wish it.

But then, as she looked over at Zavier and saw the admiration and attraction in his face, she wondered if it had to be thus. If she really did have to be alone and keep anyone who might care about her—or whom she might care for—at arm's length. The last vestiges of her annoyance filtered away.

"I hope that ye will forgive me," he was saying, and somehow he'd taken her hand in his large warm one. The one that wasn't holding the stake. "'Tis just that I am—that a man is—bound to protect a woman. And I dinna think of you as a warrior, yet I ken that you are a fierce one. 'Tis hard to reconcile that with . . . well . . . " His voice trailed off, and Victoria would have believed he was blushing if his face weren't already a bit ruddy from the cold.

"I'm not angry," she said, when he appeared unable to select the words to finish his thoughts. "I'm glad you understand. Zavier, if ever I need assistance, it will be obvious."

He was looking down at their joined hands, her small white one in his, and when he raised his face again she felt her heart begin to pound.

Before he could speak, a rustling in the bushes near a

large tomb drew their attention. Zavier's hand tightened on hers in warning, and then released. They both moved silently across a fenced expanse of grass toward the stone structure. It was nearly as large as a small home, its cream-colored stucco appearing gray and forbidding in the sliver of moonlight.

The front of the mausoleum was grand, its upper edge topped with a wide, jutting cornice and studded at its corners with curling plaster leaves. The family name carved into the frieze was covered with moss, and illegible from where Victoria stood. A square cupola that might have contained a bell was perched in the center of the flat roof. What must be the main entrance, set partially below the ground and reached by a few descending steps, was flanked by two columns. The bushes that had rustled were part of a large clump of pines and holly oaks that grew in a thick cluster close to the tomb, casting the area in wide shadow.

Victoria's neck was no colder than the February air made it naturally, so she was certain the only vampire in the vicinity was the one Zavier had staked. Perhaps there was no threat at all, and it had been merely a hedgehog or hare that bounded through the foliage.

But then she saw a flash of something light in the brush, and then heard more rustling as she and Zavier drew closer. To his credit he didn't try to hold her back, or even to take the lead. They hurried together, following the rustling bushes, but suddenly Victoria sensed something—or someone— behind her.

She whirled just in time to see a large black canvas whipping down toward her. With a shout to warn Zavier, she ducked away and spun back around to see two large men swooping toward her again. They'd come from the other side of the mausoleum.

Using a gravestone to leverage herself, Victoria kicked out and caught one of them in the gut, sending him sprawling, along with the blanket he'd been brandishing. The other reached for her arm, and she twisted away with such force she went sprawling into the bay laurel bush where she'd seen the flash of white.

The branches were tough and prickly, and it didn't help that her attacker had followed her and was trying to manhandle her out of the bush. She heard a shout, and looked up to see Zavier standing behind the man, hands on his hips, watching.

At least he'd learned.

But then something leaped on him from behind, and then another large body crashed into the fray, and she saw Zavier go down in a mass of fists and legs.

With a howl Victoria kicked out at her assailant, the force propelling her farther into the brush. But she managed to roll to the side, off the bush, and onto the ground. She swept to her feet and, as she spun around, caught sight of something in the dark foliage behind her.

A pale face, with light hair. A body that moved away through the bushes, using the same lithe movements as the one who'd thrown the sugarplum at her.

But before she could react, something shoved her to the ground again, and she landed with a whump, face-first into the slick grass. The black canvas came flying down over her, covering her face and down over the front of her before she could roll away, and it clung to her when her attacker lifted her up.

Strong arms wrapped around her, holding the canvas and her own arms close to her body. Suffocating under the heavy material, Victoria kicked and twisted until she landed two good blows against the legs of the man who held her, then slammed her head backward.

The satisfying crunch and the sudden loosening of her person told her she'd hit the mark, even as her head swam. She tumbled to the ground, and it took her more than a moment to fling off the folds of the canvas and scramble to her feet.

By the time she was upright, Zavier was standing in front of her. His red hair stuck out in tufts at the edge of his crown, and he was breathing heavily. "All right?" he asked with a satisfied grin.

She looked around. Their assailants were gone and it was just the two of them, panting in the middle of a dark graveyard. She turned toward the brush, where she'd seen the face she was sure she'd recognized. Nothing was there but flattened bushes and broken twigs—both from her own tumble into the foliage and whoever had been watching.

"They got away," she said.

"Aye, they did. Surprised me—three of them all at once. A stake wasna much use against 'em," he said companionably.

He was right, and Venators didn't generally fight with guns or knives. Their prey was the undead, not human threats. But it didn't seem to bother him that their attackers had gotten away.

"Who were they?" she asked, looking around. "And why did they want to abduct me? Did they try to kidnap you too?"

"No, it just seemed they wanted me out of the way so they could get to you. They all ran off when they saw they couldn't get the best of us."

Victoria looked up. The wall of the mausoleum stretched above her, and she could see the impressions of the family name. She couldn't make out all of the letters, but she saw enough to know that the face she'd seen in the bushes, the person who had caught her attention by throwing the sugarplum so hard, had indeed been Sarafina Regalado.

But the question was, what was Max's fiancée doing at her family tomb in the middle of the night?

Five

In Which a Message Is Delivered

On the last night of Carnivale, the Corso was filled with a blaze of light.

The entire population of the city seemed to fill the broad *strada* and its connecting piazza to bursting before it spilled into the narrower Ripetta and other streets. Each person held tightly in one hand to a large twisted candle, or *moccoletto*, and a long switch topped by a handkerchief in the other. The small blazes danced and glowed, painting the buildings and masked faces and elegant carriages in a yellow-white splash as the partygoers used their handkerchiefs to flick at the flames of nearby candles.

The game was to extinguish someone's light or have one's own extinguished, all in a frenetic, rollicking mass of milling Romans.

Victoria had never seen the like, this blast of illumination from thousands of Romans crowding the street. They even called down from crimson-draped balconies—one of which hosted Lady Melly and friends—holding their *moccoli* aloft. Victoria could barely breathe, the area was so thronged with bodies and carriages, and tinged with the scent of burning wax, the smell of so many people packed so tightly in the street, the overriding crispness of the cool air. Victoria was thankful the propellants of last night's plaster sugarplums had given way to the friendlier, softer touch of flapping handkerchiefs.

This final night of revelry, the eve of Ash Wednesday, was the wildest, loudest, most beautiful festival she'd ever experienced, and although she would rather have been seated safely in a high barouche where she could gape all she liked, Victoria had other responsibilities.

Her switch, in fact, was more than a bit thicker than the ones other revelers were holding. In fact, it was not only thicker, but had been whittled to a lethal point on the bottom end.

Eschewing the long-beaked peregrine mask she'd worn the night before, Victoria had donned a more manageable one tonight. The upper part of her face was covered by a gold mask painted with glittering streaks of blue and green, sparkling curlicues of orange and pink, and had no protrusions that would catch on nearby shoulders. White feathers sprouted from the top and sides, and long curls of red ribbon hung from the edges to her shoulders. Only her mouth and chin were free, which made eating those delicious roasted chestnuts and speaking much easier than the previous evening's disguise.

"Senza moccolo!" a man masked as a *banditto* shouted in her ear, and he flicked his switch toward her candle.

As she had quickly learned to do, Victoria shielded her flame whilst grabbing at the handkerchief, and plucked the switch from the person's hand. With a nod behind her own mask, she tossed away the handkerchief, but left off from dousing the switch holder's taper.

Zavier looked at her. "You are very quick," he said with a smile beneath the heavy-brimmed sombrero he'd chosen to wear this night. She wasn't certain how he'd gotten away without wearing a mask when Ilias had insisted she do so. "You protect your candle like you protect those of this city."

"This is madness," Victoria said, looking about. All she could see were large, painted masks and acres of shoulders and necks and throats everywhere, everywhere. Cast in shadows below arm level, lit from above, glowing and stark by turns in the night, loud and more of a crush than any ballroom back in London, the extinguishing ceremony was by turns breathtaking and horrific. "Even if I knew a vampire was about, I'd never be able to identify it, let alone get to him or her." She had to raise her voice to be heard above the din.

"Aye, so perhaps we ought to just enjoy the festivities as much as possible until the candles are doused at midnight and everyone begins to go home. After that it will be much easier to move about." The way he looked at her, so intently for a moment, as his hat brushed the feathers of her mask, made her stomach do a little flip.

But before Victoria could reply, a sudden prickle at the back of her neck intensified into a chill. She turned quickly, sensing the presence of an undead in close proximity, and her shoulder slammed into the angel next to her, and then into a gypsy, and then into an owl, as the masked people pushed past her.

Glancing back toward Zavier, she saw him starting off in the opposite direction as if he, too, had felt something and was pursuing it. Despite their agreement about the difficulty of identifying undead in this crowd, neither of them would stand aside and do nothing when a vampire was near.

They were well separated by now, and as Victoria turned once again and tried to move in the opposite direction from the people near her, she scanned the crowd, looking for red irises behind the masks that streamed past her, or for a disguise that could be covering the face of Sara Regalado.

She closed her eyes for a moment, trying to sense which direction to go after the creature that skulked nearby, and finally set off toward the left, through the milling people. The chill at the back of her neck began to intensify as she made her way through to the edges of the crowd. Suddenly, not so far from the darkness that lingered beyond the revelry, she saw the glowing red orbs in a masked face two persons away.

Edging her shoulder through the throng, playing the *senzo moccoletto* game, Victoria squirmed along until she was close enough to touch the vampire. Her neck was frigid, and she felt the odd rush of the presence the undead gave in close proximity. Angling her switch cum stake, Victoria turned to face him—or her; she wasn't certain of the creature's gender—and closed her fingers around an arm.

The crowd was so thick and full of shouts and movement and the flicking of switches that Victoria could have slammed the stake into the vampire's chest before he realized that she was a Venator, and without drawing any attention to herself, but she didn't.

Instead she said, "Tell Beauregard the female Venator is looking for his grandson."

He looked down at her, fangs gleaming. "I'm no message boy."

"You aren't? Well, then, my apologies." She moved easily, angling her stake, plunging it up and into his chest.

The vampire disintegrated, as vampires did, into a poof of ash that burst over the partygoers, causing a dainty little shepherdess to forget about protecting her *moccoletto* for a moment in favor of brushing away the sudden gust of dust.

The chilly prickling at the back of Victoria's neck had eased, but had not disappeared completely. There were other vampires in the vicinity. Perhaps one of them would rather be a message boy than a pile of dust.

Even so, she'd already given the message to two others last night, after returning to Carnivale from the graveyard and Sara Regalado's aborted kidnap attempt. Perhaps that would be enough to get the message to Sebastian.

Her neck still prickling, she began to push her way back through the crowd in search of Zavier. Behind her Victoria heard the shepherdess's shriek of annoyance as her candle was doused.

Suddenly something slammed into her from behind. She stumbled and would have fallen to the ground had she not knocked into a Pulcinella. Her flame guttered in its pooled wax, and the Pulcinella whipped his switch-laden handkerchief down on her *moccoletto*.

When Victoria regained her balance and turned, her now-dark candle still steady in her grip, she found herself face-to-face with a masked man. His eyes weren't red, and she couldn't see the shape or color of them behind his black domino. But she recognized the angle of his chin, and the crop of fair curls that brushed the side of his neck. The smile he gave her was bemused, and laced with challenge.

Apparently the message had been delivered.

Before she could speak he moved sharply, yanking a nearby Joan of Arc between them and pushing off through the crowd.

Victoria shoved a laughing Saint Joan out of her way and followed, her heart pounding. She didn't hesitate to go after him, even though she certainly recognized that she'd been followed twice in as many nights, despite wearing two different masks. It was a risk, but not an unexpected one.

Her stake was in her hand, and another was in a deep pocket where she also had a metal dagger Kritanu had given her when she started her *ankathari* training. The *kadhara* had a curved blade and was about the length of her forearm. She was also protected by the large crucifix she wore beneath her costume, not to mention her duo of *vis bullae*.

Watching the back of the shadowy domino and following its irregular path through the crowd was no easy task. He didn't carry a taper and Victoria's had been extinguished, so as they neared the edge of the light-filled festival, she paused to catch a flame from the fat wick of a donkey's candle.

When she pushed through the last barrier of people and found herself in a small, narrow *viuzza*—what she would call a mews back in London—Victoria stopped and looked around. It was an odd setting: behind her thousands upon thousands of people laughing and shouting with their glowing yellow candles, and here, in front of her, a dark alleyway lit only by her single flame, and silent. Still as death.

Her neck was still cold, the hair still raised to attention, but she saw no one. He'd been there a moment before, just as she burst free of the crowd, but now she was alone.

Ripe for another black canvas cloth to come wafting down over her head.

Victoria braced herself, half crouched, turning slowly and peering into the shadows. Then she saw one of them move.

"Ah, it *is* you. I was not altogether certain, but the way you wielded that stake convinced me." The voice was soft as the figure moved into the dim light.

"Beauregard." Victoria stepped toward him, warily casting about to see if he was alone, or if someone lurked nearby to pounce on her from behind. Sebastian, perhaps. Her stake was firm in her palm. The back of her neck remained cold and prickly. But it itched, as though there were something else watching them. "Did you receive my message?"

"But why else would I seek you out?" His response was easy, but she could sense the respect and wariness in his demeanor as he flipped back the hood of his domino.

"Perhaps the message was garbled, then," she replied. "It was your grandson I wished to speak with. Not you."

"You needn't brandish that stake as though you are a novice Venator out for her first hunt," he said, crossing his arms over his middle in a picture of nonchalance that pulled up one of his sleeves and revealed a strong, elegant wrist. The stance, the expression on his face, reminded her again of Sebastian.

Although the two shared a similar, elegant facial structure and thick, curling hair, there wasn't a great resemblance otherwise. Beauregard, who must have been in his forties when he was turned, had a slightly wider nose and more delicate lips than his grandson, and his hair was more of a silvery blond than the tawny color of Sebastian's. He was handsome enough in his own cool fashion, and that, along with his persistent charm, and the fact that he was exceedingly well dressed, was what reminded her of the younger man.

"I've done nothing to threaten you or to harm anyone," Beauregard continued.

"You've been undead for four hundred years; I'm fairly certain you've mauled at least one mortal during that time. And once you've fed from one mortal, your sentence of eternal damnation is assured. I thought I might help you more quickly on your way there."

"Er . . . almost six hundred years, my dear Victoria. Six hundred. Yet, a pittance when one looks at the age of the elegant Lilith, yes?" He shifted, his eyes beginning to glow ruby, narrowing with annoyance. "Put the stake away. After all, you did send the message, and it's not as if I've tried to bite you."

"I expect it will be only a matter of time until you do," Victoria replied.

"As you wish." Beauregard grinned, and now his fangs

flashed. They were no longer than a man's first knuckle, but sharp as a razor. So sharp that the feel of them sinking into one's flesh would hardly be noticeable, more pleasure than pain. His lower fangs were much shorter, but just as lethal, and hidden by his lower lip.

During their banter she'd foolishly allowed herself to relax enough that her gaze drifted too directly to his, too tightly to his ruby irises. She was snared.

Guardian vampires, the ones with ruby eyes who also made up Lilith's personal guard, had especially strong enthralling powers. As Beauregard's control crept over her, Victoria felt her limbs begin to soften and her head to swim. The blood in her veins surged, swelling the vessels so that hot pressure pounded through her body.

His breath began to match hers, then fought to control their merging breathing. Victoria was sluggish, but she still held the stake, and the candle in her other hand. She had enough presence of mind to realize how incredibly strong his pull was, and how difficult it would be to fight it off.

Dimly she forced herself to blink, trying to break the connection. Drawing her eyelids down was like wading upstream neck-deep in a river: slow, deathly slow. She felt movement around her, then the brush of his hand against her neck, warm and strong. . . . She tried to blink again, tried to recover her own breathing and slowly force herself out of the pulsing red tunnel into which she'd begun to fall, clawing back to her reality by focusing on the feel of the stake in her hand and the force of the *vis bullae* at her belly.

Suddenly the thrall was broken. She snapped free and pulled in a breath all her own, then raised the stake, plunging it down toward his chest—a chest that had moved closer to her in those few moments of confusion. Everything in her mind was clear and crisp again—the night, the darkness, the smell of the city, the buildings looming over them. As the stake plunged, he threw up his arm to stop her blow, stepping back.

Their forearms collided with a force that would have broken bones had they not been Venator and vampire, and she drew in her breath in annoyance, twisting away. "I knew you were not to be trusted," she snapped, whirling back toward him, stake at the ready. "Despite your grandson's arguments to the contrary." She dropped her candle and leaped.

He blocked her again, and the force of her blow sent them into each other, breast-to-breast, in a parody of a lovers' embrace before she ducked down, seeking to surge up behind him.

He feinted away, but she launched at him. Beauregard caught her by the waist and shoved her so hard she stumbled backward, catching herself against a plaster wall. Her candle flame, still burning on the ground, flickered wildly as she looked over at him, recognizing that they were at an impasse.

"Strong, brave, stubborn . . . and beautiful. Once again, I can understand my grandson's attraction for you." His lips, thinner than Sebastian's, but of the same shape, curved in a familiar smile. The movement couldn't help but remind her of the many times she'd kissed lips rather like them. Beauregard's eyes gleamed behind his mask, sweeping a pink gaze over her, trying again to capture her. "'Tis a shame he saw you first, Venator. But if he does not treat his ladylove with care and attention, perhaps you will tire of waiting for him and cast your affections elsewhere. Toward power. And immortality."

"I'm as likely to be his ladylove as he is to be a Venator himself," Victoria replied with a derisive snort, stepping back, but ready to propel herself forward. "I trust him no farther than I do you; perhaps even less. At least I know where you stand."

"I see." The way he looked at her, as though he were contemplating some great question, was so different from his earlier gaze when he'd tried to enthrall her that Victoria almost looked him straight in the eye. But she remembered how easily she'd fallen moments before and resisted. "Ah, well, at the least, as you said, you know where I stand. Now, do not strike at me again," he added when she gathered herself up to do just that. "Now that you've proven just as enticing and capable as I'd hoped, let us get to business."

Wary, but no longer breathing hard, Victoria didn't relax her stance. "Business? Was that your vampire that I staked earlier? A lure sent to pull me from the crowd? As you did last night?"

She could almost see his eyebrows rising behind the hooded mask of the domino. "I'm afraid you must be mistaken. I was otherwise engaged last evening. It was a tedious thing, but one must feed at least occasionally. Although I will admit to using that young man you slayed as one of several . . . what did you call them? Lures? To help me locate you in the crowd. So that I could answer your call, so to speak."

"Apparently he was expendable."

Beauregard shrugged. "The young ones are so bloody sure of themselves they think they are invincible once they have been turned. They do not realize that a Venator can just as easily end their immortality as they believe they can take from other mortals. It was a lesson for some of his other companions. It's fortunate for me that most of those young, weak ones have allied themselves with Regalado and his Tutela members."

"And so the battle rages on between the two vampire factions." Victoria swept up the candle, then straightened from her offensive stance.

"Battle? I'd hardly call it that. Regalado and his followers are no match for me, even with their new ally. Indeed, I have my own plan for dealing with them."

Victoria pretended to yawn. "Vampire politics: not something I'm terribly interested in—I'd just as soon stake all of you, regardless of who allies with whom. Instead, let's talk about why you've enticed me to this dark alley. I can only assume the purpose is to exact some kind of payment for telling me what I want to know."

"Ah, good. You've alleviated the awkwardness of the topic by mentioning it yourself." Beauregard laughed, sounding uncomfortably like Sebastian. Then his charm vanished, and his eyes burned pink again. "Why do you wish to see him? I did not expect a woman of your stature and confidence to be chasing after the noncommittal rake that is my grandson."

She bowed her head, taking care not to look directly into those dangerous irises. "I think that the rake is more like an apple that has fallen not so far from the tree. Ancient though the tree might be. And the matter concerns my aunt." There was no sense in being coy with Beauregard—she needed his help to find Sebastian.

"Your aunt?"

Then Victoria realized her mistake. She should have let him believe it was Sebastian himself that she, playing the woman scorned, was after. But perhaps she could yet save it. "He . . . sent me something that belonged to my aunt, and I . . . wished to thank him."

She knew Beauregard was too smart to be fooled by a complete reversal of personality, but perhaps subtlety would be more effective anyway.

"Thank him? Ah." The way he allowed that last syllable to ease from his mouth in a low sigh told her he had taken the bait. The pink glow faded from his eyes, to be replaced by smugness. "It has been months, hasn't it? And you wish to *thank* him."

"I need to see him." She allowed the desperation in her voice—let him think what he would. Let him tell Sebastian she was pining for him. It wouldn't matter in the end.

"As you might imagine, gratitude is something my grandson and I both appreciate. I might be inclined to pass on the message to Sebastian, in exchange for some from you."

She didn't reply, merely tightened the grip on her stake and waited for him to continue. It was nothing more than she'd expected.

He bowed in acknowledgment, spreading his hands as if he had no choice. "I find that I have a curiosity . . . and a craving . . . that I desire to satisfy."

Victoria knew exactly what he meant. Her palms grew clammy and her heart began to thump harder as she felt his control begin to swirl about her. He was very powerful, and likely as strong as she was, even with her two *vis bullae*.

"You cannot feed on me," she said, shifting the long stake at her waist. "I'll send you to Hell first."

Beauregard looked affronted. "Feed? My dear, you needn't be crude. Feeding is like the rutting between hogs, or the mindless fucking of a whore. What I wish from you is much more than a mere gorging on your hot, thick blood. Your Venator blood." His eyes were blazing ruby-pink, and she felt the insistent tug toward him. "Your sweet, female, Venator blood."

His voice was hypnotic, but she remained clearheaded enough to feel the wood under her fingers, even the hot splash of wax that spilled down in a trickle from the taper in her hand.

"No," she said, making her voice firm even as her mind softened. "You cannot bite me."

"Then kiss me, Victoria. Let me taste you," he said softly, but it felt as though the words were there, all around her, filling her ears and insinuating into the blood suddenly rushing in her veins. "Let me taste what it is that my own blood desires."

She blinked, focused on the feel of her weapon, forced herself to draw in the scent of rotting garbage nearby, willed her heartbeat to settle back into its own rhythm. "No," she said sharply, breaking the gentle lull between them. "You can't enthrall me, Beauregard. I'm too strong."

"I ask for nothing but a kiss," he said, his voice still calm and low, but his eyes dimmed. "Mouth-to-mouth. You might hold your stake between us if it would make you feel more at ease, Venator."

"Perhaps I would slam it into your heart and send you to Hell, then," Victoria replied, her voice easier, more normal. "Then Sebastian would surely seek me out, angry that I sent his grandfather to his eternal damnation."

Beauregard lifted his chin. "Please, Victoria, do not remind me of my fate. I prefer not to dwell on it. You would have no cause to do so, for if you give me what I wish, I'll bring your message to Sebastian. Just . . . let me taste you."

She didn't respond for a moment, and perhaps he sensed her weakening—after all, it was merely a kiss . . . and she would keep her stake poised and ready. And if his lips were on hers, that meant his fangs weren't at her neck—or delving into any other area of her flesh. This wouldn't be the first time she'd kissed a vampire.

"One kiss," she said at last, feeling the slam of her heart. "And I keep my stake between us."

"If it will make you feel better," he said, stepping toward her almost before she was ready.

His strong fingers closed over her shoulders, his head with the silvery blond curls bent toward her, the shadow in his cleft chin deepening. She rested her candle hand over his shoulder, kept the stake between them, and lifted her face, closing her eyes.

She started at the strangeness when his mouth touched hers, when she felt the bizarre sensation of one warm, soft lip and one cold, firm one closing over her own. Cool and hot, slick and soft . . . the myriad of sensations flooded her, and her head tipped back even more.

The hand holding the stake between them was smashed between their torsos; Beauregard's hand slid up from the back of her neck, which was still freezing cold, and his fingers worked up into the base of her simple braid. Victoria was kissing him back, tasting the warmth and wetness, feeling the slide of lip to lip, the pull between them, the pressure of her mask's edge cutting into her cheek. He moved, pulling slowly away, and suddenly she felt a scrape, a tingle over her lower lip, and then the warm iron of blood.

Beauregard had her head cupped in his hands, and he held her there, his mouth fixed on hers, the gentle sucking at her lower lip tugging through her body, spiraling down into her middle, curling warmly between her legs. She twisted her face, tearing away, bringing her stake hand up as he released her, stepping back.

His chest was moving up and down, and he looked at her, his fangs gleaming like blue-white daggers. "By Lucifer's blood," he murmured.

She would have lunged toward him, but he held up a hand. "I will give your message to Sebastian." Then he eased into the shadows. She heard the last remnants of his voice as it faded: "It has been a pleasure, Victoria. I look forward to doing so again."

She was alone.

Instead of turning her back on the place where Beauregard had disappeared, she edged along the plaster wall of the alley, back the way she'd come, keeping her attention behind and in front of her while she tried to pull her heartbeat back under control. Blood still dripped down her lip from the little nip he'd given her. If there were any other vampires nearby, they might sense the blood and come looking for its source.

She'd be ready.

She came to the end of the alley and saw, in the distance, the yellow glow of the *moccoletti* oozing onto the walls of the next block. The back of her neck was still cold, but not frigid, not as if a vampire were very close. But there were some in proximity, perhaps a few streets away. She wondered where Zavier was, if he'd found some undead. One thing was certain: She'd never find him again tonight. She was on the hunt on her own.

But as she moved away from the protective shadows of the alley, she realized someone was watching her. Slipping her hand into her deep pocket, she closed her fingers around the *kadhara*'s handle and walked briskly back toward the Corso. It must be near midnight, and with the new moon the Corso and its surrounding streets would soon be dark and full of drunken revelers.

Ripe for a vampire's plunder.

The crazed noise of the festival seemed to have, if it was even possible, grown louder during Victoria's absence from the candlelit streets. As she rejoined the crowd, she no longer needed the taper in her hand, for she was surrounded by soft light again, and then drawn into the flow of revelers and their shouts of *"Senza moccolo!"*

Wading through the crowd, Victoria felt isolated. She blew out her candle, and she alone was silent and watchful as the rest of Rome, or so it seemed, shouted and pushed about her. Positioned in the midst of the throngs, she stood apart, alert for danger or the emergence of malice on a night of festivity, alone in the knowledge that there was much more to their world than these others could comprehend, more than even the evil of their mortal counterparts.

A Venator—one who would never wholly be part of that world again.

The sudden deep tolling of bells from every church in the vicinity startled Victoria, for though the crowd was deafening, the funereal sound rose above the shouts. With the tolling of midnight, the street went from raucous and glowing to silent and dark in an instant.

The tapers were duffed with such immediacy it was as if a great wind had blown through the Corso and doused them all in one forceful breath. And with the light went the last bit of gaiety.

Suddenly the street was filled with silent people, leaving in quiet droves so that the avenue emptied more quickly than Victoria could have imagined. The Corso became ghostly. The back of her neck prickled with chill, and she heightened her attention, watching for the glow of red eyes, still trying to shake that feeling of being watched.

She walked along the street, her fingers around the handle of her dagger, still deep in her pocket. Then she remembered her mask and pulled it off. She needed it no longer. The festival had ended; now started the forty days of Lent. The days of dancing and revelry were over until Easter Sunday.

The raucous city had grown quiet, bereft of even the murmur of voices or the scuffle of footsteps. Here and there a pair or trio or small cluster of people walked quickly, as though hurrying to their homes now that the fun had ended.

A movement out of the corner of her eye was accompanied by a waft of cold over her neck. Slowing her walk, Victoria began to pick her way along the street, making herself an enticing target for the undead behind her. She felt rather than heard him move toward her, and deep in her pocket she changed from dagger to stake before turning to meet him.

Her. It was a woman with long dark hair and glowing red

eyes, and she gave a surprised squeak just before she disintegrated into a cloud of ash. She must have been one of the young vampires Beauregard had disdained earlier.

Whom had she called master, Regalado or Beauregard?

South along Via del Corso, away from the piazza, Victoria walked purposefully, but in no great hurry. It was many hours yet until dawn, before she would return to the Consilium or home.

More than once she felt that sense of being watched, but her neck didn't chill again, and she heard nothing. Smelled nothing. Fewer and fewer people were about, and she'd walked two blocks without hearing the sound of carriage wheels bumping over the street.

Soon she passed the slender bell tower of Santa Francesca Romana, and she approached the curved, jagged wall of the Colosseum. It loomed ahead, its countless arches deeply shadowed.

The world was silent. Even the last of the revelers had gone to their beds, ready to start the stark weeks of Lent. She was alone.

Then she felt someone behind her. Close behind her.

She pulled the dagger from her pocket, whirling around.

And though she hadn't even raised her arm to strike, he caught her wrist with strong fingers and said, "Not quite the greeting I'd expected."

Six

Wherein Victoria Encounters a Stubborn Chin

"Max?" Victoria's free hand automatically grabbed his arm, jolting him toward her, as if to be certain it really was him. "It's you!" Relief and a wave of gladness washed over her as she felt the solidity of him under her fingers. He was alive. He was back.

"Perhaps you were expecting Sebastian Vioget," Max added, releasing her wrist and stepping away from what was as close to a welcoming embrace as she'd ever given him.

In truth, she *had* expected it to be Sebastian—now that she'd sent the message through Beauregard.

"Where have you been?" she asked, her heart still hammering from the surprise of his unexpected appearance. She looked up at him as if the answer would be in his countenance. And perhaps it was.

Even in the mediocre light from a smattering of stars and the occasional lantern on the street, she could see weariness there in his face, and a sort of hesitancy. His cheeks seemed more pronounced, his thick hair more out of place than usual, his sharp jawline set and harsh and with at least three days' stubble. Max's dark clothing, although never as perfectly stylish as Sebastian's, was rumpled, and there was no sign of a mask, costume, or *moccoletto* anywhere on his person.

"It's been almost four months, Max. Where have you been?"

"I've been in various places of no import." He stood back from her, but could not seem to remove his attention from her face. "You don't appear to have suffered any great mishap during my absence."

Victoria realized how she must sound—needy and uncertain, and as though she and the Venators could not function without him. She straightened, becoming more aloof to match his style. "Have you been following me? Or perhaps you were looking for someone else tonight."

Max's handsome, angular countenance appeared even sharper than usual in the bluish glow of night. Because he was so tall, when he looked down his long, straight nose at her, his eyes were little more than dark hollows in the shadows of his face. "Following you? I'd have no reason to do such a thing."

"You certainly weren't lurking about in the shadows trying to protect me."

He paused, then replied in an odd voice, "You'd lost your *vis bulla.*"

"So you were watching to make certain I was safe? How very nice of you, Max. But I don't know what you thought . . . "

. . . *you might do to protect me without your own* vis bulla.

Victoria quickly changed the subject. "You've cut your

hair." The last time she'd seen him he'd worn his hair clubbed back in a brief stub. Now it was too short for that.

"I couldn't be more gratified that you noticed."

She ignored the comment and responded with one of her own. "Is Sarafina lurking in the shadows? Why not invite her to join us? I didn't get to speak with her last night."

"I've just arrived, so I haven't any notion where Sara is, but undoubtedly you have some point to make by mentioning her. If so, then make it, Victoria. Unlike Vioget, I prefer to cut to the quick of the matter rather than banter around it like a May dance."

"It sounds as if you're bantering now," she replied smartly. Then she thought better of continuing the game and said, "Your fiancée attempted to have me kidnapped last night. Do you have any idea why?"

He didn't respond immediately; nor did he deny that Sara was his fiancée. Max just looked down at her, as though deep in thought. "What happened?" he asked at last.

"She lured Zavier and me from Carnivale up to the Regalado family plot in a graveyard, and four or five men tried to wrap me in a big canvas and spirit me away."

"And fortunately Zavier came to your rescue."

"And fortunately I was able to rescue myself and didn't stake Zavier when he tried to get between me and a vampire," Victoria replied, realizing Max was succeeding in annoying her already, and wondering why she continued to let him—and why he continued to try.

"Zavier came betwixt your stake and a vampire? Did he get the harsh side of your tongue for his troubles? At least you never need worry about that happening with Vioget." Then he, too, appeared to ease. "No matter, I'm certain you instructed Zavier on the proper way to accompany you when on the hunt . . . but back to the important matter, which is: You saw Sara at that time? Has she turned?"

The question startled her, but after a moment Victoria wondered why it should. After all, Sara clearly enjoyed interacting with vampires, and her father, the Conte Regalado, had been the leader of the Tutela in Rome before he was turned into a vampire just before Akvan's Obelisk was destroyed. "I don't believe so. Were you expecting her to? It would make for a considerably interesting marriage bed if she had."

Max looked at her sharply, his mouth opening as if to say something just as cutting. Victoria cringed inside, knowing he would have every right to do so after she'd baited him. Instead he stated, "It's obvious you're wearing a *vis*."

Her face blossomed warm and, even though she was certain he couldn't tell in the low light, she looked away. She was suddenly acutely aware of the fact that his *vis bulla*, the one that had at one time pierced him in the intimate area of his areola, was now one with her flesh and dangled warmly in the curve of her belly. And she would swear the tiny silver cross suddenly felt warmer and heavier, shivering in her navel.

Would he be able to sense that she was wearing it? Since it was his?

"Yes. I'm wearing Aunt Eustacia's," she added.

At the casual mention of her great-aunt, a pall fell over the already awkward moment. Max turned toward the ragged Colosseum, which was only a few yards to her right, and she saw his shoulders lift as he took a long, deep breath.

"Kritanu? How is he?" he asked finally in a different voice. "The others?"

There were many other questions between the lines of those particular ones, and Victoria wanted to answer all of them—but couldn't fully answer any of them. "He is philosophical and uncomplaining, as only Kritanu can be," she replied, choosing the easy one. "He grieves, as do I—"

"And I." The words were a challenge, as if to dare her to presume he didn't.

"And the others. But she lived a long life, a dangerous one, in which she devoted more than sixty years to the Venators. We miss her—we all do—but . . . it's past, Max."

"Is it?" Now he looked at her fully. Still challenging. And he was right to be so.

Although she finally understood that he'd had to execute Aunt Eustacia, the fact remained that he had actually done it—and she'd witnessed it. There was no glossing over that in her memory.

Once again her gaze skittered away. Victoria was no shy rabbit, no cowering woman . . . yet the expression on his face made her want to alternately rage at him for his coldness and fold him in her arms to erase whatever it was that gave him the hard edge.

What an odd thing to think about Max, of all people.

She'd once accused him of being unfeeling, emotionless, of being envious of the loving relationship she'd found with Phillip. How ironic that now she was the one who felt cold and empty, while he seemed to be almost tentative, with the slightest hint of vulnerability.

But no, it was grief for the loss of Aunt Eustacia and guilt for the part he'd played in her death that made him seem less harsh. And he was asking her if she'd yet forgiven him for setting in motion the events that had resulted in that horrible ending.

She truly didn't know if she had. She tried not to think about that night and the part he'd played in Aunt Eustacia's death, the risks he'd taken, the danger they'd faced. The fact that there had been only a sliver of hope of destroying Akvan's Obelisk, and that he'd risked everything to do it. And had succeeded.

But she still couldn't answer him.

When she remained silent, he asked, "You have Eustacia's *vis bulla*? How?"

"Sebastian sent it to me. I don't know how he came to have it."

He drew back, looking beyond her, toward the ruined amphitheater. "Very clever. I'm certain you thanked him appropriately, just as he no doubt intended."

Victoria did not mistake *his* meaning, as Max himself no doubt intended. But she forbore to respond. Now that he was back, they had other important things to discuss. "Max," she said. "Have you spoken to Wayren? Do you know about *la Porta Alchemica*?"

"No . . . I haven't spoken to her since . . . since the night the obelisk was destroyed." His demeanor changed. "What happened?"

She told him about the door, and the missing keys, taking several steps toward the Colosseum as she spoke.

"Eustacia's armband that holds the key is missing," he commented. It wasn't a question, but more of a thoughtful statement. "And so you're looking for the unreliable Sebastian in the hopes that he might know, since after all he somehow obtained her *vis bulla*."

"You were there when I spoke to Beauregard, weren't you?" she said, continuing to walk across the grass-filled cobblestone square that surrounded the large amphitheater. The ruined building loomed over her, its ragged outer wall cutting in a jagged diagonal to the ground.

"Spoke?" He didn't appear to be surprised, and suddenly Victoria knew why. He'd been there. He'd seen Beauregard try to bite her. Seen them kissing.

"I knew someone was watching. So you needn't even bother to ask me what he said."

"I told you, Victoria . . . at first I didn't know if you were wearing a *vis bulla*." She paused for a moment to look at him, and he stopped next to her. "But what about you? You don't have yours."

He looked steadily at her. "You need not trouble yourself over it."

She began walking briskly again, but with his long legs he easily kept pace, continuing to speak. "You're looking to Sebastian for help, but there's something else afoot. Someone—Sarafina, perhaps, if you didn't mistake her in the shadows—arranged for what amounted to an ambush. You were lured away and could easily have been outnumbered and killed."

"I'm not foolish, Max. It was clear they wanted me alive. They must believe I know where the key is. No one raised a hand to injure me, and even the single vampire, who was nothing but a lure, simply ran away. Otherwise would it not have been easier to slay me—or attempt to—right there?"

"Wishing for death already, Victoria?"

They'd reached the Colosseum's wall. Its three rows of arcades, circling the arena one atop another, rose like dozens of black eyes staring down on them. In the shadows Victoria could see that the walls were overgrown with foliage, sprouting tall plants and grasses along the top and from the sides. It gave the amphitheater a bushy, messy appearance.

"You're the one who has a wish for death. I have too much left to do here." She cast him a sidelong glance. He'd had no gratitude when she saved his life the night Aunt Eustacia died; he'd told her it would be easier not to live with the guilt—despite the fact that he'd done what he'd done for the good of their race. What he'd been ordered to do by Aunt Eustacia herself. That was the only reason Victoria couldn't hate him—she knew he'd had no choice.

"I'm still living, am I not?" He looked at her as she gawked up at the wall. More than four months she'd been in Rome, and she'd not had the opportunity to visit the

Colosseum until now. "Do you want to go inside? There will be no vampires there, for all that it's been consecrated for nearly a century, but if you can step aside from your duty for a time, we can walk through."

"Yes."

She felt odd walking companionably with Max into the dark recess of one of the archways, instead of being on guard for a battle with undead. Inside the outer wall they were in a passageway that curved around the entire perimeter of the building, with more arches leading to the seats.

Victoria strolled along the dark passage, Max close enough to brush her sleeve. They were silent, and despite the openings on either side of them, the high ceiling loomed above in a vast cavern.

"Do you plan to walk around the perimeter all night?" he asked brusquely. "Or would you like to see the battlefield?"

Victoria gave a small laugh. She felt a bit nervous, and wasn't sure why she should. After all, this was just Max. "Yes, of course." She turned abruptly toward one of the arches just as Max stopped walking, and she bumped forcefully into him. Her forehead slammed hard into his chin as her sudden movement pushed them into an unexpected embrace.

He caught her as they collided, his strong hands finding her arms and steadying her in the moment of her silent mortification. She'd forgotten how tall he was. "Pardon me," she murmured formally, and pulled away to continue walking through the passage to the interior of the amphitheater. Her heart was beating harder; she couldn't feel more foolish and clumsy.

"This entrance is called a vomitory," Max was saying as if nothing untoward had happened—and indeed, nothing had, she reminded herself, except that for a moment she'd lost all of her Venatorial grace. In front of Max. "Because of the rapid ease with which the masses of people can enter or exit. Did you hurt your head?"

His chin had been just as hard and stubborn as it had always appeared, and it had indeed been painful to crash into. "I'm a Venator, so I think there will be no bruise." Her voice was light with humor.

"The moss that grows here can be slippery," he added as they emerged from the short tunnel. "Take care."

"There's moss everywhere, and plants," Victoria commented, looking over the shadowy interior of what had once been a pristine arena. "It's so overgrown."

"Hannever finds many of the herbs and plants he uses in his medicinal treatments at the Consilium growing here. There are hundreds of them, presumably brought here purposely or accidentally from the far reaches of the Roman Empire over the centuries. It's very fortunate for us that there is this great variety."

She looked over at him. His face was turned to gaze over the field below, and his profile struck her. With his long, straight nose, prominent forehead, and sharp-planed face, he looked like one of the very gladiators who might have fought below. Or perhaps he looked more like a senator, who might have sat in this very same section. In either case he looked strong and powerful and Roman.

Max must have felt her staring, for he shifted and turned toward her. "What is it?"

"It's just that you sound a bit like Zavier, expounding on the history of this place. I hadn't expected it."

"Yes, Zavier is quite fascinated with the history of our female Venators, among other things," Max replied, his voice dry. He looked back out into the darkness. "But it is this place in particular that appeals to me. Down there, somewhere"—he cast his arm out to encompass the arena—"Gardeleus—the first Venator—died at the hand of a vampire. And set in motion this battle that has lasted for centuries."

She looked down at the oval-shaped field, tufted with untouched grass and bushes on one side, and on the other rumpled and disrupted by a series of excavations in the form of dark holes. Aunt Eustacia had told her the story of Gardeleus and his final midnight battle with Judas Iscariot, the first vampire.

Max continued to stare down in silence. "It's been a long time since I've visited this place," he commented at last. "Born and raised a Roman, and yet I've forgotten the sacrifices made by him and the others through the ages."

His words were so uncharacteristic and quiet, Victoria wasn't certain that she'd heard them properly. She didn't speak, didn't want to break whatever spell had turned him into this pensive, thoughtful being.

At last he seemed to pull out of his thoughts. He turned and looked at her, and for a moment, as their eyes met, she couldn't breathe. There was this vast area around them, this great space, and yet she felt small and crowded. As though everything had circled down to the space between them.

"Victoria," Max said at last, "I never told you how sorry I am about what happened with Phillip."

That was the last thing she'd expected him to say. He'd never mentioned Phillip, except to decry the fact that she'd planned to marry him, claiming that Venators couldn't marry and that it would distract them from their duty.

Victoria was so shocked she couldn't respond at first. Then, breaking his gaze, she looked down at her hands, small and pale and deadly. "I think of him every day. And Aunt Eustacia too." Tears stung her dry eyes.

He moved, shifting his tall, graceful body so that he leaned back against the wall. "And yet you go on as if nothing has happened. You're a strong woman."

Victoria didn't feel so very strong at that moment.

There were times when she was able to keep the grief at bay, to move through life as though she were whole, as if she'd never been torn apart as she had been that night she realized Phillip had been turned. There were even hours and perhaps, occasionally, a day where she might not have felt the weight of her loss—losses—and when, for a brief time, she could pretend that her life wasn't preordained by duty to be defined by loneliness.

She let her knees buckle gently and lowered herself to the ground. Even when she was sitting, the sides of the walls were at her shoulder height, and she could still see around the arena. But she had something to lean against here, and suddenly she needed it. "How could I turn my back and walk away? Evil and danger are everywhere, and their power must be stopped or eventually it will take over the world. Of course I go on."

She'd said nearly the same thing to Sebastian only months ago. He hadn't understood.

"I know." His voice was a low rumble, almost a breath, but she heard him.

She looked up at him looming above her, and her head brushed against the wall. Tiny crumbles of stone and a small shower of dirt and dried leaves filtered over her shoulder as the vampire dust had done earlier that evening. It was much easier to brush that away than the remains of an undead, easier to clean up a bit of dirt than the mess left by an immortal, damned for his desire to take and rape and devour the mortal version of itself.

They were silent again. This time it was a comfortable quiet, laced with sorrow, but without the underlying tension that always seemed to crop up between them. At last Victoria was moved to ask something that had been niggling at her mind.

"Did you truly intend to marry Sarafina Regalado?" she asked, thinking of the months he'd spent pretending to be a member of the Tutela and being engaged to the young woman, remembering the time she'd come upon him with his neckcloth loosened and his hair mussed after an obvious tête-à-tête with his fiancée.

Instead of looking down at the field, he'd turned his face up and was looking toward the dark sky. She wasn't certain, but it appeared as though his lashes closed and his lips moved into a slender line. He gave one bare nod. "If it was necessary, I would have."

She wasn't surprised. Max would do what had to be done in the fight against Lilith and her vampires, no matter the sacrifice or pain. Would she ever be that cold and emotionless?

She nodded, and more dust sprinkled over her shoulder.

"The right decision isn't always easy or evident. You'll find yourself making more and more of those choices as time goes on."

"I know it."

Max drew in his breath, and there in the silent, dark night let it out slowly. "I miss her too, Victoria."

"I know." Victoria realized he meant Aunt Eustacia.

Again they were quiet for a time. At last, Victoria saw the faint lightening of the sky in the east and realized dawn was near.

How odd to have spent a night in Max's company without once wielding a stake, and with very few razorlike comments. She began to pull to her feet, her legs stiff, and he reached his hand to offer her assistance.

Strong fingers and an impossibly warm, square palm closed over her small hands, easily bringing her to her feet. He released her hand immediately and started toward the exit, the vomitory, and she followed. All without speaking.

As they walked, she realized something that had been glossed over: He was wearing a *vis bulla*.

"Max." Her voice stopped him ahead of her in the dark passageway. Victoria looked at him, studying him closely. "How did you get a *vis bulla*?"

"It's of no consequence. The sun is rising, and it's time for me to find my bed. Good night, Victoria." He turned away, walking with his confident, long-loped stride.

"Max." Her quiet voice stopped him, and once again he turned to look at her. "Does this mean you're back?"

His arms hung from his sides in an uncharacteristically useless way. "I don't know."

Seven

In Which a Small Red Jar Becomes the Topic of Conversation

"You went to Lilith? Alone?"

Max looked at Wayren, who'd straightened up in her chair. Unsure how the other Venators would react toward him after Eustacia's death, he hadn't wanted to go to the Consilium to see her. He had invited Wayren to the small room he'd rented.

"That's what I said. I had nothing to lose, Wayren."

"I know, Max. I know how much you want to be rid of her. But to take such a chance!"

"It's not as if I haven't been alone with her in the past." He knew his words came out harshly, but, bloody hell, the memories weren't pleasant ones. Blast it that he had to remind Wayren of them.

For all her calmness, all of her knowledge and wisdom, she was a bit absentminded at times. Now, realizing what she'd said, Wayren softened and merely looked at him. Behind the perfectly square spectacles she wore, her wise eyes filled with understanding. "Of course. I'm sorry."

"She gave me a salve she claims will release me from her thrall . . . but at a price." He pulled the small garnet jar from his coat pocket and set it on the table between them. Though his fingers itched to open it, he'd not done so yet. During the last months he'd kept it with him at all times, but had never opened the shiny pot, which was made from a walnut-size jewel.

It had weighted his coat. Burned his hand when he brushed it. Called to him when he emptied his pockets at night. One morning he'd awakened with it clutched in his hand.

That was when he knew it was time to return to Roma, to speak to Wayren.

Wayren looked at it, but made no move to pick it up. Then she shifted her attention back to Max, and contemplated him as if she knew what he was going to say next.

"If I use the salve I'll lose my Venatorial powers, and because her bites have tainted my blood, I cannot regain them, even if I attempt the trial again. I'll forget everything I know of that world. As if I never had the knowledge in the first place."

"Like a Gardella who has been called and refuses the call—as Victoria's mother did—you'll be ignorant and simply a man."

Simply a man.

He couldn't even imagine what that would be like.

"You wish to be free of Lilith, but you haven't used it yet," Wayren commented.

"I've decided not to."

There were times, as now, when he was convinced Wayren could read minds, perhaps even see the future. God knew she'd been around long enough to have learned the skill, if indeed it could be learned. She looked at him, her blue-gray eyes calm and penetrating. "You've done enough, Max. You've given seventeen years of your life in penance for what happened to your father and sister. You can be free."

Dear God, Lilith had said nearly the same thing. The vampire queen had tempted him. Now Wayren was giving him permission.

He knew it was true. He'd meditated on it, prayed on it, agonized over it . . . all these weeks since leaving Lilith's stronghold he'd thought of little else. But . . . "Free? But what would I leave behind? More deaths? More destruction and evil?"

And what would he lose in the process?

"You'd no longer have the memories. It would all be gone. You could truly be free."

"Don't you think I know that? How tempting is the thought of not having this bloody nagging on my neck all the time? The pain that comes at her every damned whim?"

Wayren gave a gentle shrug. "Max, to live with guilt for one's entire life, to use it as a shield against truly living, an excuse for feeling . . . is that so much better? It's not something anyone is required to do for all his days."

He looked at her and realized she didn't really understand. "The guilt doesn't burden me any longer, Wayren. It's Lilith's thrall that burdens me. I don't flay myself for what I did, for the choices I made. Those decisions are in the past and cannot be undone, and I've done everything I can think of to atone for them.

"But as easy as it might be to contemplate the freedom of ignorance, I can't do it. I know I'm needed. How can I live in ignorance when I'm needed? How many deaths can I prevent by staying? I have no right to turn my back when I am one of the few who can prevent them."

Wayren had folded her slender fingers in her lap and was

watching him during this impassioned speech. "You were not called to be a Venator. You made the choice. You aren't obligated as those Gardellas who are called."

"Do you not understand? I became obligated the moment I turned Father and Giulia over to the Tutela." His jaw cracked beneath his teeth.

"You were barely more than a child. You thought you were giving your family a gift—immortality—which is precisely what the Tutela led you to believe. That's how they draw in strong, smart young men like yourself."

"You dare to excuse what I did? Feeding my father and sister to the vampires? At sixteen, I knew what was wrong and what was right. Yet I was blinded by the chance for power and wealth and immortality."

"And for the next seventeen years, at the risk of your life, you've worn the *vis bulla*. You've paid your penance, and then some."

Max stopped suddenly and glared at Wayren. Wayren, who had been as close to him as Eustacia. Wayren, who, with her wisdom and calm, gentle ways, had been more of a mother figure to him than even Eustacia had. Eustacia had mentored and challenged him as a fighter; Wayren had touched and taught him as a young man.

She had been the one to help him through the life-threatening trial of attaining the *vis bulla*. She'd been there when he reached the point where he would either live and wear the amulet of the Venators, or die when it was pierced into his flesh.

"Why do you want me to use the salve?" he asked abruptly. "Do you think I'm no longer fit to be a Venator? After what happened with Eustacia?" His throat was dry, his hand tightly fisted into itself.

"No, Max. *No.*" She stood, coming to him, resting her slender hand on his arm. Some of his tension eased at her touch, as it always did. "I fear only that one day Lilith's hold on you will become too strong for even you to fight. Already she has caused you to do her work of destroying Akvan's Obelisk, bringing about the death of her rival and son. You could just as easily have failed as succeeded. What will she require of you the next time? And the next?"

The anger and annoyance that had whipped up inside him settled as he listened to her reasoning. "I do not know. But she has yet to control me as she would like." Max stepped away and walked across the small room. On a small table next to the narrow bed was his favorite black-painted stake. It was sleek and heavy and it fit his hand perfectly. A cross was carved into the blunt end and inlaid with silver. "Victoria told me about the Door of Alchemy. You'll need me if they get the keys."

"You spoke to Victoria?"

"Last night. Briefly."

"I'm certain she was glad you've returned. It's not been an easy few months for her—losing her husband, and then Eustacia, and you as well. Just as you disappeared after Phillip died, you disappeared after Eustacia's death. This inconstancy is becoming a habit of yours." Her head tilted to the side like a little wren's, her bright eyes watching him.

Max put the stake back with a soft clatter and glowered at Wayren. "I was not fit to be here, to wear the *vis*."

"It was very difficult for her to lose you, someone she knows and trusts, during a time of such pain and upheaval."

"Trusts? I hardly think she's foolish enough to trust me any longer. And she was not alone. You were there, and Ilias, and others."

Wayren stood abruptly. "That is true, Max. You're right. She has taken over her role as *Illa* Gardella with little trouble. A bit of grief, perhaps, some sorrowful moments . . . but overall, she is an amazing Venator. It's become her life.

She's made some difficult decisions. In fact, she insisted that no one know that Eustacia died by your hand—in order to protect you and your legacy. She carries on with her life as though unburdened with grief. It's rather astonishing how well she has adapted to the sacrifices and changes this life has brought her."

Wayren looked down at the little jar on the table, reaching to touch it with her slender finger. "I would like to take this, if you do not plan to use it, Max. Perhaps I can learn what it is that would sap your Venator powers while severing your ties to Lilith."

"Take the damned thing."

She picked it up and slipped it into a small pouch that dangled from her silver-link girdle. "I presume you will join us at the Consilium tonight, now that you have returned. And are wearing a *vis bulla* again." Behind her square spectacles, she looked at him shrewdly.

Max picked up his favorite stake and traced the silver cross. Victoria had protected him. Bloody hell. "Of course I will be there. I am ever the dutiful soldier."

Victoria was in a quandary by the time she reached Santo Quirinus late the next day.

Having been awake until dawn, she'd slept well past noon and met up with the ladies Melly, Winnie, and Nilly over a lunch filled with raptures about the hospitality of the Tarruscellis, the lovely view of the extinguishing ceremony from their balcony, and regret that there would be very little society during the next forty days of Lent.

Oh, and sympathy for poor, dear Victoria, who'd been in bed the night through with the megrims and had thus missed the most riotous, beautiful, exciting night of all. How could she bear it?

Victoria explained that she'd borne the annoying

headache rather well, knowing that the ladies weren't inconvenienced by her illness. "And it is very unfortunate that I cannot remain here with you ladies this afternoon to hear all of your adventures," she said, rising from the table, "but I promised to meet with a portrait artist about doing a new painting of Aunt Eustacia."

"You poor dear," Lady Winnie said, her pudgy fingers flashing rubies and emeralds as she patted Victoria's smaller hand. "After being ill so often this last week, I should think you'd be able to rest instead of gallivanting off."

"You still look a bit pale," Lady Nilly added. "Perhaps a brighter color gown would serve better to pinken your complexion. I shall have my Rudgers have a word with your maid."

Despite her hurry to get to the Consilium and tell Wayren about meeting Sebastian and Max last evening, Victoria's smile was genuine. The ladies could be dithering and overbearing, but they had only her best interests—and those of her mother, of course—at heart.

"Perhaps we shall be gone before you return, if you are very late into the evening," Lady Melly said. "The party . . . er . . . meeting begins at eight o'clock."

"Party? But it's Lent," Victoria replied, trying to keep her lips from twitching. Yet she was relieved to hear of their plans. Anything to keep the ladies occupied, and from worrying over Aunt Eustacia's personal effects, was fine in her book.

"It's *not* a *party*," Lady Nilly squeaked, her bright blue eyes wide with innocence and sparse lashes. "No, we wouldn't go if it were a *party*. Of *course* not."

"It's a meeting," the duchess added, nodding vigorously. "Definitely a meeting. With dinner. But no music or dancing."

"How unfortunate that I couldn't join you at your meeting," Victoria replied, dropping her grip from the chair and taking that all-important first step away from the table. "But it's probably best if I rest again tonight. You ladies have a wonderful time."

"I'm certain we will," Lady Melly said, smoothing the napkin in her lap. "I haven't any idea why the Palombaras chose to have their par—*meeting* on Ash Wednesday, but— What is it, darling? Your head again? Benedicto, some tea for the young madam, please."

"Palombara?" Victoria had swiveled from the door so quickly it was, indeed, partly her head that spun. Her mind was the other part. "Tell me about this party, Mama."

"It isn't a party at all," Lady Winnie remonstrated. "Dear me, Victoria, have you not heard what we've been saying?"

"Never mind, Winnie. The pope hasn't been here in Rome since the war, so you needn't worry that he can *hear* you," Lady Nilly returned, one charcoaled eyebrow arching.

"What's this about the Palombaras?" Victoria asked again, a bit more insistently. And she sat back down. The Consilium would have to wait.

"To be sure, it may not be the Palombaras themselves who are hosting the . . . *meeting*," Lady Melly said primly. She was twining one of the wispy curls that dangled along her cheek around her left index finger. "It's quite exciting, really, Victoria. What a shame it is that you cannot attend. I'm not certain how many people will be there, though I doubt it will be such a crush as we might have seen back home, you know. After all, it is Ash Wednesday. Even though it *isn't* a party."

"But perhaps I won't want to miss it, if you would please tell me what this meeting is." Victoria noticed that her jaw was beginning to hurt, and she eased off before she cracked something. The strength of a Venator's gritting teeth could have lasting effects.

"It would be delightful for you to attend," Lady Winnie

crowed, sounding rather unlike a duchess in that moment. "The family villa that has been closed off for decades is being opened tonight for a pa—meeting. It shall be an adventure, for the Palombara villa hasn't been occupied for years, and the family has been gone and—"

"It will be rather like a treasure hunt," Lady Nilly chirped. "They've invited only a select group of friends to help in the search, and the Tarruscellis insisted we join them."

"A treasure hunt?" Victoria felt a shiver across her shoulders. "Whatever would you be searching for in an old, empty house?" But she had a sneaking suspicion she might know.

"A scavenger hunt," Lady Melly interrupted. "And we don't know exactly how to find what we're looking for, but it should be frightfully amusing. Well, perhaps not so *amusing*," she added, looking abashed. "It will be nothing more than a *good deed*, helping the family find a key that has been missing for more than a century. I'm certain even the pope would approve. If he were here."

Indeed.

"It does sound intriguing," Victoria said. "I have decided I will attend after all."

It took her another several minutes to extricate herself from the ladies' enthusiasm, and then nearly forty minutes in the barouche with Oliver driving a roundabout path from the Gardella villa to the small church of Santo Quirinus.

Thus it was past five o'clock when she entered the small, unassuming church where a bowl of ashes sat in the vestibule. Victoria crossed herself with the gritty soot, leaving a dark smudge on her forehead and bits of dust floating down to catch in her lashes.

There were several penitents in the church, and she

paused to kneel in prayer before slipping past the rail at the altar to the confessional.

Inside the small confessional, she closed the door behind her as if to meet with the priest. But instead of kneeling, Victoria felt for the small latch to the hidden door next to her seat. It slid silently open to reveal three steps that led down to a long, narrow hall studded with icons.

Victoria closed the door behind her and entered the passageway, taking care not to step on the middle stair as she did so. That middle stair was connected to an alarm in the Consilium below, warning when an unauthorized presence approached.

The hall in which she stood appeared to be nothing but a gallery of images that dead-ended in a brick wall. However, if one knew that the last icon on the left, the one depicting Jesus with the angels Gabriel and Uriel, concealed a subtle pattern of bricks that must be pushed in the proper order, one could release the rope-and-pulley mechanism that opened the dead-end wall and reveal the spiral staircase that led to the chambers below. After she'd opened the hidden door, Victoria started down the curling steps that were lit by several sconces.

She walked through the marble archway into the main chamber of the Consilium, where the fountain of holy water splashed and sparkled, and she stopped.

On the other side of the circular font was gathered a group of Venators: Ilias, Zavier, Michalas, Stanislaus. They were all talking in earnest. One tall, dark head rose above the rest, attached to a set of broad, black-clad shoulders facing slightly away from Victoria, and that man seemed to be at the center of the conversation.

Zavier saw her first, and retreated slightly from the little group to hail her toward them. "Victoria! At last you've arrived. I couldn't help but be a wee worried after we were separated last night." He gestured toward her, his face bright with pleasure, nearly matching his hair. "And see who's returned."

Max turned, and their eyes met briefly until she focused her attention back on Zavier, who, for all of his muscular bulk, looked as excited as a child with a new toy.

"Hello, Max," Victoria said, walking toward the group. For some reason she wasn't certain whether she should acknowledge that they'd spoken the night before. The expression on his face was devoid of the soberness he'd worn then and instead held the aloof, almost annoyed expression she was more accustomed to seeing. "Good afternoon, everyone," she added, smiling at them all. The other Venators responded with nods and warm smiles, making her feel as if she were a long-lost sister returning to their midst.

But when Max arched a brow in that way of his and nodded in casual greeting, Victoria couldn't help but feel a spike of annoyance. Why did his face seem to blank and sharpen now that she'd arrived when, before he saw her, even from behind, she could see that he'd been relaxed and engaged in conversation?

"I didn't mean to be late," she said, then was irritated with herself for apologizing, because she felt as though it was only for Max's benefit that she'd done so. "But there's a problem that has arisen, which delayed me, and it must be dealt with. Ilias, do you know where Wayren is? I should speak with both of you."

"She is in her library, of course, and was waiting for your arrival," Ilias replied.

Victoria had reached the group of Venators by now and found herself next to Zavier, who'd taken her arm and drawn her into the group. "Max," she said, looking at him again, "welcome back. Are you indeed back?"

"For now, yes, I am."

Victoria looked over the others and asked, "How was the last night of Carnivale?"

"Fifteen vampires slain," Ilias told her.

"Then seventeen in all," Victoria added with a smile. "And I saw no evidence of victims."

"Where did ye disappear to?" Zavier asked, still holding her arm. "I was worried that whoever attempted to grab ye the night before had succeeded."

Victoria felt Max looking at her, likely wondering if she would share her conversation with Beauregard. But since none of the others knew about the Door of Alchemy, nor about the missing armband belonging to Aunt Eustacia, she felt no need to go into the detail of her evening. They would find out soon enough, if it was necessary.

Instead she gave Zavier the smile she'd learned was helpful in distracting a man from his purpose and replied, "I went after a vampire, and when I returned you were gone. But, more important, I have need of your assistance as an escort this evening. Are you free to help me?"

"Aye, and with pleasure. Tell me only what I can do."

"Thank you," she replied, turning the smile just a bit warmer. Having Zavier with her to watch over her mother and friends would leave her free to do her own tasks at the estate.

"Did you say you needed to speak with Wayren?" Max interrupted.

"Yes, and Ilias as well," Victoria replied, catching the elderly man's eye.

Zavier looked disappointed when Victoria removed herself from his grip, but she said, "I won't be long. Ilias, I have to do one thing, and then I'll go to Wayren's library to speak with you."

She excused herself and hurried through the long gallery of Venator portraits, this time passing the newest one of

Aunt Eustacia. At the other end of the hall she reached what appeared to be a dead end, but actually contained three hidden doors. One led to an old spiral staircase, one of several secret exits from the Consilium. These steps took one up to the ruins of a tumbledown building that appeared to be nothing more than an abandoned house on the small street of Tilhin. It was located many streets away from the main entrance at Santo Quirinus.

A second door led to Wayren's private library, and the third door was the entryway Victoria sought. The doors were not secret to keep out other Venators; they all knew this chamber existed, and many of them had visited it.

They were hidden merely as a precaution. In the event the Consilium should ever be breached, the important and valuable items kept in this room and in Wayren's library would remain safe and would be able to be evacuated through the nearby alternate entrance if necessary. Thus, Victoria reasoned, this would be the safest place for Aunt Eustacia to have hidden the armband with the key.

Perhaps she'd had the opportunity to secret it here before going to the meeting that resulted in her death. It wasn't likely, but Victoria wanted to make certain all other possibilities had been exhausted before she talked to Sebastian.

She pushed on the marble relief of a trail of vines, her fingers sliding one of the leaves to the side. The heavy marble wall rumbled and opened enough for her to slip through.

Inside this chamber, which always had torches ready to be lit, the Venators kept their greatest secrets, their most valuable weapons, and the most dangerous souvenirs of their history. Victoria held her candle aloft, showing cabinets with deep cupboards and shallow, wide shelves that lined the walls. Display tables with glass tops that enclosed some of the objects sat adjacent to one another. A desk with curling manuscript papers and a large magnifying glass was positioned in a corner.

On display here was the stake given to Gardeleus when he was called to his destiny of fathering the generations of Venators. It was made of aspen wood, and had been part of the True Cross. Lady Catherine's emerald ring, which she'd worn during her days in Queen Elizabeth's court, was in a small, silver-cornered box made of ash. A head-size egg that belonged to the serpent demon Pithius was locked in an iron cage. It had never been incubated, but for security's sake it was locked up, just in case it might someday spontaneously hatch. So far it had been there for centuries with nary a wiggle, according to Ilias.

There was the gold clasp that Eustacia and Kritanu had seized one Christmas Eve in Venice, thereby saving the city from horrific destruction at the hands of a powerful vampire. The golden anklet that had belonged to Dahhak, one of the *divs* of long-ago Persia. A twining copper ring, one of the five that had been given by Lilith to her most trusted Guardians centuries ago. An odd-shaped box made of jade that Victoria had never had occasion to see opened sat next to the egg. And, there on one of the tables, a long, obsidian object.

A shard from Akvan's Obelisk.

Victoria walked over and looked down. The piece of shiny blue-black stone was no longer than her forearm from wrist to elbow, and perhaps as thick as three fingers. It was splintered to a lethal point at one end and a wider, jagged edge at the other. One side was smooth and curved; the opposite was fragmented and ridged.

It had been a part of a large obelisk that had contained a great, primitive evil harnessed by the demon Akvan. When the obelisk had been destroyed, it had shattered and disintegrated in a great explosion. Victoria had found the piece of obsidian during her escape with Sebastian from the aftermath of its destruction, and she had brought it here for safekeeping.

The gleam of her candle flame flickering on the shiny object reminded her of the blue and black flames that had erupted from the obelisk when it was still whole. As she looked at it, Victoria felt the shimmer of evil that had once been contained therein and placed her hand over her belly, where the *vis bullae* dangled, protecting her.

Stepping closer, Victoria smoothed her hand over the length of the shard and felt the prickle of evil present. She wondered, belatedly, if it was safe to leave it here, in the deepest, most remote part of the Consilium.

"What are you doing?"

Max's voice caused her to jerk her hand away and whirl around. "Stop sneaking up on me," she snapped, hating that he'd surprised her. She stepped away from the table, refusing to look at the shard behind her. "What are you doing here? I thought you weren't sure if you were back. And now you are everywhere, as if you had never left. As if you have the right."

He'd stepped into the doorway, filling it, casting a long, dark shadow from the brighter hallway behind him. "I'm back for now," he said. "Are you looking for something?"

"Just making certain Aunt Eustacia didn't leave her armband here before going . . . that night. It was a possibility," she said defensively as he raised a brow. "Now, if you'll excuse me, I'm late for my meeting with Wayren."

Brushing past him, forcing him to back out of the entrance, she went into the small vestibule, closing the storage chamber door behind her. But to her surprise, when she turned to enter the library Max was right there in her wake. "What are you doing here?" she asked rudely.

"As an adviser to the *previous Illa* Gardella," he said

smoothly, "I was invited to attend. Ilias felt that it was appropriate for me to be here."

Wayren interrupted any response she might have made. "Please sit down, Victoria, and Max, perhaps you will take that seat." If the mild-mannered woman was surprised or upset by the barbed comments of the Venators, she gave no sign of it. "Now, tell us what has happened."

With a glare at Max, Victoria had no choice but to speak. "My mother and her friends have been invited to a gathering at none other than the Palombara villa tonight for a treasure hunt."

"Perhaps they're searching for the missing key," Max said. He was settled back in his chair, nearly lounging, with his long legs crossed before him and his wrists resting on the arms of his seat. Almost as if he knew that the more relaxed he looked, the more irritated Victoria would be.

And she was.

"Yes, of course, that was what I thought—that the missing key is likely somewhere in the villa. I'll be attending tonight as well, however, to make certain all goes well . . . and to perhaps find the key myself—"

"On the capable arm of Zavier," Max interrupted. "A good plan, indeed, to have someone to watch over your mother. But not the best plan."

Victoria took a deep breath, forcing her bubbling annoyance to simmer and settle. She was *Illa* Gardella now . . . no longer the naive amateur Venator that Max had had the ability to pique so easily a year ago. She was the one; she'd proven herself; she had the blood, the skills . . . the two *vis bullae*.

This was her life now.

He might have more experience than she, and it was valuable. But she still had her own merit and could listen to his suggestions without feeling challenged.

Even if it irked her. But as she released her breath slowly and evenly, as Kritanu had taught her, she merely lifted her eyebrows—both of them, in direct contrast to Max's single eyebrow lifting—and waited for him to continue.

"We know that Sara Regalado attempted to kidnap you, so it's likely that she and her father are interested in the key, or something else related to the villa. There are no Palombaras in Roma, yet there are vampires—we presume—who are attempting to find the keys and open the Door of Alchemy. It is possible, do you not think, that someone is pretending to be the Palombaras, and opening the deserted villa up to this . . . party tonight in the hopes of finding the key?"

"And that they might indeed be vampires or Tutela members?" Victoria added. "Yes. Which is why I have asked Zavier to attend . . . as my mother's escort."

Now it was her turn to settle back in the chair. "I will be attending, Max, but anonymously. I don't particularly wish to be recognized by any vampires who might be at the treasure hunt tonight. And especially since my mother was invited by the Tarruscelli twins, whom I already know to be acquaintances of the Regalados, I was well aware of the dangers of promenading up to the villa unsuspectingly."

"So you plan to sneak into the villa yourself?"

Victoria nodded. "I'll make up some excuse in the carriage on the way to the party that will allow me to leave Zavier as escort for my mother and the others while I pretend to return home."

"Brilliant, Victoria. You've thought the whole thing through." Max nodded as if bestowing a great favor on her. "I'll meet you there and we can find our way in together."

She didn't say anything. It would have given him too much satisfaction.

Besides, she'd expected nothing less from him.

Eight

In Which Our Heroine Is Forced into a Gown and Its Accoutrements

Victoria slipped her hand through Zavier's arm after they alighted from the carriage at the entrance to the Villa Palombara.

She was dressed as if she were attending a ball at Almack's, attired more formally and finely than she'd been in months. Despite the inconvenience of wearing a gown in a situation that could become anything but sedate, deep in the most feminine part of her it had been worth it to see the expression on Zavier's face when she came into the sitting room, ready to leave. She'd almost forgotten what it was like to dress for an evening out.

That part of her life was so far behind her now, so submerged, it was like a dream.

Lady Winnie had indeed spoken to her maid, Rudgers, who had unfairly taken poor Verbena to task. That had given Verbena at last an excuse to dress her mistress as befitted the marchioness she was. Her gown was a pink pearl hue, made

of silk and trimmed with dark pink rosettes in two rows
along the flounced hemline. More rosettes clustered at the
tops of her sleeves in small red-and-white bouquets with
long, grass-green ribbons dangling to brush her arms. The
sleeves were short caps, but Victoria had pink gloves that
reached from fingertip to past her elbow, so despite the fact
that her wrap was little more than a cobweb of white lace,
her arms were not chilled.

Rather than the simple plait she'd taken to wearing, Victoria's coiffure was an intricate gathering of tiny braids, spiraling curls, and pink pearls at the back of her crown. It left
her long white neck bare except for pale rubies that dangled
from her ears, and the silver cross that sat at the base of her
throat.

Into the coiffure, Verbena had slid one of the decorated
stakes she and Oliver had taken to creating for their vampire
hunter mistress. This particular one was long and slender—
but thick enough to be deadly to a vampire—with roses
carved on the handle and the whole stake painted pink. Victoria had been able to convince Verbena to leave off the
feathers this time, although two pearls had found their way
into the centers of the roses.

Beneath all these accoutrements of feminity was Miro's
latest creation in the battle against the undead: a special
corset. The idea had come from Verbena initially. Not only
did she take her mistress's fashion seriously, but she was
also the only maid in London who fussed over weapons and
tools.

Flimsy slippers allowed every little stone to poke through
to her soles as she and Zavier, with Lady Nilly on his other
arm, walked up to the entrance of the villa. They followed in
the wake of the ladies Melly and Winnie.

"It isn't very festive," Lady Winnie said, her comment
loud enough for Victoria to hear from behind, and obviously

forgetting that they weren't attending a party. "It's as if there's hardly anyone here. Not even a footman to help us down from the carriage! I know the family hasn't lived here for decades, but one would think they would have cleaned up a bit before having us."

"It's a treasure hunt," Lady Nilly trilled, edging closer to Zavier. "It's the atmosphere! Intriguing, foreboding, haunting . . ."

"And it isn't as if it's to be a crush of a ball," Lady Melly added, glancing back at her daughter. "It was made very clear that tonight is not a celebration of any kind, and only very few were invited. We were lucky enough to be asked. If it weren't for *Barone* Tarruscelli, who gave us their own invitation, we shouldn't have been included at all."

It was indeed an eerie, strange atmosphere. The mansion itself was hidden by the same tall wall Victoria and Ylito had climbed through to get to the Door of Alchemy, which was at the opposite end of the vast grounds of the estate, set away from the main building of the villa. Behind the crumbling wall, the manor house was gloomy and dark.

Instead of the great light spilling from numerous windows that would accompany most fetes or dinner parties or soirees, the building had only a small yellow glow from the front entrance. The door opened, giving just a brief glimpse of a butler, and then closed behind a cluster of people, as though loath to waste its illumination on the night.

Indeed, the line of carriages dropping off guests was hardly a line at all, for there weren't so very many guests. This was a fact that had not escaped Victoria, and as they approached the door and it opened again she paused, edging into the welcome shadows so that no one inside could see her. She wondered not for the first time whether it had been by accident or design that the mother of a Venator had been invited to attend.

Zavier stopped, urging Lady Melly to go on ahead as

Victoria pretended to adjust her loose slipper. The older woman, thrilled by the same environment that set her daughter's instincts on edge, did not hesitate and gladly entered the door, opened by a butler who barely stepped far enough away for them to enter. She was followed by Lady Nilly and Lady Winnie.

The door closed without the butler even looking about, and Victoria and Zavier were alone in the darkness together.

"Ye'll take care now," Zavier said, capturing Victoria's gloved hand as she straightened from pretending to fix her slipper, a task meant to keep her from being recognized by anyone inside the villa.

"Of course. Thank you again for coming, Zavier. I know my mother will be safe in your care, and I'll be able to slip into the building without being noticed. If you see anything—"

"Aye, I'll tend to her. And I'll keep watch for anything odd, though I don't ken what it is we might find. I canna believe the key is hidden in this house any longer."

"I begin to wonder myself. It could be a perfectly harmless, foolish little event meant to slip under the notice of the priests during Lent . . . but I do not believe it. However, I don't sense any undead nearby. So perhaps all will be well."

She would have turned away to melt back into the shadows so Zavier could enter the house, but his hand, rough from the calluses on his palm, stopped her, brushing over her cheek. "Your lip's nearly healed. Best take care not to run into more door corners," he said, reminding her of the lie she'd given to excuse the nip Beauregard had given her the night before.

"It was very clumsy of me," she replied, thinking of how she'd bumped her forehead into Max that same evening . . . and then she realized Zavier's intention.

He was going to kiss her. She tensed in anticipation.

Zavier moved closer and brushed her mouth with his, leaving a gentle scrape of whiskers and the musty smell of tobacco in the wake of the kiss. When he pulled back to look at her, their eyes were nearly level. Though it was too dark to see his expression, she could feel the faint tremble in his fingers against her chin. "Och, now," he said, a smile in his voice, "how does that feel?"

"I think it feels much better," she replied lightly, smiling back, hoping that Max wouldn't appear from the shadows and ruin the moment. It would be just like him.

"Victoria," Zavier said so softly his brogue was hardly noticeable, and then leaned forward to kiss her again. This time it was more than a brush of lips, yet there was still gentleness about it—as if he still wasn't certain she'd allow it, or as if he wasn't sure it was real.

The kiss was brief, as kisses went—certainly not as long or involved as others she'd experienced. When Victoria realized her hand had somehow made its way to the front of his massive shoulder and felt the slamming pounding of his heart all the way up in his neck, she drew back.

He pulled in a breath as if to speak, but she forestalled anything he might have said. "My mother will be wondering what's keeping us. Perhaps you'd best make your way inside. Give her the excuse that the strap on my slipper has broken and I've returned home to get a new one."

He nodded, his shaggy hair falling forward. With a sweep of his hand he brushed it back over his brow and stepped away. "Ye have a care," he said, and turned to walk back toward the main entrance, which had, during this interlude, remained closed and deserted.

Victoria watched him go and waited for Max to emerge from the shadows as she stripped off her gloves. She didn't like to wear them when there was the possibility of a fight.

The world remained silent, however—silent and empty,

filled with shadows and looming walls. Since Zavier had entered the villa there was no further activity. A few more lights had winked on in various windows, accompanied by moving shadows.

Victoria's neck was warm, but she was beginning to feel a little chilled everywhere else. It was, after all, February, and though milder than it would be in London, it was still cool after sundown. Dressed as she was in flimsy evening clothing, she knew she couldn't wait much longer, when a tussle in the overgrown bushes caught her attention.

Max emerged, coming from the opposite direction she'd expected—not from the drive, but from behind the villa.

"Another key has been inserted," he said without preamble, stepping like a long black shadow into the circle of light cast by a lone lantern.

"Do you mean to say you looked at the Door of Alchemy and there are two keys now?" Victoria said, stepping toward him.

"That is what I said, yes. I've just come from there. I wanted to see it for myself." His sharp nod indicated the direction behind the villa, off to the right and toward the back of the estate. "There's an old servants' entrance into the building back here."

"Which keys?" Victoria asked, starting off after him into the darkness along the wall of the house. "Which ones were turned?"

"Eustacia's wasn't one of them."

She felt a wave of relief; then something wet seeped through her slipper as she made her way along. Pursing her lips in annoyance, she continued on, not altogether certain it had been an accident that Max had led her this way.

At last he stopped in front of a door much less grand than the main entrance. A few sharp movements, the sound of splintering, and one powerful angling of his shoulders—and the door opened into a dark room.

"I'll go first," Victoria said, stepping past Max into a musty entryway. At least part of the information about the party wasn't a lie: The villa had obviously not been opened for years. If anyone had inhabited the place, the servants' entrance, at least, would have been well used.

"Be my guest."

It was dark, and Victoria paused for a moment to let her eyes adjust to the unfamiliar environment. Then, without a word to Max, she began to walk quickly, silently, but cautiously down the hallway toward the main part of the house.

She'd taken no more than three steps in her soggy slippers when a strong grip pulled her back. "Where are you going?" he asked.

Shaking off his hand, she looked up at him. "Blast it, Max, where do you think?" She managed to keep her voice low, although it was hard. "To the parlor or ballroom, where they've likely all gathered."

"Then perhaps you might wish to follow me. That direction"—he pointed where she'd been going, his hand boldly in her face—"leads to the servants' quarters."

She said nothing more, but turned and trotted off after him, annoyed with herself for getting her directions confused now that she was inside the building. Of course the servants' quarters were toward the back side of the villa.

The passageway was deserted, and there were cobwebs and dust everywhere. Victoria had to press her fingers over the top of her nose to keep from sneezing when Max brushed past an old drape that must have sent up a cloud of dust. She couldn't tell for sure, because of the darkness. There were voices in the distance, and as they moved along the servants' hallway the sounds grew louder.

Max stopped when they came to one of the back doors that

obviously led from the servants' area to the main part of the house. He cracked the door and peered inside, deliberately—Victoria was sure—positioning himself so that she couldn't see around him.

Or maybe she was just falling back into that old habit of being perturbed by everything he did or said.

Certainly he'd intentionally tried to irritate her when she'd first become a Venator and they'd had to work together. And last fall, when he'd been pretending to be part of the Tutela, he'd had to be even ruder and more snide than usual in order to keep her from asking too many questions.

But perhaps he really had come to respect her as a Venator, now that Aunt Eustacia was gone and he'd had a chance to think about things. In any case, despite his blunt ways, she was glad he was back.

Victoria realized he'd stepped away from the doorway and was looking at her. "They've gathered there in what must be the ballroom," he said in a quiet voice. "I'll sneak in and listen to what's being said. I saw a flight of stairs that might lead above for a better look."

"I'll go up and see what there is to see," she said, and started toward the door, but his hand on her upper arm stopped her.

"Go to the left, stay in the shadows, and you'll find the stairs."

She nodded once, then turned back to add, "Meet at the servants' door if we're separated."

Without waiting for a response she did as he'd suggested, opening the door that, by virtue of the fact that it was designed to be an unobtrusive servants' entrance, was set in the darkest corner of the room beyond it. She found it no difficult feat to move quickly and rapidly along the wall to a flight of stairs that led to a balconylike alcove above.

As she scurried along the wall, she saw that the main

room was not the ballroom, but an anteroom that offered three wide arches that led to the ballroom.

The people Victoria saw gathered barely constituted a crowd at all; perhaps twenty or thirty people stood about. They had sparkling goblets that looked out of place in a gloomy room lit not with lamps or sconces, but with only candles—although there were nearly as many candles tonight as there had been last night on the Corso. And since there was no music to act as a backdrop, and their voices were low murmurs, the occasion had a rather eerie feel. The furnishings were spare. A small table presumably held the drinks the guests had received, and another long table across the room was covered with what appeared to be scrolls of paper.

Victoria reached the stairs without incident, but as she rested her hand on the filthy balustrade she bumped into a small metal vase that had been hidden in the darkness. It tumbled off the bottom step and clanged to the floor. She caught it before it bounced again and, still holding it, dashed up the steps, seeking obscurity in the darkness above.

At the top she paused, looking back down the steps, privately berating herself for not being more careful. She held her breath, waiting to see if she'd be discovered.

After a long moment she saw two figures down below her moving purposefully toward the spot where the vase had banged on the floor. One of them pointed up the steps, into the darkness that concealed Victoria, but the other shook his head. Easing back even more, Victoria watched the two men converse while looking around nervously. Since she'd taken the vase with her, there wasn't anything to indicate the source of the noise they'd heard, and at last they walked back toward the main room.

She set the vase on the floor well out of the way and looked around, finding herself on a curtained balcony that overlooked what would have been the dance floor if, indeed, there had been dancing. The space was all shadows, for the only light came from the half-drawn curtains at the balcony's rail, hiding her presence from the room below. Very convenient.

So convenient that it made her wonder what the area had been used for when the villa was fully inhabited.

After a quick look around to ascertain that she was indeed alone, and that there didn't seem to be any other entrance or exit from the small alcove, she moved to the drapes and peered down through the large gap between them. Carefully pulling them closer together, so as not to draw attention to the movement of the velvet, she took advantage of her bird's-eye view and watched.

Although the group was small, the gathering looked no different from any other party Victoria had witnessed. It was certainly nothing like the Tutela meeting she'd had the misfortune to attend last autumn. There was no hypnotically scented incense burning, no chanting, no dais with a Tutela leader urging the attendees to support and save the vampires.

It was merely a party. People talked, and although their voices seemed to echo loudly and eerily in a relatively empty room, and there was a sense of unease creeping over Victoria's shoulders, nothing else seemed amiss. She still sensed no vampires.

There was Lady Melly . . . and Lady Nilly, too, hands flapping like spiraling birds as she made some urgent point. And Lady Winnie approached just then, holding a small plate of the dry Italian biscuits she claimed to disdain.

At that moment someone stepped behind Victoria, silent, sending her hair prickling.

Max.

Victoria didn't turn, didn't acknowledge his presence as she looked down from her hidden view, watching the people mingling below. The edges of the velvet curtain crinkled under her fingers as she pulled it taut from its moorings, positioning it in front of her face so she could look through the narrow opening. Max moved closer, brushing her shoulder as he peered through the same slit.

Now she saw Zavier in the center of the room below, talking with two men, and she focused her attention on him rather than on the man behind her, crowding her against the drapes.

Somehow Max must have known her thoughts, for he said in a low, amused voice, "A nice lad, Zavier. A good Venator." He was standing so close behind her his words whispered over her temple. If she drew in her breath, Victoria was certain her shoulders would brush against his chest.

She continued to watch Zavier, watch the way he gestured grandly, his large arms and broad shoulders setting him apart from the willowy dandies with whom he spoke: men who could be expected to parry a few fancy steps with an epée, and perhaps throw a punch or so if caught in an unpleasant situation . . . but who hadn't one iota of the power and strength in comparison to the more casually dressed Scot before them.

She looked down, turning her attention to count the people below, to give her something to focus on, willing her heart to slow its jagged pounding, and wishing Max would step away before she had to.

But he didn't move. His voice rumbled again. "Take care with him." There was an edge to his words, a warning that hadn't been there a moment before.

"Take care?"

He nodded, and she felt the movement of his head against the top of hers.

"You'll break his heart."

Victoria started in surprise, but her grip on the curtains—which had suddenly become deathly—kept her from spinning around or even turning her head. Still looking down, she tipped her face slightly to the side so he could hear her cool words. "Break his heart? What on earth do you mean? Never say you are attempting to advise me on my intimate affairs, Max. The closest you've come to any matter of the heart was an engagement to a lover of vampires."

"Zavier is a good man." Max's voice was calm and even in her ear. "You're too strong for him. You'll merely tread upon him with your silk slippers and trounce his heart, which he wears much too openly on his sleeve."

"You never cease to amaze me—"

"Victoria," he interrupted, still smooth but very firm. "The man is in love with the idea of a woman Venator. Any woman Venator. Had Eustacia been a few decades younger, he would have courted her."

"You're crude, Max."

A short, sharp laugh rumbled. "Perhaps. But at least I speak honestly."

"Disgustingly so."

"You would be better off with the likes of Vioget than that milksop Zavier."

"I begin to wonder why you continue to push me toward Sebastian. Is it some form of punishment?"

"Push you toward Sebastian? I wouldn't go so far as to say that."

"It was you, after all, who ordered him to kidnap me last autumn to keep me out of your way." Max had known well enough that she'd want to be involved in destroying Nedas, but she'd had no idea how tenuous and risky his plans were, and how much her interference could have jeopardized them. So he'd arranged for Sebastian to get her out of the way.

"A task that he accepted with embarrassing alacrity—but, of course, he had his own motives for cooperating. I'm certain he found the rewards worth the risk. That carriage must have been quite comfortable."

Victoria's face burned. How could he know she'd allowed Sebastian to seduce her in a carriage? Thank God he couldn't see her cheeks; they must be red with fury and embarrassment. And how *dared* he say such a thing?

Did he think that since she'd seen and experienced so much more than other women that her sensibilities weren't as delicate?

"At least Vioget can recognize your faults," Max continued in that steady voice, as though he hadn't just insulted her. "And, aside from that, I wouldn't bloody care if you were to tear out Vioget's innards and screw your heels into them. In fact, I'd applaud it. Zavier, on the other hand, the blasted fool, wouldn't see your faults if you engraved them on his stake. He's already anointed you and ensconced you on a pedestal."

"I still fail to see why you should be concerned about my affairs."

"You misunderstand. It isn't your affairs that concern me. It's Zavier's. I should hate to see a Venator incapacitated due to a broken heart. And you will break his if you continue on this path."

"You're so certain of this?"

"He's not strong enough, Victoria. He's an exceptional Venator, but he's not equipped to manage his heart. He cannot see your faults; he will let you run roughshod over him . . . and, finally, he will bore you with his easy ways, his pathetic doggedness of wanting to make you happy—all the time knowing he could lose you to this dangerous world we inhabit. And that's what I do not wish to see. For his sake. For ours, as Venators."

Tears had begun to sting the corners of her eyes, blurring her view of the party below. Burning tears of anger and grief. She blinked and took a long, slow breath, resisting the desire to spin a slap onto his aristocratic cheek like the Society miss she no longer was. "You would have said the same about Phillip had I listened."

"No." His voice became sharper and more serious. "Phillip was strong enough. He just didn't understand the world you live in. If he had . . ."

Max didn't need to finish, and Victoria didn't want him to. She released the curtains and slipped to the side, away from him. She knew very well that if Phillip had understood her life even a little, things would have been so very different. Her eyes stung and her throat felt as though she'd swallowed a ball.

"Victoria, you of all people know what it is like to suffer a broken heart. Take care not to bring the same onto one of your men. You have the power to do it."

"You forget that this Venator wasn't incapacitated with a broken heart."

"Weren't you?"

She drew herself up to reply . . . and then deflated. Oh, God, yes, she had been. For nearly a year after Phillip's death she'd been afraid to raise her stake for fear she'd turn berserker and annihilate anything in her path. The gifts she had, the powers, the strengths, the instincts: They could all be wielded for bad as well as for good. And the rage that had simmered beneath her calm exterior—the rage and hatred and loss—could have brought her down the wrong path.

The tears, silent and thus hidden in the darkness, were streaming down her cheeks now. Victoria had moved away from the gap in the curtains, away from Max and his insistent opinions, his ruthless words.

She drew in a long, deep breath, struggling to keep it from hitching and giving away the fact that he had brought her to this, and moved farther away. She wanted to get away from him, away from his damned truths.

Max turned, and the small slit in the curtains closed, leaving them in total darkness. The only relief was a dark gray essence that came from the direction of the stairs up which she'd come.

"Victoria?" His voice was quiet.

"There's nothing more to see here," she replied, relieved at how steady she sounded. "And I've seen no members of the Tutela." She was moving quickly and silently toward the exit and the stairs, focusing on the barest sense of light and her outstretched hands to find her way. "I'll go down to see what I can find."

"Victoria." Max was moving behind her; she could hear him. But she kept going toward the stairs, moving as quickly as she could, her eyes now able to make out the faintest of shapes.

She came to the top of the stairs, her hand on the balustrade helping her to feel her way around the corner at the top of the landing. Suddenly something came out of the darkness in front of her.

It was strong and metal, and someone was poking it into the front of her shoulder. "How serendipitous," came a familiar male voice. "What an unexpected prize our little trap has sprung."

A candle flared to life in front of her, revealing Mr. George Starcasset . . . and Lady Sarafina Regalado.

Nine

In Which Three Ladies Are Set Loose upon the Villa

Max heard the soft click of a pistol being cocked, and he froze just as he realized the back of his neck had begun to prickle and chill.

Vampires . . . somewhere . . . but not in close proximity.

The sudden flare of a candle lent a soft yellow glow from down the steps, just out of his sight. Then the light grew stronger and more yellow as three shadowy people moved up the stairs, into his view.

"And who were you—Ah! Maximilian!"

He knew that annoying voice all too well. Blast the chit.

"Sara." He couldn't bring himself to sound as delighted as his former fiancée did. "And Starcasset. What an unpleas-ant—yet not wholly unexpected—surprise."

He saw that Victoria—whose face was streaked with two narrow rivulets of . . . tears?—was under the control of George Starcasset and his pistol. She was also giving him, Max, a most loathing glare, as if it were somehow his fault she'd stormed into the barrel of the firearm.

Before he could move Sarafina came toward him. She was the buxom blonde, with pretty brown eyes and a head filled with little but fashion sense and coy comments, that he'd squired about Roma and engaged in many more tête-à-têtes with her than he'd cared to do. She was a lovely, fluffy piece—just the kind of woman he should marry if he ever actually thought he would do the deed, except for her affinity for the undead. But her voice and simpering mannerisms tended to grate on his nerves when he was exposed to her for any length of time.

Of course, at the moment, that simpering, fluffy chit had a pistol in her hands, so he was going to have to watch his tongue.

When she reached toward his right shoulder he merely looked down at her in annoyance and faint amusement, wondering if she was about to pull him into a reunion embrace. But when Sarafina yanked on his collar, pulling it back from Max's neck and exposing the raw bites there, he pushed her hand away, heedless of the pistol flailing about in her other grip.

"Good gad, watch that thing," he snapped, flipping his wretchedly stiff collar back into place. "You'll hurt someone, Sara. Put it away."

Unsurprisingly, she kept the pistol and steadied it, pressing it right into his middle. Painfully. "So it is true. You did go to her."

Max remembered belatedly that there was no fury like a woman scorned.

"Perhaps you could settle your lovers' quarrel some other time," Starcasset luckily interrupted. He must have jabbed his firearm into Victoria's skin a bit more harshly, for she winced and jolted. Looking at Max, he added, "I'm certain you can appreciate the benefits of coming along quietly."

Max nodded. "Indeed. It would not be in our interest to involve the other parties below in a skirmish." He glanced at Victoria to make sure she understood that she couldn't go blazing into a fight, but she was studiously looking away, her lips firmed with annoyance.

Surely she wasn't concerned about their current predicament.

"Well put, Mr. Pesaro. Now, if you and your jilted fiancée would be so kind as to lead the way, Lady Rockley and I will follow."

Thus they moved down the steps in pairs, remaining out of sight of the presumed party in the chamber beyond the anteroom where the stairs ended, Sara prodding him along in the opposite direction from which he and Victoria had come.

Max was armed with several stakes, including his favorite black one, and his own firearm, as well as a dagger sheathed in his boot. It was the mark of the amateurs who led them away that neither Starcasset nor Sara Regalado thought to check either of the Venators for weapons. Likely they thought vampire hunters would merely be carrying stakes and little else.

He would make certain they were far enough away not to alert or alarm the partygoers in the parlor before making his move. The last thing they needed was a hoard of frithering ladies and blustering would-be heroes getting in their way.

As they progressed, the sensations at the back of his neck grew colder and more intense, telling him that they were being taken to some conglomerate of vampires. They walked through a door, entering a large, dank room that appeared to be at least partially underground, if one judged by the greater chill in the air.

Obviously a contingent of undead had gathered in the

Villa Palombara. Apparently that was the true purpose behind the ostensible treasure hunt: a harvesting of victims by the Tutela, likely for Sara Regalado's father, the *conte*—and whatever minions he'd managed to gather around him after he was run off by Beauregard last fall in the wake of the destruction of Akvan's Obelisk.

An argument could be made, Max reflected as he ambled along next to Sara, that being brought closer to where the vampires were waiting would make their efforts to subdue them more efficient.

A sudden movement behind decided him. Knowing it was Victoria who'd somehow managed to catch Starcasset, the brainless devil, off guard, he swung into action as soon as Sara's attention was diverted and the pressure lifted from his ribs.

There was a fine line between disarming a woman and causing her hurt, and so Max allowed himself a bit of flair in this battle. He slid to the side, his feet lifting from the ground in the long, gliding leap of a *qinggong* movement, and came up and around Sara, Victoria, and Starcasset, executing the maneuver even in the low-ceilinged chamber.

The room was a blur as he spun and floated, leaped and glided, clocking Starcasset neatly at the back of his head with a well-aimed boot toe (he had no such qualms about injuring the dandy), and then coasting around to snag Sara around the waist and toss her through a nearby doorway.

In the midst of this effortless and liberating activity, Max saw a flash of pink that was Victoria, dashing away in the frilly gown she'd chosen for this occasion. It wasn't like her to run from a fight, so he knew precisely why she'd taken off.

Feet back on the ground, Max tossed Starcasset in after Sara, then shoved a heavy table in front of the door, wedging it under the knob, and started off after Victoria. His neck was cold; his fingers tingled. There were undead nearby, and many of them, if his senses were accurate.

And they always were.

The only reason he caught up to Victoria was because she'd taken a wrong turn—no surprise—and ended up in a dead-end hall.

He didn't have to ask where she was going; she turned on him and said, "My mother!" Her eyes were worried and her mouth set in an anxious line as she pushed past him.

"This way."

However, they'd not gone very far back when they turned a corner and were running down yet another hall just as a second door opened. More than a dozen creatures streamed in, at least some of them vampires.

Max saw Victoria run right into one of them, and before she could react another creature had leaped on her from behind. She went down in a bundle of pink lace and red rosettes, bringing the vampire with her and helping him on his way over her head.

He saw nothing else after that, however, for he was, of necessity, fully engaged with the four who leaped on him. He quickly dispatched one with his stake, but two more took its place. Something slammed into Max's legs from behind, sending his knees buckling and him collapsing to the floor.

He reared up, swinging, just as a sharp report echoed through the room. A blinding pain drilled into his shoulder, just above the scapula, and then another flash of pain skimmed his boot top, above his knee. Breathless with agony, Max lurched forward, bringing his injured leg up behind to slam into the creature as he tried to catch himself on his good arm.

Rolling to the side, he jerked to his feet just as something crashed onto the top of his head and the world went black.

*　　*　　*

"I vow, I expect a vampire to leap out at us any moment!" Lady Nilly whispered loudly. She was clasping a slender hand to her flat bosom as she led the way down a dark, dusty hall, lit only by the candle she held aloft.

The passageway was wide enough for the three of them to walk abreast, if they so chose, although the occasional table they passed might have necessitated that one of them temporarily fall behind. Vases or statues, many of them broken or lying on their sides, decorated the random furnishings. The ceiling was high, the walls lined with wainscoting, and everything was cobwebbed and dusty. More than once the ladies were startled by the sudden appearance of a cloudy mirror reflecting their progress along the hall.

"Vampire?" Lady Winnie gasped, slapping her own hand to her chest with a loud thunk and a poof of powder. She crowded up behind her slight friend and the safety of her light. "I'm not wearing my cross! And I've left my reticule with garlic at home! And my stake!"

"Hush, Winnie," came Lady Melly's voice behind them. "I scarcely need remind you that there aren't any such things as vampires, and it's just as well you aren't wearing that ridiculous cross. It's too large and bangs against you every time you move. It sounds like a morbid heartbeat, and it's so big it's dangerous."

"It was supposed to be dangerous," Winnie replied, her voice bordering on a wail. She'd grasped the back of Nilly's gown and was holding a fistful of silk. "To the vampires."

"This is just the perfect house for the undead to be lurking about," Nilly said, turning to look back at her friends with wide eyes. The single candlestick she held made a yellow glow about her face, lighting her wispy blond curls. "I can feel it! The restlessness in the air . . . the sensation of dark shadows, moving toward us . . . the sound of bat wings flapping—"

"Stop," squealed Winnie, releasing her friend's gown to clap her hands over her ears. "I don't know why we came to this dark, horrible place anyway. And why ever did we sneak away from that nice Mr. Zavier?"

Melly's hand on the duchess's plump arm nearly sent her friend through the cobwebbed ceiling, but her strident voice was sharp enough to penetrate the duchess's hysterics. "You're making a cake of yourself, Winnie. Do cease your wailing. And it was your idea to send Mr. Zavier for drinks whilst we sneaked away to start on this treasure hunt. Now, Nilly, let me look at that map. And do stop prattling about vampires. I don't know why we're letting you be in the lead."

Lady Melisande pushed her way past her hysterical friend, who had twisted about to grab onto Melly's arm and was now clinging to her like a good corset.

"I don't hear anyone else," whispered the cowering duchess fearfully. "We must be far away from the rest of the people. Oh, why did we come? We'll be found tomorrow with our throats torn open and three big Xs marked on our snowy white bosoms."

Melly had snatched the map, which was really nothing more than a crude drawing of the villa's floor plan. She struggled to aim it at the illumination of Nilly's candle, all without catching the large, curling paper on fire. "How badly have you lost us?"

"They won't tear our throats open," Nilly remonstrated the duchess, ignoring Lady Melly's question. "Vampires don't do that unless you fight them, or unless they are very angry. They just bite your chest or your shoulder and drink your blood."

Winnie's hands moved up to cover her alarmingly bare throat, her small eyes goggling as wide as they could, darting about as if to see the lurking vampires before they leaped. "But—"

"My cousin's wife's sister's friend's mother was bitten by a vampire," Nilly continued, peering into the darkness ahead of them. "She said it hardly hurt at all . . . and that it was rather pleasant, in some ways."

"I don't see how big fangs cutting into my neck would be almost pleasant," Winnie replied fearfully, bumping into a low table. "I do believe I should faint dead away so that I wouldn't feel a thing."

"May I help you ladies?" came a genteel voice.

All three heads snapped toward the man, who'd suddenly appeared from . . . well, it was unclear from whence he'd appeared.

Winnie gasped and squeezed Lady Melly's arm so hard the other woman gasped too. "Wh-wh-wh—" was all she could manage.

"Do not be frightened," he said, stepping closer, smiling gently, his hand outstretched as if to put off their fears. He wasn't a young man, but appeared to be of an age with them. He seemed harmless enough, dressed in dusty evening clothes and carrying his own candle. A cobweb clung to his sleeve, suggesting that he, too, had been digging his way through the house in search of the treasure. The man wasn't particularly handsome, but despite his trim mustache and beard—likely grown to make up for the lack of hair on his head—his face was pleasant. He certainly didn't look like he was about to sprout fangs and leap upon them.

"We're not frightened," Melly said in a strangled voice, trying to free herself from Winnie's death grip. "We just stopped to look at the map. Are you on the treasure hunt?"

"Of course. Perhaps I can assist you? Did you wish to go back to the parlor, where everyone else is waiting?"

"Has everyone returned to the parlor already? Has the

treasure been found?" Winnie forgot her nervousness and stepped toward him, disappointment oozing from every pore.

Before he could answer they were interrupted by a loud sound, as if an altercation was happening, perhaps a short distance away. "What is that noise? Are they celebrating the treasure being found?" Winnie demanded.

"No, no, I do not believe so," the bald man replied, offering an arm to Melly. "It's too early for that. Please, let me be of assistance. If you would come with me, I shall take you ladies on your way."

Melly started off with him in the direction he indicated, followed by Nilly and Winnie.

"But what if he's a vampire?" Winnie squeaked softly to Nilly. "He could turn into a bat at any moment and swoop down over us and get caught in our hair."

"If he is, he's likely going to take us somewhere and ravish us," Lady Petronilla replied, her voice pitched nervously. "I wonder if it will be in a bedchamber, or if he'll take us to his coffin and chain two of us up inside while he bites the other one?"

Lady Winifred stumbled. "Ravish? Chains? Coffin? Oh, how could I be so foolish as to leave my cross at home!"

"I shall offer him to take me first," Nilly said bravely. "Then perhaps there will be a chance for you and Melly to escape whilst he is ravishing me."

"A stake. Perhaps I can find something to use as a stake. It must be wooden, mustn't it?"

"Oh, dear! But he *cannot* be a vampire," Nilly suddenly said.

Nearly fainting in relief, Winnie turned to look at her companion. "No? But are you certain?"

"See—he carries a candle. Of course, everyone knows that vampires can see in the dark. Why should he need a candle? And he isn't nearly handsome enough," she added. "Not tall enough either, I venture to say."

"Oh . . . yes, not tall enough. And he doesn't need a candle. Indeed, I am so relieved you are such an expert about vampires, Nilly," the duchess said, picking up her stride and jouncing along merrily now.

Lady Petronilla didn't appear to be quite as relieved as her friend. "But, of course, I could be wrong. After all, I never have met a vampire," she added. Perhaps there was even a bit of wistfulness in her voice.

"We must have gotten very confused," Lady Melisande was saying to their guide, her voice carrying back to her two companions. "I don't recall walking this way at all."

The gentleman's soft laugh was easy and full of humor at the ladies' confusion. "No, indeed, madam. This is the way to the parlor. Unless you wish to see where I think the treasure is hidden."

"Treasure?" Lady Winifred bounded forward to walk on the other side of their guide. "Do you know where it is hidden?"

He smiled ruefully. "I didn't mean to—ah, you have caught me out, madam. I shall take you, if you vow not to tell a soul it was I who led you there."

"But of course not! And if there is treasure to be found there, you can rest assured we shall share it with you, kind sir," Winnie soothed him. "Besides, it is best to bring us there posthaste rather than wait until after you have taken us to the parlor and then come back . . . for someone else might have found our treasure before your return. And then what a fine fettle we'd be in."

"Indeed. Your logic, though intricate, is quite—er. If I am to take you there, then we must turn on this hallway here," he said, ushering them along.

This passageway was smaller and closer than the other

ones through which they'd traveled. It was spare of furnishings and decor, which would imply that the area the ladies now traversed was part of the servants' quarters.

Winnie noticed this and thought it was a brilliant deduction. "Of course! The treasure should be hidden in the back of the villa, where no one ever goes." Forgetting, of course, that the servants who ran the household would have quite outnumbered the residents of the villa.

Nilly had begun to lag behind her two friends, who'd placed the gentleman guide betwixt them. So when she felt a hand on her shoulder, her soft gasp of surprise was lost in the treasure-hunting conversation ahead.

She turned and found herself facing a tall man with black hair and fair skin, dressed like a gentleman on his way to the theater. He smiled, and she saw the glint of very white teeth behind his lips.

His eyes glowed red.

Nilly opened her mouth to scream, then thought better of it. Instead she closed her eyes and turned her head away demurely, fully aware that between her coiled-up hair and the low cut of her gown, there was quite a lot of skin exposed. Holding her breath, she let the candle fall and heard it roll away on the wood floor.

Her skin prickled as she waited, her veins fairly leaping, her heart trammeling in her flat bosom. Then the air shifted, and she heard something that sounded like a shove, and then a faint little pop followed by a soft poof.

And then a very smooth, mellow voice said, "Are you quite all right, madam?"

Nilly's eyes flew open. The man standing in front of her was no longer dark haired and pale visaged; nor did he have glowing red eyes.

He was just as handsome, but in a golden sort of way, with curling tawny hair and skin that glowed like toffee in the light of the candle he held. He was looking at her with one cocked eyebrow and a humorous twist to his sensual mouth.

"I . . . you . . . he . . ."

"He is gone, and you are quite safe, madam. Or should I say mademoiselle?" He gave her a melting smile. "But what is such a lovely woman like yourself doing—"

"Nilly!"

Her attention was drawn back along the dark, narrow hallway to the bustling of gowns and the rustling of paper heralding the approach of her two friends, their gentleman guide nowhere in sight.

"Oh!" wailed Nilly, her disappointment firmly sinking in.

"Why are you dawdling?" demanded Melly. "As we've found, it's much too easy to get lost in this vast house."

"And you're keeping us from finding the treasure," the duchess informed her. "I vow, if we get there too late because of your mooning about, I shall never forgive you, Petronilla."

"Now come along. Our lovely gentleman friend is waiting," Melly added, pointing down the hall into the darkness.

"Where is your candle? Now we shall have only one light, and you know how weak my eyes are in the darkness," said Winnie. "I vow I cannot see past my own fingers even in my own bedchamber at night unless Rudgers leaves the fire blazing."

Nilly turned to the golden-haired man and found he was gone. Her mouth opened, then closed once again without making an intelligible sound.

There was nothing about to indicate that either of the men had ever been there, except her dropped candle—which had gone out when it landed—and a small pile of dust that she hadn't noticed earlier.

"But . . ." Nilly gave up trying to speak and, with one last glance backward, followed the others.

"I begin to wonder if Victoria has made her way back to the party," Melly said suddenly, as she and her companions started back down the hallway. Their gentleman guide had been left standing at the corner of an intersection of two passageways when the ladies had realized Nilly was no longer with them.

"I hope she's found that nice Mr. Zavier," Nilly said, finally having obtained control of her tongue. "Perhaps they are becoming better acquainted."

"I certainly hope *not*." The Lady Winifred straightened up as though Nilly had suggested Victoria might have fallen in love with a vampire. "As kind as he might be, he's much too coarse and . . . and . . . unshaven, and he certainly isn't up to snuff for our marchioness. After all, she stepped up from being a mere miss to become the wife of the Marquess of Rockley—God rest his soul—and it won't do to have her sliding back into a dank, drafty castle in the Highlands. Why, there're probably vampires flapping—"

"Ladies," called the gentleman guide's voice, beckoning them toward him. "Are we all together again?"

"Indeed we are, sir. Please lead us on," Melly replied, conveniently ignoring the fact that they hadn't yet been introduced to their savior.

Just as they rejoined their guide, a pretty blond woman came bursting on the scene from a different branch of the hallway. The man turned in surprise, and the young woman grasped his arm, pulling him away from the older ladies. "At last! I have been searching the whole villa for you!" And then her voice dropped very low, and it sounded as though she said something about a . . . senator?

"I shall not abide it if that chit insists on accompanying us," Winnie fumed, glaring at the pair, who'd moved far enough away that she couldn't hear what they said. For, despite her complaint about failing eyesight, her ears worked perfectly well. What was so important about a Roman senator that the chit had to interrupt their treasure hunt?

And then from behind them came the sound of heavy, rushing feet. The three ladies turned to see Mr. Zavier hurrying down the hall toward them. With him was another gentleman—unknown to Winnie and Melly, but perfectly familiar to Nilly as the handsome blond who'd interrupted her tête-à-tête with the dark-haired, pale-skinned man.

"There ye ladies are," Mr. Zavier exclaimed, his brogue thick with emotion. His cheeks were flushed enough that they showed their ruddiness even in the low light, and he was holding something in his hand—something long and thin and pointed—but before anyone save Nilly could take notice, he shoved it in his pocket. "We must take our leave now," he said, looking about.

The blond man, who was also approaching, peered beyond them into the darkness. But when the ladies turned to follow his gaze, they saw that their gentleman guide and the young blond woman had disappeared.

"We've almost found the treasure," the duchess complained as Mr. Zavier offered her his arm. "We cannot leave now."

"I'm afraid the treasure has already been located, and that it is well past time to leave. All of the other guests have gone," said the handsome blond man in his comforting voice.

"And what about Victoria?" Lady Melly asked Mr. Zavier, taking his other arm, yet still looking behind her to find out what on earth had happened to that handsome man who'd been leading them about. "How vexing that he should have disappeared so suddenly," she muttered. "He was quite charming, and I didn't even learn his name."

"Victoria, thinking ye had done so, has already returned home after joining me for a short time in the parlor. After ye disappeared"—Mr. Zavier fixed a dark look at Winnie, and she returned his glance with all the haughtiness she could muster—"she had come with her slipper fixed and was quite disappointed that ye'd gone on without her. Come, ladies, 'tis best that we be on our way."

"May I?" The blond gentleman offered his arm to Nilly, and when she accepted it, began to hurry her along the hall.

If the two gentlemen happened to look back over their shoulders, the older ladies didn't appear to notice; they were much too intent on keeping their footing alongside the agile men and their long, rapid strides.

"But this is not the way we came in," Melly exclaimed when they came to a door—a small, unobtrusive one that was most certainly not the grand entrance they'd been welcomed into.

The night air was cool, and the half-moon glowed down on them as they stepped out of the villa onto . . . grass.

"My slippers," shrieked Nilly, lifting her feet one at a time in a mad, hopping manner. "They'll be ruined!"

"Come, come," Mr. Zavier said, ushering them along the dark building toward the front of the villa where their carriage was waiting.

As the ladies climbed in, their creaking joints reminding them they'd had hardly a spot of rest in the last week, with Carnivale and all of the other excitement, they noticed that theirs was the only carriage in sight. Mr. Zavier handed each of them in and then followed with an energetic leap, slamming the door shut behind him.

Rapping harshly on the roof, he settled back into his seat, surrounded by gowns and panting ladies. Not, perhaps, his preferred environment to be surrounded by such feminity . . . but it was his duty, nonetheless.

It wasn't until the carriage pulled away from the street in front of the villa that the ladies realized the blond gentleman had disappeared.

In fact, none of them could recall seeing him once they came outside of the villa.

"Well, I never," snapped Winnie, looking back out the carriage window. "That man! He tricked us into leaving so he could have the treasure."

And she settled into her seat, plump elbows crossed over her just-as-plump bosom, and brooded all the way back to the Gardella villa.

Ten

In Which Our Heroine Finds Herself in a Compromising Position

Victoria slowly came to consciousness, aware that her entire body ached.

The last thing she remembered was seeing Max collapse under a cluster of vampires; then something struck her from behind and her world went dark.

Now . . . she had no idea how long she'd been lying here . . . wherever she was. She couldn't see anything; it was pitch-black. Even after she blinked her eyes numerous times to adjust them to the night, she could make out little but vague shadows.

She couldn't move. Her wrists were tied tightly behind her, and when she uncurled her fists the pads of her fingers pressed into something that felt like dirty stone or brick behind her. She felt the same underneath, suggesting she was in a chamber belowground. A dungeon, perhaps.

That in itself didn't bode well.

Then there was the fact that the back of her neck was cold. Freezing, in fact; the prickles there felt as if a cold wind were blasting over her skin. Her hair sagged, falling over her shoulders, but provided no protection from that barometer of the undead. Her gown was disheveled, and she was quite certain that at least several rosettes and perhaps some of the flounces had been torn from its hem.

But that was the least of her concerns, for . . . She paused, forcing her racing thoughts to slow so she could concentrate. She closed her eyes, even though she couldn't see anything, and listened.

No. No, she hadn't imagined it.

Apprehension crept up her spine, spreading over the back of her shoulders. The smell was faint, but it was there: that musty, rotting, malevolent death-smell of a demon.

Demons and vampires? Here together?

They were mortal enemies—at least, they would be if either of them were mortal. The battle for Lucifer's favor had raged between the vampires and demons since he'd turned Judas into the first vampire.

Demons were, of course, fallen angels—of which Lucifer was the greatest of all. They had been purveyors of evil and death since time dawned. But after Judas hanged himself, certain that he would never be forgiven for betraying Jesus, Lucifer had wooed him and his soul to the side of Hell and used him to create a new race that was half demon and half human.

Being the devil's own creation, the vampires felt they should take precedence over the demons; but the demons had existed for so much longer, they believed their race was the more powerful and should inherit the reign of Hell.

Either way, Victoria knew, it was very rare for the two races to be together, or to cooperate in any way.

Then she remembered her mother, and her apprehension

exploded into full-force terror. Lady Melly and her two friends could still be in the villa, under the control of the vampires and the demons. Zavier could not have fought off all of the undead that had attacked her and Max. Her only hope was that he'd sensed the presence of the vampires in time to bring the ladies—and the other guests—to safety.

Or . . . a new thought alleviated her anxiety a bit. If Regalado was after the key, perhaps he meant to use her mother only as a hostage or bait. In which case she wouldn't be harmed.

She hoped.

"Max?" she said softly. She thought she'd heard a faint shuffling sound, perhaps even a groan. It was either Max or some other creature—either of which was preferable to other options, such as the undead . . . or those of the eight-legged persuasion.

There was silence, and Victoria closed her eyes again and listened this time for something closer to her. She was sure she heard something, sensed some other presence.

One thing was certain: If Max was indeed here, he must be badly hurt if he made no sound. This greater worry galvanized her into action.

Her legs weren't tied, so she used her splayed hands on the floor behind to help shift herself from the ground and move onto her knees. Her head began to pound angrily above her brows as she came upright, and there was something wrong with her right leg . . . it was stiff and it ached. Horrendously.

Victoria tried to follow the wall so she could keep her bearings in the chamber and investigate every part of the room.

Suddenly she heard voices, and the cold prickles at the back of her neck increased. Before she could think of anything to do that might be proactive, a door opened across the room from her. Immediately Victoria sagged against the wall, half closing her eyes, pretending to be unconscious. Even a moment's reprieve could help her make a decision or gather more information that would help her escape.

With the opening of the door a bit of light spilled into the room. Shadows blocked the entrance, and the rotting death-smell of the demon became a bit stronger—but not enough to alarm her. Whoever or wherever it was, it was not standing in the doorway.

Through her slitted eyes, Victoria saw that the chamber was not much larger than a parlor, and it was fairly empty. There was a large, lumpy shadow halfway across the room that spiked her concern for Max; if she'd kept going on her path around the perimeter, she would have brushed against it at one point. There were no furnishings, one door, and nothing else.

All of this she had taken in during the instant after the door opened. Now Victoria waited, her muscles tense, forcing her breathing to steady.

And suddenly something large and unwieldy came tumbling into the room. It landed on the floor in the middle of the chamber in an ignominious heap, barely illuminated by a small lantern hanging beyond the door.

"Do not fear," said a voice from the entrance. It sounded familiar, but Victoria couldn't see enough to recognize the speaker. "You won't be here long. Akvan will soon be ready for you."

Akvan? Good grief . . . was that the demon she smelled?

Before Victoria could react, the door closed. She heard the heavy grating of a bolt being drawn.

"Ouch," grumbled the heap on the floor. "Wasn't beating me enough? Why did they have to pitch me in like a horse-shoe?"

Victoria's mouth fell open; fortunately, it was too dark for him to see what must be incredulous shock on her face. "Sebastian? Is that you?"

"In the flesh. Or, rather, what's bloody left of me."

"How on earth did you get here?"

"Why are you so surprised to see—er, hear—me? I was under the impression that you were looking for me. Or, be still my heart . . . was that nothing but a false rumor?"

"I had hoped to see you in a more . . . conventional situation. But, yes, I was looking for you. I have to ask you something." She was scooting on her rump as quickly as she could toward where she remembered seeing him fall. The room was, of course, dark now, but that short while of illumination had helped to orient her. At least she knew the location of the door, and how large the chamber was. And if that big lump was indeed Max, she could do more to help him if her hands were untied. "Did he say that *Akvan* was ready for you?"

"Yes, he— Ow!" he snapped when her shoe rapped sharply against something . . . soft. "I appreciate your delight in seeing me, Victoria, but can you take a bit more care? That was my . . . er—"

"Never mind," she replied, feeling her face heat in the dark. "If you would untie me? Then perhaps we can figure some way out of here."

"Despite the fact that I find the thought of you tied up and restrained remarkably titillating, I would be happy to release you . . . if only I could. You see, I am just as bound as you are. Perhaps more so, as apparently my feet are tied, while yours are not. Which was why I found it remarkably insulting that they had to throw me in here."

Blast it. She'd realized when scooting across the floor that the knife that had been strapped to her thigh was no longer there . . . and she hoped, profusely, that it had been Sara Regalado who had removed it instead of George Starcasset. Or anyone else. "Sit up then, and we can move back-to-back and work on each other's knots," she said.

With much groaning and huffing of breath, Sebastian managed to hike himself up into a sitting position, leaning heavily against Victoria, who'd planted her feet on the ground, knees bent, in order to stabilize herself for him. He was warm and solid against her, smelling familiarly of spicy cloves and a tinge of sweat, along with a faint rusty scent. Their shoulders brushed, the fabric of what must be his shirt against the bareness of her upper back. It was damp.

"I thought Akvan was dead," she said after he seemed to be settled against her. She groped around behind, feeling his arms as he did the same, and at last their fingers touched. His were slick, but he managed to curl them around to gently stroke the center of her palm in a tantalizing caress. Slip, swirl, stroke.

Surprised at the innate eroticism of this unexpected, simple touch, Victoria swallowed as the light tickle traveled from her palm up along her wrist and arm and made her feel . . . warm and sensitive, even here in this dark, dank dungeon.

Then his fingers—and again she realized that they felt wet—began to move with purpose, feeling around for the knots in the rope. She sniffed and smelled blood. "Is that blood all over your hands? And your shirt?"

"Ah, well," Sebastian said lightly, although she noticed a bit more strain than usual in his charming voice, "the vampires became a bit overzealous in their attempts to keep me from finding y—where they were hidden, and I became rather . . . bloody in the process. I will endeavor to keep from staining your gown, but our positions might make that difficult."

"They didn't bite you," Victoria said. It wasn't a question.

"No, they didn't dare. I am, after all, the grandson of

Beauregard, as you well know. A fact that didn't keep me from being relegated to these unwelcome accommodations, but at least it kept me from getting my throat torn out. At least for now. And . . . Akvan *was* dead, or at least living in Hell," he said, at last addressing her question, "until Pesaro destroyed his obelisk. When it was shattered last autumn, Akvan was recalled back here to earth—to Rome, to be more precise, in a weakened form, as I understand it. He's spent the last four months building up his strength."

"So he is here? And so how did you get here? Do stop it and let me try your knots, Sebastian," she said at last. "You've done little but pinch me in the . . . well, somewhere you shouldn't be pinching me, and you're obviously hurt."

"Ah, the hero fails to save the damsel in distress." Sebastian sighed dramatically, but his fingers fell away and she thought she sensed an air of relief in his voice.

"Well, it isn't the first time, and I'm certain it shan't be the last," Victoria replied, groping around to try to locate the knots at his wrists. His skin was warm, but sticky, and even with the tips of her fingers she could feel the brush of hair that grew under his cuffs.

"But of course . . . since you are the Venator," Sebastian replied in a cool voice. "I am here because my grandfather set me to watch the Door of Alchemy over the last days. Apparently he is certain someone is about to open it—and it appears that Akvan and his fiends are the ones. I saw Pesaro skulking around it earlier this evening, and when I learned that there were several . . . shall we say, civilians invited within the villa, I thought perhaps I should investigate. I didn't expect to find you here as well."

Victoria had found the bulk of rope and begun to try to pry it loose, but the knots were tight and she was in an awkward position. "You decided to investigate, or was your real intent to find some way of bedeviling Max?"

"Why should I bedevil him?" Sebastian asked, his voice properly shocked. "In fact, he owes me his life."

"Indeed? Somehow I cannot imagine that." She couldn't get a good fix on the knots; her fingers were chilled from the dampness, and her wrists sore from bending nearly double and trying to manipulate the rope, which was thick and difficult to grasp.

And then, with a twinge of annoyance with herself for forgetting, she remembered the special corset Miro had made for her, the corset he'd executed at Verbena's suggestion. Her maid and Oliver had tried to create something similar at first themselves. But without the skills of the weapons master, it had been a disaster. Knives and stakes had protruded from every angle, and when she tried it on a blade had slipped from its place and sliced through the delicate shift to her skin. However, Miro had taken the idea and created the corset, and Victoria was wearing it right now.

But the problem was . . . she would need help accessing it.

"Max wasn't terribly pleased," Sebastian was saying. "In fact, I do believe he offered to damn me for staking the vampire that was about to maul him—it was last autumn, that night the obelisk was destroyed."

"You?" Victoria couldn't help a chuckle—it was a nervous one, partly because of what she was going to have to ask him to do. "You don't stake vampires, Sebastian. Even if you could, you wouldn't. Now I know you're lying." It was true—Sebastian loved his grandfather Beauregard, and as a result of his relationship with him and the knowledge that every single vampire had once been a mortal being, with family and loved ones, Sebastian refused to stake the undead, because of the eternal damnation that awaited them after their demise.

I can't send someone's father or sister to Hell for eternity, he'd once told her. *I won't be responsible for that.*

"Shall we stop this nonsense?" she said sharply. "I want to get out of these ropes, and I think that might be Max over there on the floor—but he hasn't moved or made a sound since I woke up. And I'm sure if he were conscious, he would have had some scathing comment for you and your melodramatics by now."

"Oh, dear. Then my sacrifice last autumn will have been in vain."

"I have a knife," she said, ignoring his comment. "You'll need to help me get to it."

Sebastian laughed. "I'm sure they've taken all of your weapons, Victoria, just as they did mine. I haven't anything but my boots and clothes."

"Well, if the pinching of my skin is any indication, I'm still wearing my corset," she snapped. "And that's where the knife is."

She felt him go absolutely still. And then, after a moment of stunned silence, she heard the soft puff of a laugh. "My God, Victoria, I don't know whether to laugh or to cry. Are you saying you want me to help you out of your corset? Here and now?"

She couldn't help her own little smile, there in the dark, at the sound of pure lust mixed with shock in his voice. Even though it was not the time nor the place, the thought—the memory of his hands on her skin and breasts and hips— made that little shiver that had traveled up her arm just a moment ago turn into a longer, deeper one that spiraled down, tangling sharply in her belly. Her mouth dried and she swallowed back the absurdity of thinking of such things when they were in danger.

As was her mother.

The sudden reminder of Lady Melly's possible fate put sharpness back into Victoria's voice. "No, not to take it off. Just . . . one of the front strips of boning, on the . . . er . . .

the left side has been replaced with a slender stiletto blade. I'll need you to help me remove it, and then put it to use. Do you think you can handle that?"

"I shall certainly do my best," he said gallantly. "Er . . . shall I start from the top . . . or the bottom?"

There was much too much relish in those words, and Victoria had to resist the urge to snap back at him, especially since the answer was, "From the bottom." Annoying how dry her mouth had become and how unsteady her voice was.

But Sebastian said nothing, nothing at all, to her surprise. He positioned himself so that he was in front of her, but with his back facing her. Thus, he was brushing up against the side of her left thigh. As he began to move his bound hands clumsily around, trying to find the hem of the skirt to slip between it and the edge of her shift, Victoria said a brief prayer of thanks that it wasn't Max who'd been required to help her. The idea of his strong, long-fingered hands sliding up under her gown made her stomach flutter unpleasantly.

She turned her thoughts smartly away from that and found herself distracted by the gentle stroking of Sebastian's fingers as he brushed his knuckles over the top of her stockinged leg, now separated from his touch by only the very thin fabric of her shift. The undergarment was of such fine cotton that it might not have been there at all. Her breathing was becoming a bit rough, and she tried to slow it, to steady and level it. She didn't want to think about the tingling that erupted between her legs as her sensitive skin was exposed from under the much heavier silk of her gown, and then as it was caressed by his finger.

"I hope that you shall put me out of my misery and tell me that the skinny stick of a woman wasn't your mother," Sebastian said, his fingers sliding beyond the crease where her left leg joined her hip.

"Skinny woman? What are you talking about?" Her voice

was a bit breathy, but maybe he wouldn't notice. He certainly seemed to be concentrating on what he was doing, if his own steady breathing was any indication.

"There were three of them together—the dry, brittle one, the loud, large, pillowy one, and the bossy, elegant one. I was rather hoping," he said, his fingers at last beginning to tug at the bottom edge of her corset, searching by feel for the blade, "that none of them was your mother . . . but since they were talking about you as if they knew you well, I realized I was bound to be disappointed."

"You saw them? If you caused them to be captured too, Sebastian, I shall never forgive you!" She focused on irritation rather than on the movements of his fingers as they felt around her stays. "It should be there somewhere. You'll feel the short handle protruding from the bottom of the corset . . . just . . . yes, there! I do wish you would hurry."

"Oh, faithless woman," he replied. "It was I, in fact, who saved the dry stick of a woman from being some undead's evening feed. And it was I who directed the man who was supposed to be protecting them—Zavier, was that his name?—to their location so that he could whisk them to safety."

"So they are safe?" Victoria breathed a long sigh of relief that had nothing to do with the gentle tickling of his knuckles as he worked on pulling the knife from its special slot in the corset. "Oh, how silly of me to forget, Sebastian, there is a little frog enclosure that keeps the blade from sliding out and wreaking its havoc on my gown. You must loosen it and the braid holding it in place will fall away and you will be able to— Oh! Stop that!"

He chuckled in his Sebastian way, low and laced with warmth. "But you liked it before, *ma chère*."

"That was when I trusted you," she replied smartly, feeling him pulling on the corset again instead of letting his fingers stray where they should not have gone. "Actually, I don't believe I've ever trusted you, but that was before you drugged and kidnapped me. And why did you say you hoped Lady Petronilla—the slender one—was not my mother?"

Sebastian gave a groan of relief as the stiletto at last came free of its place in her stays, and he pulled it away.

"Take care you don't cut me with it," Victoria ordered, glad that the moment was over as she rustled her skirts back into place by shifting her legs. "I'll move so you can slice my ropes—no, no, on second thought, I think it would be best if I did the cutting. If you would put the blade down, I'll move so I can pick it up and saw your ropes."

"What a splendid idea. At least the blood you'll draw will mingle with what's already there. And, to answer your question," he said as she maneuvered herself slowly around so that they were back-to-back again, she sitting on her haunches so that her hands were that much higher, "I was particularly hoping the dried-up stick wasn't your flesh and blood because it is a well-known adage—at least to the male population—that a woman, when aging, takes after the looks of her mother."

Victoria had levered up the knife and was sawing delicately, and awkwardly, against the ropes. "And whatever is wrong with the way Lady Petronilla looks?" She couldn't keep the little grunt from her voice as she felt soreness and pain radiating up her wrists from the tense, awkward motions. Her injured left leg screamed under the weight of her body as she knelt there, working as fast yet as carefully as she could.

"She is as flat as a board. Flatter, even."

"Flat as a— Oh." Victoria bit her lip and rolled her eyes in the dark.

"Ah, at last! I can feel my fingers again," Sebastian said, and he wiggled said fingers against hers.

"Take care," she warned, "else you'll get them cut and then you won't feel them at all. This blade is wickedly sharp."

"It is indeed, for I'm free already."

She felt a jolt as he pulled his wrists apart, brushing against her as the ropes fell away. He gave a relieved exhale as he took the blade from her aching fingers. Victoria heard the unmistakable sound of friction, as if he were rubbing his wrists and arms to get the blood flowing again. Which was something she longed to do herself, as soon as she was untied.

"Now what are you doing?" she asked, impatient to be free.

"Cutting apart my ankles. You do realize," he said with a sudden, low chuckle, "that I am free and you are still bound, my lovely Venator. And that I have the rare advantage over you?"

A little squirm started in her middle, making her feel ill. Or . . . perhaps it was something altogether different from nausea. "Sebastian," she said in warning, then remembered. "I have to ask you something about my aunt."

". . . and that you are at my mercy?" His voice had taken on a low purr, and suddenly he was next to her, moving with such freedom that she knew his legs were also unbound.

"Sebastian, when you took her *vis bulla*—"

His hands found her face easily—how, in the dark, she didn't know—but when his elegant yet sticky fingers curled under her chin and around the back of her neck, the only thing she could do was try to pull back as she lost her train of thought.

She had no leverage, nothing but her aching wrists and chilled fingers to hold her steady, propped behind her. When Sebastian moved closer, bringing that familiar scent of clove that always clung to him and setting her heart to pounding,

Victoria had nowhere to go except down to the floor . . . and that was one place she didn't want to go.

He missed her mouth that first time, his lips brushing just above his fingers, in the middle of her cheek. But he soon rectified the error and drew her forward, up on her knees and toward him, chest to bosom, as he covered her mouth with his.

Eleven

In Which Michalas's Wish Is Granted

As so often occurred when kissing Sebastian, Victoria found herself more helpless than not, with her hands still tied and her balance precarious. Yet she closed her eyes there in the dark and opened her mouth when he opened his, accepting his slick tongue and offering her own. The aches in her hand and leg eased, fading away in the wake of the deep kiss that reminded her how much she had missed this—intimate touching, passionate kissing, Sebastian himself.

She couldn't see him, just barely the dark shape of a shadow close to her, blocking her vision. But she pictured his handsome face and the sensual curling of his tawny, lion's-mane hair, surely tousled from battle with the vampires. His eyes were a darker shade of the same hue, a chestnut, and his skin—so unlike his grandfather's pale visage—was golden. He looked like a bronze angel, she'd often thought. An ironic description.

His lips were soft and smooth, fitting to hers and then drawing closed to lick and then nibble at the corner of her mouth, his teeth gnawing gently at her bottom lip, right where his grandfather had bitten her the night before. Victoria started when she realized this, when she felt his teeth on the tender part of her lip, and tried to turn away. But he was cradling her face in his hands and only kissed her more deeply than ever.

"I thought . . . you preferred . . . carriages," came a raspy, annoyed voice from across the room, "Vioget."

Victoria started and twisted her face violently from Sebastian, who seemed to have no inclination to release her. "Max? Oh, thank God, you're alive!"

"Your . . . concern . . . overwhelms me." There was a soft shuffling sound, a sharp intake of breath. "Perhaps . . . you could be . . . so kind as to . . . bring that knife . . . here. When"—his voice trailed off, then picked up more strongly—"you've finished . . . of course. I cannot . . . imagine . . . it should take . . . very long . . . at all."

"Carriages, parlors, dungeons," Sebastian said carelessly, "wherever the opportunity presents itself. Which it does rather more often than I would expect you'd imagine—or be familiar with."

But as he spoke Sebastian had released her, mainly, Victoria thought, because she'd mutinously kept her face away from his seeking fingers and mouth, twisting back when he tried to renew the kiss. Now he moved behind her, his hands on her hips as he found his position.

Too late, she realized she was at an even greater disadvantage with him kneeling behind her, knife in hands. "Don't move now, Victoria," he said, his voice curling in her ear like soft smoke, his breath warm on her skin. "This knife is very sharp, and I cannot see what I'm doing. I'd hate to slice into your beautiful flesh . . . the fresh blood would draw the hungry vampires here in a moment."

One of his hands moved aside the great mass of hair that had fallen down from her coiffure, when her stake had been removed, and now his lips pressed gently to the sensitive skin there on the top of her shoulder, at the juncture of her neck. Featherlight at first, then heavier, then with a sleek brush of tongue, he kissed her flesh while he sawed away, one-handed, at her ropes.

She couldn't help the smallest of gasps when he mauled and sucked at the tendon there, where he knew she was most sensitive. And Max couldn't help but hear her reaction, the faint sound of breaking suction, the quiet lapping of Sebastian's mouth.

He did it purposely—whether it was to titillate and arouse her or to annoy Max, she wasn't certain, but the only thing she could try to do was ignore the swipe of his lips, the warm slide over the top of her shoulder, up along her neck. But when one of his hands—the one not holding the knife, fortunately, slid around to cover one of her breasts, Victoria couldn't hold back a sudden intake of breath.

Sebastian laughed softly against her skin, leaving a hot, moist puff there at the side of her throat, and Victoria pulled so hard to the side that she lost her balance and tumbled to the floor. But as she fell her hands moved automatically to catch herself, pulling at the ropes. She was strong enough— and they were already frayed enough from the knife—that they tore free, and even though she landed half on her cheek on the cold, gritty floor, her hands were loose.

She rolled away from Sebastian before he could grab her again, though she felt his swipe through the air. "Your games are at an end, Sebastian. May I have the knife back?"

Half expecting him to taunt her with it, to demand a kiss

or some other payment, Victoria was surprised when she heard it drop to the floor in front of her.

"If we only had something for illumination," she said, feeling on the floor until her fingers brushed the stiletto. Gingerly she followed the blade until she found the handle and picked up the knife. It was no longer than the length of her longest finger to the end of her palm, and about the same width as her little finger. The entire dagger was nearly as flat as the piece of boning it had replaced, but was deathly sharp.

Miro had made the weapon specially for her, casting it to certain specifications. The silver handle was very short, extending only one knuckle's length from the small, flat hand guard. This was so that the blade could slide into the slit in her corset, and the handle would protrude just a small distance past the bottom end of her stays, keeping the metal from poking into her leg when she walked or bent. The other unique thing about the knife was that for perhaps another inch past the hand guard, the blade itself was covered with the same silver as the handle, so that Victoria could wrap her fingers around the hand guard and allow the blade to protrude between them without cutting herself. Since the handle was so short, it was the only way she could comfortably hold the dagger.

It certainly had worked, cutting easily through the ropes.

"I have something for light," Max's voice rumbled, a bit stronger now. "But I'll need . . . some help."

Victoria felt Sebastian moving, but he seemed to be farther away. "Sebastian? What are you doing?"

"I'm examining the door to determine whether there might be a way to open it, of course."

Victoria wanted to protest that she would need his help with Max, but she did not. Instead, she felt around on the floor and finally brushed against something solid and warm. And very, very wet. Stickily wet.

"My God, Max . . . " She started in shock, moving her hands frantically around, trying to determine what part of him had been injured, and accidentally poked him in the face.

"Christ, Victoria . . . are you trying to blind me?"

She slowed her jerky movements, brushing over his warm, moist cheek and down along his neck, staying far away from his sharp mouth. "You needn't be so profane. I cannot see a thing!"

"Obviously," he grumbled on a long breath. "I have a light. After you cut these blasted ropes." His breathing was heavy, and she could feel it now, feel the exertion in his body as he struggled to keep it steady.

She quickly sliced through the ropes that held his wrists behind him, and heard his moan of relief when his arms fell back into place. With trepidation she asked, "Where is the light?" The last thing she wanted was to be groping around Max's long, powerful body. Especially when he was injured.

"My left boot."

Relieved, Victoria gingerly skimmed her hands lightly along the side of him, taking care not to investigate anything mortifying, and noting with increasing anxiety that there were several places that were soaking wet. The stench of blood was strong, and she could nearly taste the iron in her mouth. "Are you bitten?" she asked, reaching the bottom of his calf and finding the smooth, supple leather of his boot. "Again?" she added, remembering Sara tearing away Max's collar.

"No, I'm shot," he replied, as if she should somehow have known. "And it hurts like the damned blazes, so if you could please . . . hurry."

Like a valet, she knelt at his feet and tugged at the boot.

"No," he snapped. "Under. In the heel."

"Heel?" she muttered, thinking that she was dealing with more heels than the ones on his boots.

"It slides off. Inside are small wooden sticks. Don't . . . drop them! And a piece of sanded paper."

"Ah, the work of the famous Miro, I'm certain," came Sebastian's patently bored voice from across the room.

"How do you know about Miro?" asked Victoria in surprise, prying at the heel of Max's boot as quickly as she could. It came off more easily than she'd expected, and then, feeling around, she could tell that it was nothing more than a little box with a lid.

"I know much about everything."

Max's breath caught audibly, as if he'd heard something humorous—or a new wave of pain had slammed into him—but he replied, "And do little with it, is that not . . . right, Vioget?"

"I have the little sticks and the paper. Now what shall I do?"

"Find something . . . to burn. One of those ridiculous flowers on your gown. Put them to use."

Victoria bit her lip instead of replying. The man was in great pain, Venator or no, so she could give him a bit of an excuse for his rudeness. Carefully she cut off one of the satin roses from above the hem of her gown and realized Max was right—it would make a good candle. How clever, and she was abashed that he had thought of it before she did.

Made from tightly twisted and sewn satin ribband, the flower was about the size of the center of her palm. It wouldn't burn forever, but she had many flowers, and surely each one would last for several minutes. "Now what shall I do?"

"Bring them . . . here. Give me one of the sticks. And the paper."

She moved back up toward Max's head and their hands found each other easily. His fingers were frighteningly cold, and they shook slightly as he took the slender wooden stick from her, and then the paper.

Victoria heard a faint *snick,* and suddenly a little burst of light illuminated Max's face. It looked like a hollow-eyed, grimy mask, his dark hair plastered to his forehead and temples, his full, angular lips tight and flat.

"Where's the bloody flower?"

Victoria pointed to the floor and watched as he shifted to the side and held the little flame to the red flower. She could see the fire dancing nearer his fingers, watching how he struggled to keep his hand steady as he tried to light it. With her own sigh of exasperation, she picked up the flower and held it to the flame.

One satin petal lit, and she put it on the floor next to them as the flower kindled to life. Lifting her gaze, she found herself face-to-face, very close to Max, and their eyes met over the tiny flame on the stick before he huffed it out.

There'd been pain there. She'd seen it in the unguardedness of his expression for a moment, the deep, bone-crunching pain swimming in his dark eyes.

"Where are you shot?" she asked in a kinder voice than she'd used recently.

"My shoulder. My right leg, though I think it isn't more than a graze."

A normal man would still be unconscious—between the chill of the dungeon and the loss of blood, not to mention the battering he'd taken under the hands of the vampires.

Before she could move he was shrugging painfully out of his heavy coat, which smelled like bloody, wet wool. Victoria helped pull it away from his left shoulder and saw the huge bloom of darkness glistening on his white shirt. It was, she realized suddenly, just above where the tiny *vis bulla* hung from his areola.

Her stomach squirmed, remembering how he'd forced her hand to touch it when she needed power and strength, and how warm and firm his skin had been under her reluctant fingers.

She reached to help him, but he batted her hand away.

"Tear the coat and I'll use it to bandage this. Then we have to find a way out of here, or it won't matter," he said.

"Your coat? Don't be ridiculous; the wool will be too prickly." She tore at her chemise and wadded up a large piece of the fine cotton, handing it to him when he made no move to allow her to bandage him herself.

"What have you found, Vioget?" asked Max.

"Little to assist us. The door is bolted solidly from the other side, and the hinges are outside as well. The door is made of wood, banded with iron, so unless you happen to be carrying some much larger accoutrements in your unmentionables, my dear Victoria, we shan't be leaving this chamber until they open the door. And we certainly don't want to wait for that."

"No," Max agreed.

"Sara Regalado and her father—and likely all of the Tutela—have allied themselves with Akvan, then," Victoria said. "And they tricked people into coming here to feed the vampires, I presume."

"Not all of the Tutela," Sebastian corrected. "A great number of them are still loyal to my grandfather." There was a bit of stiffness in his voice.

After Akvan's Obelisk had been destroyed—and with it Nedas, who'd been the most powerful of the vampires in Italy—there had been a great power struggle between Beauregard and Sara's father, *Conte* Regalado. As a newly turned vampire, the *conte* wasn't nearly as powerful as Beauregard

. . . but by allying himself with Akvan the demon, perhaps he thought he could overcome Beauregard.

Not a bad strategy.

And now she understood what Beauregard had meant when he spoke of Regalado's new alliance.

"And not only for the vampires," Max said. "Akvan will feed . . . from the mortals trapped here."

Victoria looked at him and read the expression on his face. "What does he do to them? Drink their blood?"

"Human heads," Sebastian said flatly. "But you're wrong, both of you." Grim satisfaction laced his voice. "It's not so much the mortals they wished to draw here. I cannot believe you don't see it for yourself."

"Of course I do. It was Victoria all along."

The understanding blossomed inside her. They'd been kidnapping mortals—and before them, dogs and cats—to feed Akvan for months. "Sara tried to capture me before . . . this treasure hunt was nothing more than a way to get me to come." She looked at Max. "They want the key, Aunt Eustacia's key."

"Or they simply want you. Which I can understand most readily," Sebastian added dryly. "It seems to be quite a common ailment as of late."

"Don't let that go out," Max said suddenly, gesturing toward the dying rose blossom.

Startled into action, Victoria quickly sliced off another flower and used the burning one to light it. When she looked back at him, he was drinking from a small vial.

"What is that?"

Swallowing, he looked at her in annoyance, then corked the tiny bottle and slipped it into a pocket. "Is that a window?"

Victoria looked up and saw, for the first time, right at the junction of ceiling and wall, the faintest rectangle of dark gray. Really, it was barely discernible from the other bricks on the wall, except that it was bigger, and just a bit lighter in color.

"Sebastian, let me stand on your shoulders," she said.

She could see the amusement on his face when he approached the small circle of light they shared. "What a serendipitous opportunity to refresh my memory about what's under your skirt," he murmured, drawing her toward the wall.

Victoria resisted the urge to acknowledge the comment. Instead she used her fingernails and the crevices between the bricks to steady herself as she climbed up onto Sebastian's bent knee, then onto his shoulders, and then even higher as he rose to a full standing position.

The top of her head brushed the stone ceiling, and she said, "It's a window. Too small for any of us to pass through."

"What can you see?"

Sebastian's fingers had moved from steadying her ankles to sliding up her calves over the silky stockings she wore, creating a delicate, delicious friction—and causing the stockings to sag. She gave him a little jab with her toe and replied to Max, "The window is level with the ground. I can see very little. A wall. The sky—it's nearing dawn, and the sky is turning gray."

"Can you see a small iron gate? Low in the wall?"

"It's very dark, Max; I can't see much of anything."

"Here."

The light below her in the small room moved closer, and Victoria reached down carefully to take the small rose from Max, who'd stood, but was now leaning against the wall. He was holding his right hand over his shoulder wound, though his face looked a bit less tense. Whatever was in that vial had begun to work quickly.

When she rested the little candle on the narrow sill of the window, Victoria could see into the yard in front of the opening. "Yes, I see a small thing—it looks like a grate. It's very small, though, Max . . . "

"As I thought. You can come down now."

She carefully handed down the candle, and found Sebastian to be exceedingly helpful in assisting her to get down from the window, his hands groping about and assisting in areas that weren't off balance in the least.

When Victoria got back on the ground and extricated herself from Sebastian's questing fingers, she saw Max on the floor by the wall.

"Max? Are you all right?"

"Stop blocking the light," he snapped.

"What are you doing?"

She crouched next to him, aware that Sebastian was standing behind, likely watching the areas he'd recently had occasion to caress.

"That iron grate is just outside of the Magic Door," Max told her. "I saw it earlier tonight." She could see that he was moving the candle around the floor near the wall. "It confirmed what Ylito and I had suspected—that this wall is next to Palombara's laboratory." He looked up for a moment, his eyes faint with wry humor. "I, unlike you, have an excellent sense of direction when inside a building."

"Whatever it is you're doing," Sebastian said from his pose against the wall, "I suggest you do it quickly, for I expect our hosts to be returning shortly. I'd prefer not to be here when they return, if we can arrange it otherwise. I'm certain my relationship to Beauregard will hold me in good stead only long enough for Akvan to ask me a few pointed questions about my grandfather before he makes use of my head and its contents."

"Then perhaps," Max said between obviously clenched

teeth, "you might bestir yourself to assist. I have reason to believe there must be a way from the laboratory to this chamber." He must have heard Victoria draw in her breath, for he added, "Don't waste time asking. If I'm wrong, I'm wrong—but there is no other way out of this room. But . . ." And he paused, then continued, "Apparently I'm not wrong, for here it is."

He pushed back onto his knees. Through the streaks of dirt and blood on his face, the hollowness in his cheeks, Victoria saw satisfaction. "A door?" she asked dubiously.

"A drop of gold. Melted gold. Going under the wall here . . . see this brick . . . here."

Victoria needed no further instruction or information. She began to work with Max, feeling around with her fingers to fit them into the groove under the brick.

But then, as a familiar, portending chill scuttled over the back of her neck, Victoria turned and met Max's gaze only inches away.

"Damn," was all he said.

"They'll be coming for me," Victoria said. "Most likely."

"Or to find out what the grandson of Beauregard might know that would be helpful to Akvan," Max said, a hint of relish in his voice. "Or for any of us."

"We'll make it look like we're still tied up," Victoria said. "Then we can take them by surprise when they come in. Max, you can still be unconscious."

"Why, thank you."

"Sebastian, if you can manage to do so without getting distracted, tie my wrists again. Quickly. Wait." She turned and slid her hand up under her skirt to the side of her corset opposite where the knife had been hidden and quickly slid out the slender but deadly stake that was hidden in the same way the stiletto had been.

Slipping it into one of the small loops at the back of her

gown (ones Verbena had insisted upon adding for just such an emergency), she allowed Sebastian to bind her wrists loosely enough that it would be no problem for her to slip free. Then, awkwardly, she did the same to him.

Max arranged himself on the floor where he'd been before, and Victoria slumped against the wall near his feet. Then she stomped her foot on the last of the burning satin flower.

Only the faintest smell of smoke hung in the air now, and the room became silent.

The back of her neck was colder, and her heart thumped faster as she felt the undead coming closer.

"Max? Do you have the knife?"

"Yes. And a stake hidden in my boot. Don't attack until we're out of the room."

"Seb—"

But a rattle at the door silenced her, and Victoria closed her mouth and waited.

When the door burst open, Victoria watched again through slitted eyes. There were only three of them. Three!

They were tall and had red eyes, and she could see their fangs gleaming, even through the tiny slit of her gaze.

Two of them stayed at the door. Max was right; they couldn't make a move to escape until they were safely out of the chamber, for fear they'd get locked back in. The third vampire, a tall woman, stepped farther in, and Victoria saw the glint of a pistol in her hand as she strode toward them.

She opened her eyes fully and looked up into the gaunt face of the female. Her eyelids were dark, her chin narrow and pointed. Long blond hair fell in ugly hanks over her shoulders, and it swayed as she slammed her boot into Max's side so hard he jolted closer to Victoria.

He didn't move, nor make a sound; even his breathing remained silent.

Now the vampire moved toward Victoria, looking down, pointing the gun directly at her. "Akvan is waiting for you," she hissed, sliding a tongue over her fangs.

Dressed in the convenience of men's clothing, she wore a jacket and a shirt that had possibly once been white, or some color close to it. When she bent toward Victoria, a leather thong around her neck fell from the opening of her shirt, knocked out by the weight of the short, black object that hung from it. Victoria caught her breath—the slender pendant was shiny, sharp, and glinted blue-black. She recognized it—a splinter, like the shard from Akvan's Obelisk that she herself had locked away in the Consilium.

With effort Victoria drew her eyes away from the glistening black fragment. The vampire was so close, breathing so heavily, she could smell the blood on her breath and knew she'd just fed.

Victoria drew in a deep breath and grieved for the mortals who'd obviously been her meal. The mortals who hadn't had a Zavier or a Sebastian to help get them out of the villa.

"Tell your friends not to move," said the female. "Or I'll shoot you. Now get up slowly."

As Victoria shifted to struggle to her feet, keeping the stake hidden, hands bound behind her—albeit loosely—she brushed against Max and felt his fingers fumble against hers. In that instant she slowed her movements, made them more awkward so that he could slip something slender and smooth into her hands.

The vial he'd been drinking from.

Victoria closed her fingers around the tiny bottle and pulled to her feet, and this time her awkwardness wasn't feigned. Her right leg was still aching, but she was able to walk on it. When she started toward the door, the female vampire followed close behind.

A quick glance behind told Victoria that the gun was still

trained on her. There was no chance for Max—or Sebastian, should he be willing to risk it—to jump to her assistance without getting her shot.

She wondered, as she stepped out of the chamber and heard the door close and its lock clang behind the three vampires, whether she would return.

And if she did, whether Max and Sebastian would even be there.

Flanked by the two silent vampires, Victoria walked down the hall, the presence of the female with the gun—and what could only be a piece of Akvan's Obelisk around her neck—slightly behind her.

They were taking her to Akvan, but she wouldn't go quietly. The female had foolishly allowed the pistol to sag away from Victoria's person as soon as the door closed. She seemed distracted and was walking faster, almost as if she were in a hurry to return.

Victoria had other ideas. She walked as slowly as possible, exaggerating her limp so as to give herself time to flip the cork from the small vial Max had given her. She'd started fiddling with it as soon as she'd risen to her feet, back in the chamber.

She wasn't sure what the liquid inside was, but at the very least it would give her an element of surprise. Max wouldn't have pressed it into her hands unless it would be useful, and he certainly didn't expect her to drink from it.

When the tiny cork popped free, Victoria carefully twisted her wrists, trying to keep from alerting the vampires to her acrobatics. But the female was muttering indistinctly—and with annoyance—to the vampire on the left, and the other appeared to be intent only on watching the placement of his feet as they strode down the gray-stoned passage. The female was obviously the leader, and her companions merely empty-headed guards of exceedingly large proportion.

Fortunately for Victoria, stakes were equally effective on all sizes and shapes of vampires, and unfortunately for them, she had a more than adequate one up her sleeve. Figuratively speaking.

Now she lifted one arm slightly, so that the ropes that had appeared to be tight around her wrists when they were crossed were now loose enough for her to free her hands.

They'd walked perhaps only a dozen paces and were still within sight of the chamber door they'd left when Victoria sprang into action.

She held the vial in one hand and the newly released stake that she'd slipped from its loop in the other. As the rope dropped away she flung the contents of the vial at the two vampires on her left. As they screamed she spun, stake in hand, to jam its slender point into the heart of the undead on her right. He poofed into dust before he realized what happened to him, and Victoria pivoted back just as quickly to face the other two.

Whatever was in the vial had splashed fully on the vampire closest to her, but some must have gotten on the female with the gun as well, for both of them shrieked in surprise and pain.

The one with the wet face clawed desperately at his skin and eyes, stumbling away, but Victoria caught him by his shirt and shoved him at the female just as she raised her pistol.

The crack of the shot snapped much too loudly in the hall. The vampire under her hands jerked as the bullet went through him, and then pain streaked along Victoria's side. As she staggered back in surprise, she saw the female fall under the weight of her agonized companion.

Pushing herself away from the wall there in the narrow passage, Victoria gripped her stake tighter and yanked the screaming vampire away from the female, tossing him aside for the time being.

The pistol had done its job but was no longer a threat, even when the female flung it at Victoria's head. She easily ducked and, despite the burning along her hip and the tangling weight of her skirts, she dove back toward the female.

Stringy hair plastered to both of their faces as they grappled on the floor. Victoria felt the wetness of her blood seeping through her gown, and the slam as the vampire landed a blow on her wound.

Smothering her cry of pain, Victoria grabbed the vampire by the shoulders and smashed her head back into the wall behind her, sending the female's red eyes rolling frantically. Her attention caught again by the leather thong and the obsidian chip that hung there, Victoria reached for it, yanking on the leather, and the necklace snapped free.

The vampire gasped, coming back to awareness, but Victoria gave her no time to recuperate. She slammed the stake down into the filthy white shirt, feeling immense satisfaction as the wood pierced flesh and bone as easily as if she'd shoved it into an egg: the slightest of hesitation whilst it broke through the outermost shell, then eased in slickly and easily. *Poof!*

The female's dust had barely begun to settle when Victoria turned toward the third vampire. She was just about to stake him when she noticed the clanking of keys at his waist. Reaching down she felt the throbbing pain at her hip more strongly and plucked the keys away before putting the stake through his heart.

It was an odd thing about staking a vampire: Not only did the creature's flesh and person disintegrate, but also all of his personal belongings—clothing or anything else on his body. The only exception appeared to be items made of copper—which was how the Venators had been able to acquire one of the five special rings Lilith had made for her closest Guardians.

Wayren had described it as a sort of imploding that happened to the undead; but even she didn't have a real explanation for it. Instead she suggested, in a rare moment of levity, that perhaps it was merely Providence's way of making the Venators' duty that much easier: no remains, bodies, or personal effects to dispose of or explain away.

Whatever the reason, Victoria was glad she'd seen the keys and snatched them up before staking the vampire. As she stood, breathing heavily and now feeling pain on both sides of her body—in her leg and her opposite hip—she saw the female's necklace where she'd dropped it moments earlier. Picking it up, she felt a sharp tingle as she stuffed it into one of the pockets Verbena had sewn inside the skirt of her gown.

Again she could feel pure malevolence permeate the splinter from the obelisk, and was relieved that she'd found it after losing it in the battle. It would be much safer with her, and in the Consilium with the other, larger shard.

Now . . . she had a ring of keys that she presumed would open the chamber door if she could get back there before anyone came to see what was delaying the delivery of the Venator to the demon. Victoria paused a moment to listen but heard nothing. Apparently no alarm had been given, and no one had heard the brief, volatile battle here in the passageway.

The demon and his court must be farther away than she'd imagined.

The third key worked to open the heavy lock on the chamber door, and Victoria called out softly as she entered. Light from the passageway behind her spilled into the room.

"Back at last," Max said from his position against the

wall, but his eyes were sharp. "It's unfortunate you couldn't manage it without getting yourself shot."

"Shot? Victoria." Sebastian was already moving toward her, his loose ropes in a bundle on the floor behind him. He didn't pull her into an embrace, for which she was simultaneously grateful and annoyed, but he did brush his hand over the huge splotch of blood flowering like an oversize rose over her waist. She was going to have a devil of a time explaining that to her mother. That and the missing rosettes.

"You can play nursemaid later, Vioget. Perhaps there will even be a carriage handy."

"I got the door open, so you can lead the way," Victoria told Max, ignoring his comments, watching as he moved carefully toward the entrance. Obviously his pain was back. "Since you have the direction of a pigeon. And I don't."

Just before Max led the way into the passage, she saw him tip a small vial to his lips again and sip from it. "I thought you gave me—"

"Quiet." And Max stepped cautiously out of the room. She noticed he held the stiletto in one hand and a stake in the other.

Curious. Perhaps he'd had two tiny bottles—one of holy water, which he'd given her, and this other one. She would find out later . . . and also find out about the bites on his neck.

She had a suspicion she knew from whom they'd come, and the thought made her stomach shudder.

To her relief, Max did not take the hallway where the vampires had led her, but turned in the opposite direction and set a surprisingly rapid pace down the hall. For all his injuries, he still moved with the grace of the hunter he was.

With an impatient gesture he motioned for Sebastian to close the door behind them, but didn't wait while he locked it again.

Apparently Max did have the directional sense of a bird, for he led them unerringly down the passage and through a door that opened to a flight of ascending stairs. Just as she stepped onto the first one Victoria heard shouts of alarm behind them, and felt the sudden wave of increased chill over the back of her neck. The door closed after them, and she followed Max up the stairs, hearing Sebastian pounding along in her wake.

At the top Max turned left and hurried off down another passage. Victoria realized he was stumbling a bit at about the same time she felt her breath drawing in more sharply, and the increased dampness at her hip. The edges of her vision were shaky, and her knee nearly buckled once as they turned a quick corner, but if Max could move like that with two more serious bullet wounds, she, with dual *vis bullae*, would keep up with him.

At last they came around another corner and up a second flight of steps and into the hallway that looked familiar to her . . . the room just beyond the ballroom, where all the people had been gathered.

She stopped, and Sebastian nearly plowed into her. "We can't go without the others." She dug into her pocket, her fingers tangling in the leather thong necklace and receiving a shock from its smooth pendant before finding the wooden stake.

"Victoria, no," he began, but Max had heard them and he spun around.

His normally swarthy face was tinged with gray. "They're all dead. The vampires fed on them—didn't you smell it? There's no one here to save but us. For now."

"Much as it pains me to say it, he's right," Sebastian said. "Most of the guests made it safely from the villa, but the ones who didn't . . . they were dead long before we were even untied."

Victoria wanted to argue. She wanted to snap at them and tell them they were wrong. The sudden wave of black fury was so surprising that her breath caught and she coughed on the malignant words she'd wanted to speak.

Max looked at her strangely; then he grabbed her arm and began to pull her after him. Not the least bit gently.

She remembered little of the next few moments, and then suddenly they were out of the villa, out into the crisp dawn air where the faint yellow in the sky brought texture and shape to the unkempt gardens.

Max whirled her around to face him, his hands on her shoulders as his eyes blazed down into hers as if trying to find something that was missing. As if he wanted to shake her. Victoria dragged in a breath of clean air, and the dull fog slid away taking with it that frightening anger. She blinked.

He released her abruptly, muttering something she couldn't hear, and turned to Sebastian, who'd stood there watching. "Go back to Beauregard," he told him shortly. And then something else, low and staccato.

"No," Sebastian said quietly, and with unusual brevity. Then he turned away. He looked at Victoria, and she realized they'd all begun walking and were approaching the wall of the villa's grounds. Beyond it was the street, and perhaps even Oliver, waiting with the carriage.

Or—Victoria's thoughts flew away as she was caught up in Sebastian's strong hands and pushed against the stone wall. He'd surprised her, and before she could shove him away, he was holding her shoulders there, pinned under his fingers as he leaned close. She drew in her breath, half wanting him to kiss her and half wanting to send him spinning away for his effrontery.

But before she could make her decision, he spoke. "I don't know when I'll see you again, but stay away from my grandfather."

"He deserves to be staked," she replied smartly, just before he bent to kiss her, catching her off guard again. When, moments later, he released her, Victoria opened her eyes to see both Zavier and Max standing there.

Sebastian was gone.

Max looked bored.

And Zavier looked as though she'd just turned into a demon herself.

Twelve

Lord Jellington Acquires a Rival

Victoria clawed her way out of the dream and came back to reality, panting as though she'd been running.

Her skin was slick and her fingers fisted so tightly she could barely pry them open. The images stayed with her, even as she tried to focus her gaze on the familiarity of her bedchamber. But all she could see were the vestiges of glowing red eyes, glittering black shards, an ebony face with twisted green horns and an evil smile. Max, Sebastian, Aunt Eustacia . . . even Phillip . . . all with drawn, elastic faces in horrific expressions, and claws, and streaming blood.

She made herself sit up, shake off the terror of the nightmare, and tried to slow the rampant pounding of her heart. She reached for the bellpull to call for Verbena.

The bedclothes were rumpled and twisted, half sagging from the bed, and sunlight—so clean and pure in comparison to the horrific malice in her dream—blasted through the filmy drapes. By the color and angle of the sunbeams, Victoria knew it was well past noon.

She started to climb from the waist-high bed, but a

twinge in her side reminded her that Verbena had put her to bed very early this morning after much clucking and salving and bandaging.

After passing through the vampire, the bullet had shaved the edge of her right hip, leaving a deep red track in her skin. Her left leg had had claw marks and bruises on it that would already have started to fade this morning.

Sitting on the edge of the bed, her toes barely brushing the floor, Victoria looked at herself in her dressing table mirror. She had dark circles under her eyes and one slight bruise on her right cheek. She didn't look that bad.

But then there was Max.

Last night, after directing her toward the carriage where Zavier and Oliver waited, he'd attempted to send her off without him. "I'm not leaving you here," she told him flatly, walking back in his direction. "You've lost too much blood and you need to have those wounds seen to."

His mouth moved in annoyance or amusement as they faced each other, both bristling with obstinacy. "Don't be a fool, Victoria. This isn't the first time I've lost a great deal of blood, and I doubt it will be the last."

"I am *Illa* Gardella and I—"

"Don't attempt to order me about, Victoria, for the only result will be your own mortification. Now be off and have your own injury seen to." He turned and faded into the shadows, and she heard the unmistakable sound of a bridle clinking, then the soft snort of a horse.

Left with no other choice, Victoria climbed into the carriage, where Zavier waited. He said little during the ride back to Aunt Eustacia's villa (Victoria didn't believe she could ever come to think of it as hers, despite the fact that it was). Zavier merely watched her, as if trying to assimilate who she really was.

It had been unfortunate that he'd seen her kissing Sebastian (or, rather, Sebastian kissing her, for she'd been more a recipient than a participant in that particular instance), but there was no help for it. Sebastian had no doubt planned it thus, at any rate, although whether his intent was to annoy Max by wasting time with such frivolity or to stake his claim, so to speak, for Zavier's sake, Victoria couldn't say.

But the thing that bothered her most about the situation was that Max had been right. Zavier was not only hurt and offended, but Victoria knew that he wasn't the right man for her to become intimate with in any fashion. He'd developed into a good friend and was a brave and skilled Venator, but his kiss had meant nothing to her. Having been kissed by two men last night, she knew there was only one of them she'd want to kiss again.

Now, however, as she slipped from her bed, feet touching the flat, hooked rug that wasn't quite as welcoming as the thick Aubusson one back at home, she realized with great disgust that she'd been diverted from getting information from Sebastian about Aunt Eustacia's bracelet.

Not that kissing Sebastian was a hardship—it wasn't in the least, for the man had very skillful lips and hands and . . . well, other means of distracting her. But there was a time and a place for that sort of activity, and Sebastian was a master at disregarding propriety.

There was a brief warning knock on the door to her chamber just before it opened and Verbena bustled in. "Yer mother and t'other ladies're belowstairs," she said. Behind her came a short parade of servants carrying a tub and buckets of water to fill it. "They're wantin' t'see you, my lady, and find out what happened last night to ye."

"Blast," Victoria said under her breath. She needed to get to the Consilium.

"And I'm wanting to know," Verbena said as she closed the door behind the last of the servants, "how th' corset

worked. Just so's I can tell that Oliver so he'll quit badger-
ing me about it. Just because he had the first thought of it
don't mean he's got t'know everything. And yer gown, my
lady . . . what happened to them roses?"

Victoria sank into the hot water and sighed a long breath
as she listened to the maid's comfortable prattle. Her
wounds burned, but it was more than bearable in conjunc-
tion with the pleasure of the bath. At some point, she'd need
to tell Verbena that her whole coiffure had fallen apart when
the vampires disarmed her and removed her stake—an inconvenience that would have to be rectified in the future.
The long sagging of her hair had been a distraction.

At last, when the water was turning tepid, she stepped out
into a large towel brandished by Verbena. As she turned to
take a seat at the dressing table, her maid reached toward the
clutter on it.

"What is this, my lady?" Verbena asked, her fingers pausing over the leather thong and the obsidian flake.

"Don't touch that," Victoria said, snatching at the shiny
black pendant, closing her fingers around it to keep it hidden
from prying eyes. It was heavy and warm in her hands for
something so small, and she felt a sizzle of awareness
prickle her fingers just as it had at the villa. "Just finish my
hair so I can get on with my business."

Verbena's eyes opened into full circles, but she wisely
said nothing. Victoria was suddenly weary of the chattering
maid, who always seemed to have to know what was going
on. Could she not simply leave her to do her duty without
trying to also be her confidante?

Images from her dream—of grasping, clawlike hands,
and the gleam of the black splinters of obsidian—suddenly
came back to her, nearly blinding her with their force.

But now, in the daylight, fully awake and away from her
bed, Victoria wasn't as overwhelmed by the dream and the

evil it portended. Shaking the images away, she recognized what it was telling her, what she must be aware of. The vampire had been wearing a piece of Akvan's Obelisk, and Akvan was back. He'd been called back to earth by the destruction of his obelisk.

If that little chip was important enough for the vampire to wear, how important must the larger shard be, the one Victoria stored at the Consilium?

One thing was certain: Victoria was going to take the small piece to the Consilium, where it would be safe from prying eyes and hands. As soon as she could make her excuses and extricate herself from her mother and the other ladies, she would remove the pendant from her home.

In the meantime, the safest place for it was in the pocket of her gown.

As she came down the stairs, Victoria heard the excited chatter of feminine voices in the parlor. She vacillated for a moment, considering whether she should ask for something to eat before joining the elder ladies, but her decision was made for her when she heard a high-pitched squeal from— it could only be—Lady Winnie, and the door opened as the other ladies chuckled in response.

"Victoria," crowed the duchess. "Come and join us."

"We feared you would lie abed all the day," her mother added. "Come, sit, and let us tell you of our adventures last night."

Victoria was swept into the elegant chamber and seated on the only uncushioned surface in the room: a straight-backed chair situated betwixt her mother and the duchess. Just where she'd prefer not to be.

Before the ladies had an opportunity to begin their interrogation, there came a rap on the parlor door, and then Giorgio stepped in.

"For the *signoras*," he said, looking at Lady Melly and her two companions as he gave a little bow. And then he stepped back, and into the room came three more servants, each carrying a bouquet of flowers larger than the one before.

Victoria watched in amusement as the three ladies dug through prickly stems, fernlike leaves, and various colored petals to find each bouquet's enclosed letter.

"For me?" Lady Winnie clasped the smallest collection of flowers to her ample bosom, burying her face in the beautiful lilies that carried their precious scent throughout the room. They were white with pink blushes down their centers, and when she pulled her face from their ivory petals her bulbous nose was streaked with yellow pollen. She didn't seem to know or care, even when she began to sneeze violently enough that the poor lilies released more pollen into the air. "It's from that lovely gentleman we met last evening," she gasped, trying to catch her breath as she finished her explosive sneezing.

"So he did not come to call, but he sent flowers in his stead." Melly, who was the recipient of the largest and most glorious of the flower arrangements, sniffed. It was made of roses of every shade of pink imaginable, and with a single white rose in the center.

"But he sent you the largest of vases," Lady Nilly said, nearly hidden behind a profusion of pink gillyflowers and red tulips. "You most certainly must be the one who caught his eye."

"But he did not come to call," replied Melly, her long, slender nose still lifted in disdain. "I shall ensure that we are not home tomorrow in the event he should attempt to show his face," she added, thrusting the massive vase at Victoria. "In fact, my dear, I believe you should accompany us to make calls."

"Make calls? On whom?" Victoria asked, startled into paying attention by the large bouquet Melly had given her, and her mother's imperious comment. "We know no one here."

"You've been in Rome nearly six months, and you know no one here? That is abhorrent, Victoria. But it's also not true. You know the Tarruscelli girls, of course."

"Yes, indeed. That is all—"

"So you will go on calls with us tomorrow. And we none of us will be here if Alberto deigns to show his face."

"His handsome face," Winnie corrected her. "His very handsome face. Although he is a bit shorter than Lord Jellington. And bald. And he cannot spell 'enchanted.'"

"Alberto?" squeaked Nilly. "He signed his name Alberto on your card?"

"He must be in love, Melly!" the duchess said, arching her brows. They were thick and wiry, and when she lifted them they looked as though they were trying to meld into one long, dark swath across her forehead. "He didn't sign *my* card as Alberto."

"What a lovely name." Nilly sighed, clasping her skinny, blue-veined hands to her nonexistent bosom. "So Italian. So masculine! And the way one must roll one's Rs when saying it . . . Alberrrrrto. Al*berrrrrr*to."

"Nonsense." Melly broke in, Victoria noticed, only when the other two ladies seemed to have run out of raptures. "He was merely being kind. If he truly had developed a *tendre* for me, he would have come calling. At least Jellington knew enough to do that, although he certainly didn't send flowers the first day after we'd met."

Victoria had listened to enough of their prattle; her mother was always in raptures over some beau or another, it seemed. The obsidian chip felt heavy in her pocket, and curiosity about Max's health weighed on her mind. And she wished to speak with Wayren about all that had transpired last night as well. "I must excuse myself," she said, standing. "I have an appointment with my . . . my Latin tutor," she added, thinking that Wayren wouldn't mind being called thus.

"Latin tutor?" her mother replied in astonishment. "But Victoria, why on earth would you wish to read Latin?"

"So that I can better study the histories of Rome as they are written," she replied primly, and, having made a quick curtsy, glided toward the door as rapidly as possible. "You ladies have a lovely day today. I do not know if I shall see you this evening for supper, Mama, for my tutor has invited me to dine with her."

Victoria arrived at the Consilium late in the day, and the main chamber where the holy-water fountain glistened was empty and silent but for the sound of rushing water.

This was not unusual, for rarely were Venators at the Consilium unless there was a meeting or gathering of some kind. Most often there was no need for people to be there, and the fewer times Venators traveled to the Consilium, the less likely it would be discovered. Venators preferred to spend their time hunting vampires on the streets.

Even Wayren and Ilias were not always about, although they each had private apartments back in the depths of these catacombs. As well, Miro, Ylito, and the physician Hannever all had their own workshops nearby, in other parts of the underground property. But they rarely made an appearance in the main chamber or galleries.

Victoria was relieved that she was able to go immediately to the secret storage room near Wayren's library. After all that had happened last night at the villa, combined with her haunting dream, she just wanted to make certain that the shard was still there, and safe. And she wanted to get the other, smaller piece hidden away before anyone else knew about it.

The fewer who did, the better. The safer.

Once inside the chamber Victoria closed the door, remembering last time when Max had sneaked up on her. After lighting a lamp on the table, she pulled the leather thong out of her pocket, the pendant dangling, jet black streaked with dark blue.

The shard she'd found still lay on the long, scarred wooden table where she'd left it. It didn't appear to have even been moved, and for some reason that knowledge eased the deep-seated worry that had niggled at her since she'd awakened from her dream. The shard was safe, and now its smaller counterpart would be as well.

When she dropped the leather necklace onto the table, the two pieces of obsidian clinked dully, and a single blue spark between them startled her. A faint aroma like old smoke, blended with something putrid, reached her nose, but faded almost immediately, just as the spark died out.

Victoria picked up the leather cord and moved the pendant so that it wasn't touching the shard any longer. Then, gingerly, she reached out to feel the bigger piece of obsidian. A sharp tingle zipped up her arm, blushing over her shoulder.

The feeling was similar to the sensation she experienced when she'd touched the smaller piece, but this was stronger, strong enough that she yanked her hand away. And she stared at the large splinter, sitting there like a chunk of black glass.

The shard looked like a weapon she would carry; it was ironic that the obsidian piece that exuded such malevolence was the same shape and size of an ash stake she'd use to destroy evil.

Of course, the source of this evil, Akvan, was not a vampire. Despite the fact that all demons—whether they be fallen angels from ages and ages ago, or half-human demons called vampires—came from Lucifer, they lived and died in different ways. Still, it was interesting that this particular piece could easily be carried as a Venator's weapon.

What would happen if she did pick it up and use it as a stake? What would be the result of slamming this obsidian pike into a vampire's chest? Or Akvan's, for that matter?

Victoria smoothed her hand over the glasslike weapon, noticing that the tingle had lessened. There were no further sparks, but the shard was warm. Just slightly.

But perhaps that was from the friction and heat of her fingers.

She wondered, suddenly whether this was what Akvan had wanted from her. This shard. This piece of his power.

A piece of the power that had called him back to earth.

It was possible, likely, even. If he wanted the shard back, what better way than to send his minions after her?

First he'd sent Sara Regalado and her cohorts to lure her to the graveyard that night. They hadn't tried to hurt Victoria, only to capture her. Perhaps they'd planned to bring her back to the villa, to Akvan, where he could demand that she produce the shard.

But how did he know she had it?

No one but Wayren, Ilias, and Ylito knew she'd found it. Even Max was unaware.

No one else except—

Victoria felt cold; then a blast of angry heat shuddered over her.

Sebastian knew.

Sebastian had seen her holding the shard when they escaped from the burning opera theater on the night of Aunt Eustacia's death.

She stood abruptly, automatically feeling for the stake under her gown.

The sun would have gone down by now, and she would take herself out onto the street to hunt down someone who could bring a message to Beauregard or Sebastian. Or she would go herself.

She'd squandered her first chance to talk to Sebastian and find out what he knew about Aunt Eustacia's armband. Now she had two reasons to find him.

And to find out if the entire scene at Villa Palombara had been a farce put on by Sebastian and his grandfather to acquire the shard.

Perhaps Akvan wasn't back at all.

No. No, he was. Or something just as evil was.

Victoria had smelled him.

She looked down at the table where the shard sat, long and black and wicked. The little pendant glinted next to it on the rough wooden table.

Now that Victoria was certain someone—Akvan, Sebastian, Beauregard, or all of them—was after the piece of the obelisk, she didn't want to leave it sitting so visibly on the table.

The heavy splinter was still a bit warm when she picked it and the leather necklace up. The obsidian stake felt good in her hand. Comfortable.

Her fingers closed around it, and Victoria positioned it as if a vampire were in front of her, making an experimental stab into the air. The swish and swirl of movement was audible in the silent chamber, and she imagined stabbing the shard into the chest of a vampire. Lilith. Beauregard. Any of the creatures with red eyes and flashing fangs.

The shard would send them back to Lucifer.

Victoria's lips tightened, curling in against her teeth, and she felt a surge of hatred for those red-eyed creatures who'd taken so much from her. Sebastian had tried to make her believe that some vampires weren't wholly evil, that they didn't deserve to be damned to Hell. But he was wrong.

And if he tried to stop her, she'd send him there along with them.

The large splinter was growing warmer, and Victoria looked down at it. Her fingers were leaving moist prints on the sleek black glass. It must be kept safe. Secret.

She had to put it away in a drawer or chest. No one would find it there.

In the darkest corner of the room she found a small wooden chest filled with nothing but fragrant wood curls, as though someone had sat and stripped them from a branch of cedar. Or had been carving a stake.

The splinter and the necklace fit easily in the box, and it was with a sigh of satisfaction that Victoria closed the lid, placing another chest on top of that one.

The pieces of Akvan's Obelisk would be safe.

Now to deal with Sebastian.

She rose to her feet and, with one last look back at the dark corner where the chest held an evil treasure, Victoria moved quickly from the chamber.

Back out in the passage, she paused outside of Wayren's library, but there were no sounds from within. No one else was about; it was just as silent as it had been when she arrived. A gentle knock drew no response, and when Victoria gently prodded the door open, she found the room dark.

The Consilium was silent and bare as she walked back toward the main chamber, where the rush of the fountain made a pleasant hum.

At least Victoria had one of her questions answered: Max had to be all right, for if he'd been otherwise he would be in the Consilium with Hannever, being treated for his injuries.

A seriously wounded Venator would be kept safe in the Consilium until he was well.

Having had her question answered by omission, Victoria left the Consilium through the secret spiral staircase that led into a hidden passage behind one of the confessionals at Santo Quirinus.

Instead of leaving through the doors of the small chapel, she went into its tiny rear courtyard and into a ramshackle old building across from the church. She exited onto the nearly empty street, where she found it was indeed well past sunset on the chilly February night.

The sky was as black as the shard she'd left below, and a full moon glowed high and small among the stars. She walked toward the unpleasantly sharp smell of wet umbrella silk. Her wooden stake felt light and weak in her hand after the heaviness of the shard, but it would do its duty if she required it.

There were no vampires about, however. Of course, that was no surprise, as this particular block of the *Borghi* was deserted of human prey.

Victoria had walked nearly all the way to the Passetto when she stopped. Had she closed the door to the storage chamber, where the shard was secreted?

She didn't remember.

Just because the door was open didn't mean that anyone would find the piece of obelisk . . . but it made her nervous to leave such important things unattended and open.

It just wasn't safe.

She hesitated only a moment before turning to make the trip back to the little run-down building, moving at a more rapid pace than when she'd been walking away from it. If any of the few shopkeepers or pilgrims Victoria passed noticed a slender figure wrapped in a dark cloak walking back the way it had just come, they gave her no second look.

Urgency built in her chest. The shard might not be safe, and she couldn't allow it to fall into anyone else's hands if Akvan and Beauregard and Regalado were after it.

Perhaps she'd move it to a different place in the chamber. A locked chest? Or . . .

By this time Victoria was moving through the hidden passage behind the confessional in Santo Quirinus. She carefully stepped over the middle stair and moved silently along the short hall hung with icons, then pressed the intricate stonework that would reveal the spiral staircase.

The floor glided open without a sound, and Victoria hurried down the curling steps, driven to get to the storage chamber to check on the shard. Make certain it was safely in its dark corner.

Tomorrow she would tell Wayren about this, but—

Someone was standing at the fountain.

Dipping his fingers into the sparkling holy water, there in the dim light, looking down into the pool. Only one sconce lit the area, as it had when she'd left perhaps twenty minutes earlier, but she recognized him. Even from the back.

Impossible.

Yet . . . perhaps not.

He must have sensed her presence, for he turned, an uncharacteristic look of shock on his handsome face.

Victoria refused to allow him to see that he'd caught her off guard as well. Instead she stepped closer, noticing the way he clamped a wet hand over his bunched-up white shirt.

"And here I was planning to tear the city apart looking for you, when all I had to do was wait for you to show up. What are you doing here, Sebastian?"

Thirteen

In Which Our Heroine Divests a Gentleman of an Article of Clothing

A chagrined expression flashed over Sebastian's face for an instant, then was masked. He stepped away from the fountain, his wet hand making a print on his light shirt. She noticed a dark coat hanging over a nearby chair.

"You returned much sooner than I anticipated," he said, recovering quickly to summon a teasing smile. "I should perhaps have waited a bit longer before coming down here . . . but I can't say that I'm terribly disappointed to have you alone at last. After all, last night in the dungeon with Maximilian was hardly—"

"Give me an answer, Sebastian." Victoria's heart was pounding, panic replacing bald shock as she realized what this must mean. Her mouth had dried; she felt it shrivel like a pea in the sun. Her fingers were shaking, and nausea curled in her belly. How could it be? "Tell me you didn't bring your grandfather," she said in a voice that didn't belong to her, even as she tried to assimilate what Sebastian's presence meant. He couldn't have done.

The Consilium, the safe, secret sanctuary, had been found.

No. Not under her watch. Not after almost two millennia of secrecy.

No.

Victoria felt fear and anger—emotions she'd struggled to keep out of her mind—envelop her, clouding clear thought as she started to dash past Sebastian, desperate to get to the secret storage chamber—and to Wayren's library—before they could be despoiled.

His teasing smile faded. "I'm here alone." His voice, urgent and low, stopped her. "I wouldn't—"

The panic eased enough for her voice to be steady when she snapped, "You wouldn't what? Infiltrate our sanctuary? How did you find out about this place? How?"

But no, of course Beauregard wasn't here, she realized belatedly, her mind beginning to function again. She would have sensed him the moment she came into Santo Quirinus. That, at least, was good.

Sebastian was staring at her, his eyes shadowed by the dim light glowing behind tawny curls that made him look so absurdly holy. He seemed to be studying her, waiting for her to speak.

His chest rose and fell easily, but the tension that skittered between them made Victoria restless and unwilling to play the game of silence. "Answer me, Sebastian. At least tell me how you learned of this place, and how it is on my guard that you've found us."

He stepped toward her. "Never fear, *ma chère*. Your secret shall remain safe with me. I've known of these chambers for a rather long time, and I've told no one yet."

A lopsided smile tilted his lips as he reached for her shoulder, skimming his knuckles over her collarbone and then drifting his fingers loosely around the nape of her neck. "Don't you yet know that I'd do nothing to endanger you? Now, since we are here together and unlikely to be interrupted, there are other activities we might find to divert ourselves. Ones that I, at least, have missed greatly." His smile, slow and sensual, mirrored the look in his eyes, a look she'd seen more than once before. Despite her anger and confusion, the desire in his gaze had its effect on her, sending flutters through her belly. "After all . . . you sought me out, Victoria."

"It was a necessity, Sebastian."

"Then perhaps you might wish to tell me what was so necessary that you had to kiss my grandfather in order to send the message?" These last words came out sharply.

Victoria shoved his hand away before it closed over her shoulder. "Don't try to play the jealous lover, Sebastian. It rings a false note. And the reason I needed to speak to you is in regard to something of my aunt's. You must have seen her . . . seen her . . ." *Blast*. Her voice was rough, and her eyes began to tingle with tears. "You sent me her *vis bulla*. But there was a bracelet she wore, an armband. It's very important. Did you see it . . . when . . ."

"Silver? Wide at the top of her arm?" he asked. "Yes, I took it also. It was the only jewelry she wore, and the only other thing I could do for her."

"Where is it? What did you do with it?"

"I didn't realize it was important to you. It's . . . I put it here to be safe from . . . behind Catherine Gardella's portrait. Apparently she liked jewelry."

A wave of relief, followed by annoyance, rushed over Victoria. "But why didn't you send it to me when you sent the *vis bulla*?"

His eyes flickered away, then came back to hers with a hint of chagrin in their expression. "I . . . ah . . . didn't think it would have quite the same . . . flair," he said with a dis-comfited expression, "to send both. The *vis* . . . well, it was more intimate." He quirked a smile.

Then, shrugging off whatever bit of discomposure he'd had, Sebastian reached for her again, and this time he caught her upper arms with both hands. "Besides . . . what if I needed a reason to contact you again?" he murmured as he pulled her close enough that her skirt swished against his trousers. "I'm not one to leave all my cards on the table."

His grip was strong, surprisingly strong. Victoria was tempted to twist away and send him sprawling to the stone floor, perhaps clipping his head on a table on the way down—but at the same time, looking up into his face, she found herself focused on his mouth. It was close, and she well remembered how it felt sliding and fitting sensually to hers. Warm and mobile, slick and coaxing.

Perhaps it would be prudent to put him off guard. Prudent and enjoyable . . . and then she could change the subject back to a more pertinent one.

But apparently, for once Sebastian had other ideas; for he sobered, the flirtatiousness fading from his face, as if he'd just recalled something important. "Victoria, you must take care. He's made it clear that he wants you for himself," he said, maintaining the distance between them . . . yet looking at any moment like he might change his mind.

At first Victoria didn't know who he meant. She looked away from his lips and their eyes met.

"Beauregard," Sebastian said, his voice tight and without its normal light edge. "I'm speaking of Beauregard. Al-though from what I understand, you've wasted no time in finding other, less dangerous men to amuse you, such as that redheaded Scot."

Now she shoved hard at his solid chest, and he released her, stumbling back a step but easily remaining on his feet.

"You *are* playing the jealous lover. How can that be, Sebastian, when you've been no lover at all these past months? When, in fact, our attachment was of the briefest kind?"

His expression changed, the annoyance easing into a knowing smile. "So you *have* missed me." Triumph colored his amber eyes, and he reached for her a third time.

This time she let him bring her so that their bodies were flush: breast to chest, thigh to thigh, feet mingling. Her skin warmed, the flush traveling from her face down to her neck and beyond. It was good to touch him again, to feel the warmth of a man's body and the strength of his arms about her.

"Hardly." They both knew she was lying.

She shouldn't have missed him—she couldn't trust him, for his loyalty was to Beauregard—but she *had* missed him, and she *did* trust him . . . after a fashion. It wasn't as if he could replace Phillip and the love and regard they'd had for so brief a time, but she was human.

And she was a woman. A woman who'd grown up cuddled and petted by Melly and her two friends, a woman who liked to be touched, who enjoyed being reminded that she was desirable, and who had made choices that kept her outside normal societal conventions so that she was a lonely outcast.

He made her feel. He'd brought pleasure to a life that had once been so simple, so normal and easy and bland, and had become stark and dark and violent. With his irrepressible charm and unabashed flirtation, Sebastian had made her heart beat faster and her body reawaken from the grief-imposed stupor resulting from Phillip's death. Even now, as they faced each other, her belly flipped deep inside, knowing there was more to come. And she was ready for it. Her heart rammed in her chest as she remembered the way his hands would glide over her bare skin . . . .

"Believe me, I didn't want to stay away, Victoria," he said, his mouth hovering in front of hers, his lips twitching in a racy grin, and the clove scent on his breath a light brush over her skin. "I wished only to keep you safe."

"Safe?" She reared her head away from him so she could look directly in his eyes, knowing that her own were narrowed in annoyance. "What did you mean to keep me safe from? The vampires I hunt every night? That is a poor excuse and another false note. Can you not even once be truthful?"

"From Beauregard." His voice had chilled, and eyes that had been soft and coaxing a moment earlier had flattened. "You have no idea—"

"I can protect myself."

"I am fully aware of your Venatorial qualities, for you see fit to remind me of them—as well as my own shortcomings—at every opportunity."

"I am who I am," she told him. "I told you this last autumn—I made the choice, and if it's too much for you to bear, knowing that I'm stronger and faster than you, that I have no need for you to protect me, that I'm *not like other women* who will sit at home waiting to be taken care of by the men in this world, then begone with you, Sebastian. I need you no more than you need me."

She realized suddenly that she was crying. *My God, crying*! Victoria, *Illa* Gardella, who'd not even squeaked in shock when her beloved aunt was killed in front of her, had tears rolling down her cheeks.

Now she was angry—at herself, at Sebastian, at the choices she'd made and the losses she'd endured—and she tore herself from his hold, turning away to focus her attention on something else . . . anything else. Anything.

The sparkling water of the fountain caught and then

mesmerized her, soothing in its rhythm, beautiful in its clarity, comforting in its holiness.

And then . . . the realization came . . . a suspicion that must have been buried deeply suddenly came billowing out. She whirled toward him just in time to see Sebastian reaching to gather her back into his arms.

She went willingly, meeting his mouth with all of the angst and anger that had built inside her since she'd had those five dreams that called her to her duty as a Venator.

Their mouths slipped and devoured as though released from a great restraint. His hands slid around to pull her hips sharply against his; then one moved up her spine, pushing her closer as he moved his lips from her mouth along the edge of her jaw, murmuring her name against her skin.

Victoria felt the dampness of his wet shirt seep into her hands, the warmth of the texture of fine linen molding to his chest under her palms, and then the direct heat of flesh beneath her fingertips as she slipped them under the hem of his shirt.

Sebastian caught his breath and tried to shift smoothly away, as he'd done every time in the past, but she was too fast for him. She'd found what she sought.

He froze and stepped back. Looking down at her, his face arrested and still, he said nothing.

Victoria's hands fell to her sides. "So, will you tell me why you wear a *vis bulla* in your navel? Or will it be more lies and prevarication?"

To his credit, he hesitated for only an instant. "I'm born to wear one just as you are, Victoria."

Her throat crackled as she swallowed. "You think I'd believe that you—a man who refuses to kill vampires—are a Venator?"

"If you don't believe me, ask Pesaro. He is well aware of it, as is Wayren."

It was true then. Max didn't lie, and Sebastian would know she'd ask him.

Victoria sank down into the chair on which his coat hung. She had so many questions, such a swarm of emotions, that she didn't know where to begin.

He must have understood, for he stood over her, abashed and sober, so uncharacteristic of the brash Sebastian she knew that Victoria nearly softened. He was like a young boy who'd been discovered swiping biscuits from the kitchen, ashamed and hesitant.

She almost smiled, but her growing disappointment and anger held it back. There were so many thoughts barreling through her mind, so many things that suddenly made sense. But she seized on one. "That was why you never undressed when I . . . when we—"

"I didn't want you to know," he said simply. The fingers of his left hand closed and opened, closed and opened as he looked down at her, still unsure, still caught.

Why? Why would he hide such a thing from her? Then she thought maybe she knew. "Beauregard. He doesn't know either."

But Sebastian shook his head, still sober. "He does know, and, as you might imagine, he appreciates the irony of it— the grandson of one of the most powerful undead in Italy is a vampire hunter."

"You don't hunt vampires because of him, even though you're a born Venator?"

"It's not that simple." Then, as if shaking off the discomfort of the moment, he bent toward her, resting one hand on each of the chair arms to bring his face closer to hers, a provocative grin lifting his lips. The charmer had returned. "But you need not fear, Victoria, that we're too closely related by blood to carry on with our . . . previous activities. The Gardella name hasn't been part of my mother's family for centuries, if not longer." He shifted to one hand, lifting the other to brush it over her cheek. "You and I are only distantly related. And for that I am immensely thankful."

Victoria jerked her face away, anger spiking through her again. He acted as if that were the most important issue at hand. "If you find it necessary to hide your calling, why do you bother to wear a *vis bulla*?" That was perhaps what incensed her the most—that he wore it, but didn't use it. It was blasphemy.

And it also explained, perhaps, the contempt in which Max seemed to hold Sebastian.

Max had handed his *vis* to her when he walked away from the Venators, and Victoria herself had removed hers when she took a year to grieve for Phillip, knowing that she didn't trust herself to wear it. She'd almost killed a man—a mortal—because she'd been overcome with grief and anger about Phillip, and the *vis* was a convenient weapon. It had been much too easy to let her fury get away from her and take over her actions. But once she regained control of herself, she'd worn it again, just as Max had done.

"I move among vampires, and among them it's known that I'm of Gardella blood, and also that I've been Chosen. Beauregard, as I said, appreciates the irony, and the others respect me. I've taken great pains to keep it a secret from everyone else."

"That was why you were so comfortable being around the undead when you owned the Silver Chalice. It was a way for you to protect your grandfather's friends."

He must have read the abhorrence in her face, the confusion in her eyes, for he took her reluctant hands and tugged her out of the chair with ease.

And this was why, she realized now, he'd always seemed unusually strong. Even from the beginning.

Anger shot through her, sparking her emotions so that her

cheeks burned hot. He'd taken care not to appear too strong or too capable as they'd faced vampires last year when Dr. Polidori was killed by the undead after writing a novel that told too many of the vampires' secrets. He'd done just enough to let her think she'd saved them both, that she'd been the one to protect them all. She'd almost died, and so had he. And he'd never told her.

And last autumn, at the theater where Akvan's Obelisk was being kept and when Aunt Eustacia was killed, he didn't tell her then.

He'd even made self-deprecating remarks about himself in comparison to her, the Venator, the warrior. Now that she thought about it, she remembered bitterness in his voice when he spoke of her skill, and her assumption that he had none.

Anyone can stake a vampire, he'd told her once.

If they can get close enough, she'd replied flippantly, clearly implying that he hadn't a prayer of doing so.

"You stood by and watched my aunt die last fall," she said, anger bursting forth. "You watched it all happen, and you did nothing!"

His hands were tight on her upper arms, and this time he didn't bother to hide his strength. "What could I have done? What could you have done? It was two of us—three, with Pesaro—there was nothing that could have stopped those events. You know it."

She knew he was right, but the anger didn't slide away. "That night—when Polidori died . . . Sebastian, if I'd known you were a Venator—"

His sharp bark of a laugh cut her off. "You wouldn't have disparaged my skill with a sword? You would have expected more from me? Victoria, it was I who held back the Imperial while you were nearly mauled by that Guardian vampire. If you'd been less self-absorbed you would have realized you could never have matched against a Guardian and two Imperial vampires on your own, and wondered how a fop such as I could have matched swords with an Imperial."

While the pink-eyed Guardians were powerful in their own right, Imperials were even more fearsome. With blazing purple-red irises, Imperials were the strongest, fastest, and most powerful beings in the vampire race. They were often centuries, even millennia old, and not only glided through the air, but also wielded deadly swords as their weapons.

"I was the one who'd been charged with protecting Polidori, until you waltzed into the picture and insisted on taking charge," Sebastian continued.

"And you were only too eager to let me! If there was someone else to do the dirty work, you'd step back and let them. If you hadn't disappeared—run away—from the Silver Chalice when Lilith sent the Guardians after you, Phillip might still be alive! You might have been able to help him!"

"Perhaps. But likely not. There were eight Imperials, along with a myriad of other vampire patrons who would have leaped to their defense, and only Pesaro and myself. I am sorry, Victoria. I've told you before that I wholly regret what happened to your husband. I would not have wished that on anyone. Believe me."

Her face was wet with tears, and she'd stopped trying to pull free from his arms. But though her muscles eased, her fury and disappointment did not. "And that night in the carriage in London . . . you tried to seduce me and then delivered me to those vampires. You let them take me away!" Once finding herself alone with Sebastian, she'd nearly allowed him to make love to her—until they were interrupted by an angry group of vampires. She'd always suspected he'd delivered her to them on purpose.

Sebastian was shaking his head. "As lovely as that distraction was, do you truly think I'd allow my attempt to seduce you to be interrupted by something as unpleasant as the undead? I realized they were present just when you did. I tried to keep them from taking you, but I wasn't able to. It was I who found your driver and told him where you were so that Pesaro could extricate you from Lilith's minions. She was too angry at me for helping you, and was watching me too closely to allow me to do any such thing."

"You mean you wished not to tip your hand to her that you were playing both sides of the game. What is it, Sebastian? Whoever is winning is the side you choose?"

He looked as though she'd slammed him in the stomach with all of the force of her two *vis bullae*. "Victoria, you cannot—"

"I certainly—"

A noise behind her had Victoria whirling to see Zavier come to a stunned halt from what must have been a run from the back of the Consilium. "How could you!" His face was tight with accusation, and he was breathing heavily. "Victoria, do ye know what ye've done? You may be *Illa* Gardella, but this is wrong."

His ruddy face flushed with anger as he strode toward her and Sebastian, his arms bunched in a threatening manner. In his hand he held a stake. "First ye kiss the man; then ye bring him into our sanctuary. And now we are found!"

"Stop yourself there, Zavier," Victoria snapped, still reeling from the maelstrom of disappointment and fury Sebastian had raised in her. Stepping between the bristling Scot and her lover—former lover—she faced the redhead. "You do not know of what you speak."

Looking in his eyes, she saw mostly pain, and she realized how it must appear to him: a tryst being held in the most secret of places. As if Victoria were compromising security and secrets in exchange for a bit of a tup, as Verbena would say.

She had difficulty not being furious that Zavier assumed the worst of her, but Victoria managed to tuck that emotion away—for the time being. Her voice gentled, but still kept a hint of steel in it. "It is not what it appears."

And then she smelled the blood and noticed the stain on Zavier's torso.

Before she could speak, a low, rolling sound, like the tolling of a bell, clanged. The sound filled the room, dull and ominous, and Victoria turned to look at a large bell high in one of the corners. She'd hardly noticed it before, but now it seemed to swell inside the whole chamber. The deep sound reverberated through her limbs, and she saw the vibration in the feather of an old-fashioned quill that sat on one of the tables. Then more running feet grabbed her attention. Ilias hurried into the room from the opposite direction Zavier had come, Wayren close behind him, her gown billowing behind her.

"What is it?"

"The warning bell. Someone has tripped the alarm above in Santo Quirinus," Wayren said, hurrying toward them. "There are trespassers near."

Victoria drew back as if she'd been slapped, whirling to face Sebastian in horror. "You!"

"I swear it was not me, Victoria! I swear it!" He looked as disconcerted as she, his attention flashing to Wayren, who did not appear at all surprised to see him. "It was—"

Wayren reached for him, her fingers closing over the juncture of neck and shoulder. "Later, Sebastian. We will talk later." She twitched her hand, and his eyes rolled back in his head as he crumpled to the floor. Obviously Wayren didn't trust him either.

Victoria looked sharply at her—she'd known all along about Sebastian! Why had she never told her?

"The vampires haven't found us yet, but there are undead

and mortals above, in the streets and buildings nearby. Something has brought them here." It was Zavier, speaking to Ilias as though Victoria were not present. His normally jovial face bore darkness and accusation when he finally looked at her. "We must drive them away."

He started off toward the alcove that led to the spiral staircase Victoria had descended only thirty minutes earlier, but she called him back.

"No, Zavier, wait. We cannot go that way, for if we suddenly appear from the church they will know our secret."

Ilias kept hidden guardsmen within the small church and in the areas surrounding it: one Venator along with two Comitators, who were martial-arts experts like Kritanu who taught the Venators their fighting skills. If there were vampires about, threatening their security—which Victoria had no reason to doubt—presumably the guards were already engaged. Still, it would be rash to come from the church and confirm to the undead where the entrance to the Consilium was.

"This way," Ilias ordered with a sharp gesture. Victoria and Zavier followed the older man, who obviously knew more about the secrets of the Consilium than anyone else, back down the steps and through one of the pointed archways that led to a chamber Victoria had seen only once before. It was bare and dusty. Trunks and several wooden crates were stacked against one of the walls, but Ilias hurried past them toward the back corner. He reached up to one of the iron sconces that were studded throughout the entire Consilium and lifted the torch from its place. Fumbling around with his fingers inside the empty sconce, he grunted in satisfaction, then withdrew his hand.

Victoria watched with increasing tension, impatience nearly sending her back to the top of the spiral stairs. At least there she could hear if the threat was coming closer.

But when Ilias removed his hand from the inside of the sconce, he also pulled back on the iron cup, and it fell away from the wall. A dull grating sound drew her attention, and she saw the wall behind the trunks shift.

Zavier was there before she was, only, Victoria knew, because he'd somehow been looking in that direction. He shoved the wall so that it opened wide enough to get through, and he dashed into the darkness beyond.

She would have followed him, but Ilias caught her arm. "You cannot come back in this way, so take care. It is only an exit."

"Thank you," she said, and ran after Zavier, noticing the splatter of blood he'd left on the floor. She didn't know how badly he was injured, but she must rely on him. It was the two of them and the three guards who watched the church above; Ilias and Wayren would stay below as a last shield in the Consilium.

The secret door had closed behind her, leaving no illumination, yet Victoria did not slow her pace.

Her huntress blood was ready, her instincts on edge, when she saw gray relief ahead. Stake steady in her hand, Victoria slowed as she came around a corner and found herself at the bottom of a set of stone stairs. Up she climbed, the heels of Zavier in front of her becoming more visible as they ascended, and the pungent smell from the nearby umbrella makers more evident.

Then she followed him through a stone doorway that led to the street in front of Santo Quirinus church. The cobblestones were covered by moonglow. The sun had been set for some time.

As Victoria burst across the *borghi* and up the five steps onto the brick street, she noticed two things: first, the bloody heap of what had been a Comitator, and second, the dank, musty death-smell she'd smelled only last night.

A demon.

Sebastian had brought demons to the Consilium!

This fact was confirmed when Victoria saw Michalas, who must have been with Zavier before he came to sound the alarm, slam his stake into the chest of a red-eyed being. When he withdrew it and stepped back the creature leaped toward him, unharmed. Victoria vaulted herself at them and kicked into the demon, sending him off balance and slamming into the side of a building.

She rolled to her feet and looked around for something to use as a blade; demons had to be beheaded. A great force slammed into her from behind, and Victoria went sprawling onto the dirt, her knee twisting as she stumbled onto a large rock. She rolled away, kicking out with all the strength of her legs and painful knee as the demon with the vampire eyes lunged toward her again.

The shouts and blows around her ebbed into the distance as she fought hand-to-hand with the demon, who matched her in strength.

This one appeared human, except for the red eyes of the undead and his foul, dank smell. Her arms ached where he grabbed them; her stomach burned when he jabbed her with an elbow. His head snapped back as she whipped her arm up under his chin, and he tumbled to the ground when she followed that up with a sharp kick behind his knee. She shoved him into a small bush and whirled around, again looking for something to use as a blade.

"Victoria!" She heard her name and shifted her attention for the barest of moments. Something flew through the night toward her, something long and gleaming. She caught Zavier's eye with a quick thanks and snatched the sword out of the air, barely feeling the blade as it sliced into her palm.

It was in her other hand a breath later, her fingers safely

behind the guard, and Victoria leaped toward the demon with a great swipe toward the creature's throat.

The blade cut through, and blood from her own wound splattered as she kept her momentum going. She didn't see the demon freeze and then shrivel into a dark mass before it bubbled into the dirt and old grass; she was already turning toward another creature bearing down on her.

A kick, a shove, a whirl and a slice, and she severed the ogre-faced demon's head from his doglike body. By the time she whirled back around, everything had stilled but for the ratcheting breathing of her companions. Michalas panted near the threshold of a building, sweat dripping from his tight curls.

"Bloody hell . . . " Zavier's barrel chest heaved as he crouched against the corner of a small building that looked as though it might tumble over from his powerful weight.

"It is Stanislaus on the steps in the Icon Hall," came a voice. Ilias stepped from the small doorway of the church, his face stern and weary. "He is dead. But the door was closed behind him, preserving the secret door in the confessional. From the looks of the blood streaking the tile, he crawled in there to die . . . and to loose the alarm bell."

"They nearly found the kirk!" exploded Zavier, staring around with furious eyes. "If we had not been here they could have found it." He rose to his feet, the man never seeming so large and ferocious as he did then.

Sudden comprehension welled inside Victoria, and she moved toward Zavier. That was when she saw there on the ground at his feet another body. This one had long dark hair in a crumpled braid, and his mahogany-colored face was turned to one side.

"Zavier, I'm sorry," she said, bending to kneel next to the man. There was nothing that could be done; the blood and the awkward angle of his head told her that in an instant.

Mansur had been a Comitator recently assigned as a permanent guardian of Santo Quirinus, but prior to that he'd
worked with Zavier. She rose and placed her hand on the
Scot's arm. "I'm so sorry."

A sick feeling rose in her stomach. Could they have prevented Mansur's death? And that of the other Venator, Stanislaus? Had she made the wrong decision by delaying their
arrival, taking the long way out?

They brought the bodies of the mortals into a nearby
building, still taking care to stay away from the church.
Their losses were one Comitator and one Venator, two-thirds
of the guardians of the church. Victoria finalized the count
of two demons dead, two vampires, and three mortals she
didn't recognize, but suspected they might be Tutela. All
were slain on the deserted street.

"You are correct. The mark of the Tutela is on the three
men," Wayren said to Victoria after Ilias examined the bodies. There was worry in the older woman's pale blue eyes.

"Mansur and Stanislaus realized too late that they were
fighting demons," Victoria said, her mind back on the loss
of her comrades. While all Venators and some Comitators
could sense the presence of a vampire, not many also had
the ability to identify demons, many of which could take
any shape. "And Stanislaus warned us the only way he
could."

"They found Santo Quirinus, but they couldna find us,"
Zavier said, his burr thick. "But 'twas a near thing." He
would not look at Victoria.

She fully understood, and accepted the blame. For, during
the heat of battle, somehow her mind had become unfet-
tered, and she realized how it had happened. How it must
have happened.

For once she believed Sebastian, and knew he had not led the way or drawn the demons to them.

For demons could mean only one thing: Akvan.

Akvan must have sent them for the shard Victoria had hidden in the Consilium.

And he would be back.

Fourteen

Wherein Wayren Reveals a Disturbing Prophecy

"No matter what you think of me otherwise," were Sebastian's first words as Victoria blazed, limping, into the chamber where Wayren had put him earlier, "you must believe me. I took great precautions that no one would follow me, especially Beauregard. I left during the early part of the day, when the sun was still out." He lurched to sit upright on the bed on which he'd been resting.

The room was small, one level below the rest of the Consilium, and outfitted almost as if it were a prison cell. There was a small bed, a table, a chair, and a thick rug on the cold stone floor. And an unlocked door. She closed the door behind her, locking it, and turned back to face him.

Still energized and alert from the fight, and filled with fury that two of her own had been killed, Victoria stood in front of the door, her hands planted on her hips. She was going to get some answers from Sebastian, and there would be no equivocation.

Wayren had done the right thing, incapacitating him so that she, Victoria, could handle the threat above. It wouldn't have been prudent to leave him mobile, for even now Victoria wasn't certain of Sebastian's loyalties or his purpose in coming to the Consilium. It was best that he, an unknown entity, not be free to walk out when they were fighting a battle for the safety of their stronghold.

"Why are you still here?" she asked, intentionally baiting him. "The door wasn't locked. You could have left when you awakened. Isn't that your usual course—slipping off into the shadows at the first sign of danger?"

"I wanted to make certain I spoke to you." He was propped up on one elbow, his legs in dark trousers stretching the length of the bed, rich blond curls winging every which way about his face. He eyed her speculatively, as if wondering how to approach her mood. "And then there was the fact that I still feel a bit dizzy from whatever it was Wayren did to me." Ah . . . now, there was a bit of that self-deprecating humor. "Perhaps you would like to take a seat? I'm afraid I'm not quite able to stand as I no doubt should. Manners and all."

"No, thank you. I'll stand. Though I'm certain that if your hide was in danger, you'd find yourself on your feet in an instant, running through the doorway." She was angry with him. She felt betrayed, and she was still reeling from the furious battle with the demons and vampires, knowing how close they'd come to discovering the Consilium. The wound on her hand had been bandaged, and her wrenched knee had screamed pain with every step down the stairs to this level. Even now it still throbbed.

Yet . . . she was here.

He was watching her, for once seeming to understand

that the moment didn't need coy comments or halfhearted jokes. He didn't even take the opportunity to mention that they were alone in a room with a bed, a fact Victoria forced herself to dismiss. After all, the last time they'd been alone they'd been on a bed. Or, rather, she'd been on the bed, tied to it, after Sebastian had kidnapped her so that she couldn't disrupt Max's plans.

Annoyance fired in her again. She felt the tingle of it skimming along her arms to her fingers. They flexed.

"It was the shard from Akvan's Obelisk that drew them here, not you," she said, focusing on the matter at hand. The shard would have to be moved. But since it was almost sunrise, Victoria knew they had at least until the new nightfall to deal with that problem. She would take the shard away today, and she thought she knew exactly where to hide it.

Sebastian's full lips tipped in half of a gentle smile. "Ah, my suspicions are confirmed. So the shard is still here. Beauregard is unaware that you have a piece of the obelisk, for no matter what you might think of me otherwise, Victoria, I did not tell him that interesting bit of information."

She believed him, because once she'd realized what had happened, everything made sense. The small piece of the obsidian obelisk on the leather thong had obviously been near Akvan, and likely he'd roused, or somehow imbued it with power. That would explain the blue sparking that occurred when the two pieces had touched in the storage room—the influence had thus been transferred to the larger one, or at least had triggered its own inherent powers.

"Akvan knew where to send his people because he could sense the location of the obelisk shard," Victoria said, trying not to notice the deep, narrow vee of Sebastian's open shirt. Somehow he'd moved, and the shirt, which she could have sworn a moment earlier had still been knotted at the neck, had gaped open, showing rich, golden skin beneath. She remembered with startling clarity that moment earlier today when her hands, sliding over the warmth of his skin and the ridges of his belly, had found the small silver *vis*.

This was not the time to be thinking of that, although from the sudden upswing in her heartbeat, Victoria knew it was too late to push the thought completely aside. Instead she focused on her anger and the vitality that still sang in her veins.

"Victoria." His voice, low and gentle, was more sensual. And it contrasted directly with her current on-edge nerves, which she steeled against his sensuality.

"It's not going to work, Sebastian. You can save your flirtations for another day. And another woman."

"Your rejection devastates me. I thought perhaps you'd come—"

"I just lost two of my own to demons and vampires who had come after the shard from Akvan's Obelisk. They could have found us, assaulted our sanctuary, and destroyed what we've built."

"And so now you've come to flay me with your frustrations and your anxieties? To vent your spleen about something for which only you can be blamed?" Blast him, but the expression on his face was much too knowing, too complacent. Yes, there was guilt bubbling beneath her animation. Guilt, and an edginess that nipped at her, threatening to burst free.

"Did you know the shard would draw Akvan out, call his people here? You knew I had it; you must know more than you divulge. As usual. You could have told me."

"I didn't know you had it here in the Consilium—"

"But you knew I had it."

He shrugged, graceful and unhurried, unaffected by her anger and her accusations. "I am not your keeper, Victoria. Unless you want me to be. In which case we can certainly discuss the terms." The smile he sent her was lascivious and meaningful.

She whirled away in frustration, nearly cried aloud in pain from her wrenched knee, then spun back, gesticulating in frustration. "Sebastian, can you never—"

Her words were cut off as she found herself suddenly pitching toward him, yanked off balance by a strong hand closing over her arm as she'd pivoted back. The combination of her weak knee and being taken by surprise landed her half on top of him on the narrow bed, hands splayed one on the blanket and the other, the one he'd pulled on, the unbandaged one, smack in the middle of his chest. She barely missed slamming her head into the wall behind him.

"Do you remember, Victoria," he said, grasping her wrist before she could pull away from touching him, "that first night in the carriage, in London? Before we were interrupted by the vampires?"

She tried to pull away, but he had no reason to hide his Venator strength now, and it was difficult. Especially since he'd quickly scissored his legs around her good knee, leaving only her injured one with any mobility, wrapped in tangling skirts. His fingers were tight over her wrist, holding her hand stamped on the warmth of his chest, half on skin, half on linen. He was leaning over her from his half-sprawled position, and she looked up into his amber eyes.

"Do you remember? You were just as angry, simmering under the surface with frustration and guilt and need, just as you are now."

"Let me go, Sebastian. I don't want to hurt you." She'd stopped struggling, but the tension hadn't left her body. His weight, half on her, wasn't unpleasant; nor was it confining or even threatening. She suddenly felt drained and resigned. And expectant. Alive.

"And you might, at that, but not in the way you imagine,"

he murmured, never taking his eyes from her face, never giving an iota of release. "You were angling for a fight then, that night in the carriage, just as you are now. That's why you came down here to me. You can admit it."

"You're mad." Her heart was thumping so hard surely he could see it, feel it, as it pounded through her body.

"Mad . . . yes, indeed, I don't deny it. I am mad." Those last words came out like a confession as, with one smooth movement, he shifted his weight and bent his face to hers.

The smell of cloves came with him, faintly, as it always did, along with tobacco and something else that was Sebastian. He was close enough that his lips hovered above hers, but he didn't touch her. "This is what you wanted, really, isn't it?" His voice was low, not quite a whisper, feathering over her skin.

"No," she replied.

She felt, rather than saw, his mouth curve into a smile. "All that passion and heat and anger . . . this is the best way to let it all out. You know that. You've missed it."

"It was only one time, Sebastian."

"Twice."

"No . . . we only . . . just once, in the carriage, last fall." He was so close, yet he still didn't kiss her. She would not lift her face that last bit to meet his.

"I seem to recall," he murmured, now brushing his lips ever so lightly along her jaw in a quick swipe, "having to stifle your cries of pleasure in that small parlor of your villa."

"But . . . that wasn't . . ." He'd moved back so that when she talked her lips brushed against his when they moved.

"It was enough for me."

His mouth, just as coaxing as she remembered, covered hers with a deliberate firmness that told her he wasn't going to let her change her mind. She kissed him back, assuring him she didn't intend to, and then she gave way and let herself enjoy the moment—and all of the lovely sensations that came with it.

He released her hands and moved her closer, driving his tongue in deep as it swept and swirled around hers. The slick movements tugged down through her belly, sending pleasant little pangs between her legs.

"I want to see your *vis bulla*," she whispered against him.

Rolling partly away and up against the wall, he smiled with such pleasure that her stomach dipped again. He pulled off his shirt, and for the first time she saw his golden chest bare—lightly haired and muscled and square-shouldered, tapering into lean hips. The dark blond hair grew down around his navel, where the small silver cross nestled, and a slender line led down into his breeches. The rest of his torso was as bare and firm as Michelangelo's statue of David.

Victoria's mouth dried, then moistened as she skimmed her hands up and over his shoulders. Pleasure indeed.

Clearly enjoying her touch, Sebastian pulled her down so that she lay on top of him, her breasts smashed against his bare skin, their legs mingling with her skirts, her left arm scraping against the rough stone wall. He kissed along the side of her jaw to her ear as his clever fingers flipped open the two fabric-covered buttons at the back of her bodice.

The neckline gaped away, and she lifted up from Sebastian's mouth as he tugged at the edges of her gown, pulling it down over her shoulders. The subterranean air was cool on her bare skin, raising little prickles there in the hollow of her collarbones. With two quick motions he yanked down her corset and her breasts tipped free, hovering and trembling above his face.

Hands sliding to hold her at the hips, pressing the juncture of her thighs into the bulge between his, Sebastian lifted his head to take her breast into his mouth. His tongue slid over the tip of her nipple, sending a renewed rush of pleasure down to where their hips ground together. She was breathing faster now, feeling the sweet build as he tugged and sucked and licked. Her arms trembled as they held her upright, and at last Victoria pulled away from his demanding mouth, sitting back on his thighs to look down at him.

His face was flushed with pleasure and his lips swollen, and when their eyes met a most mischievous grin quirked his lips. "Well, now," was all he said as he groped under the mess of cotton and lace and muslin to slide his hands up her bare thighs. She lifted so he could pull the skirts up, placing her hands on the center of his chest for leverage and rustling her nails through the hair covering it . . . but when he slipped his fingers in and around the moistness between her legs, Victoria bent forward to kiss him with a ferociousness that spoke of her impatience.

They breathed together, gasping for air between kisses that moved from mouth to mouth, and then along jaws and cheeks and with teeth and delving tongues . . . and then he moved his hand, and they were both fumbling at the fastening of his breeches, the string of his drawers. She rolled to the side as he shrugged out of them, his legs solid and muscular, just as tanned as the rest of his skin.

"Shall we?" he murmured, standing over her, for the first time completely undressed, looking lean and toned and all shades of gold and bronze. Her legs hung off the edge of the bed, and with a half smile he lifted her skirts again, parted her thighs, and, his hands on her shoulders, fitted himself into her in one smooth slide.

Victoria caught her breath, sighed, and closed her eyes as the sweetness blazed through her. She met his rhythm, rose and fell, greedy and demanding—if she were going to take pleasure, she would take it all—until the wave finally rolled over, undulating through her core to her belly and out to every limb.

Sebastian arched into her with one last stroke, his hands leaving her shoulders to curl into the blanket, tangling painfully into her hair as he matched her.

And then there was nothing but their bodies collapsed together, breathing heavily, hot and damp and sated.

After a while Sebastian moved, lifting his face to look at her and using one finger to trace along her jaw. "Feel better?" he asked, his voice low and full of amusement.

Victoria shifted, and he let his weight slide onto the bed next to her. She smiled over at him and saw the way his eyes darkened from gold to brown when she did. "What is it?"

"Your smile is quite entrancing—all those tiny dimples— yet you don't show it often enough."

She sat up, working her chemise and corset up to cover her breasts again, and shrugged. "Perhaps I find little to smile about as of late."

"At least you're smiling about this. I thought perhaps you might hold my little secret against me, and deny both of us this pleasure."

She looked at his *vis bulla*, the only cold, silvery relief on his bronze and gold figure, and some of her pleasure slid away. "You deny your fate and your duty. I can't understand that any more than I can understand your leaving your grandfather—and other undead—to exist. You have a responsibility to take them out of this world."

"And send them to Hell? For eternity? No, Victoria, I told you . . . I won't have that on me. They were once mortals, fathers, sisters, lovers. I can't damn them for something they cannot control."

"But you have . . . you've done it, Sebastian, or you wouldn't have this." She brushed her fingers over the warm silver cross. "You had to have killed at least one vampire to get this."

"Two. I'd killed two before . . . before last autumn, when

the obelisk was destroyed. Exactly two vampires. And then . . . I killed another the night your aunt died. I told you, but you didn't believe me." He reached for his breeches, no longer looking at her, but at them.

It took her a moment to realize what he was talking about. "You said you saved Max's life. That night? You killed a vampire to save him?" She paused in the action of reaching around to button her dress. Impossible to do alone. "Why? You and Max . . ."

"Despise each other? Hmmm . . . that word might be a bit strong. . . . No, no, it isn't. Yes, there is quite a history between us. I didn't do it to save him, Victoria."

"Then why? Why shatter your own moral code, nonsensical as it might be, for a man you dislike?"

He pulled the trousers up over his hips, busied himself tying them. She waited until he looked up. And then she saw the answer in his eyes.

"For me?"

He reached over to pull on his boots.

"Sebastian."

"He can be what I cannot. You need him."

She stared at him, felt her face warming and stupefaction letting her jaw drop, just a little. "Need Max?"

"If you're going to persist in this battle against the undead, you need someone like him. It pains me greatly to admit it, but he's the best Venator alive. He can be what I cannot."

"Will not, you mean to say. You *will* not."

Suddenly the door rattled, sending Victoria leaping guiltily off the bed, her loose bodice flopping. She'd locked it, and a good thing, too, for they could have been interrupted at a much more compromising moment.

Dear God, she hoped it wasn't Max on the other side, she thought as Sebastian quickly buttoned her.

But when she opened the door, it was to find Ilias there. "The sun is up," he said. To his credit, he barely glanced at Sebastian and his dishabille. "You are needed, *Illa Gardella*."

"I must go," Sebastian said, standing and swiftly pulling his shirt back on.

"Wait," she said, noticing the mark on the back of his shoulder. "What is that?" It was a small black mark, intricate and circular. It looked like the tattoo Max wore, signifying his membership in the Tutela. But the symbol on Sebastian's golden skin was much different, and smaller.

"Beauregard's mark."

He looked at her steadily, and she understood. Her stomach soured, sending a nasty taste into the back of her mouth. He might wear the amulet of the Venators, but he also wore the mark of the vampires. And he would not choose between them.

Before she could stop him, he pushed past Ilias and strode down the passageway, leaving Victoria to gather up her shoes.

"Why didn't you send for me?" Max growled, trying to shake off the grogginess. "And what in the bloody hell did you give me last night?" He hadn't slept so hard and dreamlessly for more than a year.

Wayren, as quiet and calm as she always was, merely looked at him. Her face was a bit more drawn than usual, and instead of flowing in long strands over her shoulders, her pale blond hair was pulled back into a wrist-thick braid.

Max didn't ache as much as he'd suspected he would, after two bullet wounds and innumerable punches and cuts. Perhaps whatever she'd given him to help him sleep had also leached away the pain. Regardless, as a Venator, he'd be completely healed within a matter of days.

Still. "I should have been there. So close to Santo Quirinus? And the Consilium? You could have sent Myza for me."

"She's a pigeon, Max. Myza wouldn't have been able to wake you, even by tapping her beak on the window."

"You made damned certain of that." He sat up and gulped down a mug of watered wine. "You said there was something else."

Wayren didn't blink. "Sebastian Vioget was in the Consilium with Victoria."

Max stopped the mental barrage of thoughts and questions that image brought and focused on the important one. "Beauregard?"

She shook her head. "No, he didn't bring him. He—"

But Max didn't want to hear her platitudes about Vioget. "If he betrayed us, I'll kill him."

"He's a Venator—"

"Then I need say no more."

Wayren pursed her lips in a sign of annoyance, but didn't comment further on his interruption. Instead she continued, "He had Eustacia's armband, Max. We have the last key to the Door of Alchemy."

"Bloody nice of him to return it."

"He could have given it to Beauregard," she replied with just a bit of archness in her tone.

Max gritted his teeth but said nothing.

"Victoria will want you to go with them to attempt to open the door, most likely later tonight, when it's still dark but nearing dawn. You'll be less noticeable, and the undead will be seeking shelter from the sun."

Ah, yes, he'd be one of the contingency: Zavier, Vioget, Michalas, Ylito, himself. Was that what Victoria thought?

Max realized he must have grimaced when Wayren asked, "Do her bites pain you?"

"Of course they do. You know that." His hand went involuntarily to the never-healing scars on his neck. There were new ones, too, only a month old, on the tender part of his shoulder.

"How often do you feel her pull, Max? Tell me the truth."

Unreasoning rage bubbled in him. "I don't want to discuss it."

"I'm not asking, Max. I'm demanding to know. We have to rid you of it." Now she was beginning to sound like Eustacia.

"She doesn't control me. She'd like to; she finds it amusing to play at it." Bitterness sat in his mouth. "She's not made me do anything against my will." At least, not to anyone else's knowledge.

"Akvan is back, Max. You know she must have realized that when you destroyed his obelisk, Akvan would be called back to earth."

The grogginess had completely slid away, leaving his mind sharp again. "At one time I would have disagreed . . . but now I know better. She would rather battle a demon than her own son. Her son, who tried to unleash the powers of the obelisk, could have taken over Lilith's reign—or at least weakened it. Whereas a demon would cause all of the vampires to unite behind her."

"Indeed. I believe you are absolutely correct. All of the vampires would unite with Lilith except those few who have allied themselves with Regalado since the downfall of Nedas. Even Beauregard and his minions would join Lilith; he's no fool."

"True. There are few vampires who will join the ranks of a demon, or support one in any way, unless they have some grief or complaint with their own vampire leader. Regalado has managed to convince only a relatively small number to join him. Then, too, there are some members of the Tutela, those who are still mortals and who were led by Regalado, who are still loyal to him."

"Indeed," Wayren agreed again. "The battle for Hell rages between the demons and the undead, and there are few who cross from one side to the other."

"Thus the threat from Akvan must be great enough to convince at least some undead—and Regalado himself—to join his ranks."

"His power is very great. When he was still ensconced in Hell and only his obelisk was here, there was the chance that the obelisk could be roused to imbue its possessor with great power—the power to raise the souls of the dead into an immortal army. Of course, that was Nedas's plan, which you foiled by destroying the obelisk—at Lilith's request. Now Akvan is here, and his presence brings that same power, but it's already inherent in his being. It doesn't need to be activated."

"Then why, if he's been back for more than three months, have we seen no sign of him?"

"He is still weak. He's gathering his strength, likely with the help of the Tutela and Regalado and his followers."

"Hence the reason for the event at the villa. He needed to feed."

"We cannot wait for the vampires to come together to fight him. He must be slain before he reaches his full power."

"I called him back. I'll do it."

"It will be no easy task, Max." Wayren looked at him so long and seriously—almost sorrowfully—that Max felt the urge to twitch.

"What is it?"

"It's written—"

"That I'll die doing it? I've no fear of that. You know that, Wayren." It was true. He'd be free, and he'd willingly give his life, as Eustacia had, as countless others had, for the mortal world's safety. "I'm bound as a Venator to give my life in the fight."

"It is written . . . in a prophecy translated from the Persian by our own Lady Rosamunde Gardella . . . 'Neither Venator nor undead immortal shall slay Akvan; 'tis only a mortal man shall send him permanently to the bowels of Hell, using his own strength against him.' "

Max's mouth dried and he felt energy drain from him. Who else would be equipped, trained, prepared enough to slay a demon? Surely not any mortal man. Only a Venator would know how, would be brave enough. Would have the skills.

Only a Venator who was not a Venator.

Wayren leaned forward to touch his hand, but he pulled away from her slender fingers, reaching for his black stake. "You knew it would come to this. You knew it when I first brought you the salve." Though he tried, he couldn't summon the anger. It was what it was. His path would be thus.

He lifted his eyes and met her blue-gray ones and gave a short nod. "Tomorrow."

Fifteen

In Which Our Heroine Becomes Quite Provoking

Once she considered it, Victoria was relieved that Sebastian had slipped away from the Consilium and was no longer around when it was time for her to leave.

They had so much unfinished business between them, so many things she wanted to say and to demand . . . but until she figured out how she felt about everything she'd learned in the last half day, Victoria didn't want to try to confront him. Her body still sizzled and hummed from the release of their lovemaking—if one could call it that.

And that was one path on which she wasn't ready to tread. Was it love that drew her to Sebastian? That caused her to open up to him, to share that part of herself?

How could it be, if she didn't trust him?

She might not trust him, but despite that and his predisposition to taking the easy way out of any situation, she found she could be happy, even relaxed, when she was with him.

It had been so much easier with Phillip. He was handsome and charming, wealthy and trustworthy. He obviously loved her, even adored her. He wanted to marry her—and at that time she foolishly thought she could agree, that she could have it all, that both sides of her life would remain intact, safely separate.

So she fell in love with him. Married him.

And destroyed him.

Victoria blinked back the tears. This wasn't the time to berate herself for her mistakes; God knew she'd done enough of that. All she could do now was continue on. And not make the same mistake again.

Which was why, if she were going to have any kind of relationship with a man, someone like Sebastian—one who knew her world, who understood it, who accepted it—would be a ripe candidate. Someday she might have to stop taking the potion that kept her from getting with child, and consider having one of her own. There was no other Gardella that she knew of to continue their lineage. But now she couldn't even contemplate how she could do so.

All of these thoughts rambled through her mind as she left the main area of the deserted Consilium. It was late afternoon. She'd slept for a few hours after Sebastian left, and she'd met with Wayren and Ilias. The others had also gone home to sleep until later that night.

She passed Wayren, who was in her library quietly studying some ancient manuscript and didn't appear to notice her slinking by, and continued to the storage room. Victoria had one more thing to see to at the Consilium, although everyone else thought she, too, had already gone. They all planned to meet at dawn to go with her to open the Door of Alchemy—Zavier, who would still barely look at her, Michalas, Brim.

Perhaps Max, whom she hadn't seen since they parted ways at the Palombara villa early yesterday morning, but who Wayren said would be there.

Victoria had already retrieved the silver armband that belonged to Aunt Eustacia. It was just where Sebastian had told her he'd put it, behind the portrait of Catherine Gardella and her boxy emerald ring. Loved her jewelry, indeed.

The thought brought a wavering smile to her lips, and a tangent on which she was happy to travel. In her portrait the woman was as bedecked in jewels as her liege, old Queen Bess. How she ever fought vampires in that massive gown and neck ruff, Victoria couldn't imagine.

The heavy armband was already on Victoria's upper left arm. As she closed the storage room door behind her, she felt its cold grip finally ease to match her body's warmth. The key was safely inside, and now all she had to do was to retrieve the pieces of Akvan's Obelisk and remove them from the Consilium.

Victoria quickly pulled the stake-size shard from its hiding place. She felt a sizzle of warmth as she did so, and its malevolence seemed to filter into the air. Victoria quickly slipped it into the large pocket of the long coat she wore over her split-skirted gown. The coat was too masculine-looking to pass muster with Lady Melly, but the gown, if Victoria was careful, might fool her into thinking her daughter was properly dressed.

Of course, the best course of action would be to keep Lady Melly from seeing her garbed in such a manner, and that was Victoria's intent. If all went well she would be returning to the Gardella villa much later tonight or early in the morning, and likely the ladies would be sleeping.

The little leather strip and its pendant of obsidian went into a small breast pocket on her coat. Victoria didn't want to chance the two pieces rubbing against each other again;

nor did she want to put it in a pocket with her other weapons. It would be too easy for it to get lost if she suddenly had to yank out a stake, for example.

Closing the door behind her, she left the storage room, but instead of turning left to return to the fountain room of the Consilium and leave through Santo Quirinus, Victoria went to the right to exit through the other hidden passage that released her several blocks from the small church.

The late afternoon was dark and gloomy, the sun blanketed by heavy clouds, and the air damp with a cold drizzle. The obelisk shard clunked against her thigh, heavy in her pocket as she hurried along transporting a piece of evil in the midst of the few pilgrims and shopkeepers who were out on such a dank day.

Victoria had a pistol and several stakes as well: one hastily shoved in her hair in a manner that would have sent Verbena into fits, and the other in a small loop at the waist of her skirt. The heavy silver cross she favored sat directly on the bodice of her high-necked walking gown, and she also had three vials of holy water in various locations on her clothing.

And underneath it all she wore her special corset.

Victoria felt confident and prepared to face whatever she might as she made her way from the *Borga* across the Tiber River to the Esquiline District, where Villa Palombara sat. She could have ordered Oliver to pick her up and take her in the hack, but someone might have seen him waiting and asked . . . and this was a job Victoria wanted to do alone.

She'd brought the danger of the shards to the Consilium all on her own, and she would draw that danger away while safely securing the pieces of the obelisk. Moving quickly through the streets, passing among shopkeepers who'd begun to close for lack of customers on such a day, staying away from the carriages that rumbled along carrying more affluent

Romans, splashing through chilly, dirty puddles, Victoria waited to feel the shift of cold air over the back of her neck, or the prickling awareness that someone—or something—followed her. Even though it was daytime, the sun was hidden, and some vampires could make their way about during cloudy days such as this.

But nothing stirred the air, tipping off her senses. She kept her head down but her eyes wary, scanning ahead and to the sides as she hurried along. Her fingers were a bit cold, as were her ears, for the collar of the coat wasn't tall enough to cover them, and her hair had been pinned up quickly and haphazardly and didn't provide any protection either. Victoria preferred not to wear gloves when she might be fighting, for they made her grip too slippery to handle the stakes.

She didn't know how fast or how easily Akvan could trace the location of the shard, but based on the speed with which the Consilium had been attacked after the shard had touched the splinter, she didn't think there was much time to spare.

If she could have waited until dawn, she would have. But to give the vampires and demons the cover of another night to track and come after the shard would be foolish. If she hurried she would have the task complete before the sun went down.

At last she reached the ragged part of the wall of Villa Palombara, at the backside of the elongated pentagonal estate. Far on the other end of the property, beyond the tops of the heavy thicket of trees, was the roofline of the villa itself.

She would have to traipse through the overgrowth again, and, just her luck, it was on another wet day. But the Magic Door was situated approximately in the center of the property, its crumbling stone wall a short perimeter around a smaller yard that belonged to the villa. Still, getting wet was better than trying to approach from the front, where someone in the villa might see her.

Climbing over the stone wall was rather difficult, even with the tree to assist, but Victoria managed it after nearly falling on her face when the heel of her boot caught in the back of her hem. As it was, she landed in wet grass on her knees, palms slamming one onto a branch and the other into a small thrush of weeds. Unfortunately, her wrenched knee landed on the corner of a sharp rock and sent a stab of pain blazing through her.

Swearing under her breath, she started to scramble to her feet when a pair of scuffed black boots stepped into view.

"I expected you hours ago."

Why did it always have to be Max to witness when grace deserted her?

"Well, foolish you, waiting in the damp for so long. What are you doing here?" she asked, standing gingerly on her weak knee and wiping her dirty, damp palms on her coat. At least the drizzle had stopped coming down, and now the moisture just hung in the air enough to keep it gray and dark and heavy.

"Waiting for you."

She looked up at him, pushing away a lock of hair that had fallen in her eyes with the tumble, and saw that he was staring at her from under the brim of his dripping hat. It made her skin tingle, the way his dark eyes scored over her as if he'd never seen her before. "What is it? A smudge on my face?"

"Right there." He reached toward her, his large, rough thumb brushing the side of her cheek before she could blink. "You've got the piece of the obelisk with you?"

She shouldn't be surprised. She wasn't surprised. "And the last key." She bumped into a tall sapling with a few leaves still clinging to it, and a light shower sprinkled over her arm and onto the ground.

Max was nodding. "A good strategy. Use the last key to open the Magic Door, retrieve whatever is inside that we want, and then lock the obelisk piece safely in. Not only can it not be removed without the keys, but Akvan's own proximity will not allow him to sense the additional source of power from the pieces."

"Or the power from any other splinters or shards he might have will mask the presence of this one." She realized they were still standing next to the large oak, the wall behind them and a trickle of wind sending its branches dripping old rain down on them. It was utterly quiet, and there among the gray and brown bushes they were well hidden from any prying eyes in the villa. "How did you know what I planned to do?"

"It was the logical thing, of course. You found the last key and you realized the danger of the obelisk. Very simple to put the two together." Normally he'd sound arrogant in such a discussion, but today he seemed rather subdued.

She thought she understood why. "You spoke to Wayren about the attack."

He nodded again. "Earlier today." Then he made an impatient Max gesture. "Well, let's be on with it. Unless you're waiting for someone else? Zavier, perhaps? Or . . . no . . . it must be Vioget who has you hesitating." Now the familiar edge was back in his voice.

Victoria had started to walk into the brush but at his words she stopped and turned back. Max loomed over her, nearly on her heels. "Why didn't you ever tell me about Sebastian?"

He raised one dark eyebrow. "About . . . Sebastian? He's not generally my preferred topic of conversation."

"He's a Venator. You never told me."

Again that supercilious brow. "What difference does it make? He might have the blood of the Gardellas, might even be called to the duty . . . but he chooses to ignore it. He's worth little of my thought or concern."

"He saved your life."

"For which I am eternally grateful." The bitterness in his voice belied that statement. "He could have saved many other lives if he'd taken his rightful place in the Consilium."

"He still wears the *vis bulla*," she said.

Now both brows rose, and she felt her cheeks warm at the knowing expression there. "Ah. That explains your delay in taking the shards from the Consilium. You were otherwise . . . engaged."

She held her breath to force away the blush. There was no reason for her to play the modest miss with him; he already knew she and Sebastian had been lovers. "And so I was. But I'm here now."

Max looked at her, his dark eyes unreadable. Then his lips quirked in a hard smile. "So it is to be Sebastian. Have you left Zavier intact, or are there pieces to pick up there too?"

Victoria couldn't feign a cool response to that, remembering the anger and pain on the Scotsman's face. Nevertheless, she lifted her chin, shoving her hands restlessly into the two side pockets of her coat. She wished suddenly for an undead to appear so she could stake it. Do something other than stand face-to-face with the man who bloody always seemed to be right.

"I warned you," Max said, correctly interpreting her silence. "And who will it be next, Victoria? Surely you won't destroy your entire army of Venators, one after another, because you cannot keep your—"

He stopped, biting the words off, and seemed to draw himself up and away from her, cloaking what had been sudden ire. "This is a waste of time. We have only a short while until sunset."

Brushing past her, he started off on those long legs, moving rapidly through the brush along the stone wall, leaving branches and tall grasses shivering and dripping in his wake. Droplets rained down on Victoria's hair and arms as she turned to follow, wishing she too had a hat.

She felt the heavy metal of her pistol and the warm sleekness of the obsidian shard in each of her pockets. The not wholly idle thought of which one would invoke the most long-lasting pain in the back of his broad shoulders entertained her as she strode after him.

She dropped the pistol back into the depths of her pocket, but did not release the shard. It felt good in her hand, solid. Weighty. She'd never noticed how well it fit, how it seemed to mold into her palm. She'd thought before what a good weapon it would be, but had never held it long enough to really notice its strength.

The stone warmed under her grip, and she pulled it out to admire its shiny black length. Wicked. Gleaming blue-black even in the low light of a dreary day, even in the shadows of the sprawling, unkempt gardens, it seemed to burn from within.

Her steps slowed as she examined it, fascinated by the shimmer and shine coming from within the opaque object.

A great weapon. Something strong sizzled along her arm from where she held it, up and along her shoulder, surprising her so that she almost dropped it.

Sudden crashing through the brush drew her attention away from the shard. She realized why Max had stomped off as he had, and she looked up as he came back into view. He was missing his hat, and his hair dripped dark and stringy in a face shadowed by a day's growth of beard. He looked annoyed.

No more annoyed than she felt.

"Victoria," he began, and then saw what she was holding. "What—"

But she interrupted him, stepping forward. "You're merely jealous," she said, stopping a short distance away, looking up into his sharp-planed face.

"Is that so?" He stared down at her. "You think overmuch of yourself, Victoria."

"No woman would allow you—"

His laugh was short and contemptuous. "I'm sorry to disappoint you, but I've never been one to practice celibacy, forced or otherwise. I'm merely selective in choosing my . . . companions. You've seen evidence of it yourself, so how can you doubt?" Sudden as a snake, his hand shot out and closed around the wrist of her hand that held the shard.

Victoria laughed, a deep, odd sound to her ears. "You speak of the time I saw you and Sara leaving a room, all in dishabille. I wouldn't put it past you to have staged such a scene; you were so determined to run me off."

"And showing you evidence of the affection I had for my fiancée would have served to chase you away? If only it had been that simple." He squeezed her wrist, smashing the bones horribly against one another, and pain shot through her hand. "Drop it, Victoria."

"Affection for Sara Regalado? You couldn't have felt anything for her." Her fingers were weakening under his grip, becoming numb and cold. She tried to jerk her arm away, but he moved too quickly and caught at her wrist with both hands. He was strong, very strong. She had two *vis bullae*, and she struggled against him.

"I'll break your arm if need be. Release it."

"You'd do it, too," she spat, anger blazing through her.

"I would." He tightened his grip, his face, his tall body

much too close to hers, his eyes dark and intense, his mouth determined. "Let it go, Victoria."

With a groan she allowed her screaming fingers to open, and the heavy shard tumbled from her hand. It thunked to the ground, landing next to her foot, and before she could reach down to pick it up, Max kicked it out of her reach.

Still holding her wrist, he drew her back up to look at him, grasping her other shoulder so he could glare down into her face. He gave her a little shake, his fingers so tight she could feel them through the heavy wool coat as they bit into her skin.

Though she had dropped the shard, her hand still felt its warmth, and a faint tingle still sputtered along her arm and through her body. She looked up into his eyes, and again she knew just what to say to goad him.

"Are you going to kiss me now?" she asked boldly. He released her with a little shove that pushed her a step back into the branch of a tree, sending a little scatter of drops down the back of her coat's collar.

"I prefer not to be one in a long line."

"What are you afraid of, Max?"

Then he smiled. It wasn't a nice smile at all, but it matched the same unpleasant feeling that was skittering through her. "So you want me to kiss you, do you, Victoria?"

His expression made her want to take a step back, but she stood firm. "Why not?"

The warmth from the shard had eased from her hand, and her fingers felt cold. He moved closer, and she felt the brush of ivy leaves that clung to the wall behind her.

"Why not . . . indeed."

As he loomed over her, powerful and tall and so close, Victoria's heart began to pound as if it were trying to burst from her ribs. Her lungs were so tight in her chest it seemed she could barely draw in a breath, but when she did she brought in the smell of Max—his damp wool coat, the faint smell of wine, and whatever it was that made him who he was.

She felt the brush of the stones behind her, her fingers pushing back into the wall as if to help keep her steady.

Then, hands planted on either side of her head, far enough away that they didn't touch her, he bent forward, his dark head filling all of her sight before her eyes closed and his lips covered hers.

Max kissed like he did everything else: with arrogance, grace, and consummate skill.

He wasn't the least bit tentative. There was no light brushing of mouth to mouth as if to test the waters, to sample her taste, or to allow her to twist away if she should have changed her mind.

Nor was it a plunder, the staking of a claim, a long-withheld passion released.

It was . . . it was Max. Just Max.

He was strong and sensual and very thorough. If she'd ever thought of his lips as stubborn or harsh, that thought was eliminated as their mouths fit together, drew apart, and parted in a sleek, choreographed motion, again and again, until it was all one smooth, slick spiral, curling down into the pit of her belly and beyond.

Her fingers were digging into the wet, dirty wall, and she let her trembling knees relax enough so she could sag gently back against it to keep her balance. Even so, there was still space between them; she sensed the warmth of his nearness in the chill afternoon, but touched nothing but his mouth matching and meeting hers.

When he at last pulled away with a long, gentle nibble at the corner of her lower lip, his nose brushing her cheek, she let her head tip back and felt the wetness of the leaves seep into her hair. Max shifted, his breath warm against her temple as he bent toward her again.

"Now that your curiosity is assuaged," he murmured, "can we get on with our task?"

And with that he pushed away from the wall, away from her, and, presenting her with his back, crouched to pick up the forgotten shard. He had it up and quickly in his pocket before Victoria had quite caught her breath or thought to demand the splinter back.

Her fingers trembled and her knees were wobbly, but she propelled herself away from the wall before he stood—or turned to see the dazed look on her face.

But she needn't have worried; he barely glanced at her before making that sharp Max gesture that told her to follow him. "We've wasted enough time. It's getting close to sunset," he tossed over his shoulder as he started off again along the stone wall.

The same stone wall of which there were now little bits of mortar wedged beneath her fingernails.

Sixteen

In Which Lady Melly's Courtship Takes on a New Twist

The *Conte* Regalado, or Alberto, as he'd insisted she call him, was the most charming man Lady Melisande Grantworth had had the pleasure to meet. Or be courted by.

And she was indeed being courted by the bald but dapper Italian count.

The first time she'd met him, when he had found her and Winnie and Nilly in the depths of that spooky old villa, he'd been gallant and gracious—and even though he hadn't actually taken them to find the treasure and had disappeared most inexplicably, he'd still been intriguing and kind.

And well turned. Indeed, perfectly groomed, with his small, trimmed black mustache and the briefest of beards. His clothing was expensive and fashionable, he wasn't too tall, and best of all, he had a lovely accent.

Then, of course, there was the day following the treasure hunt at the Villa Palombara, when, instead of calling on her, he'd only sent flowers . . . that had had her sniffing in disdain. The men in London had done the same; even Jellington had thought to woo her interests by plying her with flowers and jewels and the like.

But Lady Melly desired much more than cold fripperies and greenery that would die after a day or two in a vase. She wanted companionship, and wit, and above all, a man who worshiped her.

"He should be here any moment." Nilly squealed, her pale face flushed with excitement. She was peering out the window of Melly's dressing room from between lacy curtains, watching the street below for a sign of the *conte*'s barouche as her friend was putting the final touches on her toilette.

"I cannot imagine where he is going to take you on such a horrific afternoon. Why, there isn't a sunbeam to be seen, and the air is positively gray with rain," Winnie said disdainfully from her chair in the corner. "Your hair will be droopy, and those bonnet feathers! They'll be plastered to your head before you climb into his carriage."

"The *Conte* Regalado offered to drive me to see the Colosseum, and perhaps to Janiculum Hill. I am certain, though we might be a bit chilly, that we shan't be wet at all."

"The *conte*? I thought you were to call him Al*berrrr*to." Winnie sniffed, but a smile hovered about her lips.

"Alberto, then." But Melly smiled at the mirror, admiring her dimples as well as the slight pink to her cheeks.

"He's here!"

Winnie hauled herself to her feet and lumbered to the window. "Indeed, he is, dressed as though he were going to the theater. Well, I hope you shall return before supper tonight so that we can hear all of the details before bedtime."

"And I," said Melly, flouncing toward the door as if she were once again a young debutante, "hope I don't." She paused to look back at them. "After all, I am a widow, we aren't in London, and he is . . . very handsome. Perhaps we shall take an extended drive."

Nilly squealed again, but this time with disappointment. "Don't frighten him away, Melly!"

Winnie laughed. "The poor man hasn't a chance with our Melly on his trail," she said fondly, watching her oldest and dearest friend sweep down the stairs with more energy than she herself had ever possessed. "I only hope this turns out better than the last matchmaking she did—with Victoria and Rockley."

Nilly nodded. "But of course it will."

The two ladies were beginning to make their way down the stairs to the parlor when Victoria's maid—the one with the unfortunate bushy orange hair—appeared.

"Excuse me, madam. Your Grace," she said, bobbing a curtsy.

Startled that she should have spoken to them, the two women swiveled their heads in unison.

"Yes?" asked Winnie in her duchess voice, pausing on the stairs, one hand clutching the handrail.

"I don' mean to interrupt," said the maid with a bit less deference than Winnie would have expected. "But . . . did ye say that Lady Melly was going with a *conte*?" Regalado's title came out sounding like "con-tayy," but Winnie knew what the bold-faced girl meant.

"Yes." Again the imperious duchess tone.

"Oh, dear . . . the *Conte* Reg'lado?"

"Yes!" Winnie was becoming impatient. "If you have something to say, spit it out. I cannot stand here all the day long. It's nearly time for tea."

"Oh . . . Your Grace . . . Lady Melly is in grave danger." The maid's eyes were sparkling blue, and her round cheeks were flushed pink.

"Why, what do you mean?" Nilly spoke at last in a soft little sort of gasp.

"The Contay Reg'lado . . . why, we must help my lady!" As if suddenly galvanized into action, she whirled, starting down the hall in the opposite direction.

Lady Winnie's imperative voice stopped her. "Young miss, I daresay you'd best not run off without telling us exactly of what you're speaking!"

"Beggin' yer pardon, Your Grace, but milady's in great danger, an' we have to help her," she said over her shoulder, then opened the door to Victoria's bedchamber and dressing room. She disappeared inside, disregarding the other women.

"Danger? From what?" Winnie didn't want to believe the little maid, but when she came back out of Victoria's bedchamber holding something that looked like a wooden stake, her heart nearly stopped.

"What are you doing with that?" asked Nilly faintly.

The maid was slipping on a large silver cross. "I'm goin' vampire huntin'."

Zavier waited in the heavy afternoon drizzle, a hat he would normally disdain tipped low over his face to keep the rain from getting in his eyes. The chankin and wet didn't bother him at all; growing up in the Highlands, he'd had enough of it so that he'd become immune. The hat, something with a curling brim a London numpty would wear to protect his sensitive skin, served another purpose altogether: to keep his face from being seen.

He wasn't certain how long he'd have to wait. Despite the miserable weather, his worst discomfort came from the memories that plagued him, since he had nothing to do but think about things as he stood there, tucked into a nook between two narrow plastered buildings.

The carnage was bad enough . . . the image of Mansur

sprawled on the brown grass, drenched in his dark blood, made Zavier's own blood churn and his stomach swish as though he were drunk from too much whiskey.

A waste. A fagging bloody waste.

And a betrayal.

Victoria wasn't seeing clearly. She couldn't be. She wasn't weak like that, and Zavier wasn't about to watch her tumble further. Aye, she'd hurt him; he could accept that, though it still burned his gut. But he couldn't accept that it had been with the arse-dicht Vioget. The boughin' bastard who couldn't dirty his hands enough to fight with his kin. Unbelievably, apparently, he was a Gardella too, from somewhere back in the ages of his family. They all were.

How could he have turned his back on them?

The arse-dicht and Victoria had been locked away for too long in the same small chamber where Vioget had been held during the battle outside Santo Quirinus. They'd been in there so long it made Zavier's fingers tighten into one another, his short, blunt nails creasing his leathery palms.

He didn't want to think about the boseying that was going on in there. But he couldn't help it.

It made his head spin as if he were rubbered.

So he took himself outside and waited in the rain, and hoped for it to help make him a bit steadier.

But the anger built inside, simmered, sometimes roaring into his ears as he remembered the deaths last night, the intimacy and the expression he saw on her face when she was with Vioget. The Venator betrayer.

He didn't believe Wayren when she said he wasn't the cause of the attack. How else could it have happened?

It was well nigh onto noon when Zavier sighted his quarry. He waited until he walked past, head foolishly bent against the rain so that he didn't notice when Zavier slipped from the corner of a building to follow.

Fool.

Perhaps it was best that he'd stayed away from the Venators if he was that careless.

Zavier stayed in the distance behind him, considering his options. He knew little about Vioget, but what he did know was enough to identify the influence behind the bastard and his defection: the legendary Beauregard.

Zavier's hand searched the depths of his pocket, fumbling for the stake there. It was just about time that the vampire met his own damnation. He'd be pleased to help him. And whoever else dared get in his way.

"Where is the key?" Max asked as Victoria approached. Her skirts were drenched to her knees and so were her shoes. She should have found a pair of boots to wear before leaving the Consilium, but it was too late now.

They had reached the stone wall on which the Door of Alchemy stood, after traipsing quickly through the tangled gardens with Max in the lead. He'd seemed to be in a great hurry to get here, and Victoria, who couldn't quite tell where the sun was because of the clouds, didn't argue. She was still more than a bit unsteady from the kiss they'd shared.

Although *shared* wasn't exactly the word to describe the experience. *Received*, perhaps. Became immersed in. Was surprised by. Nearly lost her balance because of.

"Victoria."

She snapped her attention back to the matter at hand, realizing he'd asked a second time. "It's here." She had to shrug out of her heavy man's coat in order to get to the armband, which was pushed up under the long sleeve of her simple gown.

Max watched as she pulled off the wide silver armband and then bent it at the small hinge that divided its two halves. When the bracelet opened, the key was there on the inside of the cuff, fitted into a small nook.

Victoria thumbed it out and handed it to Max, who kept looking darkly at the sky. "Let's hurry," he said, taking the tablike key and pushing the scrubby bushes away from the door.

He knelt as Victoria had done a week ago, when she'd come with Ylito and Wayren, and scratched away the moss and dirt so that the small metal tab would fit into its place.

As he worked Victoria examined the other two keyholes—one had been filled before, and the other she hadn't seen until now. She could see only the back edges of the flat little keys—for once slipped into the narrow openings, the thin metal rectangles fit into place and couldn't be removed until the door was opened.

"Ah." Max pulled to his feet and glanced at her. "Shall we?"

He grasped the round stone disk in the center of the door and began to turn it. When the circle actually moved in a clockwise direction, Victoria found herself holding her breath. She couldn't quite believe the door would actually open.

There was a dull clunk, and Max glanced at her with a sharp nod. And then the door rolled to the side.

To her surprise he stepped back and let her enter first. Doing so, Victoria walked directly into a screen of cobwebs. Hiding an automatic shudder as she pushed away the stickiness, she brushed furiously at her arms and hair to make certain none of the spiders were crawling on her.

"You're afraid of spiders?" Max said, amusement coloring his voice.

"I'm not afraid . . . Ugh!" She barely held back a shriek as one danced across her hand and she whipped it to the floor. "I don't like them. They're like little vampires, sucking blood, and they have too many legs."

Once she'd cleaned herself off she stepped completely through the door and stood inside a dark chamber that smelled of age and damp. But she needn't have feared, for just at the edge of the doorway was a sconce. Below it was a small tin kettle and a little table with flint and a coil of very old thread to start a flame.

There was oil in the kettle, she presumed, and she lifted it off its hook, pouring it onto the dry, brittle sconce. Max stepped in to help light a small piece of tinder, and only moments after the door was opened they had a blazing torch.

"Let's close the door," she said. The back of her neck wasn't chilled, but it was best to take no chances. She had no idea how long they would be here.

The stone door rumbled back into its place, and Max said, "Bring the light here. I think we can remove the keys from the inside."

She did, angling it over his shoulder as he bent toward the inside of the middle of the door. A few quick movements, the dull scrape of stone on stone, followed by a small grunt, and he produced the little silver key they had just slipped into its place on the outside of the door.

"Clever . . . so that one cannot get locked inside," he said. She held the light and he removed the other two keys—one in gold and one in bronze—and slipped them into his pocket.

Then he stood and they were facing each other in the small circle of light dancing around the dusty chamber.

"Let me have the shard," she said, resisting the urge to step away even as her lungs constricted.

"No. Didn't you learn anything from last time?"

Victoria bristled, drawing herself back to argue, but he reached out, captured her left wrist, and said, "Look."

He lifted her hand, palm up, and brought it into the light.

When she uncurled her fingers Victoria saw with a shock that the inside of her hand—the one that had held the shard—and her fingers were marked faintly with blue.

"What is it?" she said, handing him the sconce and opening her other hand to compare. When she saw that the bluish cast on the skin that had gripped the shard was no trick of the low light, she tried to rub it away.

"When the obelisk touches flesh for any length of time, its power begins to seep in, leaving such a mark. If you're lucky it may fade in time." He looked at her, his dark eyes flat and hard. "Don't touch it directly again. Or who knows whom you'll beg to kiss the next time."

And he turned away, taking the sconce with him, leaving Victoria with burning cheeks and a flood of annoyance . . . and embarrassment. Beg?

Beg?

But he'd wanted to. She'd seen it in his eyes.

Giving her head a little shake, Victoria turned around to look at the chamber for the first time and saw now that it wasn't a small chamber at all. The room was quite large and had been set up as a well-equipped laboratory. The single torch that Max held did little to light the room, but when Victoria saw another sconce on the wall she moved to light that one, and its illumination showed more details: long tables, five or six stools of varying height and condition, utensils, and scatterings of metal shavings and curds. There were shallow wooden bowls, deep metal ones, round and softly triangular, large and small. Goblets, corked jars, tiny carved boxes were all littered about, covered with dust, and some of them with dark stains. Larger chunks of silver, bronze, copper, iron, quartz, and marble were piled on the tables or littered on the floor, which was filthy with dust, dirt, and most definitely animal droppings.

She walked along one of the tables flanking the wall,

quickly examining the remains of *Marchese* Palombara's alchemical experiments for whatever it was the undead—and others—wanted so badly. But there was nothing that caught her eye, nothing that looked important enough to be notes or journals about the mysterious pilgrim's work.

As she turned to look at another of the worktables, her wet slippered foot knocked against something on the floor. It made a soft metal clink, and she would have disregarded it as just another piece of scrap metal if it hadn't rolled in front of her, spinning in smaller circles until it spiraled to a halt. Victoria bent to pick it up, the hair on the back of her arms lifting.

She'd seen this . . . something like this before.

It was a band—similar to Aunt Eustacia's plain silver armband that had held the silver key—but this was made of copper, and it was more distinctive. While Aunt Eustacia's ornament had been solid silver, as wide as three fingers, this band was made of three tendrils of copper, each perhaps the width of a finger and woven into a solid band. A smooth, elliptical shape had been formed where the ends of the three copper strands merged together, as if they'd been melted down and pressed flat. A symbol was etched into it.

One she'd seen before. Somewhere.

"Ah. And here we find our friend the *Marchese* Palombara," Max commented from across the room, drawing Victoria's attention.

Slipping the bracelet into her pocket, she walked over to find him standing above a skeleton, still dressed in the rotting clothes of two hundred forty years earlier. "Is that what we've come for?" she asked, noticing the yellow, curling packet of papers clutched by two bony hands. "I see nothing else that could be of interest to vampires and mortals alike."

"I would suspect." Max bent forward, the lantern casting long, eerie shadows over the gray bones of the long-dead *marchese*. When he touched the skeletal arm it fell away, bone and fabric crumbling to dust in the same way an undead disintegrated when staked. And yet . . . not.

He lifted the papers gingerly, taking care to keep them intact, and handed them to Victoria. They were sewn together by a leather cord, and, when she gently lifted the top page, she found faded ink writing, mathematical equations, and diagrams and sketches.

"Ylito will be overjoyed to see this," she commented with a smile.

"Indeed. So, now that we've retrieved what we came for, shall we get it safely back to the Consilium?"

"Were you planning to take the obelisk shard with you?" she asked sharply.

"Of course not. While you were gawking about the room like a girl at court, I've already placed it over there."

She looked and saw a small trunk in a dark corner. With a withering glance at him, she walked over and lifted the lid, still carrying the sheaf of papers. Inside the trunk was the shard of Akvan's Obelisk.

"You didn't believe me." Max's voice behind her was soft and . . . she could only describe it as menacing.

"You of all people ought to understand duty," she replied coolly, looking at him. "I needed to make certain that the evil that I brought upon the Consilium has been contained. I needed to see for myself."

He gave a short nod, and when he replied there was satisfaction in his voice. "You've begun to learn, Victoria."

She started to turn away and noticed that his dark shirt, which was cravatless, had gaped away from his throat. "Those are new bites."

His hand jerked slightly, as though he'd begun to raise it to close his collar and stopped himself in time. "Unfortunately."

"Was Sara right? Did you go to Lilith?"

"Let's go. We're wasting time."

"Why would you do such a foolish thing?"

He spun away as if to start to the door, and she reached out and grabbed his arm. Hard. "Max."

His muscles flexing under her fingers, he turned back, his expression flat except for furious eyes. "Yes, I went to Lilith. Yes, she left me with yet more marks of her possession." This last word came out with rank bitterness. "Why it can make any difference to you, or to our current task, is not clear to me. Let's go."

"Alone? With her? Surrounded by all her guards? Max, she could have killed you." She couldn't let it go; she couldn't drop the subject. How could he risk himself that way?

What would have happened if he'd not come back?

Or . . . worse? *Dear God.*

At her rapid questions he paused and looked down at her. Now his eyes were bleak. "You understand nothing of her, do you? Victoria, if I were to give you one last piece of advice, it would be this: Find out who Lilith *is*, or she will beat you as she has beaten so many others before." He pulled firmly away and started toward the massive stone door.

Victoria followed, anger still spiking through her. He was so high-handed, so reticent. So cold and removed. Why did he still act that way, treat her like a naive girl, after all they'd accomplished together?

He had the door open before she reached him, and the pale gray that came through the crack was ominous in its dimness. The sun was nearly down, and Max was right— they needed to get the papers safely back to the Consilium before Akvan or his followers realized they'd come and gone from the very chamber the demon had been trying to gain access to.

Just as she was about to walk through the door, where Max waited on the other side, Victoria remembered the leather cord in her pocket, and its small splinter of obsidian. Although she had considered keeping it as a potential way to draw Akvan out of his lair, after what Max had shown her in regard to its power, she realized it would be foolhardy to take that chance.

No one could say she didn't learn from her mistakes. Even Max.

But when she reached into the small breast pocket of her man's coat, it was empty. Empty! The cord had fallen out somehow . . . sometime since she'd left the Consilium.

It had to have been, she realized, when she removed her coat just outside the Door of Alchemy in order to take off Aunt Eustacia's armband. The necklace must have fallen on the ground then, when she slung the coat over her arm and worked the bracelet down from her upper arm. It had to be on the ground outside.

"Are you coming?" Max, at the door, sounded impatient as usual.

She didn't respond, but instead, with one last look about the laboratory, she slipped out through the narrow opening. It was going to be difficult to find in the lowering light, but they would have to try. She couldn't leave it for someone else to stumble upon. "Max, I—"

"Shh!" he hissed suddenly, coming to attention.

She would have heard it too if she hadn't been focused on the loss of the little splinter: a crashing in the brush very nearby. Coming vaguely from the direction of the villa, it was loud enough to portend either a cluster of newcomers, or a very large, very careless person.

And then Victoria heard voices. Shrill voices, raised much too loudly in argument.

Her entire body went cold and then rigid.

And it wasn't because there was a vampire sending a chill over the back of her neck; indeed, there weren't any undead in the near vicinity.

No, this was much worse.

Max's face changed from one of arrested expectation to one of confusion. If Victoria hadn't been so disconcerted, she might have found it amusing. As it was, she started toward the noise just as something—someone—blundered through a pair of overgrown bushes spreading over an old path.

". . . daresay, you should have stayed home, Nilly! That little stick— Oh!" Lady Winifred, the Duchess of Farnham, shambled to a halt so quickly that her companion plowed into her from behind, sending her curls and jowls jouncing. The reticule-size silver cross around her neck bounced into the air, then thunked heavily onto the duchess's bosom. "Victoria, what on earth— Oh! Oh, my!"

"Oh!" squeaked Lady Nilly, peering from behind the duchess's broad shoulder.

Victoria had stepped toward them, followed by Max—whose dark look had been the catalyst for their choked gasps.

"Stand back," Lady Winnie said fiercely, brandishing an unwieldy wooden pike the length of her forearm and thick as her wrist. She aimed the pointed end at Max. "Has he hurt you, Victoria? One further step, and—"

"Did he bite you?" asked Lady Nilly, her voice breathless and her eyes so wide that white appeared all around her irises. "Did it hurt?"

"What are you two doing here?" Victoria asked, gently taking the duchess's wrist and lowering the ridiculous stake.

"We're hunting vampires," replied Lady Winnie in a stage whisper, still eyeing Max balefully. "You poor dear. I don't mean to frighten you, but I'm certain that man is a vampire."

"He's not a vampire," Victoria told her, trying to keep her lips from twitching. A quick glance at Max told her he was not finding the situation amusing in the least. "Although I can understand the mistake."

The sound he made could only have been described as a growl. "Victoria, it's nearly dark," he said, warning in his voice.

"Indeed. Duchess Winnie," she said, using her pet name for the woman, "what on earth are you doing here?"

Suddenly there was more crashing in the bushes—although, to give her a bit of credit, it wasn't quite so ferocious as that from before—and a puff of orange hair appeared, followed by the flushed-cheeked face of Verbena.

"Beggin' yer pardon, my lady," she said to Victoria, giving a brief curtsy. "I tried t'keep 'em from doin' it—"

"Hmph." Winnie sniffed. "If it weren't for her, we would be back sipping tea and preparing for dinner."

"What are you all doing here?" Max thundered.

Lady Nilly squeaked, her eyes popping again. Lady Winnie drew herself up bravely, but scuttled back a few steps as she closed her fingers around the crucifix, brandishing it like a talisman.

"A bit on th' huffy side," Verbena said to Victoria, casting a glance at Max. She must have seen the impatience in her mistress's own expression, for she hurried on. "Lady Melly's been taken off by th' *Conte* Regalado. 'E's been courtin' her, milady, an' I didn't know until t'day when I heard 'em talkin' about it."

"Regalado has my mother?" Cold fear rushed through her, and her mouth dried. *No,* was her first thought. *No. Not again. Not like Phillip . . .*

Verbena nodded vigorously. "An' the ladies there—they

d'cided t' come wit' me when I come 'ere to see to 'er." Now she produced her own stake, which, again to her credit, was much more of a comfortable size. And it looked a bit familiar, with its pink sequins and the remnant of a white feather still attached to the blunt end.

"When did they leave? How long have they been gone?"

"N'more than two hours," Verbena replied earnestly. "He said he'd take 'er for a drive. Th' ladies 'ere thought he'd bring 'er h'ere, if he was gonna—y'see—hurt 'er, and since they'd been here for that party, they insisted on coming wi' me."

Her mother, in the clutches of Regalado. The thought made Victoria's insides churn like a sea storm.

She focused her sharp mind, pushed away the worry that threatened to turn her senses frantic.

Were they at the villa? If so, it was a blessing that she was already here herself . . . but there were any number of places he could have taken her. Victoria realized Max was looking at her, that he'd stepped closer, almost as if to offer assistance. He'd help her comb through the villa, go with her to delve down into the underground lair of Akvan and search for her mother.

Victoria looked directly at him, her veins singing and her mind working furiously, and pushed the numbing worry back. She could fret later. It was getting darker by the moment. She made her decision in that instant.

"You'll have to take that back to . . . back," she finished firmly, looking at the bundle of papers he still had. "I'll see to my mother."

He looked as though he might argue, but it was only for a moment. Then he nodded. "It's important that we get this safely to Wayren," he said.

"Take them with you," Victoria added, gesturing to the

ladies, feeling the brittleness in her movements. "I don't need them—"

"I ain't leavin' ye alone, milady," Verbena said, stepping toward her.

"I daresay, you cannot think to order me about," said Lady Winnie, looking down her humped nose at Victoria. "Melly could be in danger! I shall not rest until—"

"Shh!" Victoria snapped to attention as the rush of a chill moved over the back of her neck. She and Max exchanged glances; he felt it too. "Go," she told him, gesturing toward the rear of the estate grounds, where the darkness seemed to be growing even faster. He would go out the way he and Victoria had come in.

With a last, steady look, followed by a sharp nod, he disappeared soundlessly into the overgrowth, leaving Victoria with three ill-prepared would-be vampire hunters.

Seventeen

Wherein the Merits of Italian Desserts Are Discussed After an Eventful Evening

Pulling the stake out of her pocket, Victoria edged along the wall in the direction of the villa.

The chill on the back of her neck wasn't alarming in its intensity; she guessed there were no more than three undead in the vicinity. Whether one of them was Regalado, with Lady Melly, she would soon find out. She prayed, firmly keeping her thoughts from worrying that one of them was . . . and terrified that it wouldn't be.

Stake gripped comfortably, she slipped between some sort of prickly bush and the old stone wall, peering around its corner. The light had grown very dim, so she could see little more than shapes of blue and black and gray. But then she noticed a faint red glow in the distance: vampire eyes.

They disappeared. Either the creature had turned away or was now hiding. In either case, Victoria was not about to let the undead get away. She moved quickly and as quietly as the sagging branches and soggy grass would allow, peering into the darkness and wishing, once again, that one of the Venator powers was night vision.

A woman screamed in the distance—or tried to, before it was quickly muffled—and that set Victoria off more rapidly and carelessly through the brush. It didn't sound like Melly . . . but, then again, Victoria had heard her mother scream only once, when a mouse had the audacity to scamper across her dressing room table.

She moved toward the sounds of struggles ahead, refusing to let herself contemplate what she might—or might not—find.

One step at a time. One battle at a time.

She ran along the side of the sprawling villa, between it and the tall enclosing wall that ran around the entire estate, toward the front, along overgrown paths and beneath unpruned trees. More screams and shouts from beyond gave her a burst of speed, and when she came near the front of the building, Victoria nearly ran into a bench that had been hidden in the lengthening shadows.

Swerving just in time to avoid cracking her leg against it, she paused, breathing heavily, and saw the cluster of moving shadows ahead. They were anonymous; she couldn't tell if one of the struggling figures was her mother. She could see six of them: three pairs of red eyes—pure red, none of them the pink of Guardians or the magenta of Imperials, fortunately—and the three pale, frightened faces of their victims, thrashing about as they were dragged toward the front entrance of the villa as if they'd just arrived.

Victoria burst from the darkness and rushed one of the red-eyed vampires. The undead looked up in surprise, then delight, then shock as she saw the stake in Victoria's hand. The female undead released her victim and roared forward, blocking the stake's downward stroke with her forearm and grasping Victoria's wrist.

Cursing herself for getting stopped by such an unoriginal move, Victoria lobbed the stake to her free hand, jerked forcefully with her other, and yanked the vampire toward her as she reached around to stab the undead's heart through the back.

The vampire poofed, blasting dust over Victoria's arm, and she spun slickly in the mud to face the others. Her foot slipped, but she caught herself in time to duck a blow from a male undead and again swiveled around to come at her target from behind, slamming the stake into the center of his back.

Just as he disintegrated into dust, the third vampire released his victim, shoving the sobbing woman to the side so hard that she tumbled to the ground. He faced Victoria, and she saw that he had a large, broken branch in his hand. With a mighty swipe he flung it whistling through the air, and it slammed into her shoulder hard enough to send her staggering back.

But she wasn't down, and Victoria caught herself against a wet, prickly bush just as Verbena and Lady Winnie burst onto the scene. What came next happened so rapidly that Victoria wasn't certain exactly how the events unfolded . . . but the next thing she knew, her target was blocked by the wide skirts covering the behind of the Duchess of Farnham . . . there was a sudden shriek of pain from the vampire . . . a flurry of activity, a splash, and then . . . suddenly . . . the satisfying *poof!* of the undead imploding into dust and ash.

And then there was nothing but the quiet sobbing of the woman—who, horribly, wasn't Lady Melly—and the gasping of breaths from the other would-be victims, a man and a second woman, who, from the looks of their clothing, were returning from an evening out.

Victoria stalked over to the scene of the last vampire's death and found Lady Winnie clutching the hand-size cross to her pillowlike bosom. "I . . . he . . . " She wheezed, her little pig eyes goggling like shiny marbles.

"I tol' ye, ye got to stab 'em in the *heart*, not the eye!" Verbena was lecturing the duchess, hands on her hips, chin raised high in the air. "Was a good thin' 'e saw your cross an' I had the chance t' throw this on 'im!" She produced a small bottle Victoria knew had held holy water.

A convenient substance, of course, and one that Victoria tended to forget to take with her more often than not, unless her maid reminded her of it.

"Now you must go," Victoria said firmly. "I have to find Lady Melly if she's here, and you can finish your good deeds"—she looked reproachfully at Verbena—"and help these poor people get home safely."

"But you cannot stay here alone," Lady Winnie argued. She had regained control of her breathing and, along with it, her stubbornness. "It's much too dangerous! And although it really isn't difficult at all to stake the monsters, I cannot in good conscience leave you here alone."

Victoria's annoyance was growing by the moment, along with the rising frantic need to get away from the babbling women and search for her mother.

She wished for her aunt Eustacia's special golden disk, which helped to remove unwanted memories from people who shouldn't have them—such as would-be vampire hunters or near victims of the undead. Such an item would have come in handy now, although it would have taken time that she didn't have.

No time. She had no time to waste.

"You must go," Victoria insisted, much more harshly than she'd ever spoken to the ladies. "Take these people and go before you get hurt yourself."

"Victoria!" Winnie sounded perfectly righteous and angry. "How dare you speak—"

"I dare because I must!" A blaze of frustration, fear, and anger blew through her, and she rounded on the plump duchess, her entire mind focused on where her mother was and what Regalado was doing to her. The back of her neck was no longer cold—which meant nothing good, in her mind, for that meant there were no vampires in the vicinity—so Regalado was either not at the villa, or was so deeply inside it that she couldn't sense his presence.

Victoria started to tell her again that they had to leave, when she suddenly realized Lady Nilly wasn't there. Anywhere. She whirled away from the slack-jawed duchess, scanning the area and seeing nothing of the stick-figured Lady Petronilla.

"Lady Nilly!" she said, streaking back into the darkness. Her neck wasn't cold, so she couldn't be . . .

Lady Winnie and Verbena crashed along behind Victoria, sounding like an entire coach and four tearing through a forest. Victoria was thankful she didn't have to go far, for several yards into the brush back toward the Door of Alchemy she found Lady Nilly walking toward her. The older woman was glowing, thin and pale, like a moon in the darkness, for by now the air was charcoal gray decorated with black shadows everywhere.

"Nilly!" shrieked Winnie, barreling past Victoria, stake in hand. "How dare you frighten us like that!"

But there was something wrong. Victoria's hands went cold as she came closer to Nilly and saw the dark streaks on her neck.

"She's been bitten," Verbena exclaimed before Victoria had a chance to say anything.

Nilly's eyes were wide and glassy, and a faint smile curved her mouth. Her hair, which was normally kept in a strictly smooth bun at the back of her crown, with two precise curls hanging from her temples, was loose and full and falling about her shoulders and past them.

"Nilly!" Before Victoria could get to her, Lady Winnie took her friend by the arms and gave her a rough shake, and to the relief of everyone, Lady Nilly's eyes fluttered.

Her lips parted, lifted at the corners, and she sighed. "Yes." She smiled. "I'm sorry, Winnie," she added, reaching for her friend.

"Don't," Victoria said sharply. A mortal couldn't be turned to a vampire that quickly . . . as far as she knew. The vampire had to drain most of the victim's blood, and then offer their tainted blood for the victim to drink to replace the loss of her own. And then the victim would fall into unconsciousness and awaken as an undead. Clearly not enough time had elapsed for that to have occurred with Lady Nilly.

Nevertheless, Victoria was taking no chances. And before she could speak, Verbena had already pulled out another vial of holy water. If, when she poured it on Lady Nilly's flesh, she screamed in agony, Victoria knew it was too late for her mother's friend.

Her mother. *Dear God.*

Victoria snatched the holy water from Verbena and splashed it over the older woman's wounded neck. She shrieked in surprise and indignance, but not in pain. Not in pain.

Thank Heaven.

"Take her home. Now." She looked at Verbena and then at Lady Winnie, and they both seemed to realize there would be no arguing. "Is Oliver here?"

"I told 'im t'wait in th' carriage," Verbena replied as they started walking back toward the house. "He wanted to come wi'us, but I told him someone had to wait there—'specially if we 'ad to leave quick."

Fortunately Victoria's neck still wasn't cold when they approached the front of the deserted villa. The three others she'd rescued from the vampires were huddled against the gate, backed into a corner. One of the women gasped as Victoria and her companions came into view, but Victoria ignored her.

"The gate's locked," said Verbena, stopping there.

"Move." Victoria realized she'd begun to sound like Max, with her blunt, terse commands—ironic, but she had no time for gentle manners. She got to the gate, saw the metal lock that had obviously been secured after her mother's companions had come through, and she started to pull on it.

That was when she heard the sound of an approaching carriage, and at the same moment her neck chilled.

Victoria froze for an instant; then with a jerk of her hand she sent the others scuttling into the shadows. Maybe . . . just maybe . . .

She adjusted the grip on her stake, eased herself into the darkness, and waited.

The carriage rumbled to a halt in front of the gates, bringing with it the faintest bit of light from its lantern, filtering through the iron bars. Victoria's heart began to pump harder. It was possible.

Her fingers tightened, her breath quickened, and she waited.

The sound of someone alighting from the barouche—a woman, she was certain, based on the faint rustle and swish—spiked Victoria's hope. If it was her mother, and she was still . . .

A titter, a coy one that Victoria would never have attributed to Lady Melly, tinkled over the night air, and a surge of relief swept over her. Odd as it sounded, it was definitely her mother.

The metal lock clinked at the gate, and Victoria eased

flatter against the damp wall, realizing suddenly that her toes were like tiny pieces of ice inside her soggy slippers . . . but she didn't care. Her mother was here.

Only a moment more . . .

The chain fell away and the gates swung open. Lady Melly came into view, her arm slipped through the elbow crook of none other than the *Conte* Regalado, she looking like a fresh young woman strolling along with her beau, he with his bare head shining in the dim light.

Before Victoria could make a move, something—some-one—pushed past her in a froth of skirts and lace and with an unwieldy stake.

"Let her go!" pronounced Lady Winnie, as though she were a patroness at Almack's, refusing to let a debutante dance a third dance with the same man.

Regalado turned to the duchess, his even white teeth sud-denly gleaming in a charming smile. "Why, if it isn't your friend, my dear Melly. Have you come to join us?"

Her mother had given him permission to call her by her Christian name? Already?

Victoria gave herself a little shake of the head at the ab-surdity of her thought; perhaps it was the sense of relief that her mother was alive and well that had sent her mind scut-tling to such a thing. Well, they were no longer in London, and they certainly had other things to concern themselves with besides the codes of propriety.

"Winnie! My heavens! What on earth are you doing here?"

"Well, now, my dear, we had a bit of a fright, 'tis all," replied the duchess in a calm voice. She surreptitiously tucked the stake behind her skirts.

Victoria saw no reason to wait for them to politely dis-cuss the situation, as they were wont to, so she stepped out

of the shadows. When Regalado saw her, the menacing edge
to his smile slipped.

"Good evening, *Conte*," Victoria said. "Mother."

"Victoria!" Her mother's voice was understandably shrill
and horrified. "What is the meaning of all this?"

Victoria had no choice but to ignore her, although she knew
she would pay for it later. Her ears began to ring in prepara-
tion. Unless she could get Wayren to use Aunt Eustacia's
golden disk, what she was about to say and do would shock
her mother far more than her unexpected—and unladylike—
appearance.

But brevity was necessary, for she had neither the wish
nor the patience to spend several minutes churning through
an explanation and its unavoidable discussion. "Regalado,
because you've managed to keep your fangs off my mother
thus far, and obviously she's had a lovely evening in your
company, I'll allow you a choice: Release her, or I'll turn
you into a pile of dust."

Regalado nearly leaped from Melly's side in his haste to
comply. "Of course, my dear. Of course. I meant no harm.
Your mother is a charming and handsome woman, I must
say. I meant no harm a'tall."

Victoria's eyes narrowed. That was a bit too easy. But . . .
her neck was still only a bit chilled—just enough to account
for Regalado's presence—and she didn't smell the horrible,
dank death-smell of any demons. Perhaps the man was just
the same repulsive, superficial coward he'd been before being
turned into a vampire.

Apparently, though the soul became mutated and malevolent in its undead form, the personality attached to it didn't
undergo any great change.

"Victoria, how *dare* you," said Lady Melly, grabbing at
Regalado's arm as if to pull it back into her possession. "I do
not know what has befallen you, but since you arrived here

in Rome, you have been not at all yourself. I cannot begin to imagine what you think you are going to accomplish by interfering—"

As her mother continued to lecture, Victoria wished desperately for Aunt Eustacia's golden disk.

The irony of the situation was that many years ago, Lady Melly herself had been called to be a Venator. She had declined the task, opting instead to marry Victoria's father, and thus not only had her mind been wiped clean of information about vampires and Venators, but all of her innate skills and Venatorial powers had been passed on to her daughter.

Regalado himself, as creepy and slimy as he seemed, also appeared to be quite disconcerted by Lady Melly's leech-like propensity. He tried to extricate himself from the woman, all the while watching Victoria with trepidation.

It was, in the end, a blessing that two more vampires arrived at that very moment; for if things had continued as they'd begun, Victoria wasn't at all certain how she would have pried her mother away from the most inappropriate of all candidates for a second husband.

But the appearance of two more undead—apparently the coachman from Regalado's barouche and a female acting, ironically, as a chaperone, perhaps?—set the next events in motion.

Unaware of the situation into which they'd entered, the newcomers bared their fangs, let their eyes light up with a red glow, and dove into the melee. Moments later, after a flurry of lace and silk and damp feathers (from Lady Melly's bonnet, after she was shoved face-first into a bush), stakes of all sizes and efficacy, along with much poofing and grunting and thunking of bulky silver crosses, there were two piles of vampire dust, three would-be victims still cowering against the wall, an indignant widow being ushered off to Oliver and his carriage, and the flapping coattails of the *Conte* Regalado as he dashed up the front steps of the villa.

Victoria wasn't even breathing hard, but she was flush with satisfaction and a feeling of well-being. Verbena wore a smug smile, and somehow her mistress had a feeling that poor Oliver was never going to hear the end of the adventure, even though he'd been relegated to stay in the carriage.

"Excuse me for one moment," Victoria said to no one in particular, eyeing the door through which the *conte* had disappeared. If he thought she was going to let him live another day to court her mother, he was severely mistaken. "Keep the carriage waiting."

She slipped away as the rest of them burrowed into the carriage, Lady Melly still screeching her outrage with her daughter and the world in general. She hadn't seen the dispatching of the vampires, for by the time she'd extricated herself from that fortuitous bush, they were nothing but piles of dust.

Victoria intended to feed her mother's ignorance by utilizing the gold disk as soon as possible.

However, she had this one last thing to take care of.

It wasn't hard for her to find the *conte*. He was under the impression that she'd allowed him to walk away a free undead, so he hadn't gone far into the villa and was peering through a side window at the ladies being helped into the carriage by Oliver.

"Curiosity killed the cat," she said as he whirled. She slammed the stake into his chest and added, "and the vampire too." His poof wasn't even especially large.

To ensure that they all returned home safely, Victoria crowded into the carriage with Lady Winnie, a pouting Lady Melly, and the dreamy-eyed Lady Nilly.

Two of the other near victims—a Miss Anne Malloren and a Mrs. Stefania Faygan, both Americans—clambered into the carriage as well. Their male companion elected to ride above with Verbena and Oliver, leaving Victoria crushed in the midst of skirts and the target of her mother's death-gaze.

There was nothing for it, however, and Victoria resigned herself to an uncomfortable—yet oh, so relieved!—ride back to the Gardella villa. Oliver had agreed to take the three others to their quarters, and until they left the carriage, at least, Victoria would be spared the lecture that was sure to come.

Instead she allowed herself to relax a bit, now that her neck was feeling normal and the carriage was moving at a rapid pace away from the horrible villa. As if unwilling to acknowledge the events of the evening, the ladies about her were chatting as if they were returning from a night at the theater. Victoria thought she heard the dark-haired Miss Malloren mention something about swimming with a shark . . . but that must have been a moment when her mind wandered and she'd misunderstood. Surely no one would be so foolish!

Although . . . when one considered Victoria's own vocation, perhaps it wasn't so crazy.

The other woman, Mrs. Faygan, who was dressed in a lovely gown of rose, decorated with matching pink pearls, seemed to be quite enamored with the Italian pasta noodles she'd become familiar with during their visit to Rome.

This launched the conversation into a direction quite distant from vampires and stakes and eerie villas . . . and the women began a heated discourse about the merits of cannoli versus English lemon biscuits.

Victoria faded in and out of the conversation, but it wasn't until they had delivered their three guests to their quarters that she realized what she'd forgotten.

The leather cord, with the splinter, was still lying somewhere in the gardens at Villa Palombara.

Eighteen

Wherein the Ruby Box Is Opened

Max stripped off his soaking clothes and slapped them over a wood-backed chair. His hair was still wet enough to plaster to his face and neck, but at least it wasn't dripping anymore, and at least it wasn't long enough to get in his eyes and mouth. He combed his fingers through the wet locks and slicked it back from his forehead and temples and over his ears.

Returning to the Consilium had taken longer than he planned. He had initially hoped to make the trip, then return to the villa in the event that Victoria needed his assistance to find her mother. But because he was carrying the alchemist's papers—or whatever it was they were—he'd decided to take no chance of being followed or spied upon and took a much more circuitous route than he would have liked. By the time he'd come dripping onto the marble floors of the Consilium, it was nearly midnight, and Wayren asked him not to go back out.

As always, it was a request, not an order. But one he could not deny.

The time had come.

He avoided looking at the small ruby box that sat on a little table next to a small lamp. It was so small, yet it beckoned. Here in this sparse room in one of the far reaches of the catacombs that attached to the Consilium—so distant and secret that no one but Wayren and Ilias, and perhaps Ylito, knew of its existence—the small ruby box was the only bit of color.

It mocked him. The life-altering box that he could no longer avoid.

The decision that was no longer his to make.

Had it ever been?

He pulled on the dry clothes Wayren had found for him, annoyed at the way they clung to his still-damp legs, hurrying because the subterranean room was chilly, and so was his skin. As he pulled on his shirt he looked down at the little silver *vis bulla*. The one that didn't really belong to him. Brushing his fingers over it, he touched the filigree cross, the impossibly dainty fingernail-size thing that hung there and gave him the power, the purpose, the exoneration he needed.

And then, with quick, nimble fingers, he slipped it out of the areola it pierced.

Immediately the strength ebbed from him. It slipped away like a quilt whipped from over a sleeping body, so suddenly that at first his fingers trembled with the loss. The bullet wounds he'd received only two nights ago, which had nearly healed, now pounded and throbbed deeply in his muscles, reminding him of what was to come. What his future would be.

Of course, he would remember none of this when he woke up.

He placed the *vis* on the little table next to a small lamp . . . and the mocking ruby box. And then, as if to counteract the blasphemous presence of Lilith's box, Max took his small leather satchel and pulled out the few items he'd stored in it.

In the morning, or whenever it was he awakened, the box, the *vis bulla*, none of it would mean anything to him. The charred satin rose, the black stake with the inlaid silver cross on the blunt end, the small glass vial of holy water, the pearl earbobs, the gold watchcase . . . the items he placed on the table. None of them.

Max looked away, annoyed that he was feeling sorry for himself. He did what he had to do. There was no question. The day he'd awakened after the tragedy into which he'd brought his family was the day he promised himself in service. For the rest of his life.

And his life was not yet over.

What would he do after this?

Max shrugged. The path would become clear. He had only to watch, and to follow it.

A knock on the door drew his attention, gratefully, from his self-pity. "Yes. Come."

Wayren entered, her gaze moving quickly over him, the items on the small table, the untouched bed. "You're ready?" she asked, still standing in the doorway.

"Have you heard from Victoria?"

Her eyes moved sharply over him, and she nodded. "Yes. She sent word by messenger bird, and asked whether you'd returned as well."

"Melisande?"

Wayren nodded again. "All are safe. Did you drink Ylito's decoction?"

Max nodded.

"Good. He claims it will ease your way—although we don't know exactly what will happen, do we? He did study the salve, Max, to determine if there was a way to use it, or alter it somehow, so that you could sever your bond with Lilith but keep your Venator powers."

"But then I would be no help in the destruction of Akvan, would I? No Venator or demon shall destroy him. And someone must."

Wayren chose to ignore his comment, replying, "I'll be here when you awaken, so that I can remind you of your task." She came into the room, closing the door behind her.

He resisted a disgusted snort and instead settled himself on the bed. She would remind him of the task he must set out to do—to somehow annihilate Akvan, and to do it as a mortal man, a non-Venator. But what he might or might not remember and know of himself when he awakened was frightening to consider.

Wayren pulled the chair next to him and opened the small cachet box. The pomade's scent—at once intriguing and horrific—wafted into the room. To his great annoyance his stomach lurched when he realized that an undercurrent of the aroma was the same rose smell that always accompanied Lilith's presence.

He closed his eyes briefly, wishing that there was another way. That he didn't have to make this choice, go through with this task, drink this cup . . . give up the life he'd built for himself, the one he'd managed to construct from the ashes of guilt and self-loathing.

She knew it, damn her. She knew this was the last thing he'd ever want to do. Ever be willing to do.

By God, she knew him too well. And he, her.

He hoped Victoria would remember his advice about Lilith. That she would learn her enemy and find a way to keep herself distant from the malevolence, the conniving, so that she could remain untrapped.

A glint of brightness caught his attention, and he willingly trod out of the depths of anger and regret and back to the present, where Wayren was holding something in front of him.

He recognized the small golden disk that spun on a web-thin chain in front of him, the lamp having been placed at such an angle that the pendant appeared to glow and glitter. The memory of Eustacia was bittersweet . . . and appropriate.

Yet it was soothing to stare at it as Wayren murmured something in the back of her throat that was just as relaxing. He tried to force himself into ease, to let it go . . . and it wasn't as difficult as he'd expected.

Cool, sure fingers smoothed over his neck and at the angle into his shoulder; the smell of roses became stronger, sickeningly stronger. He tried not to breathe too deeply, watching the golden disk, letting himself feel light.

Lighter than he'd ever felt.

But then it came to him: the ugly, evil tug, the insistent snakelike tendrils pulling at him, forcing, smothering. . . .

She was there . . . her blue eyes rimmed with glowing bloodred . . . her hair a copper nimbus around her pale, blue-veined face. He could see the delicate markings on her cheek . . . the five marks that formed a crescent shape from temple to jaw . . . the pale lips . . . one warm, one chilled like death. . . .

He fought it, fought to come out of it, just as he had before . . . tried to swim up from the deep pull of an ocean floor, an ocean of blue and glowing red, heavy and cloying, dragging him down. . . . Any moment now those lips of cold and warm would be on him . . . the smooth knife glide of sharp incisors into his flesh . . . her hands, chill and strong, over his skin—

"Max . . . Max!" A voice penetrated his delirium. He tried to listen. "Max . . ." And then somehow, through the whirl of darkness and evil, he heard the throaty murmur, the calming chant. It sliced through the lowering darkness, the enveloping horror of memory, and he allowed himself to slide back into the bath of golden light and the gentle lapping of relaxation.

There was one more thing . . . one thing he had to know. . . .

"Victoria," he managed to say, trying to focus, pulling his attention away from the gold gleam and instead to the sand-colored wall.

"She has returned . . . she's safe, Max. You can go now."

He nodded, felt his head lighten, his eyelids grow heavy. "Tell her. . . ." He couldn't speak. The words were too heavy, but his lips, sluggish and slow, formed them silently.

The scent of roses, now warm on his neck, grew stronger, suddenly putrid.

And then he let go.

It was nearly three o'clock that morning by the time Victoria extricated herself from her still-furious mother and her two twittering companions, not late at all by London Society standards, and certainly not unusual for Victoria herself. But because of everything that had occurred in the last few days, she felt utterly exhausted.

She needed to go back to find the splinter she'd dropped, but first Victoria wanted to change into warm, dry shoes and perhaps a split skirt. She'd sent Verbena to bed, neglecting to tell her of her plans to go back to the villa. Oliver could drive her. She sat down on the stool in front of her dressing table and began to strip off her soaked stockings.

Last night had been the attack near the Consilium, the deaths of Mansur and Stanislaus, along with the horrible moment when Zavier found her and Sebastian . . . and the night before that she and Sebastian and Max had been locked in the cell at Villa Palombara.

If she'd been bored and impatient a few weeks ago when she was without her *vis bulla*, now Victoria felt as though she'd been plunged back into an uncontrollable whirlwind of battles. Not to mention how forcefully she was being reminded of the impossibility of keeping one side of her life separate—and safe—from the other.

It had been a near thing, her mother and *Conte* Regalado. The very thought made Victoria's stomach lurch and churn. She could not have borne it if she'd lost a third person she loved to the vampires, especially one like her mother, who had no concept of the darkness and evil that pervaded their lives.

She had to find a better way to keep those two parts of her life safely apart. She had to keep her mother and her friends away from the vampires, and hide the fact that she was responsible for fighting them.

How had Aunt Eustacia managed? How had other Venators? Surely they all had had parents; some of them had siblings and other loved ones, either before or after they became Venators. How?

If Aunt Eustacia were there, she could ask her. It was something they'd never really talked about, even when she'd married Phillip. She knew Aunt Eustacia hadn't approved, but at the same time her aunt hadn't tried to convince her otherwise. Unlike Max, who'd argued with her and warned her every step of the way.

Why hadn't her aunt stopped her? Was it because she wanted to give Victoria the chance to try to find love—and happiness—as difficult as it might be?

At least Aunt Eustacia had provided Victoria with a means to keep herself from getting with child.

But now she was gone too.

To her chagrin Victoria's eyes filled with tears, and she felt the telltale sign of a dripping nose. She hated to cry. She was a Venator, and she'd cried more in the last few days than she had the year after Phillip died.

Died?

No. Not *died.* She had to acknowledge the truth. It hadn't been an accident. And he hadn't simply died.

She'd killed him.

She'd killed him with her naivete, her selfishness, and her bravado. Her lies.

Her lies.

And with her own hand.

A stake to the heart, as she'd done so many other times before—and since.

Blindly she reached for a handkerchief and wiped her nose, her cheeks, her chin. It was soaking when she pulled it away. In the dim light from the moon that shone through the villa window, Victoria could see her wet face reflected in the dressing table mirror. Her eyes were dark and shadowed, and her dark hair fell in horrible snarling curls around her face and neck. She looked like a Medusa. A hollow-cheeked, sad Medusa.

The only thing she had to be thankful for was that she'd killed him before he'd fed on a mortal—thus before he'd damned himself and his soul.

Suddenly, she became aware that the door of her bed-chamber had swung silently open just a bit. Just wide enough for her to see a narrow, pale face glowing in the low light.

"Lady Nilly?" Victoria asked, hastily swiping the back of her hand over the last trails of tears.

The door opened enough for the slender woman to come in, silent and thin as a wraith in her lacy white night rail. A prickle began at the back of Victoria's neck . . . not a chill, but an apprehensive sense.

"What is it?" she asked, coming to her feet, reaching automatically for one of her stakes, even though she knew . . . she *knew* Nilly was all right. But . . .

"I'd forgotten . . . I have a message for you," said the older woman, her voice oddly hollow. Her eyes were wide and luminous in her long face, her fragile hand clasped to the fabric of her wrapper, her pale hair falling behind her narrow shoulders in a ghostly shadow.

"From the one who bit you?"

"Beauregard. Master Beauregard," breathed Nilly, and Victoria saw a hint of fanaticism in her eyes. They lit like candles, her lips tipped up at the edges, and she seemed almost as if she were in a dream. "Master Beauregard . . . says . . . he has returned something that belongs to you . . . and that he expects you will return what you have . . . of his. Or . . ." Nilly's voice faded. Her words launched Victoria to her feet, suddenly scrabbling through the pockets of her man's coat. Of course! At the mention of Beauregard's name it came back to her. She pulled out the copper armband, wondering how she could have forgotten where she'd seen the etched insignia: on Sebastian's skin.

Perhaps she'd not wanted to remember seeing that mark on him.

But it was there.

"What does he have of mine?" Victoria asked as she turned back, just in time to see Lady Nilly slip silently to the floor.

She was at her side in an instant, feeling the older woman's neck on the unwounded side. Her heart was still thumping, and the odd, tense smile had faded from her lips. Reaching up onto her dressing table, Victoria fumbled for a little vial of smelling salts and pressed them under Lady Nilly's nose.

Almost immediately the woman stirred, coughed, and twisted her face away. Her eyes fluttered open. To Victoria's relief they were clear, and she seemed surprised to see Victoria.

"What are you doing?" she asked, pushing herself into a seated position.

"Are you feeling well?" Victoria asked, helping her to her feet.

"I'm quite all right. I don't know how I . . ." Lady Nilly looked around in bewilderment.

"Let me help you back to bed." Victoria did, and as they moved at a snail's pace down the hallway, she realized what Beauregard had that belonged to her.

The answer was not something she wanted to contemplate, but it was more than possible. It was likely.

After all, she'd dropped the necklace near the Door of Alchemy, and Lady Nilly had been near the door when she was bitten.

But that meant that Beauregard had been there when she was fighting the other vampires near the front of the villa.

And he'd left.

By the time she helped Nilly back into bed, she saw the faint tinge of gray in the east. The sun would be up in less than three hours, perhaps sooner. Beauregard had the necklace, so there was no need to go haring about the city tonight.

Tomorrow, in the daylight, she'd take the copper armband to Wayren and Max and see what they thought. If copper rings were important to Lilith's Guardians, what would an armband mean?

She didn't consider showing it to Sebastian, Victoria realized as she began to drop off to sleep, clothed only in her shift and with cold, bare toes. She'd shown and shared so much more with Sebastian . . . yet she wouldn't seek him out for help in relation to Beauregard.

Suddenly she was wide-awake again, staring out her window at the dark gray night.

Sebastian loved Beauregard. Last autumn he'd asked her

if, knowing how he felt about his grandfather, she'd kill him in front of Sebastian. Victoria hadn't known the answer then . . . and she didn't know it now.

She knew that Beauregard was malevolent and selfish . . . but some of Sebastian's arguments had crept into her mind and sat there, mocking her. He couldn't bear to know that his grandfather, whom he'd learned was a vampire only once he'd grown to adulthood, would be damned to Hell for eternity with the well-placed strike of a stake.

Would Victoria hesitate to place that stake because of her feelings for Sebastian?

Her fingers had grown cold. Her feelings for Sebastian were nebulous and wispy, and she dared not contemplate them now . . . perhaps ever. But surely, surely . . . they weren't strong enough to keep her from doing her duty, should the moment arise?

Of course not.

Beauregard was an undead. He deserved to die, or at least to be turned into dust and sent to wherever he must live out eternity. It was Victoria's responsibility to rid the world of vampires whenever she had the opportunity.

Nothing would keep her from her task. Not even the golden angel named Sebastian.

Victoria must have dropped off to sleep at some point in the labyrinth of her thoughts and debates, for she dreamed of things: slow, sensual, curling, arousing things . . . dark, strong, metallic, angry things . . . loud, putrid, frightening things.

She woke, not because of the dreams, she realized belatedly, but because Verbena stood over her bed. Her hands were on her shoulders, as if she'd been shaking her.

"My lady. My lady, you must awaken."

Victoria sat up abruptly, the last vestiges of the nightmares dissolving and clarity resuming in her mind. "What is it?"

Verbena handed her a small paper. It was tiny and rolled, as if it had come from the tiny container on a bird's leg. A quick glance at the window told Victoria that Myza wasn't there, waiting to bring a response back to Wayren. It was daylight, well past sunrise.

She unrolled the paper, her mouth dry. *Come at once.*

She didn't wait to change her damp, wrinkled clothes, just yanked on the man's coat she'd worn the night before and left. It took Victoria less than thirty minutes to get to the Consilium. Oliver drove her in the carriage and let her off many blocks away, after ensuring that they hadn't been followed.

Crossing herself as she dashed onto and then off the altar inside Santo Quirinus, she hurried through the secret door of the confessional, leaped lightly past the rigged middle step in the hidden hall, and ran down the revealed spiral staircase.

Ilias was waiting for her near the fountain. His face was grave, the lines next to his mouth deep and cutting. "Follow me."

She hurried behind him down a stone-cut corridor through which she'd never had cause to go before. When he stopped in front of a door and gestured for her to precede him in, she did.

As she opened the door, Hannever looked up, gave her a brief nod, and moved his short, wiry body out of the chamber as if to leave her alone.

The room was small, but well lit and warm. A rug covered the floor; a bed lined one wall. Victoria's chest felt tight as she walked in, toward the unmoving figure that lay under the blankets. Harsh breathing filled the room, as if it were the last gasps of life coming from the man on the bed.

Indeed, when she stepped closer and saw his face, smelled the blood, she knew that was exactly what it was.

The last gasps of life.

A small cry escaped from the back of her throat, and she reached out to touch him: his straggly, half-braided red hair, the brawny arm that lay crossed over his barrel chest.

"Zavier," she murmured. "What has befallen you?"

A quiet movement behind her told Victoria she was no longer alone; whether Wayren had already been in the room when she'd arrived or had just come in, she didn't know. "'Tis desperate he is," she said in her calm voice. "Ylito and Hannever have done all they can. We will know by tomorrow if he will stay with us."

"Or if we will be hanging another portrait in the gallery." Victoria's voice cracked. Not another. Not so soon. She lifted her face to look at Wayren. "What happened?"

"He went after Sebastian. And Beauregard."

Victoria's stomach dropped like a stone. "No." He wouldn't have.

Oh, God, yes, he would. She hadn't forgotten the look of betrayal on his face. The stunned hurt. The disbelief.

Was this another death that would be laid at her door?

Another that could have been prevented if she had made different choices?

Bloody hell, she'd done nothing wrong! She'd not brought Sebastian here. She'd not betrayed them.

"I do not know all that happened. . . . He was barely conscious when we found him. He said only the words 'Vioget' and 'Beauregard' . . . the rest we have surmised. But"—she gestured to the patient—"as you can see, the evidence is there."

Victoria looked again and saw that he'd shifted, revealing tears in his flesh, ribboning through his neck and down beyond the blankets. It wasn't only fangs that had caused such destruction.

Whoever—or whatever—it was had meant to leave him near death . . . yet not dead.

Enough that he would be found. But unable to be saved.

The thought plunged Victoria into burning fury. She stood, barely keeping her fingers from shaking, and made herself move slowly and deliberately . . . because if she didn't, she'd explode.

She bent, placing her hands over Zavier's head, whispered a small prayer in his ear, a plea for him to forgive and to return . . . and then placed a gentle kiss on his cheek.

When she stood, Wayren's gaze caught hers, and Victoria knew the other woman understood.

She started toward the door and was out in the corridor, just entering the empty main chamber of the Consilium, before she heard Wayren behind her.

"Victoria."

"I need to find Max," she said, pausing near the fountain, realizing that of anyone, Wayren would know where he was. She fingered the copper bracelet in her pocket. "I'm going to find Beauregard and kill him. I want him to go with me."

Victoria drew in a deep, calming breath, pushing away the fury and grief, reminding herself of Kritanu's admonishments never to let her emotions carry her away. "I need Max. Do you know where he is?"

Wayren's face did not change, but she reached out and gently grasped Victoria's arm. "There's something else you need to know."

Victoria's breath caught at the expression in her eyes. "What is it?"

"Sit down, Victoria."

Nineteen

Wherein Michalas's Other Wish Is Granted

Sebastian heard voices just in time to slip into one of the empty rooms—at least, he hoped it was empty. It would be exceedingly difficult to explain why he was lurking in the catacombs of the Consilium, near the workshop of the dark-skinned man the Venators called a hermetist.

He wasn't quite certain he could satisfactorily excuse his presence even to himself.

A little chill lifted the hair on his arm as he recognized Wayren's voice. He didn't want to be found, and he certainly didn't want to be found by her. Before yesterday's brief, un-satisfactory meeting, he hadn't seen her for years . . . but he remembered that she had a way of looking at him, at anyone, that gave the impression she could see right into their deep-est hearts.

Not that Sebastian was ashamed of what was in his deep-est heart. No, if nothing else, he had a loyalty to those he loved. Perhaps one that was inconvenient, or too strong at times, but it was all he had.

That and his good looks, which he was, of course, never shy about using to get his way.

As soon as Wayren walked past—on her way out of the workshop, and quite fortuitously accompanied by the owner of said workshop—Sebastian made a speedy, silent beeline to the closed door.

Holding his breath, he tapped the door open slightly, listening in both directions.

Silence greeted him, so he pushed harder, making a large enough gap for him to ease through.

The papers should be here—it was the logical place, and if Wayren was anything, she was logical. The hermetist—Sebastian wished he could remember the man's name—would be the one studying them, so it made sense.

The workshop was well organized: clean, neat, spare. A small pile of books rested on a slanted table, one of the tomes propped open with a curious metal object in the shape of an elongated S. Where were the journals from the villa's laboratory? Was he wrong in his assumption?

Then . . . he saw something that had to be it.

Thick brown papers, shiny, and coated with the thinnest possible layer of protective wax, bound together by a thin leather cord like a book.

Sebastian smoothed his fingers over it, then flipped quickly through the papers. He needed only the one page. Just one page, and it would hardly be missed. Especially since it had been locked away for nearly two hundred and fifty years.

But it could make all the difference to him. And Beauregard.

Ahhh.

This must be it.

He paused, quickly perusing the page. There was a drawing of an odd-looking plant—a flower, really—with a swath of petals that grew up and curled out like the inverted skirt of a woman, and a massive, upright stamen. *Amorphophallus pusillum*, read the faint script under it. And then a list of other ingredients, or so it appeared. Yes, this was most definitely it.

Carefully he tore the page from its leather moorings, trying to keep the wax cover from cracking, and taking care to make it as unnoticeable as possible. No one would see that a page was missing. Then he returned the journal to its position.

Slipping out of the laboratory as quickly as he'd eased in, he began to hurry along the corridor. This was the trickiest part now, as he traveled back up to the area where he was more likely to come across Wayren or Ilias, or, God forbid, Victoria.

Once he thought he was caught, but he managed to duck into the dark corner of an intersecting corridor in time to keep from being seen. Good thing, too, for Victoria strode by in an angry swish—he could almost feel the fury blasting from her. Fury and something else.

But she didn't see him, and she was gone in an instant.

With a relieved breath, he slid out of the darkness and followed her. For she was leaving the Consilium, and, now that he'd retrieved what he came for, so was he.

By the time Victoria reached the fresh air of the street above the Consilium, she was out of breath. Her throat was tight. The need to vomit lingered in her belly. But damned if she was going to shed tears again.

There'd been too many.

Her last conversation with Wayren, having begun with an air of desperation and determination, had ended with Victoria stunned speechless with disbelief and grief, and then great fury.

Max too?

She was filled with such blazing anger—at Beauregard, at Zavier, at Sebastian, and Max and even Wayren and Phillip and Aunt Eustacia—such blinding and numbing emotions that she blundered out onto the street several blocks from Santo Quirinus, exiting from the entrance on Tilhin that she'd used only once before. At first she didn't know where she was.

Only when she tripped over a broken step in front of the empty building she was skirting did Victoria gather herself together. She stopped and hugged herself under the coat she wore, blending into the shadows between two buildings to lean against the plaster wall . . . and mentally she pulled her thoughts, her scattering emotions, and her wayward instincts into line. She took a deep breath and closed her eyes and asked for guidance.

It was a while before she opened them, and she forced herself to focus. These were not the actions of *Illa* Gardella, this shattering of concentration, of instinct. She was glad no one had been there to see these moments of insecurity and loss.

She already knew what she had to do. And she'd hoped, planned, for Max to come with her.

But Wayren had told her it was likely she'd not see him again.

She explained that his memory of her, of them, along with his Venator powers, were gone. He'd had to do it to free himself from Lilith, and he would slip into the rest of the world to live out the remainder of his life.

He hadn't wanted to see her.

Perhaps that was the biggest blow of all.

Victoria didn't understand why . . . and yet perhaps she

did now, as she drew in long, steady breaths and focused her attention on the smattering of stars above her.

He was so proud. So arrogant and proud and confident that he didn't want her, or anyone—she needn't take it all on herself—he didn't want *anyone* to see him weak or confused.

In spite of her anger with him and his high-handed ways, she understood, after a fashion. For if she had to give up part of herself in that way, she, too would be lost.

Being a Venator had become the largest part of her. Perhaps the only part.

Victoria felt her mouth twist bitterly as she remembered how blithely she'd attended balls and soirees, fending off suitors, flirting with Phillip, alternating her courtship with him and her nighttime adventures of staking vampires. Now being a Venator defined her. Almost wholly.

There was very little left of Victoria Gardella Grantworth, debutante miss, wife—and now widow—of the Marquess of Rockley.

If she had to give that up, who would she be?

So, yes, she understood.

Now, there in the cool evening, she understood and she wept and she grew angry and determined again.

She looked up when a shadow went by, hurrying along the street in front of her.

He didn't notice her, for she was backed into the shadows in the dark, but she saw him and recognized the smooth movements, the elegant stride. She knew the tousled, curling hair and the sweep of that well-tailored coat.

The nasty feeling swirled again in her belly, making the back of her throat dry and scratchy. He'd come from the same direction as she—from Via Tilhin, on which sat the abandoned building that gave access to the Consilium. So she *hadn't* been mistaken when she thought she saw a flash of movement in that deserted corridor.

It couldn't be a coincidence that he'd been back there again. Not tonight.

Not after what had happened to Zavier and Lady Nilly. Not after what Beauregard had done.

Firming her lips, she followed.

The moment Max stirred Wayren put aside the delicate, curling manuscript she'd been studying. She slipped it into her ancient leather bag, followed by her square spectacles, and waited.

She didn't know how long it would be until Max woke, but since this was the first time he'd so much as altered his breathing, she knew it wouldn't be long. She knew she had to be on hand when he became aware. The only thing that had taken her away was when Zavier's unconscious body had been brought to the Consilium hours ago, and then Victoria's subsequent arrival.

Wayren wasn't given to sensitivity, but the recollection of Victoria's face when she'd seen Zavier, the shock, anger, and fear that had passed over her beatific countenance, would long be in her memory.

Such anger.

It worried her.

Max groaned softly, drawing her attention again. The golden disk lay on the table next to him, its chain coiled around it in serpentine fashion. He shifted again, becoming restless, his large hand rising as though to ward off something, then falling heavily onto the table, sending the lamp and the earbobs that had belonged to his sister jiggling.

Hoping to calm him, Wayren took his warm hand in her smaller ones, noticing scraped fingertips and cracked nails that looked as if he'd tried to climb a stone wall.

She knew many things of past and future, of possibility and truth, of good and evil . . . but she did not know whether

Ylito's plan would succeed. She wouldn't know until Max awakened, and she used the golden disk into which she had collected his memories.

As if she'd called him to waken, his eyes fluttered open, suddenly clear and dark. He looked around. She released his hand, watching as he curled his fingers closed.

"Max."

He looked at her, half sitting, the blankets falling to his hips. "Yes. Where am I?"

The bites were gone, she saw. His neck was smooth and clean, sweeping gracefully into powerful, broad shoulders. But he recognized his own name, seemed comfortable with his body.

"You're safe, Max. I'm Wayren." She waited.

He nodded, but she knew he didn't remember. "Wayren. What am I doing here? Have I been ill?"

"In a fashion, yes. Please. Drink this and let me talk to you." She handed him a metal cup filled with another of Ylito's concoctions.

He hesitated, sniffed at it. Hesitated more.

She smiled. "If I wanted you dead, I had ample opportunity while you were sleeping."

He nodded and drank.

When he looked back at her, she had the golden disk spinning eerily in her hand. She began to murmur again, calling down the power of the Spirit, asking for help, and watched as his eyes were drawn irrevocably to the flat pendant.

Wayren knew the moment he remembered it all . . . a tightening of the face, a tension in the shoulders, a return of the sharpness to his eyes. He reached for the tiny, delicate *vis bulla*. Closing his fingers around it, he picked it up, shuttering his eyes, and drew in a slow breath.

And then opened his eyes. They were bleak. "Nothing. I feel nothing."

Wayren nodded. "But you remember."

"Yes." He swung his feet off the bed. "What time is it? I must go."

"It's midday. But you cannot go hurrying off, Max."

He'd half risen, but at her words he sat back heavily. "Of course not. I'm the shell of a Venator now. I have the knowledge and the skills, but not the strength or the powers. A shell."

"You'll not go alone."

His beautiful lips snarled. "I may not be a Venator any longer, but I'm not helpless. I killed vampires and at least one demon before I earned the *vis bulla*, Wayren. You know that."

"Do you remember what you told me to tell Victoria, just before you went to sleep?"

He stilled, his face blank. "You didn't bring her here."

Wayren shook her head. He'd made her promise not to let anyone see him—anyone, especially Victoria. "Only Ylito."

"What did I say? Did you tell her?"

She felt his tension; it was as if it hung in the air over them like a heavy blanket. She knew much, but now she knew even more. "You wanted me to tell her you were sorry."

Because they were bare, she could see the slight shift in his square shoulders, the bit of ease that came over him. "I can only imagine how she received that bit of information."

Wayren couldn't hold back a smile. It wasn't amusing, not at all, not in these moments, not ever. But the look on his face . . . it was the Max she knew. *Thank God.* "She had a few choice words."

He stood again, energy simmering below his muscles so that she could feel his need to move, to do, to get out of there—almost as if she were inside his skin. "One person to go with me," he said, reaching for the clothing that lay folded on a chair. "White? It's too easily seen at night," he said, frowning at the shirt. "It glows. Zavier. I'll take Zavier with me."

"Briyani and Michalas will go with you."

He must have read the expression on her face, for he didn't pursue it. There would be time to tell him about it all later. But for now . . . "When you've finished dressing we will make our final plans—not to worry, Max. You'll leave soon enough."

"This afternoon. I want this done and over with."

So that he could get on with his life. Get away and get on with life.

He didn't say it, but he didn't need to. She understood.

Max hadn't realized how much he'd missed the companionship of Briyani, who was not only the nephew of Kritanu, but also Max's own Comitator. Kritanu had trained both of them together, enhancing his nephew's fighting skills as he taught Max, eventually turning over the training to Briyani when he himself became older and less flexible.

He'd certainly not stinted in his training of Victoria, despite his age and proclaimed lack of flexibility, but Max didn't begrudge her that. It made sense that he should personally teach Eustacia's niece and the future *Illa* Gardella.

Having Briyani back with him reminded Max of those early years, when he'd been much more of a loner and kept away from the Consilium while fighting his battles with the undead—and within himself. Not quite thirty, Kritanu's nephew was a bit younger than Max, and had the same wiry build and wide-jawed, tea-colored face as his uncle. He wore his straight black hair in a single braid that reached to the middle of his back, and he was wickedly talented with a *kadhara* sword. Now, as the two of them crept along through the back of Villa Palombara's grounds, for Max's third time in the last four days, they needed no words to communicate.

Michalas brought up the rear. He was as silent as fog, and thin and tall and quick. Wayren had chosen well for the team, but it was all up to Max. He led the way through the brush and between the unpruned trees, hurrying with nary a glance past the wall against which he'd kissed Victoria.

They reached the Door of Alchemy without incident, and with much dryer clothing and boots than last night. Max had the door open quickly and easily. When he was here with Victoria he'd found the traces of an opening that led to the cell in which they'd been imprisoned. Although he hadn't opened it, he decided it was the best way to gain unnoticed access to the place where Akvan lived.

Akvan. Thanks to Wayren's studies, and assistance from Ylito and Miro, Max felt as prepared as he could be.

"The trick with Akvan," Wayren had told him, "is to remember his great weakness: He will always do the exact opposite of what he thinks you want him to do. Use this against him, and you will outsmart him."

Ylito had added, "But you must make certain that there are no remnants of the obelisk left. They must be destroyed in order for Akvan to be destroyed. Remember the prophecy."

The prophecy. " . . . 'tis only a mortal man shall send him permanently to the bowels of Hell, using his own strength against him."

A mortal man.

Closing the Door of Alchemy behind them, Max and his companions worked quickly to locate the mechanism that opened the door to the cell. Either the *marchese* hadn't known about it—which was absurd, since it was his laboratory—or he hadn't had the opportunity to use it that night he'd disappeared.

Briyani had excellent hearing and nimble fingers, and he was the one who located the lever behind one of the stones. Max was at his side in an instant, and they peered through the narrow opening and saw only darkness.

Michalas brought one of the sconces over, which illuminated the cell in which he, Victoria, and Sebastian had been imprisoned. And when he looked at the floor, he saw the same telltale splotches of melted gold spattered on the stones beneath his feet.

This had been the simplest part; now he had to move forward.

But before he did, Max slipped quickly back into the laboratory and retrieved the long shard from Akvan's Obelisk that Victoria had found. His hands were gloved for protection from its power, and he slid it into a hidden pocket Miro had sewn inside the leg of his trousers. When he lifted it, he saw the leather thong with a small splinter of the obelisk he'd seen fall from Victoria's coat yesterday. He'd placed it in there for safekeeping as well, but now he snatched it up and stuffed it in his pocket.

Max had had two reasons for accompanying Victoria when she came yesterday afternoon to open the Door of Alchemy. First, to confirm that there was a way into the villa, and second, to ensure that she left the shard there, for it was crucial to his plan for destroying Akvan.

"Come," he said, and led the way into the cell.

After testing to make certain they could reopen the door back into the laboratory—the process of which wasn't at all instinctive—they closed it behind them and made their way across the small cell.

Max had explained the first part of his plan to Briyani and Michalas, and so when they stepped out of the unlocked chamber into the corridor they paused for a moment. Max looked at Michalas, who shook his head that he didn't sense the nearby presence of any undead.

But as he took a few steps, Michalas tilted his head, closed his eyes, and pointed. Silent, they moved along the passageway in the direction he'd indicated, Max taking the lead. As they approached a corner, he felt Michalas touch his sleeve. When he looked back, the Venator gave him a nod.

Max continued around the corner, filled with sudden anger. His neck felt the same—no prickling or tingling to announce the presence of the undead that Michalas could sense as easily as taking a breath. It was true: His abilities were gone.

Lilith had succeeded in taking everything from him.

The vampire was there, probably meant to be guarding the hallway in which she stood, leaning nonchalantly against the wall. But when Max came into view she straightened, her eyes gleaming red with interest.

He remained relaxed. He'd been bitten both before and after becoming a Venator . . . and he'd slain undead both before and after as well. Still, it nagged at him that he'd had to bring Briyani and Michalas as support. Doing so was smart and logical—and by God if he hadn't told Victoria more than once that their duty was to do what was right, not what they wanted.

So, when he faced the vampire, he let her come toward him, let her grab at his shoulders, let her eyes attempt to enthrall him. She wasn't very powerful, which was not surprising, since Regalado's followers were young and inexperienced. Her breath was clean—she'd not fed recently—which made it easier for him to entice her to bite his neck by tipping his head and baring it suggestively, pretending to be completely under her power.

Perhaps the vampire guards were supposed to bring any

potential victims to Akvan or Regalado, but since she hadn't fed, and since he'd offered his flesh to her so openly, the female undead didn't hesitate.

Her fangs ripped into his neck with none of the easy, seductive slide of Lilith's, and Max jerked a little in surprise. Or perhaps it was because he was weaker now. Weak and lost. He was weak, and the world was dimming.

He fumbled for his stake, feeling the familiar weight in his hand, and pulled it out from under his coat as the blood pulsed from him. She sucked roughly, greedily, and if he didn't act soon he'd lose consciousness or, worse, need to be saved by the others.

It wasn't the most powerful thrust, nor the smoothest, but Max felt the echo of satisfaction slam through him as he staked the vampire, driving the ash pike into her back.

The world was spinning, and his neck ached and dripped, but he was still on his feet when he blinked back the darkness and found Briyani there, stake in hand, as if he'd just come around the corner. Michalas was right behind, his stake at the ready as well.

Max bristled at the concern in their faces, and he turned to start off somewhere—in any direction, he didn't bloody care—but Briyani stopped him with a hand on his arm.

"Wait."

The gentleness in his voice and touch caused Max to tighten his jaw in annoyance, but Briyani was right.

The flush of salted holy water over the open wounds was a painful but necessary shock, and Max was glad his friend had acted. It would slow the bleeding and, once the initial pain had eased, would help to stop the wound's incessant throbbing.

"Now," Max said, ignoring the lingering pain, "you must go back and wait for me. It will do me no good if you are found, so hide as we discussed, and I will return. Or I won't."

"I will attend you," said Briyani, his face determined. "You cannot go alone."

"I can and I will. That was our agreement." Max fixed his sharpest glare on him, willing him to understand.

Briyani's brilliant white teeth flashed in a humorless smile. "You agreed; I did not. Michalas and I have discussed it, and he will wait. I will come with you. Either with you or behind you—but you can be certain I will be there."

"I am no child in leading strings."

"And I am no dog to be ordered about."

As Max glowered at him, once again damning Lilith for driving him to this, and cursing Wayren for giving him back his bloody memories but nothing else, Michalas stepped forward. "They're coming. Now is not the time for arguments. I will be in the chamber as planned, and if you do not return in two hours I will search for you." He fixed bright blue eyes on Max and said, "I fully intend to walk out of here alive, so you'd best return, Pesaro."

He pointed to the left, and then took off on silent feet in the opposite direction.

With a murderous glance at Briyani, Max stalked off down the hall Michalas had indicated. His fingers closed tightly into his palms, the stake still clutched in one hand, and he felt the tension all the way up his arms.

And then he forced himself to relax. There was a time when he would have easily accepted Briyani's presence, and now was an instance when he might need it more than ever. As much as it made him furious to admit that he was weak, the truth was that he was.

He was no longer the man he'd been.

Yet, when they came face-to-face with the cluster of four

vampires, Max greeted them with great boldness and confidence, Briyani at his side.

"I am Maximilian Pesaro," he announced, looking at the undead with all the haughtiness of the Venator he no longer was. "Take me to Akvan."

Twenty

Wherein Our Heroine Finds Herself in Yet Another Dark Tunnel

Victoria moved silently down the stairs, staying well out of Sebastian's sight as he descended into the cool cellar beneath a slender three-story house. The plaster-walled building that overlooked a small courtyard was unexpectedly familiar to her, for it was the same place he'd imprisoned her last autumn when he and Max tried to keep her away from Nedas, the vampire who'd planned to activate Akvan's Obelisk. Fortunately Sebastian's attempt had failed, and she'd freed herself by climbing out a window, and had thus been able to witness not only the destruction of the obelisk, but also to slay Nedas.

Perhaps he'd been staying here all along, all these months, and Victoria could have contacted Sebastian if she'd been able to find this building again . . . but it was a moot point now.

She was here, and vengeance was on her mind. Blood

pounded in her temples and reverberated in her chest as she moved along, flush with the wall, gun and stake within easy reach. The back of her neck had been chilled for quite some time, and she guessed there were a good number of undead nearby, doubtless fawning at the feet of Beauregard.

The passageway was cold and dark and very narrow. It occurred to her as she stayed far behind Sebastian that she had spent an inordinate amount of time sneaking, running, or being chased through deep, dank tunnels since she'd become a Venator. That was one of the hazards of hunting the undead, but it was becoming rather predictable. Stalking a vampire? Follow him underground. Searching for the undead? Look in a dark, damp cave. Seeking a potentially evil artifact? Follow a tunnel to find it.

These absurd thoughts served to distract Victoria and tame her urge to barrel ahead and confront Sebastian. If she showed herself, or was discovered too early, it would make things much more difficult. When outnumbered, as she surely was, Victoria preferred to have the element of surprise on her side.

It also occurred to her as she paused at a corner that, for as powerful a vampire as Beauregard was, his accommodations were rather primitive. She discovered close, dark corridors, rough walls, scattered stones underfoot, and more than one swath of clinging cobwebs that brushed her face and hair.

A rat scuttled near her foot; no, there were two of them; but Victoria didn't react even when she felt the brush of a small furry body against the hem of her skirt. Rats coexisted with Beauregard? She couldn't imagine Lilith—or even Regalado—putting up with such an affront.

But when she finally heard voices ahead and slunk her way along the dirty wall to peer around the last corner, Victoria had to revise her private thoughts. The wall that she came upon ended in a neat doorway that appeared to be covered by some kind of tapestry; it wafted back into place, indicating that Sebastian had just slipped through there. So she sneaked forward and pushed away just a corner of the cloth in order to peer in.

Beauregard's lair, instead of being simple and inelegant, was as nicely apportioned as Lady Winnie's parlor—albeit a bit less lacy. Rugs covered the floor. Candles and lamps shimmered from sconces and tables and shoulder-height candelabra. The ceiling was surprisingly high, nearly as tall as men of Max's height. The furnishings included a harpsichord, and were of fine dark wood and plump brocaded upholstery. A large wooden door on the opposite side of the chamber told Victoria that Sebastian had led her to the hidden rear entrance to the room. Based on the size and strength of the other door—not to mention the frigidness on the back of her neck—she presumed Beauregard had friends located on the other side of that main entrance.

Inside the room two fair heads, one the color of wheat, the other more of a lion's-mane shade, but both with the same thick curls, were bent over a table examining what looked like a single piece of paper.

Victoria chose that moment to step fully into the room. "It appears that I have yet another grievance to air with you, Beauregard."

To her immense satisfaction, both of their heads snapped up in surprise. Sebastian's face wore a frozen, chagrined look, rather like the one he'd had when she'd found him in the Consilium. But Beauregard . . . after the initial shock evaporated, his was replaced by a sly, pleased expression that made the hair on Victoria's scalp lift.

"Welcome, my dear, welcome to my humble abode." Beauregard made a sweeping gesture, inviting her in.

Victoria moved past the tapestry door, taking care to keep

her back to the wall so there wouldn't be any nasty surprises creeping up behind her. She remained calm and focused, reining in the fury that vibrated through her muscles and veins. One step at a time.

"How did you get here?"

Sebastian's voice drew Victoria's attention to him. He was all too appealing in the flattering candlelight, with a boyish curl falling on his forehead and that guilty expression on his face. But before she could speak, Beauregard interrupted. "I presume she found her way here the same way in which her paramour—Zander, Zavier, what was his name?— did. Surely he gave her the direction." He smiled, now looking directly at her. His eyes were still a normal shade of blue, and his fangs were out of sight, but Victoria was properly wary. "Or perhaps you recalled your stay here last autumn, before all of that unpleasantness occurred."

"Unpleasantness?" Victoria said, refusing to look at Sebastian. She couldn't afford to be distracted. "I rather thought you welcomed the destruction of Nedas and the thwarting of his plan to activate Akvan's Obelisk. After all, it put you in a much greater position of power."

Beauregard bowed his head in acquiescence. "Indeed it did."

"If this is a battle of wits, you shall find yourself overmatched. In fact, I rather think you might find yourself overmatched on all counts." She allowed him to see the stake in the hand at her side.

"Well, then, if that is the case, let us get to business. I trust you're aware that I've returned your possession, and thus you've come to return that which is mine."

"I have your copper armband, if that's what you mean," she replied. "But you've yet to return that which you took from me."

"Did he not make his way back? I do hope Gardriel and Hugh weren't too rough with him."

He? Then, with a cool rush of understanding, she realized that Beauregard didn't have the splinter necklace she'd lost, but that he'd been referring to Zavier all along. Or what was left of him. What had happened to Zavier had been purposeful and malevolent violence meant to send her a message.

Her head pounded as anger surged anew, setting her fingers to trembling in her effort to keep from attacking now.

Victoria drew in a steady breath and glanced at Sebastian, who was watching them sharply. She had no illusions about which side he would take . . . and she was glad she had a gun.

"He must have been in no condition to tell you how to find us then," Beauregard was saying. He'd stepped from behind the table and moved casually toward her, the piece of paper they'd been examining curling in his hand. "So you came upon us quite by accident."

Victoria's attention was caught, no doubt as he'd intended, by the piece of parchment he gently wafted against his leg. It reminded her of the journal Max had taken from the laboratory at Villa Palombara.

The journal that had been taken back to the Consilium.

Her attention flew to Sebastian, and their eyes met.

"Let me see that paper."

The alacrity with which Beauregard proffered it to her confirmed her suspicions before she even glanced at it, but she did take a moment to examine the single page. Then she looked back at Sebastian. "A coward and a thief."

He met her gaze boldly, and for that she had to give him credit. But that was all.

"It was a necessity, Victoria. A matter of life and death."

"Damn you, and your excuses," she said, the darkness of anger closing in on the edges of her vision. She'd actually begun to trust him, to believe in him. To let him close. "Damn you, and your grandfather too, Sebastian Vioget." She turned to Beauregard. "And you nearly killed Zavier— merely to turn my attention away, so you could send your grandson to do your dirty work."

Beauregard smiled at her. "By the devil, you're quick, my dear. Quick to understand, quick to judge, quick to blame. And quite appetizing when you're angry."

She raised her stake, flying across the room at him, no longer willing to restrain herself.

"Victoria, no!" Sebastian leaped between them, and her stake slammed into his shoulder. It was much more difficult driving it into mortal flesh than a vampire's heart; she felt the unpleasant give as it pierced skin and muscle. "Don't do it," he said, gasping in surprise, his fingers closing over her arm to propel her away. "He wants—"

"Get away," she said. He grunted as she pulled out the stake. Blood colored its tip and seeped quickly through his shirt, an unfamiliar sight. There wasn't supposed to be blood.

But she couldn't let that stop her now. She pushed at Sebastian with all of her strength, sending him stumbling backward as he reached again for her.

"Victoria, don't," he said again, coming toward her, the bloodstain blossoming on his shirt. "He wants to fight you. He wants to come between us."

She turned to look at him, empty and angry and determined. "Either get out of my sight or you'll go with him. I'm through with your games and lies."

She turned back to Beauregard, who was watching them with a half smile and a glint in his gaze. "Do you really want him gone?" he asked.

"What I want is you dead."

"But you forget, I am already dead these last six hundred

years." He lifted his hand in a nonchalant gesture, his eyes turning pink. "Begone, Sebastian."

"No." He moved like a large cat. He carried no weapon, nothing but himself, and stood solidly between them.

Victoria looked at him, scanning his pale face, the determined look in his eyes, the dark patch spreading beneath his left collarbone, seeing that his breathing was faster than it should be. Still handsome as sin, still appealing, still able to tug at her because of all they'd shared. Thank God he wasn't a vampire with the strength of the thrall behind him too. "You stole from us. You betrayed us, Sebastian. I don't . . . want . . . to . . . see . . . you."

Beauregard had moved away toward the wall behind his desk as Victoria and Sebastian faced each other. She heard a faint, low sound in the distance.

"You've chosen, Sebastian," she told him. "You made your final choice when you did this—sneaking in while we worried over Zavier, while Max was—" She stopped herself. "It was your choice. Now get out of my way so I can finish this."

The large door burst open and four massive vampires—three men and a woman—surged in. Victoria spun to face them, her heart knocking suddenly harder and faster. The stake was in her hand, but it would be a tough battle. She crouched, ready.

Sebastian had turned too, also taking a defensive stance, but he kept talking to her. "Victoria, the armban—"

His words gasped away as the first of the undead slammed a fist into his gut, and a second came from the other side and threw him to the floor as he spun to defend himself. Instinctively Victoria raised her stake, but a strong hand grasped it from behind, holding her wrist aloft, sliding an arm around her waist, and squeezing her so that her breath was caught. She struggled, kicking backward, watching Sebastian rise to his feet, only to be knocked back down by a boot to the jaw. On a normal man the blow would have cracked the bone. Another vampire dragged him back to his feet, and Sebastian managed a well-placed punch, but he had no weapon with which to stop them.

"You said you wanted him out of the way," Beauregard said in her ear.

Victoria slammed her head back and felt it crash into Beauregard's nose, at the same time trying to twist away from his strong grip. But he held on tightly and slipped his other hand around the front of her throat, pulling her back against him.

The hand tightened, cutting off her air, sending her struggling in his arms, stomping her foot down, slamming back with her free hand to jab her elbow into him, kicking, trying to breathe. . . .

And then suddenly she was released with such force that she stumbled against a chair; then her hand clashed onto the keys of the harpsichord. She turned in time to see the door close, leaving the room silent but for the last echoes of discordant notes.

Silent, but not empty.

Her neck was cold; her fingers were trembling. "After all he's done for you?" she said in a shaking voice that she abhorred.

Beauregard, who bent to pick up the paper she'd dropped, placed it on the table and looked at her. "Is it not what you expected from me? No loyalty? Manipulation? Where do you think Sebastian learned it?"

"You wouldn't kill him. He's worth too much to you."

Beauregard looked horrified. "Kill him? Of course not. I merely assisted him in complying with your wishes. You should be grateful, for now we can converse without his interference. Now, shall we get to business? You were going to kill me. Or attempt to." He looked pointedly at the stake that had fallen from her hand and rolled across the floor. "But I think that will have to wait. You have something of mine."

"And you have something of mine." She would play his game for the moment. Until she had the chance to cut the bastard's head off.

"It was only one page," he said, lifting the paper from the desk. "And you mustn't blame Sebastian. The man would do anything for me—loyalty is his great flaw, much as I've tried to teach him otherwise. But I'm all he has, and he just cannot abide the thought of me burning in the fires of Hell for all eternity." Beauregard gave a genteel shudder. "It's not a particularly pleasant thought to me either. And so when at last the door to Palombara's laboratory was reopened, I was understandably interested in obtaining not only my missing armband, but also this particular page."

"So, will you tell me what is so important about that page?" Victoria kept her tone easy, unconcerned, even as she divided her attention between the details of the room, any potential weapons, and the undead himself.

His eyes were pink when they looked at her, and she turned her gaze firmly away.

"I think you can guess, if you put your mind to it." His voice was soft and seductive, and she felt the tendrils of his thrall reach out gently and brush over her skin as if he'd actually touched her.

"It's a plant. It must have something to do with your immortality . . . or your destroyed soul, if Sebastian was willing to help," Victoria replied. She heard her voice as though it were in a tunnel, far away and hollow, and she blinked and took a step. Her fogged ears cleared, and she felt steadier.

She couldn't forget the image of blood soaking Sebastian's shirt. Blood she'd drawn.

"It's a very useful flower," Beauregard told her, "to the

undead, in particular, and, if one believes the work of the alchemist pilgrim who came to Palombara, to mortals as well.
But it grows rarely only once or twice per century. I needed
the page to identify it, for this year is a year it's expected to
bloom. And with your aunt's death, I knew the key to the
workshop would be more readily available."

He smiled. "You must appreciate my brilliance. It was
my intent all the while to divert your attention to Akvan as
he and his worthless followers tried to find the keys. I made
sure he knew about the journals and about the keys, and I
even made certain the key Palombara had kept—which I, of
course, had stolen from him that last night—was found by
one of Akvan's servants. I knew once the door was opened I
could retrieve my armband—one way or the other."

Victoria kept her gaze far away from him and his pink
eyes. She moved so that the desk remained between them
and she was a good distance away. She wasn't frightened;
she'd been in worse situations before, much more overmatched. But if he called for help again, as he'd obviously
done when he moved behind his desk earlier, she would find
herself in the same situation as Sebastian.

Or worse.

"You wanted Sebastian to steal the key, didn't you?"

He inclined his head. "He didn't realize he'd actually had
the key in his possession until much later, when you described it to him."

"But you allowed me to use it."

"He refused to steal it, if that is what you're asking. But
it didn't matter to me—once you got the door open I could
get what I needed. Except that you and that bloody Pesaro
were too quick and he went off with it."

"And you actually thought that by mutilating and nearly
killing one of my men that you would get what you wanted
from me?"

"You're here, are you not?"

She didn't like his smile. Didn't like the way she suddenly remembered his mouth covering hers, sucking the warm flow of blood from her lip.

"Of course you would come to avenge your friend. Your fellow warrior. What else would you do?" he said, his voice alluring and coaxing, as if he were trying to lull her. "You are a Venator."

What else would you do?

It was as if he'd read her mind and her private thoughts earlier. She *was* a Venator—only, wholly, and without reservation. Of course she would come to avenge the death—or near death—of one of her own.

What else would she do?

Nothing.

"I want my armband." He'd moved closer to her, and she tensed.

"I don't have it with me."

He smiled. His fangs were long and sharp and brushed his lower lip. His silvery-blond hair curled becomingly about his handsome face, and his pink eyes gleamed. "Of course you do. I can sense it."

She dodged and spun away, scooping her lost stake off the floor. "Come and get it." She bared her teeth and crouched, waiting. She'd finish him now.

He looked at her, then turned back to the desk, his back toward her.

And that challenge, that careless dismissal, was her ultimate undoing.

Victoria, bold and angry, ready to end the standoff, launched herself at him, stake outthrust in her hand, poised to drive it into his chest. He turned, caught her wrist, and with a snapping movement used her momentum to jerk it behind her, slamming her body full-force into his.

He looked down at her with burning eyes, and she closed hers, turning her face away, tilting her head back, and then bashing her forehead into his chin before trying to spin away.

He was strong, and she barely pulled free of his grip, but he was after her in an instant, grabbing at the hem of her man's coat and hauling her back. She pulled, twisting, and its three buttons burst off, scattering to the floor. For a moment she was trapped, the sleeves capturing her hands behind her as Beauregard pulled the coat off. But she shrugged quickly out, spinning away, leaving the length of coat in his hands, and managing to keep the stake in hers.

The sudden release sent her stumbling, but she righted herself quickly and turned back around, stake ready, pulling the crucifix she wore from beneath her bodice so that it hung in plain sight.

He flinched when he saw her pendant, cowering back, and she jumped toward him, the blood racing through her body with the thrill of the fight. But he managed to dodge at the last minute and avoid the stake. It slammed into his shoulder in the same place she'd struck Sebastian, easily and harmlessly. Pain jarred her arm as the stake went through and into the stone floor, but Victoria recovered, finding comfort in the weight of the cross thumping freely on her bosom.

As they faced each other, the desk between them again, she realized with a start that he still held her coat . . . that he was turned away from her and her necklace, fumbling with the fabric, feeling for the pockets.

Before she could lunge toward him to rip it away, he removed his hand from the folds, holding the copper armband he sought. "Ah," he said, still holding back, but satisfaction rang in his voice.

Victoria somersaulted across the table, kicking him aside as she landed on the opposite end, and he pulled her to the floor with him. The cross bumped up against him, and he gasped, recoiling in pain, but held on to her nevertheless as they rolled on the floor. Then the cross slipped up and over her shoulder so that it fell behind her, out of sight.

With a quick jerk he snapped the chain and the necklace broke at the back of her neck, leaving the cross under her as they shifted over the floor, grappling furiously with each other. His fingers closed over the wrist with the stake, squeezing, while she fought to reach the armband he held in the other hand. She didn't know why he wanted it, but it was for nothing good.

Their legs were tangled like lovers', and he rose over her, hips pressing into hips, suddenly releasing the wrist and letting her plunge the stake down. Beauregard rolled away and the stake whistled past him, grazing his arm, jarring Victoria as she smashed it into the floor. Her arm was still reverberating from the blow, and she tried to flip herself away when she felt hands closing around her other wrist, pulling her back. She kicked out, but it was too late—something smooth and cool latched into place on her left wrist.

And then a soft clink and her arm felt sluggish. She felt stopped, slowed, heavy.

She raised the stake again, rolling toward him where he held her arm, but he caught her blow in midair and they were locked, straining, face-to-face.

"And so it is," he said with great satisfaction.

Panting there next to him on the floor, she looked over at her right wrist.

The copper armband clasped her flesh.

"At last I have you where I want you," he said, looking at her with glowing pink eyes.

"No . . . you . . . don't!" she cried, fighting to look away, whipping her stake arm about with all of her strength, struggling to snap his hold.

They were at an impasse for a moment, hand to hand, he squeezing, she fighting to drive the stake down, lying on the floor next to each other with her braceleted arm, extended by his grip, above them.

She felt her heartbeat begin to slow to match his. Their breath mingled, and everything seemed to ebb into a fog, or an underwater, slow-moving world. The copper on her arm felt warm, as if its weight burned into her flesh, and she couldn't move it without dragging his hand with it. The relentless pressure on her other wrist had numbed her fingers as he fought to loose the deadly weapon.

With a last scream of exertion she bucked her whole body and pulled her arm free, the stake slipping from her numb fingers as her hand slammed harmlessly onto his chest. She heard the stake rattle to the floor, the dull sound as it rolled away, somehow so loud in her ears that it drowned out everything.

"Now . . . at last . . ." Beauregard said, yanking her closer. His pink eyes captured her, and she couldn't breathe. His face moved closer, blocking out her view as she struggled to break free of the thrall . . . of his hold . . . of the sluggish, wanton feeling that moved through her.

He bent toward her, his mouth closer, darkening her vision as she lost her own breath and her heartbeat became one with his.

Twenty-one

In Which Max Befuddles a Contrary Demon

Akvan was just as Wayren had described him: ungainly, horned, and tailed. His body was a solid trunk with thick arms and legs, both of which ended in curved claws. His face was jowled and porcine, with tiny eyes, puffy cheeks, and a large pug nose. Fangs protruded from his mouth like small tusks, and his skin had a bluish cast.

The stench of rank evil hung in the air as Max was ushered fully into the room where the demon was holding court. The room was large and simply furnished. Perhaps ten people were standing about, clustered loosely in front of a low dais on which the demon sat. Max couldn't identify exactly which ones were vampires any longer, but he recognized some of those present as members of the Tutela, and knew that there had to be at least a few undead among them.

On the dais next to Akvan was a slender stone table, hip high, and on it was a cluster of obsidian shards.

Briyani had been made to stand at the doorway, but Max was allowed to step forward into the center of the chamber.

"So you demand to see me?" Akvan boomed from a large chair. With his return to earth he had taken human form, but in a horrific, distorted manner in that every aspect was exaggerated and awkward. And, by any definition, horrifically ugly. He was much larger than any man, easily half again as tall as Max himself. "And who are you?"

"I am who called you back to this earth," Max told him, facing him boldly.

"He is a Venator," came a voice he recognized all too well. "A powerful one. You are right to keep him at a distance."

"Sarafina," Max said, turning as the blond woman he'd nearly married appeared, pushing her way through the small throng from the side of the room. George Starcasset was close by her side. "I see you have wasted no time in finding another companion."

"Do not be jealous, Maximilian . . . no one could replace you." She smiled in a manner that was much less naive than any expression she'd worn when he'd first met her, more than a year ago. The glint in her eyes reminded him of the one he'd seen when he'd been unable to extricate himself from a shopping trip with her: sly and covetous. "I'm delighted to see that you've returned to us. I was quite annoyed to find you missing after our visit. Is it perhaps too much to hope that you've seen the error of your ways and have come back to the Tutela?"

"A Venator?" Akvan's low, grating voice drew Max's attention back to the matter at hand. "No Venator can harm me—it is written in the *Shah-Nameh*. Let him approach."

"But he is the concubine of Lilith," Sara, ever the gossipmonger, insisted. She was moving toward him as if she owned the chamber, not Akvan.

"You know nothing," Max said, turning away from her. "Be still."

"Hold him," she ordered, gesturing sharply at four of the others, "and I shall prove it, Master Div." She gave a short, almost insolent bow to the demon as the guards she'd summoned swarmed toward him.

Max's skin crawled as four pairs of hands grasped his shoulders and arms, but he stood stoically as Sara's delicate little fingers pulled at his shirt, opening the collar to show the new bite.

"See? She has marked him, and the bite never heals . . . and no undead dares to touch him for fear of bringing her wrath down upon them." Her hands were warm and smooth over his skin, brushing his neck and dipping down beneath the fabric of his shirt as if she owned him. "And here— Hold him, I said!" She yanked on the ties of the shirt, and then the two halves, opening it over his chest, flicking her finger over the *vis bulla* that hung uselessly from his areola. "How I've missed this," she murmured cannily, giving it a tug—without noticing that it wasn't his.

It was painful, but he kept his face blank and his breathing steady. He hadn't expected Sara to be such an asset to his plan, to move things along so quickly and easily. "Tell your fiends to release me," he ordered Akvan. "I came of my own will."

Akvan waved his hand and the four men stepped away, but Sara remained. "Begone," Max told her. "I have things to discuss with your master." Sara did not like being mastered by anyone; now that her father was gone she was the heir apparent to the Tutela leadership. The flare of annoyance in her eyes told him he'd hit the mark.

"Get away from him." George Starcasset, the cowardly weasel, spoke. Jealousy colored his voice. "Or you will drive Lilith's anger down upon yourself."

"But I am safe here with Akvan," Sara said pertly, her eyes sliding over Max one last time as she glided back toward her companion. She shot a coy look at the demon, and Max was certain he saw her flutter her eyelashes. "She'd not dare to show her face here, for she's been hiding in her mountains for almost two years now."

Max would have laughed at her innocent comment if he'd been in any other situation. How little she knew Lilith.

"Why have you come?" Akvan boomed. "Only three days ago you escaped from my . . . hospitality." His laugh was deep and raspy.

"I've come because I called you back from nothing when I destroyed your obelisk. And for that you owe me a boon."

"A boon? I owe you a boon?"

"Without me you would still be trapped in nothing, whilst the son of Lilith would wield your power here on this earth." Max felt the cool air over his bare skin, but held off the urge to draw his shirt back together.

Akvan's jowls were shaking, and his eyes had nearly disappeared among the folds of their lids and his crinkled skin. His laugh was silent, yet condescension exuded from every one of his large pores. "And what favor is it that you demand?"

The demon was obviously just humoring Max's conversation, but that served the plan. Weave the web, one thin skein at a time.

For the first time Max allowed himself to show a bit of a falter, a hesitation. Now he pulled the edges of his shirt together. "What I have to say is for your ears only." And large, malformed ones they were.

Akvan looked at him, his eyes visible again, and sharp. "No. You speak aloud, here, among all."

Indeed. "There is no love lost between you and Lilith," he began, letting his eyes flicker around. "And I bear her no love myself."

"I knew it was so," Sara hissed from the side.

"Shut up," Starcasset snapped back.

Ah. Division among the ranks.

"Those pieces are too small to reconstruct your obelisk," Max said, gesturing to the small pile of obsidian. "I can obtain a much larger shard that you can use to rebuild and restore your power."

"The one in the possession of the Venator?" asked Akvan. "I do not need it."

Max shrugged. "Then our business is concluded." He turned to leave, his eyes meeting Briyani's at the back of the room. The other man gave a bare nod of readiness. Now they would see.

"Wait."

Max turned and faced Akvan, allowing a trace of apprehension to show on his face. "Yes?"

"You have this shard?"

"I can get it for you."

"Why would you do such a thing?"

"I wish to ally myself with one who has greater power than Lilith. I desire to destroy her hold over me. She promised to release me if I destroyed your obelisk, but she has refused."

"And if Sarafina is to be believed, once you are set free, Lilith will bring all of her wrath down upon your ally. I am not foolish enough to step into that trap."

Max nodded, allowing even more concern to tinge his expression. "I presumed she would be no match for you, in any regard."

"She would not! I merely do not wish to concern myself with her and her puny, half-demon creatures. I have enough of them about me now." His voice grated harshly. "But I will have the shard. And when you give it to me, I will allow you to leave."

"I do not wish to fight you," Max replied, his face tightening. "Not you."

Akvan considered him again. "A fight, then. A fight for your freedom. If I win, you give me the shard and you serve me. If you win, I allow you to go free."

"No, Maximilian," came a shout from the back of the room. They turned to see Briyani straining against the hold of two men. "I will do it! I will fight him. You are still—"

"Silence him," Akvan thundered, his command reverberating off the walls. "I shall fight him. And if he dies, you die as well."

"But you cannot endanger yourself," Sara cried from the side. She ran to Akvan's chair, her little hands grasping his bulky arm.

Max could have kissed her at that moment, not only for her confidence in his skills, but also because the timing could not have been more perfect had he paid her. "I will give you the shard," he said. "I do not wish to fight you. Only let us go free."

"I have no fear of you, Venator. You cannot harm me, but there is nothing writ that says I cannot draw you into pieces. But perhaps I should fight your friend first, and then when I win, you shall tell me where the shard lies."

Blast.

"If you wish," Max said, trying to sound a bit eager. "That is more than fair."

"But he is not a Venator," cried Sara. "Is he?" She spun a look at Max, who refused to answer. "You are not fully recovered from your return, Master Div," she said. "And he is not a Venator. Do not jeopardize our plans by putting yourself in danger."

Akvan had pulled his bulk from the large chair and now

he towered over all in the room. His muscles, bare beneath a short-sleeved tunic and traditional Persian skirt, rippled. If he was not fully recovered from being recalled to earth, Max was loath to imagine what he would look like when he was.

"I shall fight you, Lilith's concubine. And when you die—"

"When I die you shall not know where the piece of obelisk is," Max said.

Akvan lumbered to a stop. "You do not wish to fight me. If you tell me where the piece of my obelisk is, I will not fight you."

"And you will allow me to go free? And my companion?"

Akvan settled back in his chair. "Of course. Now tell me."

"I will tell it aloud, where all can hear." Max looked at him, tensing inside. This was about as far as he could go; they'd gone back and forth, around in circles so much that he hoped Akvan was now thoroughly confused about what he wanted and what he feared. "So that you may send them out to obtain the shard and wait here with me for them to return with it in their possession."

Akvan's eyes narrowed. "Draw near to me, Lilith's concubine."

Max blanched. "I cannot. The bites . . . she can sense it, and they sting and burn if I—"

"Draw near! I command you, or your companion will be my next meal."

Max looked around, visibly disconcerted, but then regained his courage. "Send your people from the chamber so I can speak freely."

"I shall not! Draw near me and speak in my ear." Akvan glowered at Sara, who peeled herself from his arm and moved away. "You as well, all of you, step back. Allow him to approach."

Max took measured steps toward the demon, gasping once and pressing his hand to the bites that still oozed blood. He stopped in front of the dais, slightly to the left side, where the table of obsidian splinters rested and looked up at the massive creature. "I cannot move . . . any closer. . . . The pain . . . is unbearable."

The stench was awful too. Max wasn't completely feigning discomfort as he drew near, but he was tense and prepared. One chance.

When Akvan's haunch-size hand lashed out, Max took the opportunity to dive to the ground, his hands busy under his long coat as he rolled. The demon grasped him by the arm and hauled him easily onto the dais as Max winced, pretending to hold an injured arm.

"Tell me where the shard is!" demanded Akvan, his breath spewing a hot, sickly death-smell over Max's face.

"It is here!" Max said, whipping his arm from beneath the folds of his coat and plunging the shard into Akvan's chest as if he were staking a vampire.

The demon shrieked, his eyes goggling, his mouth gaping; but Max didn't hesitate. He was already pulling the short sword from his other trouser leg and, as the demon remained paralyzed by the stab of the shard, he sliced through his meaty neck with a blade barely long enough for the job, and then he turned to the pile of splinters.

Everything happened so quickly that before anyone in the room could react, he had the time to dump the table and its cache of obsidian, as well as the splinter necklace, onto the shriveling, blackening mass of Akvan as the demon bubbled into the floor.

But no sooner had he done that, letting every piece of the obelisk melt into its maker, than Max was turning to defend himself from the hoard of guards that descended upon him.

He didn't know who was a vampire and who was a man,

and therefore what weapon to use against each—but the question became moot as a massive explosion erupted from the back of the room, sending scatters of stone blasting through the air. At last, Briyani!

Max took advantage of the distraction to slip away from the red-eyed creature he'd been battling, using the cover of the sudden smoke to duck low and scuttle his way toward that end of the chamber. Their plan was to meet outside of the room if possible, with Michalas rushing to meet them as soon as he heard the explosion.

He ran into something small and soft, and from the familiar grasping fingers knew it was Sara. She was still a mortal, misguided as she was, but a mortal. Instead of shaking her off, as he wanted to do, he dragged her after him through the smoke and over the piles of rubble, past the bodies buried under it, and out into the hall. Smoke filled the passageway, but when he felt the grasp of sure fingers on his arm, he turned and recognized Briyani.

His face was covered with soot, but his white teeth shone in a complacent smile . . . and as Max turned to follow him, Michalas emerged from the darkness too.

"Come," he said, leading the way. Max followed, and as they hurried down the hall, Michalas turned twice more and lobbed something behind him. Explosions followed them, and a sudden loud rumbling told Max that something had finally collapsed the ceiling behind them. The whole villa was going to come down.

"Run!"

They ran, the smell of stone dust billowing through the narrow hall behind them as the ceiling caved bit by bit, each topple bringing down the section after it. He still had Sara by the arm, and she was running as fast as they were, even in her skirts.

They finally reached the cell and burst into the secret

laboratory, then more slowly through the Door of Alchemy and out into the night that had fallen.

"You killed him," Sara said as Max flung off her grasping hands. "How did you do that? It was against the writings of the *Shah-Nameh* that a Venator could hurt him! It is never wrong."

He ignored her, looking over the wall that housed the Door of Alchemy. Half of the villa had collapsed in upon itself, sending puffs of smoke that were visible even in the low moonlight.

"How, Max?"

"Let's go," he said, turning to Michalas and Briyani. "We've finished here."

Without another word or glance he turned and they started off, leaving Sara Regalado staring after them.

"How?" she called again. "At least tell me that, Max."

He kept walking away. He would never see her again. Never deal with this again.

His chest was tight. It was over.

Sebastian cursed as he opened his eyes. At least, one eye. The other one was swollen shut. His shirt was wet with blood, and he felt as if a cart had driven over him, more than once. What had he done to himself?

Then his eyes widened, even the painful one, and he scrambled to his feet.

Good God.

Victoria.

He was unsteady, but he'd felt worse before, and the throbbing didn't stop him from rushing toward the door of the room in which he'd been tossed. It was one of the extra chambers that Beauregard used, and Sebastian's immediate fear that he'd been locked in was unfounded, for the door opened easily. The hallway was empty, and Sebastian hurried out and down the passageway, refusing to think about what he would find.

Gardriel and Hugh, two massive vampires particularly loyal to Beauregard, stood outside the door to his private chamber—not the one with the harpsichord, but one adjoining it through yet another hidden door. Sebastian, however, was fast and determined, and managed to push his way in.

As strong hands locked around his upper biceps, whipping him back to a halt, he stared at the scene before him. His vision dimmed at the edges as he gave a single, futile jerk to try to free himself. "No."

His grandfather looked up casually from where he reclined on the large, pillow-strewn bed, stroking Victoria's dark hair. It was long, and rich and thick, and it covered her bare shoulders, streaming over the lush red velvet bedding. Her skin was white, pale in the light cast from a roaring fire—a comfort for her, not for Beauregard—and her mouth was curved in a sensual smile. She looked at Sebastian from her position curled up with his grandfather. Her eyes were horribly bright and seemed deep in her skull.

"You've arrived rather more quickly than I anticipated."

"Let her go." Sebastian struggled again, but the two who held him were taller, bulkier, and much stronger than he. "Beauregard, let her go."

Sebastian couldn't take his eyes from Victoria, his heart slamming in his chest, his gut twisting painfully. Her lips were dark red and puffy, as if they'd been well kissed, and her gown . . . it sagged at her bodice, leaving no doubt what his grandfather had been doing, what he had planned.

Worst of all, her ivory skin seemed paler than usual, the hollow at the base of her throat darker and deeper. As she moved to kiss Beauregard her hair fell away, and he saw the streaks of blood on the side of her neck. Dark, but still glistening, still thick and rich.

He knew that there was still a chance, yes ... he'd drained a good amount of her blood, but as long as she hadn't drunk from Beauregard, Sebastian could save her.

His grandfather pulled away from the deep, thrusting kiss he'd been sharing with Victoria, a kiss that made Sebastian's vision dim further and his struggles more desperate. He saw tongues slide and lips mesh, and it was horribly erotic and disturbing and shocking all at the same time.

Beauregard lifted his face, pulling away from Victoria's lips with a loud smacking sound, and looked directly at Sebastian. She continued to kiss his chin and on down his neck, her small, powerful hands smoothing over the front of his chest in the same way she'd done to Sebastian himself only days ago. "You certainly may join us, if you promise to behave," Beauregard told him.

Nausea flooded him, and Sebastian couldn't speak for a moment. This couldn't be happening. "Why?" he asked finally, his voice low and broken. "Why?"

"I could no longer chance your divided loyalties, Sebastian. Now there will be no question, will there?"

Sebastian just stared, the world falling away and leaving him standing on the edge of a precipice in a cold and angry wind. "Victoria!" he said, his eyes never leaving her as he kicked futilely at the undead who held him. If he could get her attention, pull her from the depths of the thrall ... "Victoria, look at me!"

"Do you not fear. She'll be just as accommodating now as she was before ... yet she'll never change. You'll thank me in a few decades. If you'd listened to me—"

"No!"

Suddenly, as she moved and her other arm came into view, he saw the copper band biting into her wrist, and realized that was how she'd fallen. It had to be. She was too strong otherwise. "Victoria." Desperation began to skim his nerves; his voice came out in an agonized whisper.

Her eyes were heavy-lidded and alluring, her dark lashes a thick fringe beneath brows and delicate lavender eyelids, her irises wide-pupiled. Her head tilted back as she smiled up at Beauregard again, reaching to brush her fingers over his jaw and chin in an overtly seductive manner so very unlike the proud, restrained Victoria he knew.

"Let her go," Sebastian told Beauregard again, hating that there was an edge of pleading in his voice. His body trembled. "Release her."

"I will not." Beauregard's eyes glowed more deeply, and Sebastian felt the edge of his thrall tickle over his shoulders. For the first time in a long while, he recognized the power of his grandfather, and the danger he represented.

"I've never asked you for anything. I've done what you've bidden; I've protected you. Now let her go."

"It's too late." Beauregard reached out his long, narrow hand and smoothed his fingers over Victoria's neck. Blood covered them when he pulled them away, bringing them to his mouth and gently tasting.

"She hasn't fed from you. It's not too late." Sebastian's neck was prickling and his head pounded. "Please."

"But she will. She will feed from me. And then you'll be happy, Sebastian, I promise. Trust me." Beauregard looked at him. "I never could understand why you did what you did to Giulia, but—"

Sebastian managed to wrench his left arm free from Hugh's grip, surprising both of the undead as he sent his fist plowing into the vampire's face, and then twisted to pull free from the other.

But they were on him immediately, pummeling and kicking, fangs bared and eyes glowing, and Sebastian felt the

room spinning as he sagged to the floor after a vicious punch
in the abdomen.

"Get him out of here," he heard Beauregard say. The
voice was dim and far away, but Sebastian fought to bring
himself back to the room, back to save Victoria.

But before he could, strong hands dragged him out of the
chamber. And as the door closed behind them, the last thing
he heard was a low, feminine laugh filled with pleasure.

Twenty-two

Wherein the Worst Possible Happening Occurs

"So you leave us once again," Wayren said, looking shrewdly at Max.

He nodded, his hand on the doorknob of her library. He hadn't said so, but Wayren was no fool. She understood him.

"Now that Akvan and his obelisk are no threat and you're useless, you see no reason to remain. Such self-pity doesn't become you, Max."

"Self-pity? I bathed in that enough in the year after my father and sister died." He turned the knob and heard the gentle click of the door's latch releasing. "I have no illusions that Lilith will not be furious when she learns of my . . . defection . . . and she'll soon be searching for me. My intent is merely to disappear for a while."

"Again."

He looked at her. "Again."

"Without saying good-bye."

"I see no need to belabor things."

"Zavier is dying."

"I know. I'm sorry for it, too. He is a good man."

Wayren nodded. Then she looked at him again with those sharp, pale blue eyes. "Will you leave Victoria's *vis bulla*?"

Max's hand tightened, but he didn't allow it to rise to his chest and touch the amulet beneath his shirt. "She doesn't need two." He knew it was an equivocation, but it didn't matter.

"She already wears two *vis bullae*." Wayren was looking at him, her head tilted to one side like a wren.

"Then she doesn't bloody well need three," he snapped. He wanted to leave this blasted place before Victoria came back from wherever she was. Before he had to talk to anyone else. "Good-bye, Wayren. I will be in touch. *Essere con Dio*."

He closed the door behind him and hurried away before he saw anyone else, or before Wayren tried to stop him with another of her blasted cryptic comments or knowing looks. The hidden entrance near the library was closer and less noticeable. He wouldn't have to walk through the fountain room and chance running into anyone.

Moments later he ascended the dark, narrow stairs that opened into a small cellar in an abandoned building blocks away from Santo Quirinus. As he stepped out of the rickety structure, he realized he might very well be doing so for the last time.

He ducked out of the small opening at the rear of the building and then moved silently through what passed as a courtyard, but was really no more than a gap five paces wide and filled with rubble and dirt. The sun had begun to rise, sending a soft glow over the ramshackle buildings, and Max drew in a deep breath of chill air, this first full day of his bloody, detestable freedom.

He was free, yet still trapped by his memories and knowledge. He should have had Wayren use the golden disk to capture them again and take them away. At least then he would have some peace.

But he kept going, walking away from the Consilium and the world that had been his life for more than a decade.

Fast footfalls from behind drew his attention, and he reached automatically for his stake before realizing he had no way of telling whether whoever approached was friend or foe.

"Pesaro!"

"What the hell do you want, Vioget?" Max released the stake and kept walking, head high, shoulders straight. He was acutely aware of his lack of power, the weakness that seemed to pervade every step he now took.

"Victoria. It's Victoria."

Max stopped, but he didn't turn around. There was something in the bastard's voice. . . .

"Beauregard has her."

Now he turned back, and what he saw made his spine turn to ice. The blasted fop's face wasn't so pretty any longer, and he limped, but it was the expression in his eyes that made Max cold.

"Has he . . . " The word dried in his mouth, but Vioget knew what he meant.

"Not yet. But he will if we don't stop him."

Max looked at him, every bit of antipathy he felt for the other man rising to the surface. He knew precisely where to place the blame for this travesty.

But instead he turned to start back toward the Consilium. If Vioget had lowered himself to ask Max for assistance, Victoria's situation must be bad, very bad indeed. They would need others. "Have you seen Wayren?"

"Yes. She sent me after you; the Venators are waiting."

So Sebastian knew.

Max closed his mind off from that path and gave a short nod. And he said words he never thought he'd say to Sebastian Vioget: "I'll follow you."

Sebastian gritted his teeth. "Yes, I am aware that Beauregard will be expecting us." Although he was a man who avoided violence, he thought he might just forget about it for a moment and plow a fist into . . . something.

But that would mean he'd have to stop, and it would waste time he already didn't have. They had no time. *No time.* Thank God they were nearly to the house where he and Beauregard lived, albeit in separate quarters, the five men half running as he explained the situation.

It was early morning, perhaps an hour since he'd stumbled out of the underground lair, and the sun was high enough in the sky that the undead would be safely below— sleeping or otherwise. The slowest-moving carriage ever had dropped them off near their destination, but not close enough to be seen by those who stood watch over their master's domain from dark buildings or underground nooks. Sebastian knew how to get there without being seen by them, but it necessitated traveling on foot.

Too slow. They were moving too slow.

"Then we cannot all go in together." Pesaro's voice had an edge to it—it always did, but this was different. There was some odd air about him.

Sebastian's fingers itched. "I was just about to say, before you interrupted me, that very thing." He turned his attention from the cold-blooded bastard and glanced at the other three Venators who had come with him to rescue Victoria. For a moment he couldn't keep away the terror of what might happen to her.

What might be happening.

Or have already happened.

How long had he been gone now?

Too long.

Long enough.

Sebastian marshaled his concentration, focusing on their path as they hurried along through courtyards and between closely built buildings. Losing his focus would do no good for her, regardless of what had happened.

Pray God it hadn't.

How long? How long would Beauregard play with her, kiss her, touch her, before making her drink?

Sebastian's stomach rolled greasily. Once that happened, there was no hope.

Gritting his teeth again, pushing away the paralyzing worry, he barreled along, keeping his mind on a straight path. What they had to do.

How they could save her.

He couldn't remember the names of two of the others who'd been chosen to go with him—it had happened so quickly—but one was Michalas. Sly, wiry, and sharp-eyed Michalas he'd met once briefly, many years ago.

"There are two known entrances to Beauregard's main quarters," Sebastian said, speaking quickly and quietly as they ducked behind the wall of the courtyard behind his house—the very one into which Victoria had dropped during her escape from his fourth-story window last autumn.

The memory threatened his control, but he recaptured it. "And a third secret entrance that only I know of—besides Beauregard."

"He'll expect you to use it."

"So we must split into two groups. One group will go to make a disturbance and draw away the undead that guard and serve him."

"How many undead?"

"Ten or more. A dozen—perhaps you can handle that

task, Pesaro. You can easily take on a dozen undead, or so I hear."

For a moment Sebastian thought Pesaro was going to strike him, but he just gave that proud, sharp nod of his.

Michalas spoke for the first time. "We now have a fine way of making a disturbance, do we not, Max? All thanks to Miro. Yes, we'll draw attention away from you so you can enter the secret way."

There was a deliberate sneer in Pesaro's voice. "And what will you do once there? Ask Beauregard to hand Victoria over to you? I'm certain he'll do that without a thought."

In this Sebastian was completely forthcoming. "He won't expect me to fight him, but I will. I'll kill him if I have to."

Pesaro looked at him sharply and gave another single nod. "I believe you will."

Sebastian gave them terse, sharp directions, and they split up appropriately: Michalas and a blond Venator accompanied Pesaro, and the other one called Brim was to follow Sebastian.

As they began to walk away, Pesaro turned back to Sebastian and grabbed his shoulder in a hold that dug in too deeply to be friendly. "Bring her back." His dark eyes, flat and cold, told him everything that remained unsaid between them—now and in their past. At least in this their wills were united.

And then he spun away, hurrying off with harsh footsteps to follow Michalas and the blond Venator.

And Sebastian, fear banding his chest, started into the deep, narrow tunnel beneath the house where he did not want to go.

Because he was terrified of what he might find within.

They were nearly to the secret entrance when Sebastian heard it: a dull, rolling boom in the distance, above and from the other side of Beauregard's private chambers. He realized it was the sound of the promised distraction.

There was no worry that the three of them, including the legendary Pesaro, would hold back a dozen undead. For all that he hated the fact that he'd had to ask for his help, Sebastian knew there was no one better for this task.

Another boom sounded a bit closer, echoing in the distance, and Sebastian knew it was now up to him to do his part.

At the secret door he turned for one last look at Brim. The man towered over him, and he was ebony-skinned, with unfashionable close-cropped hair; he wore his *vis bulla* through a slender, well-tended eyebrow. Like his name, he brimmed with energy. He gave a brief nod of understanding, and Sebastian turned to the door.

He hesitated then, again afraid of what he might find, then steeled himself and barged in, feeling the entrance of Brim behind him, hearing the flap of the tapestry as it closed. A vampire waited just inside, grabbing for him, but Brim had his stake out, and Sebastian heard the quiet poof as he charged toward the red velvet bed and the two figures on it. The sounds of struggle behind him told Sebastian that Brim had found others waiting for them, and was holding them back—but Sebastian had no goal except to get to Victoria.

He couldn't tell. He couldn't see—his legs didn't seem to be moving him closer fast enough. . . . It was as though he were slogging through a river, trying to rush through pounding water. But the stench of blood was deep and metallic in the air.

Suddenly Beauregard was in front of him, his eyes pink and his fangs long and sharp. "You are too late. Pardon me if I don't offer my condolences, but that's because I know that someday you will thank me."

"No," Sebastian said, his attention flickering to the prone

figure on the bed. Her long hair obscured her face, and a blanket covered her body. "I don't believe you." He couldn't. Wouldn't.

"Believe what you must, but she is mine now. See?"

He showed Sebastian his arm, a long lean one, bared by a rolled-up sleeve, corded with muscle and decorated with the damned copper band. A deep cut above the wrist, between it and the armband, still oozed dark, glistening blood.

"She drank willingly, greedily. She enjoyed it, Sebastian."

"No . . ." He started toward the bed, and to his horror Beauregard didn't try to stop him. That was the worst sign of all.

So then he knew.

"With her power and my blood, by Lucifer's sword, she'll be as powerful as Lilith."

"Damn you." Everything slowed again, but this time Sebastian was focused on his grandfather. The stake, the weapon he'd disdained for more than a decade, felt light and useless in his hand after the guns and swords he'd taken to using in hunting and fencing. But it was lethal, and he would use it.

By God, he would.

Beauregard stopped the blow, blocking Sebastian's wrist with the flat of a sword that seemed to come from nowhere. "Sebastian, you are overwrought," he said with a calm that burned Sebastian. "I'll share; I promise you this. And now, with the page you obtained from the journal, we'll have the power—"

With a grunt Sebastian reared toward him again, caught his grandfather by the neck in his long fingers instead of in the chest, as the older man had expected. With a shove, with power long dormant and a strength he'd forgotten he had, he slammed him back against a tapestried wall. The bed curtains next to them brushed their legs as Beauregard struggled, dropping his sword with a clatter, and trying to pull Sebastian's hand from his throat.

"Damn you," Sebastian said, readying his stake.

"You cannot do this," Beauregard wheezed, his fingers still pulling at him. His sharp nails tore into the tender flesh on the back of Sebastian's hands. "After all I've . . . done for you."

"You took her from me."

"She was pulling you from . . . me. I did it for both . . . of us."

Sebastian tightened his fingers, ignoring the blood that was streaming down onto his wrist. He steadied the stake. One plunge and it would be done.

"I raised you . . . when no one else . . . would." His eyes were no longer pink; his fangs had retracted.

"Because my father was taken by your lover!" Sebastian spat. "She mauled him, remember?"

"She was . . . jealous . . . of him." Beauregard's throat convulsed under his hand as he coughed. Sebastian wasn't fooled. He couldn't strangle a vampire; this would merely slow him down, cause him pain enough to hold him until he could stab the heart. "And he . . . like any Vioget . . . could not resist . . . a beau . . . tiful . . . woman."

Sebastian became aware that the sounds of struggle behind him had ended. He glanced back and saw nothing but the signs of their battle. Brim was nowhere in sight.

They were alone.

"Don't, Sebastian. Don't do it." Beauregard's breaths were stronger now. His hand wrapped around Sebastian's wrist instead of pulling at it, scratching at it. Gentle. Imploring. "You'll regret it. You know it. You've lived with it for—"

"Stop." Sebastian felt his fingers cutting into the flesh beneath them, tearing into his grandfather's throat. He lifted the stake. "I do love you."

The door burst open at that moment, and Pesaro charged in. His arms and shirt were streaked with blood, his face hardly recognizable in its intensity.

He didn't hesitate but went straight to the bed, and Sebastian watched as he yanked back the blanket with a bravery he himself hadn't had.

Victoria murmured, moved sinuously, and her eyes fluttered, then closed completely. The hair fell away from her face when Pesaro lifted her, her head falling back to show the bites and blood streaks on her throat and shoulders. Her lips curved in a sensual smile, and a quick trickle of blood spilled from the corner of her mouth.

"Christ Jesus," Pesaro breathed. He lifted his face, and Sebastian was struck by the loathing there. The stark fury. The same madness he knew was on his own face, grinding in his own gut.

Everything else fell away, and Sebastian plunged his stake.

The soft poof resonated, the ashes scattered, and he heard the tinny clatter of the copper armband as it fell to his feet.

Twenty-three

In Which There Occurs a Bedside Vigil

"There's nothing we can do." Wayren looked around the room. The Consilium's fountain rumbled behind her, all of its sparkling, blessed water of no help in this instance. "Do you not feel it? You can sense her, even here."

She knew they recognized the presence of an undead—a destroyed one of their own, brought into the sacred and secret halls of the Consilium; she knew because of the stark hopelessness on Sebastian's handsome face, the self-loathing and guilt that certainly churned inside him.

And the murmurs and exchanged glances of Michalas and Brim, who, though injured and knocked unconscious during their battle with the undead, still stood strong at the back of the room.

And Max, whose face was devoid of expression. Who couldn't sense it any longer himself, but who knew. Who kept in the dark alcove as if he would separate himself from them all.

Perhaps it was best if he did, now that Victoria was gone.

"I'll wait with her until she awakens. Ylito, too. The rest of you"—Wayren glanced at Sebastian, and then Max— "can do as you wish. It won't be sundown for hours."

She turned from them, from the dark, hopeless faces and the simmering undercurrent of rage. She hoped, prayed that it wouldn't be directed at Sebastian—for as much as Max wanted to place the blame there, and as much as Sebastian himself did, Wayren knew it was not that simple.

Sighing, she passed by the portrait gallery. There would be the need for more paintings, for Zavier would expire soon. And Stanislaus's had not yet been completed. And Victoria . . .

Footfalls drew her attention, and she turned to see Sebastian in her wake. "I want to be there when she wakes," he said. Gone was the charm, the light, flirtatious manner. There was deep sorrow and angry regret, but determination as well.

He would be a good Venator. His time had come at last.

"Do you intend to fully join us now?" she asked, making way for him to walk abreast with her.

"I have no reason not to. If I had . . . I've been foolish and irresponsible."

He had been, but she understood, as she was wont to do. He, as Max had done, would find his place here, and learn to grow beyond his faults and mistakes.

"You dispatched your grandfather. Don't think I don't know how difficult that was for you. You will grieve."

Sebastian looked at her, his face set and haggard. Despite the weariness and pain there, he reminded her, as he always did, of the great Uriel—but with an extraordinary sensuality she didn't think Uriel would appreciate. "Is there truly no hope? Nothing that can be done?" he asked.

"There's nothing." Max's voice was flat and sharp behind them, startling Wayren. "She drank from him."

She paused so that Max could join them, then replied, "He drained much of her blood—she was very weak, and by drinking from him she replaced hers with his. She'll awaken and be an undead."

"Then why not stake her now and relieve us of the waiting?"

"Because you must see her as she's become so that you can say your farewells," she told Sebastian. "And know that it is so, and irreversible."

They had reached the room where Victoria lay. No one had been allowed in since Max burst into the Consilium carrying her unconscious, blood-streaked body. He'd then relinquished it to Ylito and Ilias.

The chamber was small, too small for five people, but Wayren knew it was futile to try to keep Max and Sebastian out. Victoria had been bathed and dressed as though she were a corpse, ready for burial. Her dark hair lay in a thick braid over her breast, and the crisp white lawn of her simple gown served only to show how pale she was. A blue-veined hand rested on her stomach, and another prominent vein lined her face from temple to jaw.

When they came in, Ylito looked up from his examination of Victoria and met Wayren's eyes.

"She needs more blood," he said quietly. "I don't know that it will do any good, but Hannever wishes to try."

"Will she drink?" Max asked, a flash of metal in his hand. He had a knife at his wrist and would have sliced into it before Wayren grabbed his arm. She sensed a viciousness, a recklessness there that boded no good.

"Wait. It must be Gardella blood," Ylito said.

Sebastian was already rolling up his sleeve to bare a muscular arm. "Give me the knife, Pesaro."

Max turned away and went to stand against the wall, watching. His arms hung at his sides, his shoulder against the wall in a deceptively casual stance. His face was expressionless.

The tension in the room was heavy and solid, and even Wayren, who usually wasn't affected by such energy, felt stifled and on edge.

Hannever came in the door at that moment. "Blood. Now." He was carrying a tray with a stack of cups on it, two small vials, and other accoutrements, and he put it down on a table. Next to the stake that lay there.

Without another word he moved to Victoria and made a small cut on her arm, squeezing a drop of the dark blood into a small bowl. The room was still and silent and tight, nearly choking in its intensity.

Anger, guilt, terror, madness . . . all simmered and swelled.

When Hannever turned away from Victoria, Sebastian offered his arm, and Hannever made a small incision, forcing the blood into one of the bowls. *Drip, drip, drip* . . . The sound was like little explosions in the tiny room.

"What good will it do?" Max's voice was sudden and harsh.

"No good, I think. But she needs it. We must try," Hannever said, busy with one of the vials. He put a tiny drop of a liquid into Sebastian's blood and used a slender reed to stir. "No. Not this."

"Try Max," Wayren said. She met Ylito's eyes.

Max's wasn't right either, according to Hannever.

"We have to get her some blood!" Sebastian said, his teeth tight around the words. He was already moving toward the door, opening it.

"Zavier," Max said. "Let Zavier try."

Their eyes met, and then Wayren looked at Ylito. Yes. It was fitting. He'd want to.

"We must have his permission."

Wayren nodded. "He'll give it. Let us go and I'll ask him."

Twenty-four

In Which There Is a Chilling Draft

Victoria murmured, shifting restlessly, moving for the first time since they'd come into the room. Sebastian brushed the hair away from her forehead, the soft, lush curls that had been captured in a braid that lay in a thick line past her breasts. Her skin was damp and clammy, and still so pale.

This would be the last time he'd touch her.

Sebastian looked at her lips, at the curve of her jaw, remembering how strong it could be—how defiant when she lifted it and pretended she didn't want him as much as he wanted her. Now he would have no one to taunt in a carriage, no one to tease and tug and coax into his arms.

His wound from her stake still ached, oozing blood, and he remembered again why she was lying there, and how she had found Beauregard's lair. Who had led her there, and why. How Beauregard had manipulated them both.

He'd sat there—it had been hours—since he and Pesaro had been allowed to enter after whatever Hannever and Ylito had done with Zavier's blood. Somehow they'd fed it into Victoria using some sort of tube, but it hadn't seemed to do any good. The back of his neck still prickled and chilled, and she still lay there, cold and pale.

She moaned again, and Sebastian looked up. He met Pesaro's eyes from across Victoria's body. There was no hope there, nothing but grim determination. A stake sat on the table near Pesaro; Sebastian had no doubt he'd not hesitate to use it.

A cold one, he was.

Wayren and Ylito had found a small corner of the room where they both sat reading or studying some old text. The sight of them brought to Sebastian's mind the fact that the page he'd stolen from the Consilium was still in Beauregard's lair.

He would have to go back and find it once . . . once this was over.

At that moment Victoria's eyes fluttered, and the sensation in the room shifted. It became closer and smothering, and no one seemed to breathe.

Wayren was suddenly standing at the foot of the small bed. Ylito took his place near the head, and before Sebastian knew what was happening he heard a soft whisk, and then a faint clink. Pesaro was doing something at his side of the bed, and Wayren and Ilias near the foot.

Restraints.

God, restraints.

How demeaning for her.

He felt and found the soft leather cuffs, the metal fastenings on the side, and let them drop. He wouldn't do it.

Victoria was breathing more stridently now, and her eyes were fluttering. One of her legs moved; her lips parted; she rolled her head. She tried to raise an arm, but it was held in place by . . . not a cuff, but Pesaro. His hand on her arm, around her wrist. Clamping it onto the edge of the bed.

All of a sudden her eyes fluttered open. Wide. They

opened wide, and she looked around. They weren't red; they were the same brown-green they'd always been.

The room seemed to hold its collective breath, waiting. Ylito shifted near the head of the bed, and Sebastian saw him reach for something on the table.

No. Not the stake. Not yet.

But when he glanced over, he saw that it was still on the table, held in place by Pesaro's hand.

"What . . ." Victoria said, looking around, her eyes moving slowly from face to face. "Beauregard!" She tried to move, and a confused look passed over her.

Ylito moved, and something splashed through the air, sprinkled down on her face before Sebastian could stop him. Not her face!

But instead of screaming and tearing at the spray of holy water, Victoria twisted around, merely turning her face to get away from it as if it were nothing more than a summer rain shower.

"Why did you do that?" she asked, her voice stronger now.

Something in the room changed. It was as if a sudden light had come on. They all looked at one another, afraid to hope. . . .

"Is it possible?" Ylito asked, looking at Wayren.

"I don't know how it can be," she replied. She'd moved next to Sebastian, and he felt her palpable . . . was it relief? Could it be? She reached down, smoothing her hands over Victoria's face, over her shoulders, her eyes closed, a low hum coming from the back of her throat.

"The two *vis bullae*."

They all looked at Pesaro, who'd removed his hand from the stake. Whose face actually bore an expression now. "She wears two of them, does she not?"

Sebastian stared at him. How the bloody hell could Pesaro know that . . . when he himself didn't?

Wayren straightened, her hands continuing to move in soft, rhythmic gestures over Victoria's body as if to soothe it . . . or to somehow measure it. "It must be. There can be no other explanation. The strength of the two overpowered Beauregard's blood, and she was not turned."

"And so that is why she needed blood," added Ylito. "When the tainted vampire blood did not take hold, it had to be replaced with mortal blood."

"What are you talking about?" demanded Victoria. "Why am I here?"

Sebastian looked down at her, a sudden jubilance rushing over him. For the first time in a long while he felt something other than doom and guilt. *Thank God.*

But then, as he took her cool fingers into his hand, he realized something horrible.

His neck was still cold.

Epilogue

Wherein We Are Reminded That Hell Hath No Fury

Sarafina Regalado walked boldly into the chamber where Lilith the Dark awaited.

Her journey from Roma to these mountains in the depths of Romania had been long, and she was exhausted. But she refused to be cowed by the powerful undead who stood before her. What was the worst that could happen?

The queen of the vampires could bite her.

And Sara would rather enjoy that.

"Do I know you?" Lilith asked after a moment. "Why have you braved my guards to speak to me?"

"My father was *Conte* Regalado, but he is dead. The woman Venator killed him."

The blue-red eyes narrowed. "Ah, so you are the one. What do you want?"

"I bring you news," Sara told her, looking around at the sumptuous furnishings, and examining the vampire's gown.

Out of style, wrong fabric . . . but somehow it suited her. "Akvan is destroyed. The Door of Alchemy has been opened."

"That is no news to me." The queen was watching her hungrily. "Beauregard is dead, too, at last. Although his armband is missing again."

From under her cloak Sara pulled a sheet of paper, brittle with age and from the thin wax that covered it. "Perhaps you would find this interesting. I obtained it from one of Beauregard's minions—the one who brought me to you."

Lilith took it lazily, but Sara saw the way her gaze sharpened when she looked at the drawing of the plant and the instructions, written in a language that Sara didn't understand. But she didn't need to. She'd brought it to someone who would know how to read it.

"And what do you wish from me?"

"How did Max kill Akvan?" asked Sara. "He should not have been able to."

The queen looked at her, and before Sara's eyes she became even paler than before, nearly translucent, so that more ribbons of blue veins showed through her white skin. "Maximilian. No."

She rounded on Sara, who was suddenly taken aback by the fury in the vampire's eyes. They burned in her skull, burned as they looked at her, burned as though they touched her skin. "Did he slay Akvan with his own hand? *With his own hand?* Tell me!"

Sara nodded. "He did."

"No. I cannot— *No*." Her mouth compressed; her hair swirled about her in a cloud of copper. "*No!* He has betrayed me!"

"And you are not the only one," Sara told her. "Although," she added hastily as the vampire spun back to her, fangs bared as though to tear into her, "his betrayal of you—

whatever it was—must be much more important than what he did to me."

"Max. How dare he!" Lilith was shrieking now, her chest heaving with anger and malevolence. "After all of the graces I've bestowed on him, all of the freedoms! And he betrays me." Her voice had dropped now, steadied. "I shall have my vengeance."

She looked at Sara. Lilith's eyes glowed, but no longer burned. All but one of the veins under her skin had faded. Her lips curved invitingly. "Both of us shall. Now come closer, my dear, and give me your pretty little neck."

Here's a sneak peek at the next volume of the
Gardella Vampire Chronicles

When Twilight Burns

Available from Signet Eclipse in August 2008

Barely a week after her return to England, Victoria found herself slogging through ankle-deep sewage deep beneath London. Stake in hand, she ducked to keep from scraping her head on a low dip of the tunnel ceiling as she followed Sebastian.

What had once been a small river tributary flowing south to the Thames had been enclosed by the city's construction during the past six centuries. The sluggish water now oozed with sewage, and only God and the toshers knew what else.

She considered herself quite hardened to repugnant images by now, but even she didn't particularly relish the thought that her boots were possibly crushing human remains floating in their own waste.

It occurred to Victoria that she could have been dancing at the Bridgertons' soiree, in a less damp—but just as odiferous—environment, if she'd listened to her mother instead of to Sebastian. (Lady Bridgerton was known for her exceedingly strong lily-of-the-valley eau de toilette.) Victoria hadn't yet concluded which was the better choice, but despite the drawbacks, she was leaning toward vampire hunting in the sewers.

At least here she could eliminate with the slam of a stake any creature that accosted her. It wouldn't be quite that easy to dissuade the gossipmongers and fortune-hunting bachelors of the ton.

"I don't sense any undead," she told Sebastian as she stepped on something horribly squishy. A rank odor squelched afresh into the air, and with her next step she felt something hard and cylindrical roll beneath her boot. A bone. A canine one, she hoped.

"Do you not?" he asked, his voice smooth and echoing over the quiet splashing made by their stout leather boots. "Perhaps there are no vampires about, then. Only the harmless toshermen, which we may come upon, if they venture this far."

"Or perhaps you lured me down here for another reason."

She could see the wickedness of his smile in the torch's uneasy light. "Why should I ruin a perfectly good pair of breeches—not to mention boots—by coaxing you here, when I'd much prefer to have you . . . elsewhere."

His blatant words caused a sudden swirl of pleasure

in her belly, and to diffuse the warm feeling Victoria gave an unladylike snort—which had the added result of filling her nostrils with putrid stench. She wondered how the toshers could make a living, working down here day after day, collecting copper, bones, rags, and anything else of value to sell on the streets above. And how vampires could stand to live among the odor when the mere smell of garlic took them aback.

"Of course," Sebastian continued, "it's not as if you'll be clutching at me and crying for protection, even in a place as revolting as this. Much to my great regret." He brandished a torch that cast sporadic shadows to break the darkness, but Victoria found that she could see surprisingly well even outside the glow.

She was just about to make a wry return when she became aware of a new sound—that of rushing or falling water—and then a faint prickle at the back of her neck. The dark, disgusting environment slid away, replaced by the familiar rush of readiness and a cold smile.

"Ah," Sebastian said, cocking his head as if to hear better. "At last. Just when I thought we were well and truly lost."

"We're not alone," Victoria murmured, the prickle flushing into a full-blown chill.

"Undead?" His voice dropped to match hers.

She looked up at him. "Do you not sense them?"

"I do now that you say it," he said. "And it's no surprise, as we're near the place I was looking for."

A sudden splash behind them had Victoria spinning to meet the red-eyed vampire who'd come from nowhere.

Presumably, he'd been expecting a slow-moving, malnourished tosherman, for the half-demon had taken a moment to roll up the sleeves of his dull shirt, and that attention to grooming was his undoing.

"You should have worn cuff links," Victoria said conversationally the instant before he poofed into undead dust. She blew off the tip of her stake and turned back to Sebastian, who was watching her with an odd sort of smile.

But before she could wonder what it meant, his expression smoothed, and he lifted the torch higher. "Take care," he said, gesturing ahead of them.

When she stepped farther in the sloshing damp, she saw why. Only a few paces ahead of them, the filthy water was dumped away, cascading into nothingness. A wall loomed beyond the falls, a clear dead-end. "What now?"

"There." Sebastian gestured with the torch, and she saw a crude ledge slanting up from the sludge. Carved into the wall, it was easily wide enough for a man to ascend up into . . . "Is that an entrance?" Victoria peered up at the dark wall rising in front of them.

"You can see it from here?" Sebastian raised the torch, illuminating it more clearly.

"What's up there?" Victoria had already started to hike up the inclining ledge, keeping her stake at the ready. Water dripped from her boots at every step, splattering quietly on the rock beneath.

"Something that I'm certain you'll be fascinated to see," he said from behind her, suddenly very close. "Per-

haps you'll even wish to reward me for showing you."
His breath was warm on the side of her neck exposed by
the long single braid she wore tucked into her coat.

"Unless it's Lilith's dust, I highly doubt that," she
replied. Her heart beat a bit off-kilter as he moved behind her. "But you can certainly continue to hope."

COLLEEN GLEASON

THE REST FALLS AWAY

In every generation, a Gardella is called to accept the family legacy of vampire slaying, and this time, Victoria Gardella Grantworth is chosen, on the eve of her debut, to carry the stake. But as she moves between the crush of ballrooms and dangerous, moonlit streets, Victoria's heart is torn between London's most eligible bachelor, the Marquess of Rockley, and her enigmatic ally, Sebastian Vioget. And when she comes face to face with the most powerful vampire in history, Victoria must ultimately make the choice between duty and love.

"Intriguing, witty and addictive."
—*Publishers Weekly*

Also Available
RISES THE NIGHT:
The Gardella Vampire Chronicles

**Available wherever books are sold or at
penguin.com**

J.R. WARD

DARK LOVER

THE DEBUT NOVEL IN THE
NEW YORK TIMES BESTSELLING
BLACK DAGGER BROTHERHOOD SERIES

"Deliciously edgy, erotic and thrilling."
—*New York Times* bestseller Nicole Jordan

In the shadows of the night in Caldwell, New York, there's a deadly turf war going on between vampires and their slayers. There exists a secret band of brothers like no other—six vampire warriors, defenders of their race. Yet none of them relishes killing more than Wrath, the leader of The Black Dagger Brotherhood.

The only purebred vampire left on earth, Wrath has a score to settle with the slayers who murdered his parents centuries ago. But, when one of his most trusted fighters is killed—leaving his half-breed daughter unaware of his existence or her fate—Wrath must usher her into the world of the undead—a world of sensuality beyond her wildest dreams.

**Available wherever books are sold or at
penguin.com**